GU1

Star-Crossed Summer

Star-Crossed Summer

Sarah Stanley

ROBERT HALE · LONDON

ISBN 978-0-7090-8395-5

Robert Hale Limited
Clerkenwell House
Clerkenwell Green
London EC1R 0HT

www.halebooks.com

2 4 6 8 10 9 7 5 3 1

Typeset in 10/12pt Sabon
Printed and bound in Great Britain by
Biddles Limited, King's Lynn

DEDICATION

For my home city of Gloucester and the beautiful nearby village of Frampton-on-Severn, which inspired my fictional Frampney. And also for the picturesque North Devon towns of Lynmouth and Lynton, with which I have taken liberties but which will still recognize themselves as Lannermouth and Haldane. In particular I mention the Rock House Hotel, Lynmouth, upon which I have modelled the Dower House.

Chapter One

'You are acquiring a top quality stallion from an excellent stud, Sir Guy.' The middle-aged widow was ill at ease with her visitor, a gentleman more than ten years her junior.

'Excellent only because of the Valmer bloodline, Mrs Tremoille,' he replied mischievously, and she looked away as if he hadn't spoken.

Their voices were deadened in the shadowy Tudor library, where centuries of candles had yellowed the decorative ceiling and darkened the oak panels. The light was scarcely better out in the park as ominous storm clouds gathered over the stillness of the Cotswold escarpment. It was a late afternoon in June, but seemed more like twilight. 'It closes in early,' she observed pointedly.

He baited her. 'Should I beg your hospitality for the night, madam?'

Her glance would have shrivelled a lesser man, but Sir Guy Valmer was indifferent. In her unrelieved black, the former Jane Lindsay might be a lady now, but her present crisp air of propriety was superficial; one small scratch would soon expose the flaunting harlot beneath. Covert enquiries had uncovered her carefully concealed past in a low Worcester bagnio, but now she had another secret, and that was why he was here. The acquisition of the stallion was an excuse; his real purpose was to assess the woman he might one day have to face in court. His dark russet hair was a dash of rich colour in the gloomy chamber as he placed a leather pouch on the desk, between a lighted candelabrum and the latest volume of *Lithgow's Journal*. 'We are still agreed on a thousand guineas?' he enquired.

'Unless you wish to pay more.' Jane watched the thin smile that played around his lips as he shook a mixture of gold coins and bank notes over the journal. Jane glanced at the publication. Did he know of the legal notice that appeared within its fashionable pages? She studied his face again. This man was a devil with whom she only dared sup with a very long spoon, and would not sup at all were it not for the need to gauge her enemy. No doubt his purpose was the same, and now that she'd come face to face with her nemesis, she prayed he would never find anything legally binding that would serve his cause. In spite of her deep unease, she had to concede that he was a dangerously attractive man. She'd heard that Maria Carberry, leading actress at the Theatre Royal, Drury Lane, was wont to warm his nights. Maybe it was true, maybe not, but if so, La Carberry was probably a sleekly satisfied woman, because something about him told Jane he would be a master of seduction.

He was leanly muscular, tall – over six feet she guessed – and possessed a lazy strength and masculinity that could almost be tasted. She had never been drawn to men with hair of an even remotely reddish hue, but on him it was quite perfect. That dark, deeply polished shade reminded her of chestnuts fresh from the husk, and such loosely tousled curls would be the envy of many a woman. His face was aristocratically handsome, with finely moulded lips, a clear complexion, and arresting grey eyes that seemed to penetrate and unsettle. No doubt those eyes could also flirt and caress to devastating effect. His clothes – a dark brown coat, white shirt, cream-striped Marcella waistcoat and fawn trousers that disappeared into immaculate Hessian boots – were such marvels of the tailor's art they might have been stitched directly on his body. Ah, that body. So slender, athletic and masculine. Her breath escaped silently as her gaze moved secretly to the trousers that cleaved so close over his buttocks, hips and thighs that his anatomy could be made out in interesting detail. It had to be said that there were aspects of modern male fashion that pleased her immensely; trousers certainly did. On the right man. Embarrassingly small proportions were there for all to see, as were larger counterparts, and Valmer was impressive. Experience told Jane he'd know very well how to put such a fine organ to exquisite good use. He wouldn't be a selfish lover – not this man – he'd take care to pleasure the woman in his bed. The thought aroused her, causing such an unexpected stab of raw craving to clench between her legs that she had to turn away. Her thighs trembled as a velvet wave of sexual excitement washed vigorously through her, becoming visible in the sudden flush of her face. It was several moments before she recovered enough to turn back again, and to her relief he was still intent upon counting the money, and hadn't noticed anything.

The voracious appetites that had served her so well in her licentious youth were still as fierce as ever, but these days she seldom found gratification unless it was self-administered. Her late husband, Esmond Tremoille, had been surprisingly adventurous for one of such frail and nondescript appearance, and in his quest for new excitement had even been known to sample four-legged partners. Ill health had eventually put paid to any sexual relief, save by her right hand or his own, and not even that as consumption began to overwhelm him. Now his frustrated widow yearned for a well-endowed swain possessed of the stamina of an ox, with whom she could copulate until her very teeth rattled.

He counted the last coin. 'There, Mrs Tremoille, a small fortune to see you through 1815's troubled summer. Tell me, what do you expect now that Napoleon has escaped from Elba and is again rousing France to his banner?'

'The vile Corsican seldom enters my mind, Sir Guy. I am confident the Duke of Wellington will soon see him off. What concerns me more is the unreasonable opposition of the masses to the government's Corn Laws.'

'Hardly unreasonable, Mrs Tremoille,' he responded, handing her the empty pouch, 'Corn is bread, and bread is life to the people. Protecting British corn prices means a vastly more expensive loaf.'

'I am aware of that, Sir Guy, but farmers and landowners need protecting too.'

'What you really mean is that farmers and landowners want more profits.'

'You are a landowner,' she reminded him.

'And I've reduced rents to help my tenants and labourers survive. Have you?' He enjoyed the way her eyes slid away, allowing him the small victory. Like far too many landowners, she lacked the foresight to help with the survival of those who depended upon her. He waited for her riposte, but it didn't come. 'Is Lancelot now mine?' he asked.

'Yes, Sir Guy. I'll have him brought around to the front immediately.' She returned the money to the pouch and sealed it with hot wax into which she pressed her late husband's signet ring. Then she rang a little silver bell.

A lanky butler of about fifty, with silky light-brown hair and spaniel eyes, opened the door immediately. 'Madam?' His voice was deep and guttural, conflicting with an otherwise soft and smooth appearance. Mordecai Bolton was Jane's creature, and had been with her since before her marriage.

'Ah, yes, Bolton. See that Lancelot is brought around to Sir Guy's carriage, and then inform Joshua he's needed to ride urgently to Gloucester.'

The door closed again, and Guy regarded the woman whose activities encroached so greatly upon his plans. She was still handsome, but as hard as nails. He'd noticed earlier how she'd observed his lower regions. Well, she wouldn't have found him lacking. Nor would he be lacking when it came to driving a legal wedge between her and the house and fortune she'd acquired through the convenient disappearance of Esmond Tremoille's final will and all proof of its existence. It was said that the final will excluded Jane and left everything to Tremoille's only daughter, Beth, whom Jane had cruelly thrown out into penury. 'Mrs Tremoille,' he said amiably, 'I still do not understand why you have sold Lancelot.'

'Sir Guy, bloodstock was entirely my dear late husband's concern.'

Dear late husband? He decided to ruffle her hypocritical feathers. 'Rumour has it you're considering marrying Lord Welland.'

'Have you been paying attention to local gossip? How very unworthy.'

'Local gossip is often a very fertile meadow.'

'Well, perhaps you need reminding that it is now more than a year since Esmond's death, and Lady Welland passed on over ten years ago.'

'So the gossip is true?' he pressed. Welland was the man she'd always wanted, although God alone knew why, for the fellow was an unpleasant bully who'd made it clear that while she was good enough to screw, she wasn't good enough to marry. Instead he'd chosen a shrinking violet of impeccable breeding. As for Welland's wisdom in offering for Jane now, it had to be wondered if he'd heard any of the whispers about Esmond Tremoille's will. Guy would guess not.

She hesitated, clearly uncertain whether or not to confirm anything, but then arrogance got the better of her. 'Yes, Sir Guy, I am indeed considering marrying Lord Welland. I have yet to accept.'

But you will, having waited more than twenty years to win him, Guy thought. 'Then my puzzlement deepens. Welland's interest in horses is well known, which makes the sale of a stallion of Lancelot's quality even more odd.'

'I am still free to dispose of my property as I see fit, and will be until such time as I again become a wife. Besides, Lord Welland already possesses Lancelot's full brother, Galahad.'

'Whose progeny may run like three-legged donkeys,' Guy pointed out.

'The same might apply to Lancelot's offspring.' She picked up the pouch and went deliberately toward the door, but he remained where he was.

'A union between you and Welland would command much of the county.'

'Our combined estates would hardly stand comparison with your vast tracts of Sussex, Sir Guy,' she answered.

'I own nothing in Sussex, madam.'

'The point is that the possible size of joint Tremoille and Welland lands in Gloucestershire will have no bearing on you, because you own nothing here.'

'That, madam, is a sorely disputed fact, is it not?' he said softly.

At last, he'd come to the heart of the matter. Alarm darted through her, cooling her skin and drying her mouth as she turned at the door to face him again.

'Tell me,' he continued, 'does Welland know there is doubt about the will?'

Somehow she was a picture of composure. 'There was nothing wrong with my husband's will, Sir Guy, it was very clear and to the point.'

'Madam, I'm sure the document you produced was all those things when it was drawn up, but it wasn't the ultimate will.' Rumours of another will had started from the moment of Esmond's passing, and had been fanned by a mysterious fire that killed his local lawyer Beswick, and razed his premises to the ground. But lawyers usually provided their clients with personal copies of wills, which in Esmond's case had probably been carefully concealed from the rapacious Jane. Did the mysterious letter to Beth from her father, announced in *Lithgow's Journal* and held by Withers, Withers & Blenkinsop, the lawyers in London, contain directions to this other copy, Esmond having anticipated the destruction of the original?

'You are wrong about the will, Sir Guy, and before you now proceed to repeat the old yarn about my late husband having tricked your late father out of this estate, let me remind you that all the deeds and other papers are in order.'

'How droll, for we both know that there was considerable sleight of hand on the part of Esmond Tremoille.'

'My husband was an honest man!'

Guy laughed aloud. 'Madam, your husband was twin to a corkscrew!'

'You came here to purchase a stallion, Sir Guy, and have accomplished that, so there is no need for you to remain a moment more.'

She opened the door coolly, but couldn't hide the tremble of her hand on the doorknob. That hand told him so much. 'This house, estate and stud belongs to *my* family, Mrs Tremoille, and I mean to take it all back,' he warned, as he passed her into the panelled hall, where he deliberately rattled her more by pausing to look around, as if he were already master.

He remembered it all so well from his childhood. With its dark oak panelling and impressive staircase, it was a perfect example of Tudor architecture, built by the Valmers during the reign of Henry VIII. His family's blue lion badge was everywhere, including the stained-glass oriel window that cast spangled lights over the black-and-white tiled floor. The only sign that it was no longer Valmer House was in the portraits, which were all of Tremoilles, including the late unlamented Esmond. The crafty old fellow wore a powdered wig and dated purple brocade coat, and didn't look robust enough for his legendary sexual exploits.

Not all the canvasses portrayed the dead, however, for the young Jane was among them, although the artist had ignored the preening strumpet, playing safe by daubing an angelic golden-haired bride with a vacuously pretty face and equally vacuous china-blue eyes. Her cloven hoofs and pitchfork were also well hidden.

Below Jane there was a much more modern, exquisitely realized likeness of a young woman aged about twenty. She wore a décolleté leaf-green muslin gown, as fine as cobwebs and gathered high beneath her enticingly full breasts. Beneath a filmy silver gauze scarf, her dark hair was piled up in a knot from which fell a number of shining ringlets twined with soft green ribbons. Here was a nymph of trees and hedgerows, Oberon's child, a woodland spirit clad in shades of willow, fern and shady pool. Her soft hazel-green eyes gleamed with innocent sensuality, and her slightly parted lips seemed to seek a kiss. Her name appeared on the frame. Elizabeth Tremoille. Sweet Beth, his quarry, was an enigma, strong but fragile, sensuous but pure, a denizen of fairyland trapped in the brittle, godless world of England's beau monde. How on earth had a debauched old lecher like Esmond Tremoille sired such a captivating creature?

'Where is your stepdaughter?' he asked suddenly, his voice finding an echo on the tiled floor.

'Beth no longer resides here, Sir Guy, nor has she since her father's death. I neither know nor care where she is.' Jane walked past him toward the outer hall. Guy followed, and Bolton supplied him with his hat, gloves and cane before opening the main doors.

Guy emerged beneath the heavy stone porch with its sentinel Valmer lions. His bottle-green travelling carriage waited, the team of greys stamping impatiently. The lowering sky cast a shadow over the country-side, and everything was so hushed that he heard a vixen barking in the woods along the park's north boundary. The house sheltered in a valley at the very edge of the Cotswold escarpment, its position affording protection from the south-westerlies that swept up from the Bristol Channel. Rising proud and golden against the menacing sky, above the valley's southern lip, was a picturesque Tudor gatehouse, from beneath which the drive descended toward the house. Beyond the gatehouse a narrow road crossed common land to a thick hanging wood on the steep western edge of the escarpment, and then wound down through the trees to the Gloucester road far below.

'Do you know anything about Miss Tremoille's movements since she left?' he asked suddenly, turning to look back at Jane.

Her eyes flickered. 'No, Sir Guy. She certainly hasn't appeared in society, or I would have heard. The creature was a viper in the bosom of Tremoille House, lying, scheming and attempting to forge her father's signature in order to steal from him. She also consorted with undesir-ables.' Guy didn't believe a word of it, and thought it more likely Jane was drawing upon her own dubious history. She confronted him. 'I can see that you are determined to think me a liar, but it remains that her father disowned her and so have I. May I ask why you are so interested in her?'

'In spite of your protestations to the contrary, I believe she is Esmond's real heir. I intend to prove as much, and then make her Lady Valmer. How better to regain what Esmond Tremoille stole from my father?'

She was plainly shocked, but at that moment an elderly manservant approached the porch, leading a sturdy dun saddle horse. 'You wish me to go to Gloucester, madam?' the man asked respectfully, keeping his eyes lowered as he snatched his battered hat from his greying hair.

'Yes, Joshua.' Jane glanced at her fob watch and then handed him the leather pouch. 'Take this to Williamson's Bank before it closes. It stays open longer on Wednesdays, so you should have time.'

'Yes, madam.' Joshua stuffed the pouch inside his coat. Then he mounted and adjusted the pouch, before urging his horse away.

Guy eased his long fingers into his kid gloves, an action Jane found so erotic that she experienced another involuntary sexual thrill. 'Mrs Tremoille,' he said softly, 'while I draw breath the past will never be over and done with. I *will* take back that which is mine, and you would be well advised to remember that.'

Jane mastered her wayward senses. 'I won't be giving you another thought, Sir Guy.' She nodded at Bolton, who promptly closed the doors.

Guy didn't care, having had enough of the Widow Tremoille for the time being. Flexing his fingers and glancing up at the dark storm clouds that now filled the sky, he approached the carriage, to the rear of which a groom was tethering a fine bay stallion. There were two things he needed now – Beth Tremoille and her father's final will, a copy of which he was firmly convinced had survived.

He reached Lancelot and, as he thoughtfully slid gloved fingers over the stallion's glossy coat, he recalled Jane's hand on the library doorknob. There'd been a recent edition of *Lithgow's Journal* on the desk, so she had to have seen the notice by Withers, Withers & Blenkinsop. It must have chilled her when, like him, she guessed the letter probably confirmed a copy of the last will. Guy straightened with a smile. His objective was clear. He had to find the lady, find the will, and then exact full revenge on all things Tremoille.

In the house behind him Jane had returned to the library. Filled with trepidation, she closed the door behind her and went to the decanter on the table by the large floor-standing globe. Pouring a large glass of Esmond's favourite single malt, she drank it in two gulps and closed her eyes as the liquid coursed down her throat to heat her stomach. This wasn't the time to lose her nerve, not after plotting so long to get what she wanted. Striving for composure, she went to the desk and opened the copy of *Lithgow's Journal* at the page displaying the legal notice.

Miss Elizabeth Tremoille. As has been done on previous occasions since the death of Mr Esmond Tremoille of Tremoille House in the County of Gloucestershire, it is hereby again requested that the above lady, only daughter of Mr Tremoille, contact Withers, Withers & Blenkinsop, solicitors of Caradine Street, London, where a letter from her father awaits her.

What was in that cursed letter? The spectre of the reputed last will loomed again. She had almost ransacked the house when Esmond died, but found no sign of it, so she'd despatched Bolton to dispose of Beswick and his records. Then she'd seen the first notice from Esmond's London lawyers, Withers, Withers & Blenkinsop. She'd written to them in her capacity as Esmond's widow and Beth's stepmother, seeking information about the letter's contents, but they would only deal with Beth. Jane sighed heavily, for there was Thomas Welland to consider as well. She had wanted him for so long that the thought of losing him again now was almost too much to bear. She had married Esmond for his money and the status he would provide, but another reason for netting him was that his land bordered Whitend, Thomas's ancient estate in the vale, south of Gloucester. The fact that Esmond was rewarding between the sheets – and just about everywhere else he could think of – had been a very pleasing bonus, but it was Thomas she'd dreamed of all along. She was under no illusion. He was considering the match solely as a means of getting the Tremoille lands and stud, not because he wanted his once-favourite whore to spread her legs again. There would be no marriage if Guy Valmer succeeded in his aim. In fact, there would be nothing at all for poor Jane.

Chapter Two

*B*eth was at that moment far closer than either Jane or Guy imagined, watching from a hiding place in a knot of sweet-scented elder high on the southern boundary wall. She saw Joshua being urgently despatched, and saw the doors closed in the elegant visitor's face. She didn't know Guy, just that he had probably purchased Lancelot, nor did he interest her, because she'd only returned to see her beloved former home.

Her patched green woollen shawl and shabby grey chemise dress had seen far better days, and her bare feet were bleeding and dirty after walking the five miles from Gloucester. Weary and undernourished, she pushed her dusty hair back from her forehead and leaned her head against a branch. It was over a year since she ceased being the elegant and beautiful Miss Tremoille, and in that time she had become a blacksmith's woman. She was Jake Mannacott's whore, because although she liked and respected him, she certainly didn't love him. That was the reality of her life, but she'd always ached for true love, silks and lace, a scented marriage bed, and a passionate bridegroom who was both handsome and wealthy. In the secrecy of her bed at Tremoille House, she'd explored her own body, arousing her breasts and stroking herself between the legs as she imagined her perfect lover. Such wild feelings had seized her that it seemed her flesh would melt with excitement, but such innocence had been banished forever when she surrendered her maidenhead on the dirty floor of Jake's hovel. There was no melting flesh, no excitement, just paying her dues.

Now the emptiness of her stomach suddenly made her feel nauseous. Beads of perspiration sprang to her forehead as the churning sensation made her retch several times. She felt weak and feverish as the spasm ran its course, and by the time it had passed Joshua was riding beneath the gatehouse. She'd known him all her life. He'd taught her to ride her first pony, and brought her fresh fruit from his tiny cottage garden, strawberries, raspberries and fine juicy apricots. What errand could require such haste? Her attention returned to the house. Jake had warned her that such a visit would be foolish and achieve nothing, but she *had* to see it again. Her father had begged her forgiveness on his deathbed, and told her it was all hers after all, not Jane's, but where was the final will that proved it? Tears stung her hazel-green eyes as she drank in the uneven, lichen-covered roofs and the windows high in their gables. The stone was mellow, and always looked warm in the sunlight. Today, beneath such heavy skies, it was subdued. A handsome deer park dotted with specimen trees and purple and crimson rhododendrons stretched down through the valley, before the land plunged steeply over the edge of the escarpment, through dense woods toward the vale, where Gloucester Cathedral was clearly visible, even in the summer murk.

She glanced up as the rain that had threatened for some time at last began to fall. It was time she set off for Gloucester. Hearing the faint crunch of wheels on the gravel drive, she saw that Lancelot's purchaser was leaving. If she hurried, she'd reach the shelter of the hanging wood before the carriage reached the gatehouse. Scrambling down from the hawthorn to the common, she grabbed the battered basket she'd brought in the vain hope of gathering wild strawberries and, after raising her shawl, ran toward the road. Rooks wheeled noisily above the woods and in the distant vale the winding Severn shone like a silver ribbon. Gloucester Cathedral shone in a narrow shaft of sunlight that pierced the clouds, but the rain quickened over the hills and she was soon soaked. The fresh prints of Joshua's horse had already filled with water, but suddenly they slithered and became random. A dead pheasant lay on the road, its feathers spattered with dirt thrown up by the rain. The bird must have started from the grass and been trampled by the frightened horse. Then, judging by the prints, the horse had veered sharply to the right, toward a bramble thicket. Beth's first thought was that Joshua had recovered control and was now well on his way to the Gloucester road. Or was he? She halted, the carriage behind her suddenly forgotten as a cold finger ran down her back. Something felt wrong. She was close to the woods now, and the rooks seemed to be shrieking a warning. But of what? Lightning glittered to the south, followed by a long growl of thunder as she scanned the common for any sign of movement, but even the cattle and sheep were sheltering in the lee of the woods. Then, just beyond the bramble thicket, she saw Joshua's horse, riderless, its reins caught on thorns. Slowly she retrieved the pheasant, stuffed it into the basket, and made her way toward the thicket.

Joshua lay among the brambles, his clothes torn, his face and hands badly scratched and bloodied. His eyes stared unblinkingly toward her, and her heartbeats quickened unpleasantly. Was he still alive? She reached through the thorns to shake him, 'Joshua? Joshua, it's me, Miss Beth.' When he didn't react she knew he was dead. A hot wave of horror engulfed her, and suddenly her stomach revolted. She turned, heaving uncontrollably. It seemed an age before the convulsion eased and she was able to raise her face to the torrential rain. Her mouth tasted sour and she shivered uncontrollably. When at last she felt able to look at Joshua again, the first thing she saw was the sealed leather pouch protruding from his coat. Reaching for it, she felt the coins and paper inside, and knew it was a lot of money. Payment for Lancelot on its way to Jane's fat account at Williamson's Bank? Breaking her father's seal, she gasped on seeing the bank notes and gleaming gold guineas. It was a fortune! Her mind raced excitedly. With a sum like this she could be free to begin a new life, with good food in her belly and fine clothes on her back. She could go to London, where no one knew her, and then choose where she wished to live from then on. One possibility succeeded another with such speed that her thoughts were blurred.

Lightning flashed again and thunder shook the escarpment like the judgement of God and, as the sound died away, she took a huge breath and tried to be rational. She could walk away now, but what good would that do her? This might be the only chance she ever had to claw herself back out of poverty. Yet taking such a sum would mean prison, maybe even the gallows. Except that it wouldn't really be stealing, because Jane had no right to anything, including Lancelot. Closing the pouch again, she hid it beneath the pheasant in the basket. For a moment she considered taking the horse as well, but knew it would be risky. Better to stay on foot, as befitted someone of her present situation. Then she realized she also risked being accused of killing Joshua, which would certainly mean hanging!

Her fearful gaze darted around through the downpour, but all she saw were the sheep and cattle, and a few goats tethered by the fringe of the wood. Her mind went blank. She couldn't think, couldn't move. A pigeon flew up from an elm, wings clapping loudly as more lightning dazzled the sky, closely followed by a roll of thunder that resembled immense skittle balls in a heavenly alley. Beth's immobility ceased, and she hastened into action, freeing the horse and sending it cantering on into the woods, then grabbing the basket to run back to the track. With more sense she'd have remained in the thicket until the carriage had driven past. The effort of running, combined with hunger, made her hot and weak again. She was overwhelmed by the sick, churning feeling of earlier, colours began to merge into a garish red monochrome and, on reaching the road, she could no longer stay upright. Her knees sagged, and the basket fell as she lost consciousness.

Guy's coachman, Dickon, was alarmed to see a young woman slumped at the roadside. What was this? A trap? His bushy salt-and-pepper eyebrows drew together, and the capes of his brown benjamin coat dripped as he half stood, grasping the reins firmly in one hand and applying the brake with the other, almost losing his cocked hat and wig in the process. Guy leaned out as the carriage lurched to a sudden halt. 'What is it, Dickon?'

'Can't rightly say, Sir Guy. There's a woman keeled over just ahead. Might be a rum do.' He spoke with a broad West Country accent, but not Gloucestershire. 'Should I drive on, or take a look?'

'Take a look. I have my pistols ready.'

Lightning forked across the distant Severn, followed by a snarl of thunder as Dickon climbed down, muttering under his breath. On approaching, he saw her eyelids flutter as the cold rain dashed her face. She was younger than he'd expected, and far too thin, but would be comely if cleaned up. He realized she wasn't pretending. 'There now, missy, take it easy,' he said, crouching beside her.

'I'm all right.' Her memory returned, and with it came panic. How had she forgotten the carriage? If only she'd stayed out of sight.

'You're not all right, my girl, you're weak and hot.'

'I've been running, that's all.' He helped her to a sitting position.

'Without food for some time, I'd guess,' he said. She nodded and looked uneasily at the basket, which by some miracle had landed upright, its contents undisturbed. Dickon mistook the unease. 'Stole that fancy bird, did you?'

'I found it dead.' Her gaze moved to Guy as he alighted. How different Jane's visitor was close to, taller than she'd expected, deceptively lithe, with a suggestion of considerable strength. In spite of her weak state, she could still appreciate his natural grace and elegance. His tall hat was worn at a slight angle on his curling auburn hair, and there was an air of fashionable ennui in the way his ebony cane swung in his gloved hand. He was the sort of man for whom Beth Tremoille would once have appeared in her most becoming attire.

Dickon hissed at her beneath his breath. 'Mind your manners now, my girl, for this is Sir Guy Valmer.' Valmer? She tried to think. Tremoille House had once been Valmer House.

Guy reached them and stood looking down at her. 'When did you last eat?' he asked, his cane still swinging. The rain spattered his hat and excellent coat.

'Last night, sir.'

'Upon what delicacy, may one ask?'

'Crust and cheese, and some ale.'

'But tonight you'll dine in style on pheasant?' He pushed the basket with a toe. 'So, madam, you've been running after missing – let me see – two, possibly three meals? It would appear inevitable to me that you are found in such a state by the roadside. Why are you here?'

His grey eyes seemed to see right through her. 'I – I've been visiting up at Tremoille House. My aunt – Mrs Alder – is the cook there.'

'You're exceedingly well-spoken for a cook's niece. What's your name?'

'Bessie. Bessie Alder.' The lies came easily. Mrs Alder was indeed the cook at the house, and had a niece called Bessie.

'Well, we cannot leave you fainting away at the wayside, so if you're going to Gloucester, I'm Samaritan enough to take you in the carriage. But do, pray, keep well away from me. You may be well spoken, and no doubt, exceedingly pretty beneath the grime – but there are limits on my goodness of heart.'

In the carriage? She was horrified. He made her feel he could read her thoughts, and he asked a lot of prying questions. Five miles was a lot of questions. 'I'm happy to sit on the box,' she offered hopefully.

'Have such a ragamuffin perched like the figurehead on the *Victory*? No, madam, you'll keep out of sight inside.'

She nodded reluctantly. 'Yes, sir.'

The rain stopped suddenly as Guy returned to the carriage. Dickon pulled her to her feet and lifted the basket. Its weight took him by surprise. 'By God, that's some bloody pheasant!'

'Yes, to make a stew,' she said, fearing he would investigate the basket's contents, but instead he handed it over and she hurried to the carriage, where Guy waited to help her inside. His hands were strong, and she sensed their cleanliness beneath the flawless kid of his gloves. All of him was clean, and he smelled so good that she was made even more aware of her own dirt, so she pressed wretchedly into the furthest corner, the basket clutched close.

After pointedly lowering the window glass, Guy took his place as well, slouching back against the oyster velvet upholstery with his Hessian boots resting on the seat opposite. She gave him a covert glance. His eyes and lips seemed chill, she thought, and yet she found him alluring. Was the chillness a façade, masking a far warmer personality beneath? After all, how many gentlemen would rescue her from the wayside as he had done? Or perhaps the attraction was simply that he represented a world that was now lost to her.

She hadn't noticed the hamper in the other corner until Guy pushed it toward her with the tip of his cane, and flicked the lid back. 'Eat, I beg you, for I cannot bear the thought of your hunger.' She saw a capon inside, with some crusty bread, slices of cooked ham and some red cheese, and lodged at the back a bottle of good German wine. Removing his gloves, Guy leaned across for the bottle, which had already been opened, with the cork only shoved lightly back in place, and poured a little wine into a glass. 'Steady now, or your stomach will reject it.' As she sipped, he broke a portion of the capon and presented it to her. 'Since you are too shy to take anything, I will thrust it upon you.'

He watched her eat. Try as she would, hunger overcame manners, and she knew she was devouring the succulent meat like a dog gobbling its one meal of the day. 'So, Miss Alder, you have been visiting your aunt the cook, who should be reprimanded for not feeding you.' Lancelot neighed behind the carriage and he saw her eyes fly to the window. 'You appreciate horses, Miss Alder?'

'I don't know anything about them, Sir Guy.'

'Then you may take my word for it that the creature I have purchased this day is worth every penny of his thousand guinea price.' Beth's heart almost stopped. She had stolen a *thousand* guineas? Guy misunderstood the change on her face. 'I agree, it's an unjust world that permits me to lavish a fortune on a horse, but denies you food. Some more Rhine wine, Miss Alder?'

'Rhine? Surely it's Moselle?' she replied unguardedly.

'So, not only do you speak beautifully, but you can distinguish between Rhine and Moselle.' He tapped his fingers on the handle of his cane. 'Who *are* you? I am not in the habit of forgetting faces, nor do I normally give aid to the ill-washed and ill-dressed, but you have aroused my curiosity.'

'I'm Bessie Alder, sir.'

'So you say, but somehow I feel I've seen you somewhere before. Quite recently. But where?'

'You're mistaken, sir.' She guessed he'd noticed the portrait in the hall at Tremoille House.

The carriage swayed on down through the steep, dripping woods towards the broad levels of the Severn vale. To Beth's relief the remainder of the journey was accomplished in silence, although the atmosphere became more and more claustrophobic. She began to feel that Guy's eyes would soon penetrate the basket and see the pouch nestling beneath its pheasant blanket. Her thoughts turned to how and when to run away to London. It was best to leave as soon as she could, while her courage was still high. Jake knew too many people in Gloucester, so she'd go to nearby Cheltenham, and buy a coach ticket at the Plough Inn.

Never had five miles in a carriage seemed to take longer, and the evening light was fading when at last they drove past the new dock basin and approached the site of Gloucester's medieval southern gate. The watery sun was setting in a horizon of carnation and salmon, edging the clouds with a fringe of lurid garnet. For some weeks now there had been unusual spectacles of colour when the sun was low in the heavens.

Dickon drove up into Southgate Street, where the carriage wheels rattled and splashed through puddles among the uneven cobbles. Everything was oddly quiet, with no one around, and no other traffic. Something felt wrong. After passing Williamson's Bank, and Dickon halted the team to ask directions of a young woman – plump, painted and blonde – leaning from an upper window in a gown so low cut it was a miracle her bosoms did not tumble out. Beth knew the house. It was a brothel, with one bawd or another always at the window, displaying her breasts and offering male passers-by a variety of services. This woman was more impertinent than most, and after telling Dickon how to get to the Crown Inn, she noticed Guy seated in the carriage. She winked at him and bared her nipples. 'Like to play with these, luvvy? Can I give you a good f—?'

Guy interrupted her. 'The only thing you're likely to give me is the clap.'

Her rouged face suffused. 'That's a lie! I'm clean and so is this house!'

'For pity's sake drive on, Dickon,' Guy said, tapping the roof with his cane.

The whore's screeches followed as the carriage began to move. 'What's wrong, molly boy? Can't get it up except for another cocker? A bugger in velvet and lace, eh? Just a limp-wristed, tight-waisted, stretch-arsed bugger!'

'How delightful,' Guy murmured, while Beth kept her eyes lowered.

The old streets of Southgate, Northgate, Eastgate and Westgate met at the Cross in heart of the city, where it was always busy. But today there was no one to see as Dickon drove over into Northgate, before turning left into Cathedral Lane, where stood two prominent inns, the Black Horse and the Crown. There ought to have been ostlers outside the Black Horse, trying to lure trade from the nearby Crown, but there was no one, although the angry murmur of voices could be heard in the taproom as someone delivered a rabble-rousing speech.

The Crown's galleried, ivy-twined courtyard was also deserted, and although the smell of roast beef emanated from the kitchen, there was no clatter of pots and pans. Only when Dickon bellowed for service did two reluctant ostlers venture rather furtively from the stables at the rear of the inn. A mist of rain drifted in the air as Guy alighted, but then shouting and general disturbance broke out at the Black Horse, and fear began to prickle over Beth's skin. This was why the streets had been so unnaturally quiet, she thought. Word of imminent trouble had kept honest citizens in their homes. Fired by drink and the troublemaking orator, an unruly slogan-chanting mob poured into Cathedral Lane. Hatred of the new Corn Laws was tangible.

A window was smashed in the lane, and Lancelot began to rear and whinny. Guy whirled around to one of the ostlers. 'Hold him, damn you!' The moment his attention was diverted, Beth jumped down from the other side of the carriage and slipped out into the dangerous lane just as the innkeeper ordered the courtyard gates closed. Guy hadn't even realized she'd gone; if, indeed, he'd care, for of what significance was a starving ragamuffin compared to the alarm of a thousand-guinea horse? A bakery window had been shattered, and there were triumphant yells as men grabbed what bread they could. When the last loaf had been seized there was a moment's eerie silence before a man in a sacking hood hurled a lighted torch into the bakery. The chanting and howls of bitter anger resumed. Mayhem was all around, and the smoke, but then came the sound of drumming hoofs, and someone shouted a warning that scattered everyone. 'The militia's coming, lads! Make yourselves scarce!'

Beth's heart raced as she followed some men to the cathedral close at the end of the lane. She hardly glanced at the great church's soaring splendour as she ran across toward King Edward's Gate, and then into Westgate at the bottom of which was the Severn and the riverside road to the new dock basin. From the docks it was only yards to Fiddler's Court, the dingy yard where she lived with Jake Mannacott and his daughter, Rosalind. The docks, barely three years old, were still busy because the Severn's notorious tides did not wait for anything. A ship canal was being built between Gloucester and Berkeley Pill, to avoid the treacherous meanders of the river between the city and the sea, but thanks to her father, among others, work on it had stopped due to lack of funds, forcing cargoes on to the river. As she skirted the timber yards on the northern side of the basin, she saw trows – traditional Severn barges – making ready at the river lock. She hurried around a wharf cluttered with coal, road stone, barrels, casks, bales, chests and ropes, and after tying the basket to her shawl, which served as a rope, climbed over a padlocked gate into the deserted street beyond.

Then she paused, clutching the basket and shawl to her breast. That morning she'd had nothing; tonight she had a thousand guineas and was on the point of leaving Gloucester for a new life. She walked on. Every night she gave herself to Jake, pretending pleasure because she felt indebted for the roof over her head. He worshipped her as a goddess, yet she hadn't stepped down from Olympus, merely from the Cotswolds, and she was flesh and blood, with all the needs, faults and frailties of her kind. Her body was no longer chaste, but her heart was. Poor Jake would be inconsolable when she left; his jealous slyboots of a daughter, however, would be overjoyed. Rosalind Mannacott was almost seventeen and didn't care a fig for anyone but herself. She worked in Poll Barker's tavern, although what sort of a barmaid she was could only be imagined. Saucy and congenial were not words that sprang to mind. Beth had heard that Poll would have dismissed her long since had not her odious, libidinous son, Ned, prevented it.

At last she reached the narrow passage leading to the yard and dirty cottages of Fiddler's Court. Jake's cottage, little more than one room with a loft, stood at the far end. With faded green paint on the dilapidated door, and a grey, moth-eaten net curtain at the single window, it was hardly an agreeable abode, yet a light, girlish voice sang sweetly inside. Beth knew there would be silence the moment she entered. Sighing, she lifted the latch. The song broke off mid-note.

Chapter Three

Beth entered a low-ceilinged room where a dim light was provided by a rancid tallow candle that smoked unpleasantly as the door closed. The cottage was a far cry from the luxury of Tremoille House, possessing three rather rickety wooden chairs, a table with one leg supported on a brick, and a shelf bearing some chipped crockery, pots and pans, a pair of iron candlesticks, a tinderbox, and Jake's shaving things. Opposite a tiny fireplace there was a ladder to the loft, where everyone slept. The rain dashed against the window, and every now and then a drop fell down the chimney to patter on the crumpled newspaper, sticks and stolen coal that were placed in readiness for a fire.

Rosalind was on her chair by the fireplace, and her face had assumed the surliness she kept for Beth. She was a pretty girl, with long straight silver-blonde hair, and large forget-me-not eyes set above high cheekbones. Her figure was slender, and her small, upturned breasts had pronounced nipples that showed through her worn lilac cotton dress. Given good clothes and a better start in life she could have been elegant, but as a blacksmith's dissatisfied daughter she was thin, ragged and sullen. 'Hello, Rosalind,' Beth said.

The girl got up and spoke with a deliberately broad Gloucestershire accent. 'I've done the lessons you left me.' She took a battered notebook from the mantelshelf and dropped it on the table as if it were a dead rat.

'The lessons your father asked me to leave for you,' Beth corrected, unwilling to take the blame for trying to educate Rosalind Mannacott. She placed the pheasant on the table before taking the basket up to the loft to hide the pouch under the straw where she and Jake slept. The rain tamped noisily on the roof just above her head, but even so she feared the chink of coins would carry to Rosalind's sharp ears. Then she took off her wet clothes to hang them on the rafter hooks, next to the fashionable togs she'd worn on leaving Tremoille House.

The clothes were still immaculate. She hadn't worn them since, because they made her look as if she were in one world, when in fact she was now in another. It had been money well spent when she used a little of her meagre purse to acquire ragged garments and a battered valise in which to hide her former glory. Glimpsing her poverty-stricken reflection in a puddle had been a dreadful moment, so awful that she sat on the edge of a horse trough in tears. That was when Jake found her. He'd been so kind and concerned – genuinely so – and offered her a roof over her head in exchange for lessons in reading and writing for his daughter. But teaching Rosalind was a thankless task, leaving Beth feeling she wasn't earning her keep; so she became Jake's lover.

Beth touched the cream muslin gown sprigged with pale rose pink flowers, and the exquisitely stitched rose velvet spencer. On a little shelf nearby were the matching velvet reticule, emerald green gloves and a pretty straw bonnet. Her white silk stockings were tucked into the black patent shoes that rested on top of a rafter. It all looked as if she'd just disrobed, and the quality was such that it would fetch a pretty penny in Gloucester, but Jake wouldn't let her sell anything. He wanted her to keep this small portion of her former life. But even though he'd always been kind and loving, tonight she was going to desert him. It wouldn't be an entirely selfish desertion, because she'd decided to leave him half the guineas. Only that way could she salve her conscience regarding the man who'd saved her and given her his love.

A draught of cool, damp air beneath the eaves made her shiver and, as her nipples tightened, her thoughts became more sensuous and fanciful, but it wasn't Jake who came to mind, it was Sir Guy Valmer. She had been very conscious of his worldly, almost feline appeal. He was sophisticated and dangerously handsome, and the enigma in his remarkable grey eyes promised things – pleasures – of which she as yet knew nothing. His hair, so richly coloured and curling, was thick and soft in a way that invited ruffling by female fingertips, and his lips promised kisses that would melt the soul. She touched her breasts and closed her eyes, recalling all she'd noticed about him, even his habit of toying with the shirt frill at his cuff. He had awakened something primitive that she hadn't known before, a need to cross the chasm between dutiful caresses and fierce desire. What would it be like to lie with him? To have him inside her? To possess him just for a few minutes? To kiss his mouth, his throat, his chest, all of him? Yes, all of him. She wanted to bury her face in the tangle of hair at his loins, and breathe in the scent of him, wanted to take the source of his masculinity in her mouth and— Shocked by the path her desires were taking, her eyes flew open again. She had never even *thought* of kissing that part of Jake, yet mere kisses were the very least of her cravings for Sir Guy Valmer! What was the matter with her? He frightened her so she hadn't been able to escape from him quickly enough, and yet now she dreamed of being sexually intimate with him. It wasn't just a dream, but a physical lust that hunted through her flesh like hunger through the starving. She drew a deep breath, determined never to think such shameful things again. Much good would it do her anyway, because although the former Beth Tremoille might have been able to reach out to him without fear of rejection, he'd been disgusted by the Beth Tremoille of Fiddler's Court.

Rosalind moved around downstairs, and Beth hurriedly donned her second dress, a poor garment of faded brown wool, and then dragged her wooden comb through her damp, tangled hair. From the top of the ladder she watched as Rosalind inspected the pheasant. The girl looked up as Beth descended again. 'Where did you get this? Gamekeeper turned poacher, eh?' she sneered.

Beth was in no mood. 'No doubt you'll be eager enough when the stew's ready.' The girl flounced back toward her chair, but Beth tossed the pheasant on to the seat. 'Oh, no, you're going to do your share of work. Pluck the wretched thing.'

Rosalind clearly longed to hurl the pheasant back, but thought better of it and began to tug out the feathers savagely. Beth used the tinderbox to coax a fire in the hearth, and then drew water from the well in the rain-swept yard and suspended a pot above the new flames. When the pheasant was gutted and ready she quartered it with a small axe Jake had made, and into the pot it went, together with the onion, carrot and few potatoes Rosalind had stolen in the market the day before. Beth was making the nourishing stew for Jake and Rosalind; she herself would no longer be here to sample it. Tonight they'd make do with dry bread and stale cracked Single Gloucester cheese. It would be tasty enough toasted.

Her tasks finished for the moment, she decided to break the silence with Rosalind. 'Did you get wet coming back from the tavern?' she asked, but her amiability fell on stony ground.

'There's no way of coming back dry when it's pissing down.'

'Why do you always have to be so bitter? And so foul-mouthed? I've been teaching you how to speak properly, so I know you can do better.'

'You're a fancy Tremoille, so you swank around with your nose in the air. Me? I'm a nobody who'll never amount to much, so why try to bully me into your snob ways? In the tavern I serve others just like me, not fine lords, so don't try to make me what I'm not!'

'I teach you because it's what your father wants,' Beth reminded her.

'And what does he know? Nothing!'

'He knows that he wants a better life for you, Rosalind. You're a pretty girl and have brains. It wouldn't take much effort for you to make a good enough marriage to put all this behind you.' Beth indicated the shabby cottage.

'Silk purses don't come from sow's ears,' Rosalind replied.

'Well, if you want to remain a sow's ear, just continue the way you are.'

Before Rosalind could think of a suitably stinging reply, familiar steps were heard in the court. They both turned as the door opened in a flurry of rain, and Jake bowed his head to come in. He brought the smell of the forge on his wet clothes as he went to sniff the stew pot. 'What's this? We've got *meat* to sup?'

'I found a fresh-dead pheasant,' Beth replied. 'But it won't be ready until tomorrow. I'm afraid it's toasted bread and cheese tonight.'

He grinned, and took off his old cloak to shake raindrops over the floor. At forty, he was still remarkably youthful, a giant of a man whose light-brown hair didn't have a single strand of grey. His brown eyes twinkled as he drew a bottle of cheap brandy from his coat pocket and set it on the table. 'This fell off a passing wagon, so we'll live well for a few hours, eh, Bethie.' He took two cups from the hooks above the stone sink. 'The liquor will turn bread and cheese into a king's banquet, and leave us with a nice glow, eh?'

Rosalind pouted. 'And what about me?' she demanded.

'No liquor for you, Rozzie, you're too young.'

'Not too young to work in a tavern!' Belligerence entered her voice.

Beth quickly diverted his attention. 'I wonder if it's quiet in town now? When I came back the militia dispersed a mob firing the bakery in Cathedral Lane.'

'How come you saw something like that?' The bottle paused over the second cup. 'Your way home from Tremoille House doesn't take you up into town.'

She coloured with unnecessary guilt. 'I – I was lucky enough to have a carriage stop for me.'

'Oh?'

'Well, I'd fainted by the roadside, and—'

He was appalled. 'Fainted? Oh, Bethie!'

'It was hot, I was hungry, and I ran to try to get to the woods for shelter from the storm.'

'Who stopped?'

'A gentlemen who'd bought a horse from my stepmother. His name is Sir Guy Valmer, and he's lodging at the Crown. He didn't know who I was.'

Jake's eyes darkened. 'And what did he want for his charity?'

'Nothing. Oh, no, Jake, don't think *that*, because I can tell you here and now that I stank far too much for him.'

'I know you wouldn't lie to me about such things, Bethie,' he conceded. 'Forgive me, I still can't quite believe I've got you.' He pushed a cup toward her. 'Here, take a draught of this, it'll do you good.'

Her guilty conscience increased, and she was quite relieved when he reverted to her earlier question. 'As to the trouble in town, all I know is what I was told by a fellow I passed on the road. He said there'd been a curfew set after a riot over bread prices, and that I'd best get home as quickly as I could, or the militia would nab me.' He sighed sadly. 'I don't know what the world's coming to. Damned unjust, that's what it is. Landlords and all the grand folks looking after their own interests as always, and leaving the rest of us poor sods to starve. They'll rue it one day, Bethie, there'll come a revolution in England like happened in France, unless they watch out in London. We peasants are good enough to fight for our country, but not good enough to get our fair share of the bounty.' He took the bottle and sat in his chair. 'I trudged to Whitton today for a couple of hours' work. Damn me, it's humiliating, Bethie. Standing around like a great girl, in case a mean-gizzard called Carter might need some help. Carter. Bloody ugly bugger he was, with an ugly disposition to match. I could have stuck his poker up his arse as soon as look at him.' Jake ran his hand through his hair. 'And all I could think of was how I'd like to buy a half-share of the village forge at Frampney. Twenty guineas are what I need, but I might as well whistle at the moon. Anyway, I'm this late because I went to Frampney to take a look. It belongs to a farrier named Matty Brown; his wife is called Phoebe. A straight couple, no nasty sides. I liked them both, and they liked me. They're getting on now, and Matty needs someone younger for the harder work. It would suit me down to the ground, suit us *all* down to the ground.' He drew a very long breath. 'By all the saints, Bethie, getting into that forge would be a neat thing. A very neat thing. And Rozzie wouldn't have to work at that damned tavern, or get groped about by that cock fool, Ned Barker.'

Beth nodded. In this one thing she sympathized with Rosalind. Ned Barker was unspeakable, yet his mother was always proudly hinting that he had a lord for a father. No one believed her, because Ned was a lout through and through, and convinced he was God's gift to womankind. His attentions to Rosalind were bad enough for Jake to have already set about him one dark night. There was a violent side to Jake, especially where his daughter's well-being and chastity were concerned. Well, Ned wouldn't paw Rosalind again, because by this time tomorrow Jake would possess enough money to buy into that forge in Frampney *and* get a nice little cottage in the village. He and Rosalind would have a new life in the country, with food for their bellies and a roof that didn't leak. She sipped the brandy, which was so fiery that she began to cough.

Jake laughed. 'A scorching mouthful, eh?' He drained his cup and poured a little more. 'You know, while I was working today, two fine lordlings came in with a dandy high-stepping nag. I had blisters on my feet, rags on my back, and a belly groaning like God knows what, and they whined on about the low price they were getting for their corn. God above, Bethie, there was no comparison between them and me. They see a poorhouse as something to walk past with a dainty nosegay, but for me, unless I get full work soon, the poorhouse is too damn close for comfort.'

At Tremoille House that same evening, Jane finished the glass of dry sherry she'd been enjoying in her private apartment, and smoothed the silver-blue taffeta gown she hadn't worn for well over a year. She was leaving widowhood behind, so rubies glowed at her throat, and there was a jewelled aigrette in her beautifully pinned hair. Thomas had called and was waiting for her in the drawing-room. She glanced a final time at the copy of *Lithgow's Journal*. It was risky to accept Thomas, but she couldn't bear to let him slip through her fingers now. With a sigh, she left the apartment to go downstairs.

He was dressed for the evening, but didn't look particularly at ease, having always preferred to slouch around in hunting pink. A paunchy fifty-two, he had never been handsome: his forehead was too broad, his eyebrows too bushy, his cheeks almost hollow, and his wiry iron-grey hair had receded to a monk's tonsure. Height wasn't in his favour either, because he was barely an inch taller than her. He was inconsiderate, testy and generally lacking in charm, and yet she remained his adoring slave. The Worcester bordello where they'd met had served gentlemen with a penchant for young girls. She'd been fourteen, and his title and money were more than enough to impress her, but then he deserted her for the dull, blue-blooded Diana, a fact that in her darker moments Jane still resented. There was no hint of any of this in her greeting. 'Thomas, how good it is to see you again,' she said warmly, her hands outstretched as she approached him.

'My dear.' He kissed her cheek and approved of the abandonment of her weeds, but she knew something was distracting him. She ushered him to one of the most comfortable chairs. Like the rest of Tremoille House, the drawing-room was all that was Tudor, with jewel-bright tapestries on the oak panelling and three cartwheel chandeliers suspended from the elaborate plasterwork of the ceiling. The large carved stone fireplace, big enough to stand in, still bore traces of its original decorative paintwork, especially the blue lion of the Valmers, and the furniture might have been used by one of the Tudor monarchs. When Thomas was seated, he took out a cigar and lit it from a candlestick on the small table at his elbow. 'Well, Jane, you won't have heard the news.'

'News?' She went to pour two glasses of Esmond's finest cognac.

'That the expected battle has taken place and Bonaparte is trounced?'

Her lips parted. 'I haven't heard anything like that. That a battle was about to be fought, yes, but not the outcome.' She handed him a glass.

'Hardly anyone knows. I met an old acquaintance who told me the banker Rothschild received the intelligence from Brussels by, well, by pigeon. It seems they not only fly home, but can bring messages too. So I'm told, anyway.' He sipped the cognac and smacked his lips loudly.

Jane sat down. 'Are you sure someone isn't pulling your leg?'

'No, I'm not sure, but I feel it's all the truth.'

'If so, what is Rothschild doing about it?' she asked, 'Buying? Selling?'

'He's too wily a fox to let that out. Damn it all, I don't know what to do, Jane. I could make a fortune, or lose it.' He leaned his head back.

'Are you asking my opinion?'

'Certainly not.' He looked at her as if she'd lost her wits.

She changed the subject. 'How is Rowan?'

'My son and heir is a mystery to me. I haven't understood him since he was sent down from Oxford for indulging in prizefighting, among other low things. How Diana and I produced him, I cannot begin to guess.'

Jane had always suspected the saintly Diana of breaking the Seventh Commandment, but could hardly say as much. 'He's young yet,' she said reassuringly, 'and as I recall, his father was not dissimilar in his youth.'

He was disparaging. 'The boy's twenty, damn it. At his age I knew control; he apparently has none. But looking at him, one can't imagine he's a hell hound.'

'I'm so sorry, Thomas, for I know you had such high expectations of him.' She spoke soothingly and with implied admiration, knowing it rarely did any harm to flatter a man's vanity. It was easy to slip back into her old whorehouse skills.

He drew on the cigar. 'You're still a harlot, Jane, with the added attraction of also being a rich and desirable widow.'

She wished he'd show less avarice and more affection. Why did she love him so much? The heart was a thing of mystery. 'Are you sure even now that you want this old whore as your wife?' she enquired a little acidly.

'You surely didn't expect me to make you Lady Welland all those years ago? Damn it, your tail was for hire at that damned bagnio!'

'Esmond married me,' she observed.

'Tremoille was an eccentric libertine who enjoyed being shocking, although I notice even he took care to bury your past. He preferred to hug himself with secret laughter when he saw society accepting you to its bosom.'

'Whereas you preferred to break my heart,' she answered reproachfully.

'Be fair! I'd have been thought a fool.'

'So you married a fool instead,' she said.

'Don't speak of Diana like that.'

'I'll speak of her as I choose, Thomas. She was a fool from the day she was born until the day she shuffled her mortal coil. Ah, but let us not forget that she was also too well-bred to say boo to a goose, which made her perfect for you.'

'I warn you, Jane—'

'You can't order me yet, Thomas. I'm a free agent, not the gullible little doxy who was dazzled by your title as she ministered to your cock.'

His eyes narrowed. 'My, my, how refined you are.'

'And how you used to like it.'

'Maybe I did.'

'Is that past tense too? I'm sure you'd still like it now.'

'You're hardly a young girl.'

'And you, sir, are a portly, middle-aged man, so let us not quibble.'

For once he saw the humour of it. 'All right, you win. Maybe I *did* make the wrong decision all those years ago. I'll never forget my amazement when I heard you'd become Mrs Tremoille, or that first time I saw you in society, dancing a *ländler* with the Duke of Beaufort. He had no idea his partner was a whore.'

'And dear Diana had no idea about anything either,' Jane replied slyly. 'I *so* wanted to tell her about your taste for young girls. Tell me, did you indulge after me?'

'Occasionally,' he answered frankly, 'but if you're fishing to know if they were better than you, the answer is no. You were in a class of your own, Jane.'

'I still am,' she said softly.

Her change of tone wasn't lost on him. 'Oh, Jane, when you speak like that.'

'Things stir?'

He put his glass and cigar aside and held her gaze. 'You've *always* stirred me.'

'It's been a long time, Thomas.'

'Claiming to be as good as ever is one thing, proving it quite another.' He unfastened his white silk breeches.

She was dumbstruck, having expected no more than a little verbal flirting, but her powerful sensuality forbade her to overlook this sudden opportunity to satisfy her lust. And his. The desires she tried so hard to suppress were suddenly released as if through a sluice, her treacherous thighs quaked and her loins softened as if they were melting. She knew he wouldn't produce a great throbbing weapon, because he had always needed working on before he stiffened enough to be useful, but she'd dreamed of this for so long that she didn't care how small and shrivelled his tool was. Her blue gown whispered as she knelt before his chair and took him in her hand. He was warm, velvet soft, and yet to respond as she leaned forward to put her lips over the crinkled foreskin and slide her tongue inside against the hidden surface within. He grew and grew until the foreskin had pulled right back, exposing the most delicious of lollipops, or so she'd always likened it. She licked and nibbled gently, then enclosed it entirely with her mouth. Oh, how she loved the taste of a man, and the knowledge that she was in command of this most precious part of his anatomy. It was his lodestar; without it he'd be lost.

Ripples of excitement began to concentrate between her legs as she savoured him, rolling him around in her mouth and sliding her tongue over him. Oh, how she feasted upon him, her body undulating erotically as her pleasure intensified. She could feel herself drifting toward the edge of consciousness, before she sank weakly against him as wild contractions of desire overtook her. He arched as enjoyment consumed him too, but he made no attempt to reach out to her as he moaned and gasped. Then he came with a force that made him cry out, and she enjoyed such tremendous gratification that she could hardly breathe. For a long moment they remained together, and then he sighed. 'By the powers, Jane, you *are* still as good as ever.'

'This old dog has no new tricks to learn,' she said, sitting back on her heels. Sexual satisfaction was so necessary to her that sometimes she thought she would go mad without it. She made a considerable effort to get up gracefully from the floor and return to her chair.

'So, Jane, are we to share a marriage bed?' he enquired, shoving his limp appendage unceremoniously back inside his breeches, and fastening them again.

'I haven't decided,' she answered with misplaced coyness.

He disliked simpering. 'Well, to be honest, my dear, I need reassurance that you're still worth offering for.'

Her cocoon of sexual warmth shattered, admitting cold shivers that slid down her spine. 'What do you mean?' she asked. 'Surely you aren't about to play the callow boy and tell me I've just cheapened myself too much for your bed?'

'Allow me more maturity than that. No, Jane, I must ask you some questions.'

'Questions?' From nowhere the ominous shadow of the missing will fell across her again, but she kept strict control of herself.

He nodded and reached for the cigar again. 'I learned this morning of a second will that reinstated your stepdaughter and excluded you. Is there any truth in this?'

'None whatsoever.' Her fingers were crossed in the folds of her gown.

'You swear it?' he pressed.

'Of course. Thomas, is your proposal solely based on acquisition?'

He gave a short laugh. 'If you expect romance from me, you'll be disappointed.'

'I think I had already grasped that fact, Thomas.'

'And you know nothing of the fire that killed the lawyer Beswick?' he asked.

At that she rose coldly to her feet. 'I do not care for the implication, sir!'

He waved her to sit down again. 'Don't be so damned prickly, woman, it's a reasonable enough question.'

She remained standing. 'Reasonable? I beg to differ. You should not lend your ears to tittle-tattle that was no doubt started by my hussy of a stepdaughter.'

'Beth? Maybe. I thought she'd left Gloucester, but apparently not.'

'If she's still here, she certainly doesn't mix in good society.'

He was droll. 'Hardly surprising when you made damned sure all

decent doors were closed to her. By the time you'd finished with her character, she'd become a blend of Lucretia Borgia, Messalina and Delilah.'

'Come to the point, Thomas. Are you withdrawing your proposal?'

'If you've told me the truth, the proposal still stands. So what's it to be?
Do you wish to become Lady Welland?'

'I thought I did, but now I'm not sure,' she replied, too disturbed by the
past moments to think clearly. She had always seen him for what he really
was, a grasping bully who would never treat her well, but *still* her heart –
and body – ruled her head.

He frowned. 'Don't forget I'm offering you a title.'

'Nor do I forget that I will be your chattel,' she answered, adding, 'I've
had a year of complete freedom, and the feeling is good.'

'But are your lonely nights also good?'

Colour entered her cheeks. 'Maybe they haven't been lonely.'

His eyebrow quirked. 'I hardly think even you would stoop to that
lapdog butler. Come on, Jane, we'll do well together.' Provided I continue
to have the rights to these estates, she thought. He took her silence for
consent. 'Then it's agreed?'

She hesitated. 'Yes, it's agreed.'

'Excellent! The sooner we're wed, the sooner I can get out of Whitend.'

She was nonplussed. 'Get out of Whitend? I don't understand.'

'It's bloody damp there, what with the moat and standing between the
river and the canal,' he replied. 'The one thing for which I really have to
thank your late lamented husband is that he put a stop to the Gloucester
and Berkeley Canal. Now it seems the canal is to be completed after all. It
passes within a hundred yards of the house, Jane, and on an embankment
too. Then I had a nightmare.' He cleared his throat, discomfited by his
own morbid fears. 'A week ago I dreamed I drowned.'

'Thomas, dreams are just dreams.'

'You don't understand. I dreamed of drowning *in* the house. There was
water everywhere, as if the sea had reclaimed the vale.' He shuddered.

She didn't know what to say. There had been a time when he'd backed
the canal scheme, seeing it as a fine way to increase his fortune. He also
enjoyed sailing on the estuary, and acquired an interest in the Forest of
Dean coal that was brought upriver to Gloucester. Now, because of a
dream, he feared water?

He drained his glass and then drew a long breath. 'You see, Jane, if the
embankment were to be breached, or the Severn tide burst the river-
banks....'

'Oh, Thomas,' she chided, getting up to replenish his glass.

'You may find it amusing, but we all have secret fears, do we not? Mine
is a horrible and lingering death by drowning.'

'Is *that* why you're marrying me, to live up here?' She managed a smile.
But he wasn't amused. 'It isn't a matter for levity, Jane,' he said gruffly.

'You have lived at Whitend all your life, and your forebears for centuries. It will still be standing – and dry! – for generations to come. So, let's forget about such things, and think of our betrothal instead. We *are* betrothed, aren't we?'

He looked at her and pulled himself together. 'Yes, and arrangements for the marriage itself can commence. I have a fancy for the cathedral.'

'Wouldn't it be more suitable to have a discreet wedding?'

'No, damn it, I won't skulk to the altar. I'll make arrangements for it to proceed as soon as possible and as grandly as possible. I want *all* of Gloucestershire to be there, every knight, baronet, viscount and earl, with a duke or so to add class.' He got up reluctantly. 'Well, I suppose I'd better toddle off to Whitend.' He looked expectantly at her, clearly hoping to share her bed for the night, but she was having none of it.

'You've enjoyed enough of my hospitality for the tonight.' There was a discreet tap at the door, and she turned irritably. 'What is it, Bolton?'

The butler came in. 'Madam, Joshua's horse has been found riderless.'

The thousand guineas! Had Joshua stolen it? 'Have someone ride to Mr Williamson's residence in Eastington, to enquire whether or not Joshua delivered the money. Well, go on, you fool!'

Thomas raised an eyebrow as the door closed. 'Who, pray, is Joshua?'

'A trusted servant I sent to Gloucester with money for Williamson's Bank.'

He found it amusing. 'Trusted? The look on your face suggests you may have made an error of judgement. You need a husband to control your purse strings.'

Chapter Four

Fiddler's Court was quiet and Rosalind was fast asleep in the loft. Fresh rain pattered against the ill-fitting window as Beth washed in a welcome bowl of warm water. She'd braved the rain a little earlier to wash her hair in water from an old butt in the corner of the yard. Now she felt clean again as she went to sit naked on the threadbare rug in front of the dying fire, Jake stripped to use the same water to scrub away the grime of the forge. He was well developed and muscular, with a hairy chest and an upper half that was deeply tanned. Everything from his waist down was pale. He had taut buttocks and strong thighs, and his male member seemed almost vulnerable as it hung from the dense forest of dark hair at his groin. He was a fine figure of a man, good-looking and virile, courageous and kind, and she wished she could love him in the way he loved her.

'Oh, Bethie,' he whispered, coming to draw her fingers to his lips and kiss them as gracefully as any gentleman of quality. Contrition gnawed through her. This man loved and trusted her, he gave himself without question, and would do anything for her, but tonight she was deserting him for a new life. Ought she to tell him, or was it kinder to leave him in ignorance and make this final evening something he would always remember for its tenderness and passion?

'I'm sorry Rozzie treats you so badly,' he said, as he sat down with her.

'It's not your fault, Jake. She doesn't like sharing you with me, and now you've insisted she learns to speak properly, she probably thinks you're ashamed of her.'

'You're her chance to make something of herself. She has to learn how to go on, and right now is too quick with her tongue. A shrew is what she is.' He smiled. 'So, what happened up at the house?'

'I just watched from the boundary.'

'A wise thing, too. You won't get anything back from that old cow. But the Devil takes his own, and one day she'll roast in a hot place.'

'Do you promise?' she asked with a smile, and leaned her head against his shoulder. Her dark curls tumbled over his skin, and the muted firelight swayed gently over the soft contours of her body and face, emphasizing the delicate loveliness that poverty had not dimmed.

'I'd promise you the moon on a stick if I could, Bethie,' he whispered, stroking her cheek. 'You're the prettiest damn thing I ever saw in my life, do you know that? Those big hazel-green eyes promise a man heaven, but it doesn't really work, you and me, does it? I can reach out and touch you when I want, but I don't really *have* you, do I? It's like grasping a will o' the wisp, or trying to keep hold of a good dream that wants to go come morning light.'

Such poetry from a man like Jake almost undid her, especially as it revealed him to have more insight than she'd realized. Tears stung her eyes, and she caught his hand. 'Don't, Jake, please don't.'

'There's no need to cry at my nonsense.' He looked curiously at her. 'It's only the liquor talking. You never promised me anything, and I know it'll end someday, sooner or later.'

'I'm sorry, Jake,' she whispered. 'I want to love you, truly I do.'

'Don't be sorry, Bethie, for you've been kindness itself to me,' he said, placing his hand on her knee and caressing it gently. 'People around here gloated when you lost everything, but not me.'

'My father's influence with the canal company threw a lot out of work, so I can understand their delight in my downfall.'

'I'll never forget the moment I saw you sobbing your heart out, looking as lost and frightened as a kitten.'

'A *kitten*?' She smiled.

'Yes,' he whispered, reaching for her hand. 'Dear God, I love you, Bethie.'

'I know,' she whispered.

'And I want you so badly right now that cocker's fit nigh to burst.'

He placed her hand on the erection rising from his groin. Her fingers closed gently around it, and she slowly teased the foreskin back to massage him with the palm of her hand. She wanted so much to give him pleasure, to show by what she did now that while it wasn't passionate love, her affection for him still went very deep indeed. Tomorrow, when she'd gone, he'd know what she'd been saying tonight. Her fingers were knowing and tender, teasing, pausing, and teasing a little more, almost bringing him to a climax, but not quite. She knew him so well, and was able to prolong his delight until it almost became too much for him. Her caresses were intoxicating, and he lay back on the floor, his whole body arching with intense gratification, until suddenly he drew her to the floor and straddled her to kiss the valley between her breasts. From there his lips moved to a nipple, while he fondled the breast with adoring fingers. She caressed him too, sliding her hands over his back and down to his waist, and then down to his buttocks. He didn't enter her yet, for that would lead to a hasty conclusion, and he wanted to prolong the exquisite pleasure.

35

She didn't anticipate thinking of Sir Guy Valmer; indeed he seemed nowhere in her mind, but suddenly Jake had changed. It was Guy she embraced, Guy who kindled exquisite excitement between her legs. Her blood ran more swiftly, her skin flushed and she met Jake's lips in a kiss that seemed to burn them both. He couldn't restrain himself any longer, and pushed deep into her. She clung to her imagination, so that it was Guy who thrust into her, Guy who impaled her with his passion. A spring tide of sexual satisfaction rushed through her, sweeping her up until she felt weightless. She had never before experienced such unbelievable ecstasy, or wanted anyone so much that she yearned for her flesh to fuse with his. The motion of his body, the warmth of his skin, the joy of his domination, all had become one in her world. Pleasure, deep, deep pleasure, please let it go on forever.

Jake gasped her name as he came in an explosion of pulsating desire, but it was Guy's voice she heard. Everything was Guy, and her emotions were so chaotic that she could barely grasp reality. Bewildered tears stung her eyes. She had just experienced the most rare and consummate sexual reward. It was the first time she had reached such a pitch of joy, and she owed it to Guy, to whom she was so strongly attracted that he took Jake's place in her arms.

Jake rolled aside and gathered her to him, resting his head against her hair. Satisfaction, the brandy and the warmth of the low fire combined to make him sleepy, and within moments his breathing had changed and she knew he was asleep. The wind gusted around the eaves, and raindrops patted the window as she wriggled out of his embrace and covered him with the blanket she'd brought down from the loft a little earlier. Then she climbed quietly up to the loft, where Rosalind was deeply asleep, and collected the money pouch and the fine clothes of her former life.

She changed downstairs, taking particular care to comb her dark hair into a tidy and acceptable style, and then counted out the money as quietly and carefully as she could. When it had been divided, she replaced half in the pouch, which in turn she put in her reticule. Jake's portion she left on the table.

Her preparations complete, she sat up in a chair, listening to the cathedral bell chime the night away. At four Jake would awaken because of the cockerel in the next yard, so she would leave at three. But as that hour approached, Rosalind's quiet voice intruded upon her silence. 'Where did you get that money, Miss Fancy Tremoille?'

Beth gasped guiltily. 'Please don't awaken your father,' she pleaded softly as the girl climbed down the ladder.

'Have you been streetwalking to set up a nice little nest egg?'

'You know that's rubbish.' Beth looked at Jake, but he didn't stir.

'Then where did the money come from? Did you have it all along?'

'It's not your business, and no, in that order. But you'll be delighted to learn that I'm leaving. The money is for your father.'

Rosalind's eyes gleamed. How much was there? It looked a lot, enough for a good life, but even now she didn't forget to show her dislike. 'Well, get on out then.'

'And good riddance?' Beth enquired wryly.

'Something like that.'

Beth pulled on her emerald-green gloves. 'Will you tell your father that I am sorry to leave like this?'

'Tell him yourself. Shall I wake him for you?' Rosalind stepped toward Jake.

'Do so, if you want to cause him even more pain. Are you really that vitriolic? Hate me if you wish, but don't use him.' Beth looked at her levelly.

Rosalind turned. 'You always have a way with words, don't you?' she said mockingly, her diction perfect, without a trace of an accent.

'Be all that he wants, Rosalind, because he only seeks the best for you.'

'I want what *I* want, not what *he* wants,' the girl replied, reverting to type.

'I couldn't care less what you want, Rosalind, because I think you are a malicious little spit-cat who should have been drowned at birth.' How good it was to speak her mind. 'Now, when your father awakens, you are to warn him to be very careful to whom he mentions this money. Very careful, do you understand? And before you choose to flout the warning, perhaps I ought to advise you that it's in your interest as much as his to keep quiet.' Without looking back, she went out into the damp, dripping dawn.

Rosalind gazed at the closed door, then at the carefully piled guineas. Only then did she glance at her father.

The cockerel crowed at four, as it always did, and Jake stirred to find his life had changed forever. Rosalind could hardly wait to tell him his beloved Beth had deserted him and left money behind. Twenty guineas. Jake stared at the notes and coins on the table, then reached for the bottle of brandy. He closed his eyes as it coursed down to his belly. 'Twenty guineas? Oh, Bethie,' he whispered.

'We're better off without her.'

'I'm not better off, Rozzie, I'm *nothing* without her.'

'Well, she's let you know what she thinks you're worth. And I reckon she had the money all along.'

He shook his head. 'No, she didn't. I knows you hate her, Rozzie, but—'

'You're right!' Rosalind cried. 'I hate her more than you'll ever know. But now she's gone, without bothering to say goodbye, or thank you!'

He looked away. 'She did,' he said softly. 'She said it last night. And the twenty guineas, well, it's what I need for a share in the forge at Frampney.'

Rosalind managed to meet his eyes. 'I wonder how much more she had?'

'For the love of God, Rozzie, can't you let up for a minute? I *love* her, and one day, when you fall in love, you'll know better how I feel right now!'

She ran to fling her arms around him. 'Oh, Dad, don't take on so, please don't! I'm still here, you've still got me!'

He paused before holding her close. 'Ah, but it's not the same, Rozzie. Bethie's my other half. My other half.' His shoulders shook as he began to sob.

'Please, Dad, don't cry, I can't bear it.'

He drew himself together with a huge breath, glanced at the money again, and then his face took on a new resolve. 'Right, Bethie left that money for me to buy into that Frampney forge, so that's what I'm going to do. We'll go there today.'

'*Today*? But—'

'No arguing, my girl. What's to keep us here, eh? Do you *want* to go to that tavern again? Do I *want* to trail around looking for work? The answer's no, so we're leaving today and that's that. But first we'll have a proper meal somewhere up in town. I've a mind to make a hog of myself.' He spoke bravely as his heart broke.

The parson kept his spirits up by singing rousing hymns. His face was round and red, and his hat was tugged low against the drizzle as he drove the dogcart along the wide new road to Cheltenham. It was still early morning, dull and dismal, the rising sun only visible as a dull yellow stain on the eastern horizon, and Beth huddled gratefully on the seat beside him. He'd taken pity on her as she walked out of Gloucester, and asked no questions about why she was out on her own so early.

She thought of Jake. Did he know she'd gone? That she'd left the money? Her thoughts were interrupted as the parson stopping singing. 'These times are bad, with radicals and reformers creeping from their vile corners, and poor John Bull threatened by the raising of the tricolour within these shores. No one is safe, as witness the terrible murder up near Tremoille House.' Her heart lurched. 'A groom from the house was done to death,' he went on, 'and the money he carried was stolen. I pray the culprit is caught and hanged.'

Beth felt almost sick with apprehension, as if the parson would at any moment seize her reticule and find the pouch. Her worst fear had been realized, Joshua's death was being regarded as murder. The rest of the journey to Cheltenham passed in a daze. She didn't rally her thoughts and composure until the pony clattered to a halt outside the Plough Inn, from where most of the mails and stagecoaches departed. The spa town, so much more modern and elegant than its port neighbour of Gloucester, was already busy, and seething with rumours about a great battle somewhere near Brussels. Some said it was a victory for Wellington, others that the French were triumphant. Excitement and panic were equally represented, quite upsetting the parson, who drove away quickly into the throng of traffic. She entered the courtyard, and approached the ticket office, from where a bespectacled clerk peered short-sightedly. 'Yes, madam?'

'I wish to travel to London on the next available coach.'

'Well, you're in luck, there's room on the Rocket stage, leaving in an hour.'

'Is it a reputable coach?'

He was affronted. 'No *dis*reputable coaches will be found at the Plough, madam. One inside seat left at twenty-four shillings. It's fifteen hours on the road.'

She tendered two of the guinea coins, and after he'd rather insolently tested them with his teeth and found no base metal peeping through gold paint, she was given her ticket and change. It was with some relief that she pocketed the assorted coins, for at least she would now be able to present sensible amounts when required. She breakfasted in the crowded dining-room with other passengers, including an anxious young couple also waiting for the Rocket. Out in the yard a noisy group of gentlemen argued about the effect a victory would have on corn prices, and in the street there was an increasing air of unrest as the rumours continued to spread. But Beth was in a world of her own. Only this time yesterday she had been walking barefoot and hungry toward Tremoille House. Now everything had changed.

Wearing a blue paisley dressing-gown over his shirt and trousers, Guy was taking breakfast by the open casement window of his rooms at the Crown. He regarded the scruffy boy a waiter had just shown in. 'I'm told you're called Weasel? Is that so?' The boy nodded nervously, turning his musty hat in his hands. He was small and thin, and wore threadbare old clothes that were several sizes too big for him. His brown hair, long and straight, was greasy and lacklustre, and he looked as if a good meal would not go amiss. Guy indicated the breakfast that was still on the table before him, and the boy sat in the opposite chair and fell upon the food, stuffing toast, butter, marmalade and bacon into his mouth, and then guzzling strong black coffee direct from the pot. Watching him, Guy was reminded of the hungry Miss Alder.

Weasel wiped his nose on his grubby sleeve, and then looked at Guy. 'What you want me for, mister?' he asked, spitting crumbs.

Guy moved the newspaper aside and placed a half-crown on the table. 'I understand you are Gloucester's best nose.'

Weasel's brown eyes widened, and his dirty hand reached toward the coin, but Guy shook his head. 'Oh, no, it's only yours if you undertake a small task for me. Nothing illegal, I just want you to find someone. Half-crown now, another if you succeed.'

'A whole crown? Mister, I'll ask across the ruddy *county* for that. Who are you after? What you want to know?'

'Miss Elizabeth Tremoille, and I simply need to know where she is.'

Weasel sat back. 'The fancy bit of muslin from up at Tremoille House?'

The look in his eyes told Guy he already had a notion where to find Beth Tremoille. 'Have you something to tell me now?'

Weasel shook his head. 'I'm not certain, and don't want to go losing a half-crown by getting it wrong. I'll make sure, then come back.'

'That's fair enough. Be warned though, my business is urgent.'

'I'll be back quick enough.' Weasel's chair scraped as he got up. He hesitated, and then grabbed a final slice of toast before hurrying out again.

Guy resumed reading the newspaper, which was full of the war in Europe and the riots at home. He'd heard the conflicting tidings from Brussels, and knew that whatever the truth of it, there was going to be trouble in the country. There was another tap at the door, and he looked up with some irritation. 'Yes?'

The same waiter as before put his head around the door. 'Mrs Tremoille has called, Sir Guy.'

Before Guy had time to reply, Jane marched in, brushing the waiter aside and halting regally before the table. 'A word, if you please, Sir Guy.'

Guy waved the waiter away and then stood politely. 'Good morning, madam,' he said, stepping around to draw out a chair for her. 'Please take a seat. Now, to what do I owe the honour of this pleasant visit?'

'You have no idea? I thought Sir Guy Valmer had a finger on every pulse.'

He went to stand by the latticed window. 'I do my best.'

'You really haven't heard what has happened, have you?' she said in surprise.

'Clearly not, Mrs Tremoille, so if you will please illuminate me?'

'My man Joshua was set upon and murdered yesterday afternoon. His body was found on the common; the pouch of money had gone.'

The sun was beginning to break through, and Guy heard the cathedral bell echoing over the city rooftops. Then his grey eyes swung back to her. 'And why, pray, does that bring you scurrying to me? You must have left Tremoille House very early to be here now. I trust you are not about to accuse me of anything?'

'It is to ascertain your innocence that I am here.'

'You have amazing effrontery, madam, and were you a man I'd call you out for what you have just said. I find your tone unpleasant, and the suggestion that I now possess the horse *and* the money is an insult to both my integrity and my honour.' Her lips pressed together, and she drew back slightly, aware that her fury over the missing money had made her rash. Guy regarded her coldly. 'You are on very dangerous ground, madam, and ought not to tread further. Someone has the money, but it isn't me.'

'Which is all very well, Sir Guy, but if you were in my place, who would *you* suspect?' she challenged.

'Oh, without a doubt I'd suspect you, madam, because that is your nature, but I do everything within the strict letter of the law, so murder and highway robbery are certainly not crimes with which my name will ever be connected. Now then, do you wish to repeat your calumnies?' She declined to answer, and he smiled. 'Ah, retreat. I begin to get the measure of you, madam.'

'Don't be too sure of yourself, Sir Guy. You hope to marry Beth and take Tremoille House and the rest of my husband's estate away from me, but I intend to keep what's legally mine. Do your damnedest, sir. You won't find a new will. If he made one, Esmond didn't even tell his oldest and dearest friend, Francis Prettyman, where it was. You are on a wild goose chase, Sir Guy.'

'So you have no curiosity to learn the contents of the letter held by Withers. Withers & Blenkinsop?'

'Letter?' She was all bewilderment.

He laughed. 'Oh, what an actress you are, to be sure. You've seen *Lithgow's Journal.*'

Her eyes slid away from him. 'It's all conjecture, Sir Guy. No one knows if my husband made another will, let alone if a copy of it is still extant.'

'So what is in the mysterious letter?' he asked softly. 'I'll warrant you have discomforting suspicions. Have you now taken the wise precaution of telling Thomas? No, of course not, you're still insisting there never was another will.'

She rose. 'Think as you wish, Sir Guy. Good day.'

He inclined his head graciously, and then looked down into Cathedral Lane, where evidence of the mob's rampage was all around. Windows were being repaired, and labourers carried buckets of water to complete damping down the smouldering bakery. Jane's carriage emerged from the inn yard, its wheels leaving tracks in the layer of wet ash on the cobbles as it turned toward Northgate Street. Returning to his coffee, he mused on the fate of the missing money, and again found his thoughts turning to a dirty, dark-haired girl in rags who not only knew how to distinguish between Moselle and Rhine wine, but was also carrying a basket that, according to Dickon, contained a remarkably heavy pheasant. Yes, it was possible that the fragrant Miss Bessie Alder knew more than she should about the stolen money. She'd been in the right place at the right time, and certainly was not what she appeared to be.

41

*

The guard on the Cheltenham Rocket blasted his bugle as the stagecoach lurched and bumped out of the Plough on time. The clouds were lifting and a watery sun shone as the wavering notes of 'Cherry Ripe' echoed along the High Street. Beth sat quietly inside, holding her reticule protectively as the team came up to a spanking pace. She leaned her head back on the drab upholstery. 'Forgive me, Jake,' she murmured, her head moving to the rhythm of the coach.

Chapter Five

At noon Guy strolled across the sunny cathedral close toward a handsome double-fronted house near King Edward's Gate. It had a stone-flagged path and colourful flowerbeds, and was, he'd been informed at the inn, the residence of Mr Francis Prettyman, the former magistrate who'd been Esmond Tremoille's closest friend. He'd also been informed that the old gentleman had suffered a seizure a month ago, so maybe there was nothing to gain by visiting him, but there might, just might, be something to be learned here. Tilting his top hat back on his head, he walked up the path to the dark-blue door and reached for the gleaming brass knocker. The rapping sounded inordinately loud in the passage beyond, as did the hurrying female footsteps that came in response. A flustered housekeeper in a large mobcap opened the door. 'Yes, sir?'

'Is Mr Prettyman at home?' Guy removed his hat.

For a moment she seemed at a loss for words. 'Well, Mr...?'

'Valmer, Sir Guy Valmer, Mrs...?'

'Ferguson. Sir Guy, my poor gentleman is in no state to make acquaintance with anyone. He is not himself, nor will be again.'

Guy was at his most sympathetic and charming. 'It is a great tragedy, Mrs Ferguson, both for Mr Prettyman and for you, so let me be honest. My desire is to look around the house.'

'The house is not for sale, sir.'

'Of course not, nor do I seek to purchase it. I merely wish to look for something, a document that is of great importance to me. I have no wrongdoing in mind, I assure you.' He dangled a five-pound banknote in front of her.

She stared at it. 'Look around?' Without further ado she snatched the note and stood aside for him to enter. 'Mr Prettyman is in his bed, sir, the third door on the left up the stairs, otherwise you may look where you wish. I'll ask you no questions, and you'll give me no reasons.' Inclining her head, she hurried away across the stone-tiled hallway, past the rather splendid staircase and then down a narrow passage toward the rear of the house.

Guy glanced around. Closed doors lined the hall, and daylight pene-
trated a fanlight above the front entrance. The smell of beeswax and
honeysuckle drifted from the only piece of furniture, a small console table
upon which stood an empty dish for cards, and a vase of flowers. He went
to the nearest door, and looked in at the dining-room. A cursory inspec-
tion told him there was nothing to be found there, for it contained an oval
table, six chairs, and a sideboard with a display of reasonable plate. There
were landscapes on the wall, and candlesticks and a garniture of oriental
jars on the mantelshelf. He looked in the sideboard, but there were no
papers at all.

The door directly opposite opened to a blue and oyster-silk drawing-
room, small but elegantly furnished. He searched thoroughly, and was
about to leave when he looked again at a small portrait, a watercolour of
Esmond Tremoille not long before his death. Something about it aroused
Guy's curiosity, and he returned to take it from the wall. It was sealed at
the back with the usual glue and brown paper, but a touch revealed the
paper to be oddly cushioned. Removing the jewelled pin from his neck
cloth, he drew the point carefully along two sides of the brown paper, and
then looked inside to see a folded vellum document. As he drew it out
carefully, he was confronted by the seals of Esmond Tremoille and the
lawyer, Beswick. Hardly able to credit his amazing good fortune, he stared
at it for a moment, before the awful thought struck that it might simply
be another copy of the will that left everything to Jane Tremoille. So he
unfolded it to examine more closely. The brevity of the contents made him
want to laugh out loud. *I, Esmond Zachary Pentewan Tremoille, being of
sound mind, hereby revoke all previous wills and leave my entire estate to
my daughter Elizabeth Mary Dorothea Tremoille.* The date was a week
before Tremoille's death.

Guy pushed it inside his coat, and then replaced the painting. Suddenly
the reacquisition of his family's stolen lands seemed much closer, and if
Fate's benevolence continued, his bride would soon be within his grasp as
well.

The team of six oxen moved slowly south of Gloucester, *en route* for
Frampney, and the heavy, cumbersome wagon trundled awkwardly
behind them. Gloucester's bustle was no more, and the oxen ambled
placidly along the causeway that crossed the sunlit meadows and marsh-
land of the Severn floodplain. Rosalind had made herself as comfortable
as possible among sacks, casks, tea chests and other necessities. She was
deep in thought, clutching her bundle of belongings, and staring back at
the city she was leaving for the first time in her life. There'd be no more
of the Barker tavern, no more avoiding Ned's wandering hands, and no
more hunger, because her father would be his own master. Prodding a sack
of grain, she wriggled a little, and then sat back, her eyes on the road,

where puddles filled the ruts and the smell of dung was released in the midday heat.

She was terrified of dropping the money she'd purloined, because her father would know in an instant what she'd done. Conscience didn't figure in her outlook. Nearly 500 guineas was hers now, so she'd bide her time, wait for the love of her life to come along, and then run off with him to live happily ever after. Dad would never know; well, not until she upped and left, and anyway he only needed twenty guineas for the forge. He'd be happy with that. She smiled a little smile, and closed her eyes. It was so easy to forget that none of this would have been possible were it not for Beth Tremoille. Rosalind didn't want to think of Beth. Ever again. Jake and the carrier walked beside the wagon, the latter a plump fellow sucking a blade of grass in a manner as bovine as the oxen. He was sixty years old, and wore a smock and a frayed straw hat. His fat cheeks were ruddy, his eyes so deep-set their colour was indeterminate, and his uneven teeth were discoloured from chewing tobacco. He wasn't much of a man for talking, but Jake made him curious. 'So, Frampney forge interests you, eh?'

'If it's still available.'

'It was this morning. Old Matty Brown's past it now, and falls asleep with that darned pipe of his. He'll have the lot up in flames around him one day.'

'I met Matty and his wife yesterday and I think they liked me.'

'Well, as you'll be the first man to come up with the cash, you'll be made very welcome. I'm Johnno Walters, by the way, and I do all the fetching and carrying for Frampney.' He extended a large paw.

Jake accepted it. 'Pleased to meet you, Johnno. I'm Jake Mannacott, and the wench in the back is my daughter, Rozzie.'

'Why did you decide to leave town for the sticks?'

Rosalind had heeded Beth's advice and warned Jake not to mention his sudden good fortune. 'Oh, what with last night's riots, and the promise of more trouble to come, Gloucester's no place for a young girl.'

'Too right. Darn me, but it's come to something when honest men feel driven to go around smashing stuff up and robbing. It's what the likes of the bloody Frogs do, not us.' Johnno shook his head gloomily, and silence returned for a while.

'Is there much trade in Frampney?' Jake asked then.

'Squire Lloyd's got some grand high-steppers, and his son, Master Robert races a lot. There's a good few farmers; the doctor's got two cobs, and there's Lord Welland at Whitend, of course.' Johnno pointed west, where the five-gabled roof and chimneys of a large old house were visible above the trees. 'He's got a racing stud, and often uses Matty when his own smith can't cope.'

'I've heard tell that Welland's hard on his nags.'

'Well, he's no angel, that's for sure. There was a fright in Frampney a few years back, when it seemed Squire Lloyd was going to sell up to Welland. My God, you should have heard the mass sigh of relief when it didn't happen.' Johnno grinned. 'There's some who say Welland's not quite right in the head these days. The Severn's in front of Whitend, and the new canal passes behind it, and someone I know well said Welland's suddenly got the frights about being drowned. He seems to have got into a rare old state, convinced the river will bust its banks and the canal too, and no one at Whitend will survive. It's a wonder he hasn't started building an ark!' The carrier wheezed with laughter. 'Anyway, yes, there's plenty of work at Frampney forge.' He cleared his throat and lowered his voice so Rosalind wouldn't hear.

'Listen close now, Jake, you're the father of a ripe young wench, so I have to tell you something important. Master Robert Lloyd's a handsome hosebird and philandering alley cat who's left many a bastard in his wake without acknowledgment. You keep a strict eye on your little wench, Jake, because you mark my words, he'll take one look and get a dick-itch.'

'If he lays one finger on my Rozzie, I'll tear his throat out with my bare hands,' Jake breathed, but nodded his gratitude. 'Thanks for the warning.'

Johnno flicked his whip and whistled at the oxen, then looked at Jake again. 'Master Robert excepted, you'll find Frampney mortal quiet after Gloucester. Squire Lloyd's a good landlord, fair when need be, and he's got prosperous farms. There aren't any manufactories or new-fangled machines to take our livelihoods away, so there's no unrest.'

Two hours later the ox-wagon lumbered slowly into the wide village green at Frampney and stopped on the corner. Jake looked from the three duck ponds to the forge, and the sheds and little wisteria-hung house behind it. A wisp of smoke rose from the forge, and the sound of metallic hammering drifted on the air. He tugged his cap firmly on his head, grabbed his belongings from the wagon, and then held his hands up to help Rosalind, but she wouldn't let go of the bundle. He was impatient. 'Chuck it down, Rozzie, What have you got in there anyway? The Crown bloody Jewels?'

'Just my things,' she replied, climbing down awkwardly without assistance.

He turned to Johnno. 'Thank you, friend.'

'It was a pleasure, Jake.' Johnno pointed the whip toward a tavern across the green. 'I'll see you tonight over at the George and Dragon, and introduce you to a few folk.' Johnno whistled and cracked the whip, and the oxen strained forward again, making for the general stores, which lay beyond the tavern.

Jake looked at Rosalind. 'You wait here with our stuff, and I'll get on over to the forge. Wish me luck.' She watched him walk away, and then sat patiently on the verge, her chin in her hands as she stared around. Were all village greens like this? So wide and long? And the houses were all so neat and tidy, with flowers in the gardens and pretty curtains at the windows. Her eyes came to rest on a mansion behind a tall wall with fine gates. It must be Squire Lloyd's house, she thought, wondering about Robert Lloyd. She'd heard everything Johnno said about the squire's son, and felt a thrill of excitement. How good it would be if he tried to seduce her. Not that she'd let him.

When Jake presented himself at the forge, where a groom was holding a bay hunter for which a new shoe was needed. Matty Brown continued to hammer for a moment, his skin shining in the glow of the roaring fire. He was a huge man with an immense belly, and was short of breath, He paused to wipe his brow. 'So, you're back again?' he asked in a rasping voice. 'You've got twenty guineas?'

'Guess so.'

Matty nodded toward the horse. 'All right, let's see your work. Finish what I've started. Mind now, for it's the squire's nag, so do a good job.'

Jake removed his old coat. 'I don't do bad jobs, Mr Brown.'

'We'll see,' rasped Matty, sitting heavily in an ancient chair and reaching for his clay pipe. Two horses he'd seen to this morning. Only two, and yet his damned heart was flapping like a great pigeon. Phoebe was right, he couldn't manage any more, and if this young fellow could shoe a horse, then there was a place for him at Frampney forge.

Jake worked the horseshoe, getting into the rhythm of the hammering, and each blow on the anvil was like ridding himself of everything. He gritted his teeth, bringing the hammer down with such force that the sparks flew high around him. The horse stirred, turning its head to watch, and then starting as the fiery shoe was plunged into the bucket of water. Steam rose, and the water seethed. Jake ran his hand gently over the horse's flank. 'Right, my handsome,' he murmured, 'let's be having a look at you.'

A shadow darkened the doorway as Matty's wife came in with a brimming mug of ale and paused a moment for her eyes to get used to the light. She was small and plump, with a pleasant, good-natured face and rosy cheeks. Her white hair was coiled into a knot and hidden beneath a simple mobcap, and she wore an old-fashioned, pinch-waisted lavender gown, with a clean white neckerchief around her comfortable shoulders. 'Well, now, Matty Brown,' she declared on seeing Jake, 'I thought from all that wild hammering that you'd had a new lease of life. I should have known better.' She pressed the mug into his free hand.

'I reckon I've got a new partner, Phoebe.'

Jake paused to smile at her, his muscular body aglow in the light of the forge. 'I'm pleased to meet you again, Mrs—'

'Just Phoebe,' she broke in quickly, 'there's no formality here. I'm pleased to meet you again too, Jake. In fact, if I were a couple of years younger, I'd make that fine body of yours very welcome indeed!'

Matty guffawed. 'Get on with you, Phoebe Brown. A *couple* of years? More like ten or fifteen!'

'I know what I mean, you old curmudgeon, and I know my way around a man's flesh. You had a body like that once, until you took to sitting around with ale and a pipe.'

'Yes, and you were a slender slip of willow once too,' he countered.

Phoebe laughed and bent to kiss the top of his head, and Matty nodded as Jake finished the horse. 'You'll do, my friend, you'll do.'

Jake's face showed his relief, then he remembered Rosalind. 'I've got the money, like I said, but I've a daughter too, name of Rosalind. I must get somewhere to live. Do you know any rooms to let?'

Phoebe brightened excitedly. 'Oh, well now, *we've* rooms, eh, Matty? The front bedroom and the back attic. Both are good, dry *and* warm in winter. How old is your girl, Jake? And what happened to your wife?'

'Rosalind's sixteen, and my wife, God rest her soul, died four years back.'

Phoebe eyed him. 'And there's no woman in your life?'

'There was, but she left. There's just Rosalind and me now.'

Matty turned to his eager wife. 'Reckon it would please you, eh?'

'Oh, Matty, you *know* it would!' She gave him a huge hug.

Matty held his hand out to Jake. 'It's a deal, Jake Mannacott. You're welcome, and so is your daughter. And I'd be obliged if you'd call me Matty from the outset.'

Jake was almost overwhelmed. This was his dream alive and shining, but wounded and bleeding too because Beth wasn't sharing it with him.

Guy returned to the Crown with the will, but on entering his room was startled by a lilting female voice. 'Well, now, if it isn't my handsome English rover.'

'Maria?' He turned to see her lying on the bed, a delightfully curved figure in a loose pink silk robe. With flaxen hair and amber eyes London's favourite actress was a very unlikely Irish beauty.

'And what other lady would you expect to take this liberty?' she enquired, sitting up and allowing him a full view of her long, shapely thighs and the cluster of dark hair at her crotch. Her breasts were full and creamy white, with dark nipples that thrust against the robe's dainty fabric.

Guy removed his coat and draped it carefully over a chair before regarding her. 'I trust you did not travel in such a state of erotic undress?'

'What, and allow the common people to ogle Puss?' She smiled. 'You are the only one I permit to see *that*, sir, although right now I'm a little miffed with you for obliging me to toddle all the way down here to satisfy my appetites.'

'Is that what I'm good for?'

'My darling, it's what you're *superb* for,' she murmured. 'So superb that I'll have you know this is the fourth inn at which I made enquiries before finding you.'

'I'm flattered.'

'So you should be, sir.'

'And how is Drury Lane managing without you?' he asked.

'My understudy is doing her paltry best.'

He smiled. 'She may outshine you.'

'That drab little mouse?' The magnificent amber eyes were scornful. 'I'll be welcomed back with laurels and roses. Besides, she has no talent for comedy, and the only laughs she will get are when she falls flat on her fanny.'

'How unkind.'

'It's not my kindness that interests you, sir.' She edged to the bedpost and then knelt up with her thighs provocatively apart. 'Come over here and show your appreciation,' she whispered, pouting her lips.

He hesitated, but it was barely noticeable. He had seldom met a woman of more earthy passions. There was nothing she was not prepared to do in the pursuit of sexual pleasure, and no male fantasy she was not prepared to indulge, but she was a difficult woman, with a ferocious temper and arrogant disregard for anything that did not fall in with her exact requirements. He enjoyed her blatant sexuality but not her character, and had recently begun to debate the wisdom of continuing a liaison that – for him – was based solely on her astonishingly varied sexual repertoire.

She pouted, and a different note entered her voice. 'Well now, Guy Valmer, I do not leave offers on the table for more than a minute. Either you take it up, or I leave.'

He felt desire stirring. 'Will you give me time to undress?' he asked lightly.

She smiled then. 'You must leave that to me, sir.' Slipping from the bed she came over as if to link her arms around his neck and lift her lips for a kiss, but, as he bent his head to oblige, she gave a playful laugh and stepped back to begin undoing his neck cloth. 'Oh, how I love the sound of a neck cloth being drawn from around a man's neck,' she breathed, pulling the muslin slowly away. 'It's so sensuous and full of promise.'

'I trust I can live up to expectations.'

'You will, my darling, you will,' she replied, reaching down to hold the swelling at the front of his trousers. 'My, my, what a delightfully big boy you are, my English rover. I vow my thighs are trembling already, and Puss begins to purr.'

'I trust you and Puss intend to wait for me?'

She laughed and began to undo his waistcoat and shirt. When his chest was exposed, she leaned close, her palms flat against it, and breathed deeply of his scent. 'You always smell so very good,' she whispered, her lips moving against his skin and the unexpectedly dark hair across his chest.

'One does one's best,' he said softly, sliding his arms around her.

She pulled away again. 'No, not yet, not yet!' He took his arms away having long since learned that the best way was *her* way. She undid the front of his trousers, and her breath escaped slowly as she touched the tip of his now rigid arousal. 'Oh, my beautiful English rover, I simply *have* to worship at such a grand altar,' she whispered, pushing his trousers down and sinking to her knees in a cloud of strawberry silk. Her hands shook as she guided him into her mouth and began to adore him with her tongue. He closed his eyes as a riot of carnal sensations spread from his groin through the rest of his body. She swayed gently, lost in enjoyment and, as she took him deeper into her mouth, her hands slid around to clasp his hips. Her fingers smoothed and explored, stroked and fondled, as if she would remould him to her own secret design, and she made little sounds of contentment as her pleasure intensified.

Guy's desire began to mount. His erection was like a rod of hot iron, and he didn't know how long he could withstand her ministering, but even now, when gratification was so close, a portion of his consciousness regretted what he was doing. This was just a sexual act; he didn't love her and never had. How much better would it be if he *did* love her? How much more rewarding and precious? But love had always eluded him.

She drew away suddenly. 'Now I'll have you inside me, if you please, sir,' she declared, thus making it plain that her own needs were all that mattered.

'And if I refuse?' he replied.

Her amber eyes flickered. 'But you won't, my English rover, because I have you in such a lather now that you'll do whatever I ask.'

'Then ask,' he said.

Their eyes met, and for a moment he saw her uncertainty, but then she gave him a pouting smile. 'Please make sweet love to me now, my dashing rover,' she begged, holding her arms up to him almost in supplication.

He smiled, and pulled her to her feet and then scooped her into his arms to place her on the bed. She lay back with her legs spread. 'Come to Puss, my fine tomcat,' she invited, slipping a hand between her legs and massaging herself. 'Make Puss happy.'

'Would you have me be ill-mannered enough to mount you with my boots on?'

'Yes, oh, yes, I've a mind to try that,' she answered.

'As you wish.' Boots and all, he climbed on top of her, his virility slipping readily between her thighs to nestle against the entrance to her sexual soul. She gasped. 'Holy Mother, Holy Mother of God.' The irreverence was torn from her lips as he enslaved her with his devastating masculinity. He, and the voluptuous pleasure he gave her, was everything in her world.

This was why she had followed him, why she ached for him, couldn't stop thinking about him; could never have enough of him.

Guy knew so well how to give her the utmost delight, and without penetrating her, slid the moist tip of his erection against her most private and sensitive flesh. She squirmed and moaned as exquisite sensations melted through her. At last, slowly and commandingly, he pushed inside her, burying himself as deeply as he could before lying perfectly still. His size stretched her, and took her to new heights of rapture. She was almost beyond reason, her muscles tightening convulsively around him, her fingernails digging savagely into his back through his shirt and waistcoat as she writhed, almost mad with gratification. His own control still strong, he moved a little inside her and was immediately rewarded by her almost delirious joy. Suddenly she reached the point of no return, and displayed the ferocious sexual aggression of a tigress. Ripping and clawing, biting and kissing, she ground herself on him in an orgasmic passion that transcended what had gone before. 'Puss is going to have your soul, your very soul,' she gasped, working her body on his erection as if she would fuse with it forever. No mortal man could have withstood such an onslaught for long. He began to drive in and out of her, and she cried out with each thrust. When he came she screamed an oath worthy of Billingsgate, her body twitching uncontrollably as she shared the climax. Her legs and arms were wrapped around him, and she held him close until the spasms had finally died away, and then she sank back on the bed, exhausted. He bent his head to kiss her nipple, but her senses were so keen and vibrant that she couldn't bear to be touched. 'No, please! It's too much. Too much.' Her body quivered, and she closed her eyes. 'You're opium, and have made an addict of me.'

He rolled on to his back. 'And you've almost skinned me,' he murmured, relieved he hadn't undressed after all.

She turned to lean over him, her flaxen hair spilling warmly over his shoulder. 'I make no bones about having had many lovers. I may be a good Catholic girl, but still confess my appetites every week. I know what a man can or cannot do for me. You are one apart, my English rover, the only one who gives me such ravishment that afterward I cannot bear to be even breathed upon, let alone touched. It's an exquisite sensation, for which I thank you.' She kissed him on the lips, and her tongue explored his mouth before withdrawing. Then she turned away from him, snuggled down, and went to sleep.

Guy was used to her ways, and got up to straighten his clothes and then pour a glass of Madeira. He had various letters to write, concerning affairs on his estates, and when Maria awakened, he intended to send her on her way. He hadn't wanted her to follow him, but now that she had, and he'd obliged her with what she wanted, he wished her back at Drury Lane as swiftly as possible.

He'd attended to three letters before she stirred, and he set his pen aside cautiously. In recent weeks her moods had swung arbitrarily between loving and loathing. The adoring Puss who went to sleep could as likely be a rabid cat on awakening, so he was seriously considering ending the liaison. He wanted many things from a woman, but not caprices so wilful as to seem unhinged, so he watched as she sat up and pushed her hair back from her face. The strawberry wrap had fallen revealingly from her shoulders. Her nipples were soft now, and her languid movements told him she was still sated, and yet she had an edginess he knew presaged another outburst. Rising from the bed, she pulled the wrap tightly around herself, as if suspecting him of ogling her as she slept. 'Do you intend to make an honest woman of me?' she asked suddenly.

He wasn't about to indulge her. 'You know that's impossible,' he replied bluntly.

'So, I'm good enough to shag witless, but not to wear your ring?'

'You're being unreasonable, Maria, because you already have a husband. You married the theatre manager who contracted you in Dublin, then left him to make your fortune in London. You are Mrs Ambrose Malone, and that is that.'

She turned away distractedly and began to pace up and down, her robe hissing over the wooden floor. 'But if you *could* marry me, you would?' she said then. When he shook his head, her breath snatched and her lips curled back. 'You slavering, misbegotten English hellhound!' she breathed.

He rose slowly from the desk. 'Maria, if your Catholic conscience is such a torment, I suggest you confess to a priest.'

'*My* conscience?' she cried.

'What else? You come to me like a bitch in heat, get what you want to feed your hunger, and then wake up with guilt weighing so heavily that you behave like this to make yourself feel better. Well, enough. Dealing with you is like dealing with a madwoman!'

'Yours is the conscience being salved, Guy Valmer! You've been callously using me, and what's left of the gentleman in you rebels at your cruelty.' Her stiff demeanour and air of wounded pride were so ridiculous that he was amazed she didn't know it herself, but she appeared to believe herself to have been gravely insulted.

'View it in that light if you wish, Maria, it's immaterial to me. Our recent encounters have almost always ended this way, and I want no more.'

'Oh, I'm sure you'd rather I just went away. You bring me here, use me, and—'

'You came of your own volition. Do stop this idiocy, Maria.'

'Idiocy? So that's what you think of my injured character?' She stalked to the screen in the corner and disappeared behind it. He could hear her dressing furiously, and then she reappeared in a rose-and-grey striped lawn gown and grey silk pelisse, her golden hair swept up beneath a silk bonnet. 'Good day to you. I will send for my luggage.'

'Goodbye, Maria.' Her steps faltered, but then she raised her chin again and swept out, leaving the door wide behind her. Guy breathed out with relief. He didn't know what was wrong with her, and had tried to be patient and understanding, but it had got him nowhere. He'd come to believe that the kinder he was, the worse she became. Now it was no longer going to be his problem.

Chapter Six

That evening, having been to the George and Dragon, where Matty and Johnno introduced him to a host of village folk, all of them friendly and welcoming, Jake leaned against the forge entrance. His coat was tossed over his left shoulder as he looked across the village green at the lights beginning to twinkle in Squire Lloyd's grand house. Sweet perfume filled the air from the white roses and honeysuckle climbing through the apple tree next to the forge, and everything was quiet, save for the squabbling of the ducks on the pond. There was no drunken brawling, no constant traffic, no shouting and street cries, no swaggering whores and no jangle of different bells. Just peace. Except for the darned cockerels. He smiled wryly. He and Rozzie had left one behind, and come here to find thirty-one! Every darned cottage had fowls, with a strutting cock to lord it over them. Come dawn it would be well nigh bedlam! Well, he could put up with that for the sheer pleasure of being out in the country at last. From his attic window he didn't look out on dirty alleys and the dock basin, but on green fields and the embankment along which the canal was to pass. And beyond that he could even see the wild estuary, where the hazardous Severn tides reversed the flow of the river.

He looked up at the stars glittering in the deep ruby that remained of the sunset. Never had he seen such a heavenly pageant as tonight's dying sun. Such wondrous colours and patterns, painted upon a sky so clear that he felt he might reach up and pluck some of the stars. Frampney was living up to his dreams, but one thing jarred his contentment, and perhaps it was the greatest thing of all: he'd lost Beth. A nerve twitched at his temple as he blinked back the tears that had seldom been far away all day. A grown man, reduced to helplessness by love.

He watched a fine carriage drive slowly around the green, expecting it to turn into the squire's driveway, but instead it passed by and came steadily toward the forge. He straightened as it halted by him. The liveried coachman addressed him. 'Would you be Jake Mannacott?'

'Who wants to know?' Jake asked uneasily, not for the first time wondering exactly where and how Beth had got the twenty guineas.

Another voice answered. 'Sir Guy Valmer wishes to know.' The carriage
door opened and a fashionable gentleman climbed down.

Jake sharpened. The gent who'd found Beth when she fainted? What
could *he* want? Beth said he didn't know her.

Guy glanced curiously over the handsome smith, of whose existence he
only knew because of Weasel's diligence. Weasel also learned that Jake and
his daughter had suddenly left Gloucester with enough money to buy into
a prosperous village smithy. 'Mannacott, enquiries have led me to believe
you may know something of Elizabeth Tremoille's present whereabouts,'
he said, flicking the lace at his cuff.

It *was* the money. Jake thought, fearing his new life was about to be
snatched away before it had begun. 'Elizabeth who?'

'Oh, come now, let's not play childish games. I'm talking about the
woman you've lived with for the past year. I know she was your mistress.'

'All right, I lived with Beth. But why do you want her?'

Ignoring the question, Guy went into the shed, looking around at the
array of tools and at the fire that still glowed red-hot. 'My finding her can
only be to her benefit, I do assure you.'

'I don't know where she is.' Jake followed him in.

'I understand you came here to purchase a partnership, and obviously
you've succeeded. Where did you get the money?'

Jake felt cold. 'I saved it.'

'Twenty pounds? Allow me more intelligence than that! Beth gave it to
you, didn't she?' Jake said nothing, and Guy picked up a poker that lay
with its tip in the heart of the fire. As he examined it, the glow reflected
in his compelling grey eyes. 'Beth gave it to you, didn't she?' he said again.

'I'm not saying anything to you, Sir Guy.'

'For fear of incriminating her?'

'I wouldn't know what you mean.'

Guy gazed steadily at him and saw that Jake genuinely didn't know
where the money came from. 'Look, I mean her no harm, I just want to
find her.'

'I don't know where she is, Sir Guy, if I did, I'd—'

'You'd what?' Guy watched the emotion on the other's face.

'I'd try to get her back! That amuses you, doesn't it? The thought that
a man like me would even *hope* she'd come back to him? Well, I hope,
because I worship that woman more than anything else on God's earth.
But I've lost her.' Jake turned his head away quickly, knowing that his love
was too naked, too painful.

Guy put the poker down. 'It doesn't amuse me in the least. True love
should never be mocked. So, you don't know where she could have gone,
but she *did* give you the money?'

'That's my business, Sir Guy.'

So she had. Guy tugged his hat low over his forehead. Pieces of the puzzle had begun to slip almost mockingly into place. Why couldn't he have realized earlier that the reason Bessie Alder looked so familiar was her strong resemblance to the portrait of Beth Tremoille at Tremoille House? Now, too late, he understood why the cook's starving niece spoke so well and understood the finer points of German wine. He'd had his prey in his grasp! A nerve fluttered at his temple and his lips pressed together. What had happened on that common? She'd definitely stolen her stepmother's money, but had she murdered as well? And where had she gone with the 980 guineas she'd kept for herself? London, of course. He returned to the carriage. 'Back to the Crown, Dickon. We'll leave for Town at first light,' he said, as he slammed the door.

Midnight struck as the Cheltenham Rocket arrived in the capital, and entered the huge yard of the important coaching inn, the Swan with Two Necks. It stood on the north side of Lad Lane in the City, and was noisy with travellers, vendors, ostlers, dogs, ticket office bells and horses. There was such a crush of coaches, carriers' wagons and post chaises, to say nothing of piles of luggage, that it was some time before the Rocket's weary team could finally be manoeuvred to a safe place to discharge its passengers. The last part of the journey had been accomplished at a snail's pace because the capital was ringing with word of a great victory for Wellington at somewhere called Waterloo, near Brussels. Crowds were out in the streets, most of them delirious with delight and singing 'Rule Britannia'. But there was dissent too, from those who feared the price of peace, and the Rocket had passed several disturbances that reminded Beth of Cathedral Lane, with hooded groups breaking windows and chanting 'No starvation! No landlords!'

As Beth and the nervous young couple climbed down, the coachman slid from his perch. 'I brought you safe and well, sir, ladies,' he said, extending his hand hopefully. It was the custom to tip drivers, so he was rewarded. The portly, balding innkeeper, Mr Waterhouse, a famous man in the coaching world, emerged from the taproom, wiping his damp hands on his apron as a troop of cavalry clattered past in Lad Lane. The young husband called out to him. 'Sir, has there really been a great victory?'

'There has indeed, sir. Word was brought from Brussels this evening, and is spreading like wildfire. Some like it, others don't. I've heard the Prime Minister's house has been stoned and the Houses of Parliament are besieged by a mob, but Hyde Park's all celebrations. I just hope there's no trouble around these parts.'

The young wife shrank timidly against her husband. 'I'm frightened, Jeremiah.'

Jeremiah put protective arms around her. 'I'll look after you, Amelia.' He turned again to the innkeeper. 'Have you a room for tonight?'

Mr Waterhouse was soothing. 'Certainly, sir.'

'And for me?' Beth asked quickly.

'Indeed so, madam. You'll all be safe in the Swan.'

The young couple hurried inside, but Beth loitered, just gazing up at the inn, which was four storeys high, with balustraded galleries to the numerous bedchambers. She had escaped, she was anonymous, and the stolen money was still in her possession. Her new life had begun! Turning, she began to follow the other passengers, just as the bells of nearby St Lawrence Jewry began to peal joyfully, drowning every other sound in the yard. Gradually every church in London seemed to join in until the joyous cacophony echoed across the starlit sky. War was over and the Corsican finally defeated; now would come the aftermath.

Once inside, she gave the name Mrs Alder and asked for a meal, a room and a hot bath for the following morning. Widows were permitted much more latitude, such as travelling alone without any questions asked, and she explained away her lack of luggage by saying it had all been sent ahead several days before. A tired serving girl led her into the dining-room where she was soon served bacon, eggs and fresh-baked bread. To Beth it was a feast fit for a queen, and she felt comfortably drowsy when at last she made her way up the external staircase to her room on the second-floor gallery. She was exhausted as she prepared for bed, and within moments was fast asleep.

The sun shone brightly the next morning, and after enjoying the hot bath she'd requested on arrival, Beth went down to breakfast feeling really clean for the first time in over a year. The yard was still busy, some church bells still pealed in the distance, and in a nearby street people cheered a military band. While taking breakfast she listened to the conversation of gentlemen poring over an extraordinary edition of the *London Gazette* that contained details of the great battle. Exhilarating as the news was, she had other things to think about. Now she was in London, she had to decide what form she wanted her new life to take. Even more urgently than that, she had to find some more clothes. One set of togs simply wouldn't do for a lady in the world's greatest city. At midmorning she set out to see what could be done. It wouldn't be easy, because buying a new dress entailed going to a dressmaker or purchasing a length of material to make up. Neither option was practical when she only had the clothes on her back, so she would need luck.

The overnight riots might have been fleeting and scattered, but the results were in evidence. Broken windows were being reglazed or boarded, dragoons were conspicuous and, lying amid the horse dung on the cobbles, she saw a torn banner bearing the motto *Bread & Blood*. A newsboy stood on a corner with a wad of broadsheets under his thin arm, chanting, 'Castlereagh's house under sie-ee-ge, Castlereagh's house under sie-ee-ge.' Nearby, a rival was yelling, 'Full account of victor-ee-e, full account of victor-ee-e.' Flags, banners and bunting fluttered from windows and across streets, and shop windows displayed laurels and patriotic slogans. Passing vehicles were decked with flags and more laurels, and every stagecoach seemed to carry young bloods yelling with excitement and throwing their expensive hats in the air. But she saw other things too, a gathering of surly labourers in a shabby yard, and a sailor and whore coupling in a damp alley.

It was in a much quieter little street near St Paul's that she saw the sign of a fashionable dressmaker, Madame de Sichel. The bow windows of the double-fronted premises displayed an array of samples, from bonnets and gloves, to chenille flowers and mannequins in modish gowns. It was as good a place as any to start, she thought, going inside. Maybe there had been some orders that had been cancelled at the very last minute. The room inside was very plain, but beautifully decorated. There were floor-standing mirrors and wall mirrors, and chests of drawers from which spilled fripperies of all kinds. Several chairs stood against walls, sheet-covered garments hung from the picture rail, and a tapestry curtain shielded the entrance to whatever rooms lay beyond. The doorbell was still tinkling as an attendant, squat, olive-skinned and middle-aged, came hastily from the back to attend her. Casting swift eyes over Beth's clothes, and probably assessing her purse at the same time, she nodded supercil-iously. 'May I 'elp you, madame?' she asked in a heavy French accent.

'I was robbed during my journey to London and have nothing left except these clothes I wear, so I need an entire new wardrobe as quickly as possible. My name is Alder, Mrs Alder.'

Suddenly the curtain jerked aside again and another woman emerged, her grandiose manner suggesting she was Madame de Sichel herself. She was in her forties, tall, angular and rather horse-faced, in a high-necked, long-sleeved mauve muslin gown that appeared to be decked with every known flounce, frill, bow and embroidery stitch. What her hair was like was the vicar's dog's guess, because she wore an improbable red wig to which was pinned a little square of very costly cream lace.

'Mrs Alder? I am Madame de Sichel, and I will attend you in person,' she said in a decidedly English voice. 'I believe you will not require the pattern books, because I am convinced I already have an entire wardrobe that will fit you.'

An entire wardrobe? Surely it was too good to be true, Beth thought, as the dressmaker produced an inch tape and began to measure her from head to toe, before declaring, 'Well, madam, you are the same size as the late Lady Harcotleigh. Such a tragedy and she so young, but it means I have been left with a wardrobe of completed garments.' The dressmaker ushered her to a comfortable chair and gave her the latest edition of the *Mirror of Modes*, one of the most important magazines of fashion. 'If you would care to examine page twenty-three. There is a new design from

Paris that is a real masterpiece of beauty. I am sure it will be exactly to your taste, and I have the finest apple-green mousseline de soie that would be a perfect thing over a shell-pink satin slip.' Madame de Sichel then snapped her fingers at the attendant, who disappeared beyond the curtain, permitting Beth a brief glimpse of a room full of seamstresses.

Beth turned to page twenty-three. The dressmaker was right, the gown engraved there was beautiful, with dainty flounces at the hem and ribbons floating from the tiny puffed sleeves. It was also going to be exorbitantly expensive to make up. Common sense suddenly prevailed as she realized her excitement had begun to run away with her. On leaving Gloucester she'd had 500 guineas, and had already spent some of them on the journey from Cheltenham and the inn here in London. What was left had to provide her with somewhere to live and support her afterward. She couldn't afford Lady Harcotleigh's wardrobe, or anything in the *Mirror of Modes*.

She was about to close the magazine on her moments of madness, when an advertisement on the opposite page caught her attention.

A gentleman of quality desires a tenant for a modest house of great beauty and solitude by the sea. Available on excellent terms due to the owner wishing to settle the property before departing for Jamaica. Particulars from Mr Henry Topweather, Agent, 15 Easterden Street. Mr Topweather answers letters post paid, and advertises if desired, not otherwise. All at his own charge, if not successful.

A modest house by the sea? Excellent terms? How perfect that would be? Away from the past with all its memories, good and bad, and from the present with its uncertainties and fears. At such a house there would surely only be a future. She would call upon Mr Topweather to ascertain what was meant by 'modest'. She was about to close the magazine again when, unbelievably, her own name leapt out at her.

Miss Elizabeth Tremoille. As has been done on previous occasions since the death of Mr Esmond Tremoille of Tremoille House in the County of Gloucestershire, it is hereby again requested that the above lady, only daughter of Mr Tremoille, contact Withers, Withers & Blenkinsop, solicitors of Caradine Street, London, where a letter from her father awaits her.

Beth was transfixed. Her father's London lawyers had a letter for her? Might it concern the lost will?

The dressmaker interrupted her thoughts. 'Behold, madam, the late Lady Harcotleigh's wardrobe.' She swept a grand arm at the wonderful garments now miraculously hanging from the picture rail. Beth struggled to collect herself. The garments were exquisitely beautiful, and she would have liked nothing more than to wave an equally grand arm and say she'd have them all, yet knew she couldn't. They were beyond her means, and somehow she had to wriggle out of what was bound to be a very embarrassing situation. 'Madame de Sichel, I am quite overwhelmed by the magnificence of these clothes, and I really would like to try everything on, but I am afraid I do not have the time now as I have realized I am going to be late for an important appointment with a house agent.'

The dressmaker's face fell, but then perked up again. 'I can have the clothes delivered for you to try on at your leisure.'

'That would be most agreeable,' Beth answered, 'I am staying at the Swan in Lad Lane.' At least she'd have the joy of parading in the incomparable wardrobe, before returning it as 'unsuitable'. Then her gaze fell upon a décolleté peppermint muslin gown, gathered softly at the high waistline by a little drawstring. Next to it there hung a grey corded silk spencer, buttonless, with a high flaring collar. Both garments were so very much to her taste that she simply had to wear them now. 'Madame de Sichel, I must have those this instant.'

The dressmaker dimpled vainly. 'Oh, yes, indeed, Mrs Alder.'

Minutes later, the purchase price having been paid, Beth emerged into the sunshine in her new clothes. With the gown and spencer she had little black patent shoes, an elegant grey silk bonnet trimmed with green and cream chenille roses, a cream silk pagoda parasol, dark green gloves, and a capacious new grey satin reticule. She was she was anxious to go to Caradine Street, and hastened to the nearest hackney coach stand. Soon she was on her way to the premises of Withers, Withers & Blenkinsop, her fingers crossed that she'd find word of her father's final will. The route took the coach down Easterden Street, and she glanced up at the name Topweather painted in gilt on a first-floor window. She would go there next.

But a great shock greeted her two junctions later, when the hackney coach halted opposite the lawyers' premises in Caradine Street, for drawn up before the stucco porch of Messrs Withers, Withers & Blenkinsop was Sir Guy Valmer's green travelling carriage, with Dickon seated placidly on the box.

Chapter Seven

*B*eth was utterly daunted. It could hardly be coincidence that Guy was here. Had he realized that Bessie Alder and Beth Tremoille were the same person? Had the solicitors' notice brought him? Did he think she'd murdered Joshua and stolen the money? She didn't know what to do, except hope he was calling somewhere nearby. When she didn't alight, the hackney coachman climbed down to come to the door. He had a bulbous red nose and bushy eyebrows, and wasn't in the best of tempers. 'How long are we going to hang around like this, miss?' he growled.

'I wish to wait a while.'

'It'll cost you. I charge double for standing around!'

It was outrageous, but she nodded. She didn't dare alight in case Dickon recognized her, nor did she want to drive on before ascertaining if she was worrying unnecessarily about Guy. Another twenty minutes passed before the doors of the building opposite opened and two men came out. She recognized one as the senior partner, Mr Arthur Withers, who had been summoned to Tremoille House on occasion in the past. He was a strangely chinless man, short and well upholstered, in a powdered wig and stern black clothes. The other man was Guy, and she was aghast, having begun to convince herself that he was calling elsewhere.

He was as perfectly dressed as before, his chestnut hair shining in the sunlight, and he was smiling at something the solicitor said. His maroon coat and cream trousers were a superb fit, and he was the personification of stylish nonchalance as he tapped his hat on his head and began to tease on his gloves. A jewelled pin flashed in his neck cloth, and she distinctly heard him laugh. He really was an extraordinarily attractive man, she thought, trying not to remember that he was the source of the sensual ecstasy she'd experienced the last time she'd lain with Jake. She bowed her head and toyed unhappily with her reticule. It would now be utter madness to approach the solicitors, because doing that would in all probably lead to her arrest, maybe even the gallows. If she simply drove away, at least she would keep her freedom.

Suddenly the coach door was snatched open and she gave a start on finding herself face to face with Guy. 'Well, now, if it isn't Miss Alder,' he declared, 'or is it Miss Tremoille?' She blanched, too intimidated to move or even think. 'Have you no swift ripostes this time?' he taunted.

She couldn't look away from his spellbinding eyes, but her wits rallied a little. 'Who *are* you, sir?'

'You know me well enough, although I admit I almost didn't recognize you.'

Beth felt completely trapped. Dread flowed over her as the worst seemed about to happen, but at the same time she experienced such a devastating sense of attraction toward him that he might have been a magnet and she a helpless pin. Her body ached, and her lips were tender and expectant, as if anticipating his kiss. She was shaken by her feelings; ashamed, betrayed and haunted by them.

He tried to read her thoughts. 'I'm curious about your transformation from beggar to fine lady. Exactly how much did that pheasant weigh, mm? Somewhere in the region of one thousand guineas?' The colours she wore reminded him of the fascinating portrait at Tremoille House. She was Oberon's daughter again, a tree spirit from the depths of an enchanted wood. He drew himself up sharply. Fantasy had no place in this. She was the hunted, and he the hunter. For him she was simply Esmond Tremoille's heir, and therefore nothing more than a matter of unfinished business. A tricky matter of business at that. What part she'd played in the death of the man Joshua was yet to be uncovered, but a common thief she certainly was, and criminal or not, he needed her in order to regain Valmer property. He'd marry her if she were as ugly as sin itself.

His silence puzzled her. 'Why do you persist in this case of mistaken identity?'

'Hardly mistaken identity. I've been looking for you, Beth Tremoille. I even found out about your blacksmith and paid him a visit.' He smiled as her lips parted. 'So he still means something to you? You certainly mean everything to him, but he's grateful for the memories. He's at the forge in Frampney now, should you wish to return to him.'

So Jake had purchased the half-share he wanted so much. She was glad, but this time nothing showed on her face as she regarded Guy. Suddenly she shouted to the hackney coachman. 'Drive on! Drive on! This gentleman is pestering me!'

Guy grabbed her wrist. 'Oh, no, you don't! You're not going to give me the slip!'

'Let me go!' she screamed. 'Drive on, for pity's sake! I'm being attacked! Help! Help!' The coachman's whip cracked, and the horse set off at a strong trot. Guy tried to pull her out of the coach, but she resisted with all her might, even going so far as to kick out at him. She felt his gloved fingers slipping, and at last he had to release her. The door swung wildly, and she sobbed as she tried to close it. For a moment her eyes locked with Guy's as he stood in the street behind. His lips moved, and she knew what he was saying. *I'll find you again, Beth Tremoille, I'll find you!* She sat back weakly on the seat, trembling and feeling sick. Guy was quick-witted enough to have noted the coach's licence, so it would be stupid to direct the driver to the Swan. Glancing out she realized she was in Easterden Street. Well, two could be quick-witted, she decided, and leaned out. 'Stop now, if you please!'

The coachman hauled on the reins and, as she climbed out, he stretched a hand down to her. 'That'll be three shillings,' he said, 'unless you want me to tell that fancy cove where I've dropped you off?'

She disguised her feelings as she took the coins from her reticule, but then held them up just beyond his reach and let them drop into a heap of fresh horse dung. She walked away with some satisfaction hearing him curse foully as he got down to retrieve the money. As soon as he wasn't looking at her, she dodged into a circulating library on the corner, and observed through the window as he wiped the coins on his coat, climbed back up to his seat and turned the coach around to return to Caradine Street. He was going to tell Guy anyway! She hurried from hiding and ran along the street toward the entrance of Mr Henry Topweather's premises, slipping inside without attracting any attention. The door gave on to a shadowy, unlit staircase to the first floor, where another door admitted her to the house agent's offices. An elderly clerk, thin and stooping, looked curiously at Beth from his stool behind a high, narrow desk. The quill behind his ear had stained his lopsided wig as well as the top of his ear, and his drab clothes were so comfortably worn they looked as if he hadn't changed them in six months. 'May I help you, madam?'

'I wish to see Mr Topweather.'

'He is engaged with a client at the moment, but will not be long. If you'd be so kind as to take a seat over there?' He indicated an upright chair in a corner, then sanded some papers and blew the excess away noisily. As Beth sat down she became aware of low male voices and the smell of cigar smoke in the adjoining room, the door of which stood slightly ajar. After about five minutes there came the scraping of chairs, and two gentlemen emerged – at least, *one* gentleman came out, accompanied by a short, fat man of about forty, with perspiration on his high forehead and a fixed smile on his wet lips. He wore a baggy blue coat and grey breeches, and his small dark eyes were like polished pebbles as he fawned upon his companion. The gentleman was maybe ten years older, tall and muscular, with a high complexion and drinker's nose. His manner was blustering and his temper disagreeable as he jammed his expensive top hat on his sparse hair. 'I've been assured that you are in Baynsdon's confidence, Topweather. I trust it's true?'

'I'm his second cousin, my lord.'

'All I want is to be tipped the wink about his decision. Damn it all, not only do I *refuse* to be defeated by my scheming bitch of a wife, but I also intend to make money out of it as well! I never imagined that my thrice-cursed marriage would cause more flutters in Belvedere's than Wellington's final tilt with Boney!'

Topweather hurried to open the outer door. 'I will be in touch with you the moment I learn anything, Lord St Clair.'

'See that you are, Topweather. Baynsdon must find for *me*, d'you hear?' His lordship stomped out angrily, and Topweather closed the door thankfully, and then saw Beth. He raked her from head to toe, and evidently found her much to his liking, for his face creased into a rather oily smile as he crossed lightly toward her, almost on tiptoe. 'Why, madam, I had no idea you were here.' He bowed over her hand, holding her fingers longer than was necessary and thus making her uncomfortably aware of him. 'May I be of assistance?' he enquired.

'You are seeking a tenant for a property?' She drew her hand away.

'I have many properties on my books, Miss...?'

'Mrs Alder. I am a widow.' He glanced at her far from sombre clothes, especially the area of her breasts. 'My husband passed away five years ago,' she said, annoyed to feel the need to explain, and filled with distaste by his obvious male interest.

'You must have married exceedingly young, Mrs Alder,' he replied smoothly, perhaps intending it to be a compliment, or perhaps to convey his suspicion that she was not telling the truth. Neither possibility was pleasing, and when she didn't answer he cleared his throat. 'I, er, I have no idea which property interests you.'

'I saw an advertisement regarding an isolated house on the coast.'

'Ah, yes. Please come this way, and I will show you the property.' He glanced at the clerk. 'Jones? Some tea, if you please.'

She got up to enter the other office, and was disagreeably aware of his hand resting against her waist as he ushered her toward a green leather chair that faced his cluttered desk. The room still hung with Lord St Clair's cigar smoke, a blue haze that floated and swirled in the draught from the door. As she sat down, she knew that Topweather was leaning over her in order to ogle her breasts. Not only that, he was rubbing his right hand against the front of his breeches. Revolted, she wished she hadn't come here, but it was too late now, and anyway, she really was interested in the house. Topweather went around the desk to sit down and rummage through a drawer. At last he brought out a document from which depended a bright vermilion seal. 'The property in question, the Dower House, is situated on the Devon shore of the Bristol Channel, at a small fishing hamlet and creek called Lannermouth.

'Dower House? So it's part of an estate?' That wasn't what she wanted at all.

'Originally, yes. The nearby Haldane estate owns Lannermouth, but the

Dower House was sold several years ago. The Haldanes have always been an important West Country family, and the village next to their ancestral home is named after them.' He spoke to her, but looked at her bosom. His right hand was thankfully out of sight, but she knew he was rubbing himself again. Was she the only young woman ever to set unfortunate foot over his threshold?

'Can you describe the property?' she asked coolly.

'It is thatched, part old, part modern, and has been got up in a gothic manner. The proportions are modest; it's tastefully furnished, with five bedrooms, three reception, a kitchen, stables and all the usual offices, a kitchen garden, hen coop and so on and so on. I understand there is also a very fashionable veranda, thatched like the house itself, around three sides of the ground floor. Oh, and a secluded pleasure garden on the landward side, sheltered from the sea winds and planted with flowers and shrubs of an almost Mediterranean nature. A housekeeper is in residence, a Mrs Cobbett. Other staff can be hired locally. If this is agreeable to you, the sum of fifty-five guineas will secure it for twelve months.' He placed the document in front of her.

It seemed idyllic, she thought, and affordable. She would take the house in spite of the agent's disgusting inclination to fondle his private parts in her presence. A year at the Dower House in Lannermouth would enable her to consider at leisure what to do with her future. 'I will take it immediately, Mr Topweather,' she said, 'if that is in order? I have the money with me.'

He regarded her thoughtfully, still smiling, and then nodded. 'Excellent.' The clerk brought in a tray of tea, which when poured proved to be weak and colourless. Topweather waved Jones out again, and placed a cup before her with his offending right hand. 'Now, I need a few personal details, Mrs Alder,' he said, wiping his damp palms on his coat as he sat back and then, reaching for a notebook and a pencil. 'Your full name, maiden name, the name and circumstances of your late husband, your present address, and so on.'

Beth was resigned. She'd already invented her surname, so why not everything else too? It was as well to be hanged for a sheep as a lamb. 'Eliza Mary Alder, née Wilkes, widow of Jacob James Alder, sea captain. Presently staying at the Swan with Two Necks in Lad Lane, but formerly of Queen's Crescent, Scarborough.' It sounded impressively plausible, she thought, pleased.

He scribbled it all down, and then rose again. 'Please excuse me while I have Jones prepare the necessary documents. It will not take long.'

The tea remained untouched as Beth discreetly counted fifty-five guineas on the desk, and glanced around the room. All was not as it should be, she thought, sensing something in the atmosphere that had nothing to do with her personal abhorrence of Mr Henry Topweather. He definitely ran an agency, because apart from the details of the Dower House, the desk was laden with letters and documents concerning other properties around the country. Why then did she feel so ill at ease? It wasn't that she was afraid of Topweather's unwelcome advances, because Jake had taught her how to defend herself. She was just aware of something yet to come.

After a while Topweather returned with the new documents, and resumed his seat to go through them with her. When she was content that the Dower House was indeed hers for the next twelve months, she appended her false signature and then pushed the money toward him. 'I trust I am now the legal tenant, Mr Topweather?'

'Indeed yes.' The constant smile continued to crease his cheeks, and she wondered if his facial muscles ever ached, but then he asked something startling. 'Tell me, Mrs Alder, why is it that a lady of your obvious quality takes the risk of carrying such a great deal of money on her person? Don't be afraid, for I am not about to seize your purse and steal whatever is left. On the contrary, I may be able to increase its contents by a considerable sum.'

'I think my business here is done,' she declared firmly, getting up.

'At least do me the courtesy of hearing me out,' he said in a reasonable tone.

'I would rather not.'

'Then I fear I may have to turn you in to the authorities, for it is clear to me that you have given me false information about your identity. It's my guess there's a warrant out against you. So sit down again, if you please, and let me tell you how we can win ourselves a splendid pile of money. I know you'd like that, because if you were already rich you wouldn't be looking at the Dower House, so far away from London. But I'm not interested in your secrets, just in your co-operation.'

The light in her eyes changed. So that was it. He wanted her favours in exchange for his silence! 'You revolt me,' she breathed.

His smile became lecherously rueful. 'Much as I'd enjoy dipping my wick in you, my dear, I fear my proposition is far from carnal. What I want is that you be an errand girl, someone who looks the picture of fashion and breeding, and who will be accepted without question. Believe me, it will be to your own advantage too.' She hesitated, intrigued against her will. Gauging her indecision, he proceeded. 'When you were waiting in the other room, you saw Lord St Clair. He and his wife are cousins in the process of divorce, and each believes they have sole right to the title and Ulsbourne Castle in Sussex. Lord St Clair is the present titleholder, but she is the only remaining member of the senior branch of the family, and has produced papers that apparently cast doubt on his legitimacy. The matter is a great *cause célèbre*. If Mr Justice Baynsdon, to whom I am related, finds for her, Lord St Clair will lose everything to her, title included, because in the absence of a legitimate male claimant, the title can go to the female side. Belvedere's Tearooms are *the* place this season, where the beau monde will bet upon anything, and the St Clair business has them chasing their tails in a veritable frenzy. Vast wagers are being laid, mostly upon the verdict going to Lord St Clair outright. But there are other possibilities; for example, Lord St Clair might retain the castle but lose the title; Lady St Clair might win everything, or the title and nothing else. Now then, what would you say if I told you I already know the judge's exact decision?' he asked.

Her lips parted. 'Do you?'

Again the smile, 'Oh, yes, my dear, and what my partner and I need is a go-between to place our bets. In short, Mrs Alder, someone like you.' Beth was no fool, and guessed that his partner was none other than Mr Justice Baynsdon himself. 'Place the bets, for us at Belvedere's Tearooms,' Topweather continued, 'and at eight o'clock tonight you, personally, could be in possession of at least two hundred times the outlay for a year at the Dower House.'

She was silent for a moment, and then regarded him again. 'You believe me to be dishonest, Mr Topweather, so surely you see that I might abscond with *all* the money?'

'You would be very foolish to try it, because my man will be following you all the time, and believe me, he is most adept at such matters. You would not escape with anything that was not yours.'

'I begin to wonder if I would escape with what *was* mine,' she countered.

He gave her his first genuine smile. 'Honour among thieves, Mrs Alder. I am scrupulously fair when dealing with associates. Do we have an agreement?'

'It's very tempting, but—'

He wagged a finger and tutted. 'That's the wrong answer, dear lady. You must agree or I will see to it that the relevant authorities know all about you.'

'Then I have no choice, do I?' She got up. 'What am I expected to do?'

'Come here at seven tonight. I will tell you what to bet, and give you the funds to place at Belvedere's Tearooms for my partner and me, under the names of Harrison and Connor, both of Richmond. What you call yourself is up to you. I will have a carriage waiting to take you there. When you have the winnings, keep what is yours and bring the rest back here for me to divide with my partner, and then we can all go our separate ways. Believe me, with funds like that you could live in luxury at Lannermouth. Just remember to be circumspect between now and then. You will be watched. Behave yourself and all will be well. I'm a fair man.'

'I wouldn't call blackmail fair, Mr Topweather.'

For the rest of that day Beth thought long and hard about the evening ahead. She dared not defy Henry Topweather because he would certainly carry out his threat. Fleeing London now was an option, of course, but to go where? The Dower House was hers for the next year, so to bolt elsewhere would mean forfeiting that precious money. And there was the rather unworthy fact that she would dearly like to have more in her purse. It had to be faced that the funds she had would not support her for the rest of her life, and no matter how contemptible Henry Topweather might be, he offered her a chance to become truly wealthy.

Chapter Eight

Beth arrived at Belvedere's Tearooms at half-past seven that evening, in the yellow-and-black chaise that had awaited her at Henry Topweather's door. By coincidence, the coachman was Billy Pointer, a post boy from the Swan, whose acquaintance she had made earlier in the day when admiring a red chariot for sale in the inn yard. He was a former jockey, lean, likeable and amiably monkey-faced, and boasted of being the best driver in London, a claim she thought justified as he skilfully wove the chaise through the crush to draw up right outside the brilliantly illuminated tearooms. A footman hastened to lower the rung for her to alight, and as she stepped down to the pavement she felt perfectly attired for her role. She had purloined some of Lady Harcotleigh's wardrobe, an emerald green silk gown with a scooped neckline, a high-collared daffodil-yellow silk spencer, and a wide-brimmed openwork hat in the same emerald green as the gown, tied on with wired yellow ribbons. After a great deal of endeavour she had achieved an acceptable knot in her hair, and was satisfied she looked her part. It was wrong to wear garments that weren't yet hers, but she told herself that soon everything that Madame de Sichel had sent to the Swan would be paid for, right down to the very last ribbon and silk flower. She was prepared for the evening in another way too, having been provided by Topweather with several thin canvas bags folded inside her reticule. They would be needed for all the winnings Topweather confidently predicted. She spoke anxiously to Billy. 'You will wait for me, won't you?'

'Of course I will, ma'am,' he answered in his cheerful London accent. 'Don't you fret, I'll be here when you leave, and later I'm to take you back to the Swan as well.'

The doors of the tearooms were decorated in honour of the victory at Waterloo. Arrangements of flags and flowers flanked the entrance, and an arch of moss and laurel leaves spanned overhead. The people arriving here tonight were the cream of society, dukes, earls, duchesses and countesses, and all other ranks of the aristocracy. Dandies strolled toward the tearooms, some accompanied by fashionable ladies, some walking in loud drawling groups. Carriages of distinction thronged the street, and the drawl of superior voices filled the air, some so affected as to resemble the braying of donkeys. She was a little worried about attending on her own, and gladly tagged on to a group of ladies from the carriage behind hers. There was a deafening racket of conversation inside, and no one noticed as she left the ladies and walked alone down the long hallway. So many people crowded the staircase to the main tearoom on the first floor that it took some time to ascend, but at last she found herself in a lofty chamber with west-facing windows that caught the extraordinary prism-hued dazzle of the early evening sky.

There was a dais at the far end, where an imposing long-case clock stood against the wall and the gentlemen in charge of the betting were seated at a table. She queued to put down a considerable bet in the names of Harrison and Connor of Hampstead, and Alder of Scarborough, and was given three betting slips that she took to a small table in a corner. Her mind was racing and she felt a little sick, because at the very last moment she'd impulsively parted with all her remaining guineas. She was either the greatest of fools or the wisest of owls, and tried not to think of it as she sat back to watch London's *ton*. Several times she encountered eyes that were quickly averted. Did any of them belong to someone Topweather sent to keep watch on her? The minutes ticked by, the room was now a press, although of Lord St Clair there was not a whisker. Clearly he did not wish to risk a public humiliation. As the clock began to chime eight, the chattering died away and the sound of running footsteps was heard on the staircase. A breathless footman in a white wig and gold livery appeared, holding a sealed note aloft as a path was made for him to reach the dais, where an elderly gentleman in grey velvet broke the seal and read. Then he glanced around the sea of impatient faces. 'I have to tell you that Mr Justice Baynsdon finds ... er, finds for Lady St Clair on every count, subject to an investigation into her ladyship's legitimacy.' The result was *exactly* as Topweather had said. There were gasps and groans, but Beth felt almost faint with excitement. She had just won almost 11,000 guineas for herself! Her fingers tightened over the precious betting slips as she got up to make her way through the suddenly noisy room. She was not alone in having wagered upon the exact wording of the verdict, for two young noblemen whooped with delight as they waved their slips at the presiding gentlemen. Beth soon found herself being jostled as the beau monde swarmed around the dais.

At last she tendered her slips, they were examined and approved, and bundles of banknotes were pushed toward her. She managed to cram it all into her reticule and the canvas bags, and then left hurriedly. Behind her the two young noblemen began to brandish their winnings tauntingly. Their gloating mirth was cut short when one of Belvedere's famous cream cakes flew through the air and hit the shorter of them on his pointed nose.

Then more cakes rained, and the ladies in the room squealed with delight as they joined the commotion.

Beth emerged thankfully to the warm evening air, lengthening shadows and glorious sky, and found Billy waiting about fifty yards along the street. As she climbed thankfully into the chaise, bets were already being laid in Belvedere's as to how many cream cakes would be thrown before the riot was brought under control. Soon she was on her way back to Easterden Street, carefully separating her winnings from the rest. She had counted with scrupulous care, making sure she did not take so much as a farthing from the vast amounts won by Topweather and his partner. Sitting back at last, she marvelled that she now had the 11,000 guineas in her reticule. She could pay Madame de Sichel, and then go to the Dower House to live well on the remainder. How unbelievably different things had been only two days ago, when she'd left her hiding place by the boundary wall at Tremoille House, to get to the woods before Sir Guy Valmer's carriage.

As the chaise drew up outside Topweather's premises, she saw a berlin drawn up by a lamppost further along the street. Mr Justice Baynsdon, perchance? The door opened next to her and Topweather's bloated face peered in. 'So, Mrs Alder, I trust the evening went well for us?' he said, his eyes gleaming as he saw the bulging canvas bags on the seat opposite her.

'As you can see, it went very well indeed, sir,' she replied, 'and I trust that this finalizes our association?'

'If that is your wish, but there could be other nights as profitable as this; they happen from time to time.' His hot gaze was fixed on the curve of her breasts.

'I want it to end here, Mr Topweather.' A sixth sense made her glance swiftly out of the chaise's tiny rear window. A green carriage came slowly around a corner into Easterden Street, and if she was not mistaken Dickon's solid figure was at the ribbons! Her breath caught and she looked swiftly at Topweather again. 'Well, I have completed my side of the bargain, and so bid you farewell.'

'Look, it's foolish to abandon what can clearly be a profitable association!'

Her frightened eyes were on the approaching carriage, and she slammed the door and called out to Billy to drive on just as Guy's horses passed the window. Then Dickon came into view, but to her relief Billy roused the chaise team into action. For a terrifying moment she saw into the other vehicle. Guy was in evening attire, with a large topaz in his cravat, at least, she thought it was a topaz because it flashed yellow in the light from a street lamp. They stared at each other, but as he sat forward in astonishment, the chaise leapt away from the kerb. She looked from the back window and saw him leaning out to yell at Dickon to give chase. Topweather realized something was up, and melted away into the shadows, discretion always being the better part of his valour. Dickon, masterly as he was, proved no match for Billy Pointer, who wove through the streets like a demon needle, and pulled into the bustling yard of the Swan without any sign of pursuit. She alighted quickly, her reticule and shawl bundle in her arms. 'Thank you, Billy. I wished to avoid—'

'There's no need to explain, Mrs Alder,' he answered swiftly.

She pressed a coin into his hand. 'I'm very grateful.'

He touched his hat and then stirred the horses into action again, skimmed past the red chariot that was for sale, and disappeared into Lad Lane. She turned thoughtfully toward the chariot, not noticing Mr Waterhouse nearby, enjoying a mug of ale. 'An excellent bargain, madam,' he observed.

'I'm sure it is, sir.'

'One hundred pounds gets you the chaise, and another sixty a pair of fine horses.'

'I will consider it,' she replied, for a notion had begun to form in her head. She had to get to the Dower House with her fine new wardrobe and how better to do it than in her own private vehicle? Especially if someone like Billy Pointer could be persuaded to leave London for the wilds of the seaside. She hurried up the gallery steps to her room, where she was brought to an abrupt halt on being confronted by an irate Madame de Sichel. The dressmaker had checked the inventory of Lady Harcotleigh's wardrobe, and noticed the absence of an emerald silk gown and various accessories. When Beth entered, wearing the missing items, the dressmaker's face hardened, and it was plain a very unpleasant scene was about to ensue. But Beth's wits were still quick enough to save the situation. 'Ah, here you are at last, *madame*. I thought you would never respond to my message.'

'I received no message.'

'No? Well, it doesn't matter. I have to leave London urgently, and need to settle my account with you before I go.'

The dressmaker became unsure. 'Settle it?'

'Why yes. You surely did not imagine I was making free with garments for which I had no intention of paying? I am pleased with everything, and will take it all.' Madame de Sichel's lips opened and closed, reminding Beth of the occupants of Tremoille House's ornamental pool. 'Is something wrong, *madame*?' Beth enquired.

'Er, no, madam,' The dressmaker dimpled self-consciously. 'Nothing at all.'

'Do you have the bill?'

The woman handed over a sheet of paper that displayed alarmingly expensive reckonings, and Beth felt quite exultant as she counted out the total. Then it was her turn to direct a meaningful look. 'There will be a receipt, of course?'

'Oh, of course!' The dressmaker went to the writing table in the corner, and used the Swan's pen and ink to scribble the necessary acknowledgement and signature. 'I trust you will honour me with your patronage in the future,' she declared hopefully, and then sailed from the room, a different woman entirely from the gimlet-eyed Fury of moments before. As soon as the woman had gone, Beth hastened out to peer cautiously over the gallery balustrade for any sign of Guy. The now customary sunset splendour stained the sky, reaching down into the yard as a dull pink light. The inn was particularly busy because a number of coaches were due in or about to depart. There was no sign of Guy, but Billy had already returned, and was engaged in a heated argument with Mr Waterhouse. They were standing by the red chariot, shouting and gesticulating, although she couldn't hear what they were saying because of the general noise. As she turned her attention to a Gloucester stagecoach, it suddenly dawned on her that she was lodging in a very obvious place. So many coaches from Wales and the West Country used the Swan that on reflection she was amazed Guy hadn't come here already. She needed to leave London immediately. Tonight! The burgeoning thoughts of earlier returned as she looked at Billy still arguing with Mr Waterhouse. Judging by the choler of the disagreement, the post boy was almost certainly out of a job. She hurried along the gallery and down the steps, and then threaded her way toward the chariot.

Billy's wrinkled face, crimson with fury, was dwarfed by the large brown beaver hat he'd tugged low over his greying hair. 'And I tell *you*, Mr Fancy Waterhouse,' he was yelling, 'that you owe me five shillings!'

'Get away, you poxy little sod, *four* shillings is all I owe!'

'Excuse me,' she interrupted, and both turned to look at her in surprise. Billy snatched his hat off respectfully. 'Ma'am.'

'Yes, Mrs Alder?' said the innkeeper a little testily, but still managing a smile of sorts.

'It concerns the chariot and pair.'

'Yes?'

'I would like to purchase both, with a view to leaving for Scotland tonight, but I also need a permanent driver.' She raised an eyebrow at Billy.

He leapt at the chance. 'Will I do, ma'am?'

The innkeeper rounded on him furiously. 'You work for me!'

'Not any more, you scaly beggar! If this lady wants a driver, then I'll go. Anything on God's earth is better than working for crooks like you!'

She interrupted again. 'Mr Waterhouse, about the chariot?'

He struggled to concentrate on her. 'Very well, Mrs Alder, but it's to be cash in hand.'

'That's agreeable to me,' she replied. 'I will take dinner here, and then settle my bill in full.' This was the second time she'd uttered these golden words, and it felt as good now as it had before.

The disgruntled innkeeper began to stalk away, but was halted when Billy called after him, 'Four shillings are better than nothing. I'll take them!'

Waterhouse turned, his eyes like flint. 'You're breaking your contract by shoving off without notice!'

'I haven't *got* a contract, so don't you try pulling that one. Four shillings, or I'll report you. Don't forget, I know more than you'd like about what goes on here.' The implied threat carried weight, because the innkeeper fished in a leather purse and handed over the money. Then he continued to walk angrily away, venting his wrath on an unfortunate pie-man who'd done nothing to warrant it.

Beth looked urgently at Billy. 'I meant the offer, Mr Pointer.'

'I know you meant it, ma'am. And just Billy will do. What are your terms?'

'Terms?' She thought back to the wages her father had paid for a coachman. 'Twenty-six pounds ten shillings a year, a roof over your head, uniform and your meals provided,' she said automatically.

He seemed well pleased. 'That's good enough for me, ma'am!'

'Billy, I'm anxious to leave tonight, not for Scotland, but the north coast of Devon. A place called Lannermouth.'

'Why, blow me, I know it! A few years back I took an elderly lady and her son posting there. A new road leads down into a river gorge that ends in a sea creek. Pretty as a picture.'

'Please remember I want everyone to think I am going to Scotland,' she said. 'How long do you think it will take to get to Lannermouth?'

'Three or four days. It depends on the weather,' he replied. She hoped he was right, because if she closed her eyes, she could already smell the salt sea air. She smiled warmly. 'How long will you need to have a meal and get the chariot ready?'

'We can be out of here in an hour and a half, ma'am, but it's not good to be on the road after dark,' he cautioned.

'I know, and I'm quite happy to stop at the first inn you recommend. The important thing is to be out of here.'

He searched her face. 'Someone's after you, eh? I'll lose them for you, ma'am, don't you fret about that. I know all the byways and inns.'

'I have to pack all my belongings.' She was thinking of her new wardrobe.

'I'll see that a good maid helps you, ma'am. After that, you have a good dinner, which is one thing the Swan does well, then we'll kick our heels of London.'

Beth returned to her room feeling able to place her complete trust in him. The feeling grew when a few minutes later a neat maid presented herself to help with the packing of the wardrobe. Two waiters carried in an old trunk that had been lying forgotten in an attic, and soon Beth's new clothes had not only been folded away, but the trunk had been taken down some back stairs to the red chariot, and a boy paid to keep an eye on it. Billy had soon sneaked into the kitchens, from where he'd have been ejected had Mr Waterhouse known, and then went to attend to the pair of geldings that went with the chariot.

It was later to prove fortunate that Beth decided to settle her now considerable bill before taking dinner, although she didn't realize it at the time. She suffered the indignity of Mr Waterhouse's excessive hair-splitting over the smallest thing, and when all was satisfactorily settled, she went through to the crowded, dimly lit dining-room. A waiter conducted her to a small table next to the inglenook fireplace, where copper and brass pans reflected the wavering flames of the candles. The windows all faced on to the yard, and the surrounding inn was quickly losing the last of the late evening light. Had it not been for the small candle in the centre of her table, the room would have been very shadowy indeed. Her dinner comprised vegetable soup, roast pork, peas and potatoes, followed by raspberry pudding, and was very good. There was a lively conversation at the next table, where half-a-dozen gentlemen, who'd dined well and consumed much wine, were discussing bloodstock, in particular the huge price paid that day for a two-year-old colt by Psalter. Beth was very interested because the colt was half-brother to Lancelot, and was from the Tremoille stud.

The sensation of being observed overtook her so slowly that at first she hardly noticed, but as the feeling intensified she began to glance around. Her heart almost arrested as she saw Guy, leaning elegantly against the jamb of the door to the entrance hall, tapping his three-cornered hat against white silk breeches of superb quality. His clothes were those she'd glimpsed earlier, a black velvet evening coat and a muted gold waistcoat that was partially unbuttoned to allow his shirt frills to push through. The chestnut of his hair had become tawny in the uncertain light, and he presented a matchless picture of male elegance, so handsome and confident, polished and relaxed, that he might almost have been a portrait by Thomas Lawrence.

She had been right, it was indeed a large topaz in his cravat, she observed numbly, as he straightened to cross the room toward her.

Chapter Nine

Reaching Beth's table, Guy sketched a bow, disturbing the gently swaying candle between them. 'May I enquire who you are tonight?' he enquired softly, holding her gaze with that unsettling directness that made her feel almost naked.

'You keep labouring under the false impression that we are acquainted, sir,' she replied. *Don't show your fear, Beth, whatever you do, don't show your fear.*

He sat facing her. 'What a consummate actress you are. I salute you, but you are still the little thief I found by the roadside near Tremoille House. I told you I'd find you again, and I have. This establishment should have come to my mind earlier of course, being so prominent for coaches from Gloucestershire. Now then, Miss Tremoille, we have things to discuss,' he said conversationally, appropriating her wine glass and taking a sip. He met her eyes again, and smiled a little. 'You tantalize me, for you are the most enterprising young woman I have encountered in a long time.' She was so conscious of his closeness that her skin seemed to tingle. She could smell his cologne, fresh and clean, and she couldn't help watching his mouth. She'd kissed those lips in her thoughts, felt their passion and tasted their sweetness. He cast a spell over her, awakening her senses so that desire began to gather between her legs and in her breasts. His glance brushed hers, lazily, almost caressingly. 'Have you nothing to say?' he asked.

'You frighten me, sir.' That at least was the truth. His allure coiled around her, passing smoothly over her flesh, finding its way to places no man had found before. Never had she imagined she would be as attracted to anyone as she was to him. It was a physical pain so intense that it caught in her breath and brought tears to her eyes. Raw emotion cut a swathe through common sense, and she knew she was within seconds of throwing herself on his mercy. But did he have any? Folly beckoned in the fascination of his eyes, the silken softness of his voice, and the beguiling essence of his cologne. She looked away in an effort to break the spell. 'Why are you hounding me like this?' *To punish me for robbery and murder?* She willed him to have some other, unconnected reason, but feared the worst.

Guy chose that unfortunate moment to remind her of his suspicions. 'Please don't ape the innocent, because that is something you definitely are not. You've been a blacksmith's mistress and you've stolen a large sum of money. Whether you are also a murderess I do not know.'

Alarm pierced her as she felt in danger of imminent capture. She had to get away from him, but how? She cast around desperately for a way of escape, but all that came to mind was the woman's weapon of making a scene, which had worked in Caradine Street and might just work here too. 'Leave me alone!' she cried suddenly, and a hush descended over the dining-room. The gentlemen at the next table turned in their seats. Her voice rang out clearly in the silence. 'If you do not stop pestering me, Sir Guy, I shall be forced to ask the landlord to have you removed!'

For a moment she thought there was a glimmer of admiration in Guy's eyes, and when he replied he was the soul of reason. 'Miss Tremoille, I only wish to speak to you.'

'I'm not Miss Tremoille, and I don't wish to engage in conversation with you, sir.' Her voice broke in distress, and she sought a handkerchief in her reticule. To her relief, a chair scraped at the next table, and one of the gentlemen arose. He was in his forties, and a dandy in the mould of Mr Brummell. A lace-edged handkerchief fluttered between the second and fourth fingers of his left hand, and he might have been described as handsome, were it not that a ridiculous hauteur required him to look down his nose at anyone to whom he spoke. Ridiculous or not, there was a decidedly chill glint in his pale-blue eyes.

'I say now, Valmer, this ain't quite the thing,' he drawled.

'If I require your interference, Newton, I'll ask for it,' Guy replied in a dangerously amiable tone.

'Well, 'pon me soul, your manners are appallin'. I'm afraid somethin' will have to be done about that.' Newton nodded at his companions, who all got to their feet. Then he smiled at Guy. 'The lady says she don't know you, Valmer, and by all the powers you've made her cry.' He took Beth's hand and raised it to his lips graciously, before turning back to Guy. 'So *we* say she don't know you either, that makes six of us in complete agreement, against your paltry one. Dear boy, your presence here is superfluous.'

'I have no desire to mix it with you, Newton, and I'm rather astonished you should be ill-advised enough to risk offending me. But then, you have the advantage of your merry men, which is more or less what I would expect of you.'

Newton flushed, and then waved Guy away with waggling fingers. 'Off you trot, Valmer, just make a dignified exit while you can.'

'Have a care,' Guy breathed, unwilling to endure much more.

77

Beth spoke up quickly. 'No! Please! I – I'd rather Sir Guy remained here and *I* left. It's better that way.'

Newton hastened to draw out her chair. 'If that's your wish, m'dear.'

She felt Guy's eyes upon her, and on taking the briefest of glances, saw his cool amusement. 'Until we meet again, Miss Tremoille,' he murmured.

Getting up, she stammered her thanks to the gentlemen, and conversation broke out behind her as she hurried out to the yard, where to her unutterable relief Billy was ready and waiting with the chariot. Billy gave a start and called through the grille behind his box. 'Mrs Alder?'

'Yes. Leave now, Billy!' she called back. 'Hurry! Stop at the first good inn you know that's off the beaten track!' He took the light carriage swiftly into Lad Lane, and from there commenced a tortuous route toward the west, turning numerous corners until Beth had no idea where they were. But the important thing was that Sir Guy Valmer didn't know where she was either. Nor would he be able to trace her, unless he spoke to Henry Topweather, of whom he knew nothing. With luck he would soon set off up the Great North Road in the hope of overtaking her.

It was nightfall four days later when they reached the last mile of the journey. Beth had just fallen asleep and her dreams took her back to Fiddler's Court, where Jake's arms were warm and his lips tender. 'I love you, Bethie, you're the most precious thing in my world.' The sweetness of his love surrounded her, and she could smell the hay in the loft. 'Give me your hand, Bethie. Feel that? Cocker's ready to do you justice. My God, he's fit to explode. Oh, yes, you stroke him gentle like. Gentle, gentle.' He exhaled with rich pleasure. 'Now then, let's get him between your legs, Bethie, so he can go about his God-given business. Aah, that's right. My God, you've got him going, he can hardly fit, he's that swelled up with love.'

The chariot shuddered over stones in the road, and her eyes flew open again. The weak light of the carriage lamps hardly made an impression on the gloom as the horses picked their weary way down the long winding gorge that led from Exmoor toward the sea. She must only have dozed for a few moments, because they were still negotiating a long gradual decline that had not required Billy to fit the drags to the rear of the chariot as he'd had to do quite a few times while crossing Exmoor. Occasionally he had also hired horses for the climbs out of deep valleys.

The narrow road, which was quite new, wound along the gorge's steep wooded side, swinging out past huge boulders and outcrops, before shrinking back into dips and recesses where secretive springs trickled through moss. It was only just passable for carriages, and before its construction packhorses would have been needed to transport goods. The loud babble of the East Lanner river echoed beneath the dense canopy of trees, and now and then she saw the stark white of rapids or waterfalls far below, while high above, an early moon shone an upturned crescent in the starry darkness. She wondered how much further it could possibly be to Lannermouth. The high moor seemed miles above and behind them, and she longed for the silent comfort of a clean featherbed.

Suddenly the noise of the carriage took on a different sound and she glimpsed the candlelit window of a cottage poised above the drop to the river. She lowered the window glass and savoured the smell of the summer leaves and moss and, for the first time, the sea. Lights shone through the darkness ahead, but she couldn't make anything out in detail until a sharp turn around another cottage took them into the glow of a porch lantern. Billy slowed the horses right down, giving her a chance to assess her surroundings. By the light of more lanterns she saw a river confluence that flowed down to a creek where a walled harbour was just distinguishable in the gloom. Lannermouth, she thought, as Billy drove carefully over a double-arched stone bridge that spanned the East Lanner at the very point of confluence. Beyond the bridge and away from the village, the road skirted a few acres of level grassland before climbing steeply north-east over a towering hill. She would soon learn that it was the coast road to Porworthy and Minehead. The grassy area was well kept and dotted with the ghostly silhouettes of handsome specimen trees, and twinkling through the graceful branches she saw a lamp shining at a gothic trefoil window.

The chariot halted again, and Billy climbed down to open gates bearing the name, Dower House. Resuming his seat, he drove down a narrow drive that ran parallel with the creek. One hundred yards later, after passing a small stable block that was built right on the harbour wall, they reached the house, which had a thatched veranda surrounding the ground floor, with scented roses twining the wooden pillars. The smell of the sea was fresh and tangy, and she was sure she could hear the splash of waves close by. The lamps swung up and down with the springs as Billy applied the brakes for the last time. Beth looked up at the lighted window. Was it the room of the housekeeper, Mrs Cobbett? Billy jumped down to rap loudly with the highly polished brass fox's head knocker on the green-painted door. After a moment the lighted upper window opened and a round-faced woman in a white nightdress peered down, her grey hair hanging in two long plaits from beneath her night bonnet. 'Who's there?' she called in a rich Devon burr.

'Mrs Cobbett? My name is Miss Mannacott,' Beth answered, 'and I am the new tenant.' Billy already knew the new name, having learned of it during the journey.

Mrs Cobbett was taken aback. 'I didn't realize there was to be a tenant, no, that I didn't.' She drew back inside hastily and after a moment candlelight appeared beneath the front door. Bolts and keys crunched, and the door squeaked as Mrs Cobbett opened it. 'Do come in, please.'

Billy touched his hat. 'I'll see to the horses and luggage, Miss Beth. Are the stables all right to use?' he asked the housekeeper.

'Everything's there. There's a mite of oats from Mr Grainger's time, and I reckon the water butt's full. It's all in good repair.' Billy led the team and chariot around toward the stable block, where the horses would be given a well-earned feed and rest, and Beth followed Mrs Cobbett into the hallway, with its whitewashed walls and red-tiled floor. The woman's candle fluttered, setting shadows leaping and fading, and Beth could smell herbs, especially rosemary, which hung in little bunches from a picture rail. The housekeeper opened the furthest door into a spacious, exceedingly clean kitchen. 'You must be hungry, Miss Mannacott?'

'Oh, yes. And Billy too. That's the coachman.'

The woman nodded. 'Of course. Now, I've not much in the store cupboard because I expected to be alone here, but I did bake today and my sister's boy brought me some plaice from his morning catch. I can fry some to take with bread and butter?'

'It sounds delicious.'

Mrs Cobbett smiled. 'Let me take your outer things, and then you sit down.'

An oil lamp was soon lit, and in a short while the light brightened over a clean, tidy room with very white walls and a wealth of oak dressers. There was a stone sink, and one of Count Rumford's patented iron ranges. Mrs Cobbett busied herself with it. 'Darned new-fangled thing,' she grumbled, 'I was happier with my old open fire and brick oven. This contraption is bedevilment. There, it's burning up at last. I'll have a good pot of tea on the brew in no time. Oh, lordy, there's so much I have to do tomorrow. If I'd known about you I'd have laid in everything, but I'll make a start first thing by going up to the village store in Haldane.'

'Billy can take you in the chariot.'

The woman blushed. 'Me? Go in a carriage?' But she was clearly pleased as she took the tea caddy from its shelf and carefully set out cups and saucers. But when she turned to ask Beth how she liked her tea, the words died on her lips, for Beth was asleep on the white-scrubbed table, her head resting on her arms.

Once again Beth's dreams were erotic, and it was with Guy that she lay. They were naked together on a dew-soaked lawn, and skeins of dawn mist threaded through hanging willow fronds. She didn't care that they were in the open air, or that they might be seen, just that she was with him in the way she yearned to be. The exciting strength of his body pressed against her as he leaned over to kiss her, dwelling over the intimacy. The dew clung to his skin, and the glow of approaching sunrise touched his hair as his tongue teased her lips, now sliding over them, now pushing between them, as soon another part of him would tease and then enter. His breath was soft against her cheek as he whispered, 'You didn't really believe I wanted you arrested, did you?'

'What else could I think?' she answered, and closed her eyes as he kissed her lips again, tracing their outline with the tip of his tongue. An erotic thrill tingled through her veins as he slid a hand to the nape of her neck and twined his fingers slowly and richly in her hair. 'You wish you found me repulsive, don't you? You wish you could hate me, but you can't. You desire me as much as I desire you, and now, at last, we are consummating that desire.' he breathed.

'I've wanted you since the first time I saw you,' she confessed, nuzzling against him and tasting the salt of his skin. All pretence was abandoned, and submission was divine. Oh, the rapture of making love with a man she desired – and the reckless exhilaration of surrendering to a man she feared. His mouth adored her throat, her breasts and her eager nipples. She held him, exulting in his hard, strong body, and the fact that for these precious moments he was entirely hers.

His lips worshipped her belly, lingering over her navel, and then moved down to the dark thatch of hair between her legs. Her body arched with delight as he pressed his face into the forest, breathing deeply of her scent. Gently he parted her thighs a little more, and then began to explore her moist, most secret places with his tongue. She writhed with pleasure as he kissed and sucked gently, gratifying desires she had hardly acknowledged. Her hands smoothed lovingly over his shoulders, and then sank through his hair. How she loved him. How she loved him! She was lost in joy, and her body was his to do with as he chose.

At last he moved from between her legs, and kissed his way up her body until his face was level with hers again. As his lips sought hers again, she could taste and smell herself, but then his hand slid down between her legs again, and as he slipped his fingers inside her, he stimulated her most sensitive place with his palm. Such a tide of ecstasy rushed over her that she thought she would dissolve with joy. Again and again the tide swept over her, until she thought she could stand no more, and yet even then another wave would carry her away into new elation. It was only when her body was so sensitive to him and she felt as if she were made of the most delicate glass, that he took his hand away and prepared to penetrate her with his arousal. He moved until he could lower his hips between her thighs, and slowly, so slowly, he allowed the gleaming tip of his manhood to pause at the gates of her body. 'Do you want me, Beth?' he whispered.

'You know that I do,' she breathed, and then gasped with renewed excitement as he pushed himself into her. He was so big that she felt him stretching her, and the feeling was almost too delicious to be believed. How could she withstand more pleasure? How many times had she already been satisfied? Oh, so many, and now he was storming her defences again, pleasuring her almost to the edge of reason. He withdrew, taking his time so that she felt every inch of him, then he was deep inside her again, so deep that it seemed he would impale her forever. Her hips moved luxuriously in time with him, and then their lips dissolved together in a kiss that threatened to rob them both of consciousness. They were absorbed by each other, becoming a single creature, with but single heart and a single soul.

It was perfect bliss, the loving embodiment of passion and fleshly delight, and all the while there was the dew, the crushed grass, and the wisps of evaporating mist among the draping curtains of the weeping willow. Their sensuous congress was warm and fulfilling, adoring and sensitive, but just as he began to pump his seed into her in a climax that transcended all things mortal, the dream was shattered.

Beth was awakened with a start as a marmalade cat jumped on to her lap. The rug over her knees was dislodged, and she found herself in the bright morning light of the kitchen at the Dower House. Sleep was slow to release her, and the dream lingered. Confusedly, she reached out for Guy, and was bereft at not finding him there beside her. There was a self-conscious bloom on her cheeks, because it really was as if she had just been physically invaded and adored by Sir Guy Valmer. How different the cold clear day. She sat back slowly on the chair, pondering the irony that the man she wanted but couldn't have when awake, was hers in every way during sleep.

After a few minutes she gathered the purring cat into her arms and got up to look out of the window, where Mrs Cobbett's potted geraniums bloomed on the sill. She was startled to see the sparkling green-blue water of the Bristol Channel apparently lapping the house's foundations, although when she leaned forward to look down, she saw there was a walled path about six feet above the high tide mark. The Dower House really was at the edge of the sea! The door opened behind her and Mrs Cobbett came in. Gone were the plaits and nightgown, and instead her hair was pinned beneath a floppy mobcap and she wore a blue gingham dress and starched apron. Her shoes tapped as she crossed to the range. 'Ah, you're awake at last, miss.'

'Good morning,' Beth replied. 'I'm sorry I just fell asleep like that.'

'Think nothing of it, my dear, for you were exhausted. You'll soon feel wonderful, because there's no better spot on God's earth than the Dower House. Now then, you go outside and have some fresh air in the garden while I see to some breakfast. Tea, toast, some boiled eggs, and honey from our own hives. And after breakfast I'll set a nice warm bath in here, so you can have a good soak after all those days on the road.'

'Thank you, that's something I would really appreciate.' Beth smiled at her. 'You're a treasure, Mrs Cobbett.'

The housekeeper beamed. 'Why, thank you, miss.'

'How is Billy?'

'That cheeky London hosebird has made himself quite at home in the room over the stables. Oh, if he *could* take me up to the village to get provisions? It's a mortal steep climb, and when I'm there, I'll engage a girl to help me here.'

The cat jumped out of Beth's arms as she emerged from the kitchen door to the walled pathway that separated her from the Bristol Channel. In the absence of a wind, the waves washed gently among the rocks not far below her. The sea was dotted with sails, and on the shimmering horizon she could see the coast of Wales and the Brecon Beacons beyond. High above, seagulls wheeled against the cloudless sky. The cat rubbed around Beth's ankles as she inhaled air that seemed to fill her lungs more than any before. She looked to the west, and saw the harbour and river mouth. Several cutters swayed on the swell of the tide, and fishing boats were setting out, overlooked from the other side of the harbour by a joined row of ancient thatched cottages that clung to the base of tree-hung cliffs that were at least 500 feet high. The cottages rose inland up a track, and ended where a much smaller dwelling was set at a right angle to the rest, so that instead of facing the harbour as did its fellows, it looked up the gorge toward Exmoor. At the top of the cliff were the rooftops and chimneys of the village of Haldane.

Looking east, Beth saw the flat tree-fringed shore of the little park against a background of the precipitous cliffs of the enormous hill over which the coast road disappeared. At the base of the cliffs the sea swirled between huge rocks and boulders. She walked to that corner of the house to see more of the park and its fine trees. Two stone steps led down to the grass, and a path skirted the little kitchen garden and then the hedged flower garden behind the house, where the drone of bees around hives was soothing. She could smell thyme, as well as myrtle, roses and lavender, and it was all so arcadian that she didn't resist the compulsion to keep walking. Leaving the path, she strolled across the park, and had almost reached the road when a horseman breasted the hill on the coast road. For a moment he was framed against the skyline, a dashing hussar on a cream horse, before he began to ride down toward Lannermouth. As he drew nearer, she admired his uniform, a blue dolman jacket with scarlet facings, a fur-trimmed pelisse over his shoulder, and a gold and red shako with long golden flounders and a bright red pompom.

He reined in on seeing her, and removed his shako to incline his head. His hair was thick and dark, and his eyes a subtle shade of deep turquoise. She thought he was in his mid-thirties. It was hard to tell. Like all hussars, he had side-whiskers and a moustache that drooped on either side of his mouth. He manoeuvred the horse a little closer and she suddenly remembered her crumpled clothes and untidy hair. 'Good morning, madam,' he greeted. 'Major Haldane, your servant.'

'I'm pleased to make your acquaintance, Major. I'm the new tenant,

Miss Mannacott. Forgive my dishevelled appearance, but I only arrived late last night and I fell asleep in a chair.'

'So, we both arrive here together? An omen of future friendship I trust.' She smiled. 'Are you home on leave, Major Haldane?'

'No, I've chosen to leave the army because my regiment, the King's Own Light Dragoons, will soon embark for India. I was there before and was at death's door due to malaria. I have no desire to risk the same again, and with the war finally over, I prefer to manage my estates. So, when I take off this uniform I will become plain Mr Haldane.' He donned the shako once more, and prepared to ride on. 'No doubt we shall meet again soon, Miss Mannacott, in fact I shall see to it, on that you have my word.' He kicked his heels and the horse cantered on over the double-arched bridge and then disappeared around the corner of the cottage where the porch lantern had been lit the night before. She walked back toward the house, and arrived just as Mrs Cobbett came out to tell her breakfast was ready. 'Ah, there you are, miss. I trust you have an appetite?'

'I could eat an entire banquet.' Beth followed her into the kitchen. 'I have just made the acquaintance of Major Haldane.'

'Master Landry's back?' Mrs Cobbett turned, clasping her hands and beaming. 'Oh, the Lord be praised! No one has heard from him for so long, we've been convinced he died in some god-awful foreign place.'

'He looked hale and hearty enough to me.'

Mrs Cobbett looked at her. 'And no doubt he still has his winning smile. He's the biggest landowner in these parts, and the biggest catch, although it's said Miss Harriet will be his bride. That's Harriet Bellamy, the rector's daughter. She's a really pretty wench, and has had eyes only for Master Landry ever since I can remember.'

Beth smiled, but in her mind's eye she could still see Landry Haldane's dashing uniform and deep turquoise eyes.

Chapter Ten

It was the morning of Friday, 13 July, and the office of Mr Arthur Withers in Caradine Street was as stuffy as the man himself. Jane paced irritably up and down, her mulberry muslin pelisse and gown swishing over the floor, her face grim beneath her wide-brimmed grey silk hat. The solicitor's refusal to divulge the contents of Esmond's letter had forced her to come to London, but so far she had achieved nothing. 'So, Mr Withers, you issue a very public notice concerning my late husband and my stepdaughter, yet refuse to tell me what it concerns?'

With an infuriating smile, the solicitor spread his hands. 'Mrs Tremoille, even if I knew the contents of the letter, it would still be my duty to treat my client's confidence as if in the confessional itself.'

'Really?' Jane raised an eyebrow. 'Must I remind you that I am here in the capacity not only of client, but also as widow of a client?'

'You are not my client, Mrs Tremoille, and I only acted occasionally for your late husband. I always discharged my duties to him to the very best of my ability, but his main solicitor was always Mr Beswick of Gloucester.'

'Then why did my husband entrust this letter to you?'

'I cannot answer that, madam.'

'And you still plead ignorance of the contents?'

'I assure you, Mrs Tremoille, that the letter was sent to me already sealed, and that your husband gave no intimation of its purpose. In his accompanying instructions he said that it was for his daughter, and *only* his daughter.'

She tried a different tack. 'Mr Withers, no doubt you have heard that I am to marry Lord Welland?'

'Yes, and I offer you every good wish for your future happiness.'

'My new husband's business could be placed your way, Mr Withers – a considerable offer, you will admit.'

His tongue passed over his lip and he toyed with the quill before him. 'I – I cannot say any more than I have already, Mrs Tremoille.'

She looked out over at Caradine Street. Would it be irrational to suspect Sir Guy Valmer's elegant well-kept finger in this particular pie? 'Are you declining to assist me, sir?'

'I fear I must, Mrs Tremoille, because my reputation wouldn't be worth a jot were it known I'd been indiscreet about a client's business.'

She knew it was hopeless, and hit back petulantly. 'I'll see to it that your reputation suffers anyway.'

'And I'll take the appropriate legal action,' he replied coldly, going to the door and holding it open. 'Good day to you, madam.' She swept past, and he closed the door softly behind her. Returning to his desk, he took up a pencil and snapped it. 'Lord Welland must be mad!' he muttered.

As she went down the twisting stairs, Jane heard low voices from the even more cluttered office on the ground floor. She paused by the door and heard Bolton's deep tones and then a milder male voice laughing. Smiling, she proceeded to her carriage, and sat patiently.

Bolton's spaniel eyes were wide and innocent as he poured from the bottle of sherry with which Jane had armed him. 'Well, here's to us, eh?'

'I was always partial to a drop of armadillo.' The solicitor's mousy little clerk downed his glass in one lip-smacking gulp. 'Fine-looking woman, your Mrs Tremoille. I wouldn't mind lying her on her back.'

Bolton was hard put not to choke on his drink, for the thought of Jane Tremoille submitting to such runtish nonentity was almost too funny for words. 'Yes, her late husband always thought she was handsome,' he managed to say.

The by now imprudent clerk pulled a face. 'He couldn't stand her at the end though, could he? I heard Mr Withers and Mr Blenkinsop talking. Your late master changed' – he stopped and glanced across the desk at Bolton, then finished unconvincingly – 'his wife's allowances.'

Bolton gave a bland smile. *Changed his will, you mean, my fine fellow.* He replenished both their glasses, and then leaned closer with a conspiratorial air. 'My friend, just between you and me, what *is* in that letter, eh?'

'Drinking friends aren't secret-sharing friends. Not yet.'

'But you do know what's in it?'

'Oh, yes, but only because I was listening at the door when Mr Withers and Sir Guy Valmer opened it.'

'So what was in it?' Bolton prompted.

'I don't know exactly. Oh, don't go looking at me like that, because *they* don't know either. It's in some sort of code that only Miss Tremoille will understand. They think it's to do with finding words on the pages of a certain book, and thus reading a message. But without knowing what book it is.' The clerk shrugged.

Bolton was taken aback. 'And there's no hint about that?'

'None, but they think Miss Tremoille will know in an instant. So, if Sir Guy wants to understand the letter, he has to find Miss Tremoille, and she's given him the slip. Beats me what it's got to do with him anyway.'

The clerk realized his tongue had been running away with him, and shifted nervously. 'Hey, look, my friend, this won't do. I've work to finish and old Withers will skin me alive if it's not done. Off with you now, tempting me like this.'

Bolton was all amiability as he took his leave, went out to the carriage. 'Well?' Jane demanded, as the vehicle pulled away from the kerb.

'The letter has been opened.'

Jane's eyes flashed. 'That sanctimonious, slippery codfish of a lawyer!'

'But they're no further forward,' Bolton went on.

'Valmer?'

The butler nodded, and explained what the clerk had told him. Jane sat back, her mind racing as she tried to guess which book it might be. Beth had always been reading something, and for the last few years of his life so had Esmond. The library at Tremoille House contained hundreds of volumes.

Bolton was sympathetic. 'At least you know they can't decipher it. They need to find Miss Beth.'

Jane nodded. 'What would I do without you?' she said wearily.

'We need each other,' he replied, with the frankness of a very old friend. 'If it weren't for you, I'd probably still be a doorkeeper at a bawdy house, and if Miss Beth inherits everything after all, you'll have nothing and I'll be out of a position.'

'Then we must both pray she has vanished forever.'

That evening, Arthur Withers leaned against the stone column and watched the two pugilists squaring up to each other. The hall echoed with the shouts of gathered gentlemen. 'I believe Jackson has made a fine job of coaching your friend, eh?' he remarked to the man at his side.

Guy pushed back his top hat and shrugged. 'Lord Welland wouldn't agree, for he dislikes pugilism, especially for his son, who drives stage-coaches as if he were the Devil incarnate, and has a turn of phrase to shame a ship's company.'

'Quite the wild young gentleman, eh?'

'I fear so, and as well as being my friend, he is also my distant cousin. We first met at Newmarket last year, and hit it off sufficiently to have remained in close contact ever since. Rowan Welland is an enigma, with the charm of an angel, the looks of a dashing pirate captain and the char-acter of a dozen squibs in a fire. The combination proved too much for Oxford, anyway.' Guy watched as the two unevenly matched fighters moved around the cleared space, fists raised. Sommers was a big carrot-headed Bristolian of thirty-five, who'd greeted Rowan's challenge with laughter. As well he might, because Thomas Welland's twenty-year-old son and heir was lean, limber and almost beautiful with his dark hair curling to his shoulders. But he was far from effeminate, taking his punishment well and occasionally managing to land a few left hooks. Some, but not enough. 'He's going to be annihilated,' Guy said at last.

'Damn it all,' Withers grumbled, 'I've got a fiver on him.'

Guy gave a low chuckle. 'More fool you, my friend, for this is one match that has always been too unequal. And today is, after all, Friday the thirteenth.'

'I don't hold with such superstitions.'

'Perhaps you should,' Guy pointed out wryly.

Withers sighed. 'Oh, I'm not a wise judge of fighters at the best of times.'

'But in other things I trust you implicitly. Why did you want to see me?'

'This morning I received a visit from Mrs Tremoille. She tried to persuade me to divulge the contents of the letter, and even offered me Welland's business.'

'Which you refused?'

'Of course. I am *your* man, Sir Guy, not hers.'

'I'll see that you're well rewarded.'

'I am content with such as this.' The solicitor swept an arm around the spartan but superior surroundings. 'I must be the lowliest member, eh?'

'Mixing with the nobs suits you? I can think of far better company.'

'Maybe so, but through you I've been given access to a number of hitherto exclusive venues where I have secured new clients of excellent calibre, so believe me, I am well pleased with the rewards that have already come my way. Besides, if I prosper on account of my own endeavours, without accepting money from your purse, I am beholden to you only for the introductions, nothing more.'

'You're a wise man, and, I know, a completely trustworthy one. You're the only one I've told about finding the missing will. I wish it to remain that way. Rowan Welland knows nothing of it. Nor does he yet know, although I'll have to tell him soon, that I'm trying to find Miss Tremoille.' Guy looked at the match again. He hadn't taken the younger man fully into his confidence because, knowing Rowan's mercurial temper, Valmer secrets might be blurted in anger.

'My lips are sealed, Sir Guy. Have you any further news of your fair quarry?'

'No. She laid a false trail on the Great North Road, but that's all I know.'

Guy's words were drowned by increased shouts at the other end of the hall, and Withers was distracted. 'Welland drove one home then, eh?' he declared hopefully.

'Don't get excited, because Sommers has landed seven to that one.'

Suddenly the crowd became even noisier, booing, hissing and catcalling as Rowan grabbed his opponent's unwisely long red hair with one hand and hammered disgracefully at his face with the other. It was despicable behaviour, totally unworthy of any pugilist, let alone the son of a lord. The crowd's disapproval was deafening, and the appalled referee and a burly assistant were forced to drag him off the sagging Sommers, who reeled semi-conscious into the arms of his seconds. Guy frowned. 'Oh, dear,' he murmured, watching as Rowan endured the crowd's vilification; or rather, ignored it. His handsome face was impassive and he didn't even glance toward his fallen opponent. He would have done better to keep an eye on the crowd, because suddenly an angry onlooker caught him unawares and knocked him cold. A rousing cheer rang out, and the approving crowd bore the assailant shoulder-high around the room. Guy tugged his hat forward again, and picked up his cane and gloves. 'Come, Withers, we have one young sprig of nobility to revive.'

He and the solicitor conveyed the unconscious pugilist to the room that had been set aside for him, and laid him on the table, where Withers set about smacking his feet in an attempt to bring him around. Guy applied a cold wet towel to Rowan's face and neck and, at last, the young man stirred. He found it difficult to focus as he squinted at the face above him. 'Guy?'

'Yes, Coz, and I can't say I approve of your version of the rules.'

Rowan grinned and rubbed his jaw. He began to get his bearings again and sat up carefully. One hazel eye was almost closed, and he was a mass of bleeding grazes and fiery bruises, but his dark good looks were still plain to see. As was his charm. 'Maybe not, but it rid me of a few tantrums I might otherwise have taken back to Whitend,' he said.

'So, you're seizing the bull by the horns and visiting dear old Pa?' Guy asked.

'I'm expected to turn up when he marries next month.'

Guy grinned. 'How do you feel now?'

'As if every mangy nag at Tattersall's had paraded over me. I'll survive. Oh, my head!' He winced.

'You have only yourself to blame.'

'Quite so,' agreed Withers.

Rowan smiled ruefully. 'A fine pair of attendants I appear to have acquired. Where's your sympathy? Look at me, a poor battered and broken thing, and you tell me it's my own fault.'

Guy straightened and counted two fingers. 'One, you shouldn't have challenged Sommers, and two, you certainly shouldn't have held him by the hair in order to beat the living daylights out of him. Now then, if you have the strength, I will escort you to my club and treat you to a fine meal. You included, Withers.'

The solicitor was regretful. 'Much as I would like to accept your kind offer, Sir Guy, I have an appointment that can not be ignored, and should leave now.'

The solicitor bowed, and then withdrew, leaving Rowan to look curiously at Guy. 'What's going on, Guy? He seems a rather unlikely friend.'

'Arthur Withers is an associate.'

'Something devious, I take it?'

'Naturally.' Guy smiled.

'Am I part of a devious plan too?'

'Good God, no! Whatever makes you think that?'

Rowan was sheepish. 'Well, on today's lamentable display, I'm far from admirable, so why do you bother with me?'

'Because I like you, damn it,' Guy answered, reaching for Rowan's crumpled shirt and throwing it to him. 'Besides, you're my cousin.'

'On a rather convoluted family tree.' Rowan donned the shirt and then struggled in a looking glass to tie his cravat. 'What a sorry visage, eh?'

'It's nothing a large sack with eye slits will not put right.'

'Most amusing,' Rowan replied drily. 'Still, with half the beau monde beating a track for Paris now, there'll be few Corinthians to disapprove of me.' He continued dressing. 'Jerry Waddington was present at a review of the Russians in Paris. One-hundred-and-sixty thousand of them, all in superb caparison. I'll warrant the British Army made a sorry sight after that!'

'Dear boy, the British – well, the English anyway – revel in being eccentric.'

'It's hardly eccentricity. The truth is that our army is the worst clad in Europe,' Rowan muttered, setting about donning his shoes again. 'By the way, I'm of a mind to visit a gaming hell tonight. Will you join me?'

'I fear I cannot, as after dinner I will be otherwise engaged.'

'Really? La Belle Maria?'

'No, actually. She and I are no more. There was one scene too many.'

Rowan could not hide his surprise. 'But, she's been your mistress for God knows how long. So, if not La Carberry, what – or who – are you doing tonight?'

'It's what, I fear. I've accepted an invitation to the Fenton House *bal masqué*.'

'Good God, what on earth possessed you? Susannah Fenton wishes to delve into your breeches, and she's a fearsome wench when her blood is up.'

Guy chuckled. 'Well, her blood is the only thing likely to be up, my friend.'

Rowan returned to the matter of his father's forthcoming nuptials. 'Guy, I find it very distasteful that the Widow Tremoille is to be my stepmother.'

Guy glanced at him. 'I hope my quest to relieve her of her fortune will not cast a shadow over our friendship?'

'It makes no difference to my regard and affection for you, Guy, because I hold both bride and groom in complete contempt.' He paused, and then looked at Guy again. 'I may be only twenty, drunk most of the time and senseless in some prize ring for the rest of it, but as yet I'm not a fool. Our meeting last year at Newmarket was an excellent thing for me, and I value our friendship above all else in this world. So, I made it my business to find out what I could about the transfer of Valmer House to Esmond Tremoille. I conclude that your father probably was tricked out of it. I don't think the Tremoilles have any legal right to it all, but in the absence of any proof that Esmond Tremoille behaved dishonestly....' Rowan spread his hands.

'I fear you'll have to take my word on that.'

'Of course I take your word, Guy. Old Tremoille was devious enough *before* his second marriage, let alone after it. Dear Jane's pretty hand worked him well.'

Guy laughed. 'She's accustomed to working men well.'

Rowan laughed too, and then became more serious. 'Guy, you will not like what I'm going to say, but I think that morally Beth Tremoille should have the estate. Don't misunderstand, for I do believe your claim to be true, but you have so much already, and poor Beth has nothing at all. It isn't her fault that her father was a crook and yours a cuckoo.' Guy was, of course, in full agreement, but not for the same soft-hearted reason. For a moment he considered confessing everything, but something held him back. He wasn't quite ready yet.

'I'll always have a soft spot for Beth,' Rowan continued, donning his waistcoat. 'I can't help it. My old man once started making overtures about a match for me with her, but then Esmond died, she ceased to be heiress, and so everything was dropped. I doubt if she even knew about it. Ah, Beth, a wench to bring out the beast in men, eh?'

'You're still a mewling boy, my laddo,' Guy murmured.

'I'm old enough to go a-fucking, and I do, often.' Rowan finished dressing, inspected his slender reflection in the looking glass, and then grinned at Guy. 'Right, I'm ready to be wined and dined.'

'I don't want to seduce you, damn it, I just want to eat.'

Chapter Eleven

In Frampney the twilight of Friday the thirteenth was warm and balmy, with long shadows darkening the green. The disappearing sun dyed the heavens with shades of red and gold that reflected from windows, and the wisteria around the gabled window of Rosalind's bedroom was sweetly perfumed as she held the rose-coloured dress against herself, her eyes shining. 'Oh, Dad, it's the prettiest thing I've ever had!'

Jake smiled as he watched her. 'You're seventeen today, and I thought it was time you got a fine dress, Rozzie.'

'It must have cost, oh, I don't know—'

'Where are your manners, girl? You don't go wondering how much a present cost. Well, get it on then, and come down to eat so we can all admire you and make you swollen-headed.'

'Dad?' Rosalind turned to look at him. 'Girls put up their hair at seventeen.'

'Oh, I don't know about that,' he began, 'there's time enough to be a woman.'

'Please, Dad,' she begged. 'I've been practising by this mirror.'

'Such vanity.' But he gave in. 'Go on then, if you must, but Rozzie, don't grow up too fast. Stay a child while you can.'

He left and she immediately slipped out of her old linen gown to look at her naked reflection in the mirror. There was nothing of the blacksmith's daughter in her pale, clear skin, or in the beauty of her face. Her body wasn't thin and scrawny any more, but was beginning to fill out because of Phoebe's wonderful cooking. Now there were curves coming in all the right places, including her breasts, which had always had large firm nipples. Slowly she slid her hand down into the dark hair at her groin, and then pushed her fingertips further down, into the moist warmth between her legs, back and forth, back and forth. Oh, how good it was; how she enjoyed the way her nipples hardened more, and how she loved the excitement that began to work through her. It was like satisfying a hunger; well, almost satisfying it. Drawing her hand away, she pouted at her reflection. Giving herself pleasure wasn't the same as going with a lover. She could have any boy in the village, but had set her heart upon Robert Lloyd, even though she had yet even to see him because he was away. Everything she'd heard about him excited her. He was going to be her first and only lover, and she'd be so dear to him that he'd ask for her hand. Then she'd be mistress of Frampney! He'd filled her thoughts since she arrived here, and when he came back, she'd be his destiny. How glad she was now that she could read, write, and speak properly. She told herself these accomplishments were her own doing, plucked from the air and polished by her own endeavours. Beth Tremoille had no hand in it. Mrs Robert Lloyd would not have a lowly background as she and her dashing husband danced a wicked waltz at court. The thought of this glittering life reminded her of the money. She'd hidden it under the bottom drawer of the chest in the corner, and had so far resisted the temptation to look at it. When the time was right, it would be her dowry.

Hearing a horse cantering slowly along the far side of the village green, she looked out of the window. The twilight was deceptive, allowing her to see through the shadows and make out a young gentleman, hatless, riding a prancing cream horse toward Squire Lloyd's house. There was something magical about the scene, an unearthliness that was due entirely to the bands of uncommon crimson sunbeams shining horizontally between trees and cottages from the far western sky. Bewitched, Rosalind held her breath. The horseman wore what she thought was a pine-green coat and grey breeches, but the colours were hazy. His shoulder-length fair hair glinted almost amber, and his horse was alternately cream and coral as he rode through the wrought-iron gates of the manor house. Was it Robert Lloyd? Yes, it had to be. A groom ran from the stables to hold the horse as he dismounted, and Rosalind melted back from the window as he seemed to look right across at her. Phoebe suddenly opened the bedroom door, and Rosalind snatched up her old gown and held it against her body. 'You gave me a fright!'

Phoebe smiled, her eyes moving shrewdly to the window, just as the young man ran up the shallow flight of steps and disappeared into the Lloyd residence. 'Here now, let me help you.' She held the new gown for Rosalind to step into, and then raised it until she could fasten the tiny bodice with its little puffed sleeves. 'So Master Robert's back again, is he?' she murmured. 'That's a real Friday the thirteenth for Frampney. Don't go looking at him now, little wench, for he's bad.'

Rosalind flushed. 'I wasn't—'

'Yes, you were. Now, I may not be your true family, sweeting, but you've no mother now and I think it's my place to watch over you, whether you like it or not. Master Robert's gentry, and gentry don't mix with the likes of you unless they've got dishonest designs. Are you listening now? Master Robert Lloyd is a wicked lot, Rozzie Mannacott. Handsome, and dashing as the day is long he may be, but there are fatherless babes in these parts that deserve his name. Do you understand?'

'Yes, but I've only just seen him for the first time!' Rosalind protested.

'Then see that you don't get to know him. I warn you, I'll tell your father if I have any cause to worry about it. Right?' Phoebe smiled. 'You're a pretty wench, sweeting, and one day you'll find a fellow who'll treasure you. Now then, take a look at the present from Matty and me. Well, go on.' She took a pair of green satin slippers from inside her apron.

'Oh, Phoebe, they're beautiful!'

'Yes, and God-alone daft for Frampney, but the sort of foolish things I'd have given my eye-teeth for at your age. Matty got old Baggy Anders to make them.'

Rosalind suddenly flung her arms around the countrywoman, tears filling her eyes. 'Oh, thank you, Phoebe, thank you, thank you, thank you!'

'Mind now, lovey, have a care, won't you?' Phoebe nodded in the direction of the manor house, and then went to the door again. 'I'll go on down now and set out the feast. I killed one of the fowls today, so we'll live well tonight. And you'd best know, your Dad's asked Jamie Webb along.'

'Oh, no!' Rosalind was incensed. Jamie was a stupid village boy who was always pestering Matty or her father to take him on to learn black-smithing. So far, thank goodness, they'd both said no.

'Jamie's got a soft spot for you, Rozzie.'

'Well, I haven't got one for him.' As the door closed behind Phoebe, Rosalind sat sulkily at her little table with its faded mirror. She brushed her long fair hair, and then twisted it up into a rather insecure knot to which she pinned a white ribbon bow. Then she thought of Robert Lloyd again. The fact that a few silly village girls claimed he got them into trouble made him even more dangerously attractive than before. He wouldn't get *her* with child until she was his wife! Humming to herself, she went downstairs to the low-ceilinged kitchen, which was filled with the appetizing smell of a cooked chicken resting in front of the fire.

Jake stared at her, and Matty took his pipe from his mouth. Phoebe smiled as proudly as if Rosalind were her daughter. 'There now, what did I tell you? She's as pretty as a picture. Come over here, Miss Seventeen, and be head of the table.'

Jake drew the chair out and she looked up at him. 'Dad? Do I look well?'

He put a hand to her cheek. 'You look like your mother, Rozzie. It's been so long now, I'd almost forgotten how pretty she was.'

'You loved her better than Beth, didn't you?' she whispered, but he didn't answer. Why did she always have to spoil things? He'd loved his wife *and* Beth. He loved Rozzie too, but there were times when she tested that love severely.

Phoebe brought a steaming pan of meat juices to the table and stirred flour into it. 'Matty, bring that cabbage water. That's it.' Stirring like a demon, she looked at Jake as he sat down again. 'When did your Bethie die, Jake?'

Rosalind stared darkly at the gravy as Jake shook his head. 'My wife was Annie.'

'Oh, I thought— Well, you talk in your sleep and one evening in that chair you spoke really lovingly to someone called Bethie.' Seeing Rosalind's stony face, Phoebe felt awkward. 'Well, perhaps I misheard. Anyway, where's that foolish Jamie Webb? Is that him at the door now? Come on in, Jamie!'

Jamie stepped nervously into the kitchen, twisting his hat around in his hands. He was a burly eighteen, with wiry mud-coloured hair and freckles, and was dressed in his best clothes, which were at least a size too big, having been his late father's. Matty sat forward. 'You saved yourself by the skin of your teeth, Jamie. Phoebe was about to come after you with a meat cleaver.'

'Good evening,' Jamie said, swallowing. 'The – the fowls got out and—'

'Never mind all that,' Phoebe interrupted briskly, taking the gravy back to the fire. She checked the bubbling pots of runner beans and potatoes. 'There, everything's ready. Get the perry, Matty.'

'We're having *perry* today?' Rosalind had thus far ignored Jamie.

Jake grinned. 'Well, you'll only have one seventeenth birthday, eh? Mind your manners now, Rozzie, and greet your guest as is right.'

She looked unwillingly at her admirer. 'Good evening, Jamie.' How she hated him. He was so ordinary and dull, so tongue-tied and awkward all the time, that she was embarrassed to be seen walking with him, and now he was spoiling her day.

'Rosalind, I've brought you something. It's not much, but I thought you'd like it.' He put a little box on the table in front of her.

She smiled stiffly, and just looked at the box, much to Jake's disapproval. 'Get it open then, Rozzie,' he said a little sharply.

She obeyed and her lips parted when she saw the carved wooden pendant inside. It was in the form of a knot of rosebuds, and was very beautiful. She held her breath as she took it out. 'Why, Jamie, it's lovely!'

'It took me a good few nights.'

'You *made* it?'

'Aw, well, I bought the ribbon,' he said, his face almost fiery. 'It's a bit of hazel, and good against the eye.'

Rosalind tied it carefully at her throat, and Phoebe beamed. 'There, now you're fit for the king's palace, eh?'

Jake laughed. 'Yes, and – what's that fancy nob place in London called? – Alma's? Yes, that's it, Rozzie. You could bend a toe with the dandies there. Well, sit down, Jamie, you look like a row of left legs.' Grinning, Jamie slid into the seat next to Rosalind, just as Matty brought an earthenware jar from the pantry and poured deliciously cool perry into five cups.

Jamie turned to Rosalind. 'A puppet show was set up by the George and Dragon about an hour ago. If you'd like to see it, I'll take you.' His voice was strained because he was besotted with her.

Rosalind would love to see a puppet show, although not with Jamie Webb. But he'd taken trouble with her necklace and she could sense her father's annoyance rising again, so she smiled as pleasantly as she could. 'I'd like that, Jamie. Thank you.'

Jake changed the subject. 'Jamie, what was going on over at the squire's bailiff's this afternoon?'

'Williamson's Bank has called in some tenants' loans.'

Matty nodded wearily. 'Yes, that's what I was told too. Things aren't looking good. It'll be really bad come Michaelmas.'

Phoebe tutted. 'Matty Brown, this is Rosalind's birthday feast!'

'I'm only repeating what's on everyone's tongue these days, Phoebe.'

'Repeat it sometime else.'

The meal went off well, and afterward Jamie took Rosalind to the puppet show. It was dark now, and the night breeze had turned unexpectedly cool, but Rosalind was determined to show off her birthday finery. Goose pimples stood out on her arms, and the chill seeped through the shawl Phoebe had prevailed upon her to wear. She told herself that maybe Robert Lloyd would come to see the show, or perhaps it was too vulgar a thing for someone of his breeding. Villagers had already congregated by the makeshift Punch and Judy stand. Nearby there were six horses tethered behind a large covered wagon, and light was provided by torches on posts knocked into the grass. Rosalind heard cheerful violin music and then saw a dancing monkey leaping about in time to a foot-tapping jig. 'Oh, look! A monkey, a real monkey, I've never seen one before!'

'I saw it in Gloucester last year. It's a clever thing. Watch now, and it'll take a bowl and go begging. See?'

Rosalind watched the tiny creature holding up the little bowl. 'Give him something, Jamie; go on, please, for I want him to come closer!'

Jamie searched in his pocket. He only had a few pennies, but to please Rosalind he'd have given them all. Bending down, he held one out, and the monkey loped over the grass, bright eyes like shining beads in its little wizened face. Jamie dropped the penny into the bowl, and Rosalind reached out to touch the soft brown fur, but the creature bounded back toward the wagon in which the show and its people travelled around the countryside. Once there, it sat on the canvas roof with the bowl.

Rosalind laughed. 'If he begins to count it all now, I won't be surprised.'

Jamie looked taken aback. 'Don't be daft, it's only an animal.'

Her smile faded. On top of all his other faults, he had no sense of humour! She pressed her lips angrily together, promising herself that this was absolutely the last time she would go near Jamie Webb, no matter what her father or anyone said to the contrary. Drawing her shawl closer, she looked around the crowd. The sooner the show began, the sooner it would end and she could be rid of him. To her relief the little curtains on the Punch and Judy stand opened and the performance began, allowing her to ignore Jamie without seeming to.

Later, at the end of the show, as a man moved through the crowd with a wooden bucket into which coins were dutifully dropped, an educated voice suddenly spoke behind Rosalind and Jamie. 'Good evening, Webb.' They turned sharply, and Rosalind saw it was Robert Lloyd. His gaze was upon her, calculating and sensuous and, as their eyes met, her heart lurched, her mouth ran dry, and she felt heat rush into her cheeks. She had never been introduced to an eligible young gentleman before and she could not have chosen to appear to better advantage than right now. A glow began to kindle deep inside and she gave him a brief smile before looking away again, as if he was of little interest. But she found him very interesting indeed; intensely so. How handsome he was, she had never seen a man more handsome in her life. His hair was so light, and his blue eyes, dark-rimmed and pale-lashed, were mysterious in the dancing light of the torches. His elegance made Jamie more oafish and clumsy than ever.

Jamie snatched off his hat. 'Master Robert?' he gasped.

Robert's eyes remained on Rosalind. 'Won't you introduce us, Webb?'

'Rosalind – I mean, Miss Mannacott – this is Master Robert Lloyd.'

Robert inclined his head. 'Robert Lloyd,' he murmured, noticing her little satin shoes. Well, she was a pretty thing, and prepared to flirt with her eyes. But was she prepared to spread her legs? He'd certainly do his damnedest to persuade her. He smiled as she deigned to offer a neat little curtsy.

'Master Robert,' she said softly, keeping her eyes lowered until the last moment and then bestowing a fleeting smile before looking away again.

Robert's glance descended between her breasts, and then moved up the graceful line of her neck to her averted face. 'Mannacott? So you're the new farrier's daughter.' The breeze caught his long hair and blew it softly across his face, caressing his skin just as she wished to caress it. 'How fortunate that I have a horse to be shod tomorrow. I trust I will see you then, Miss Mannacott.' He bowed and was gone, moving away through the dispersing crowd.

Jamie breathed a sigh of relief, and looked at Rosalind. 'Come on, or your Dad will be after me.' He tried to take her hand, but she pulled it away. Walking hand-in-hand would imply they were sweethearts.

He was embarrassed, but tried not to show it. 'Did you like the puppets?'

'Yes, I suppose so,' she replied, then added, 'Master Robert's very hand-some.'

Jamie realized she had more than a passing interest in the squire's son, and halted to look intently at her. 'Have you got notions for him?'

She flushed and took refuge in indignation. 'Don't be stupid, Jamie.'

'I'm not stupid; I leave that to the wenches. Master Robert's always getting his dick out and giving it exercise, as more than one wench around these parts has got lasting proof. Nothing will stop him while his father owns practically everything around here. Someone will get him one day, though, those with womenfolk like my sister Jenny, who was messed about with good and proper. I tell you this for nothing: if he goes near you, *I'll* get him!'

She pushed him away. 'And what right do *you* have to say who comes near me and who doesn't?' She ran toward the forge, and didn't look back.

As masked balls went, Lady Fenton's was a wild success, but it was a pity the invitations to her home in Kensington had not specified that it was also a fancy dress ball. Consequently the hostess, her family and close friends were all clad in extravagant costumes, whereas the rest of the guests arrived in conventional ballroom finery with masks and dominoes. A country dance was in progress as the clock neared two in the morning, and there was a great deal of stamping, clapping and whooping. The blue, pink and gold ballroom was a sea of jewels, plumes and fine silks, of medals, uniforms and tasteful black velvet. Unfortunately the whirling sets were also dotted with fancy dress; here a knight in shining armour, an Arab sheikh and a horn-helmeted Boadicea, there a cavalier, an Othello and a plump fairy queen.

Lady Fenton was Diana, complete with leopard skin and quiver of arrows. She was of Amazonian proportions, and had it not been that she was considered one of the finest hostesses in the capital, her costume would have been judged lewd and improper because sufficient bosom was displayed to do justice to a fashionable King's Place brothel. Her brown doe eyes had been angry all evening because she had no one to blame but herself for the mistake on the invitation. It was especially galling because she'd wanted tonight to be perfect for the seduction of Guy Valmer. He was marked to be her next lover now that he was blessedly free of Maria Carberry, and if she failed to lure him to her bed, she would be ill; positively, indubitably, unavoidably ill! She observed from the side of the ballroom as the country dance ended, but he was nowhere to be seen. Then she remembered the card room. Ah yes, that was his likely lair. She began to make her way toward a fine Ionic colonnade that marked the way to the great vestibule and most other rooms, including the card room, where he had indeed been, deeply engrossed in play, until a chance glance out through the colonnade made him pause.

A young woman in the nearest set of the country dance was laughing and clapping as she wove in and out, and she was so like Beth Tremoille that he left the table to lean against one of the columns. Dark-haired and beautiful, she wore a silver-green tissue gown that he felt Beth might also have chosen, but there the similarity ended, because the dancing lovely lacked Beth's grace, style and, he'd lay odds, her wit and intelligence. There was something rather vapid about this young woman, and vapid was something Beth could never be. Even when dressed like a beggar and plucked from the wayside fainting from hunger, Beth Tremoille had a certain something, a glint in her green-hazel eyes, a tilt to her jaw, and a quick word. Beth was a woman to conquer, and the conquering would be very enjoyable. He considered returning to the card room, but then Lady Fenton whispered in his ear. 'Now, sir, why are you interested in that simpering miss in green?' She sidled around him, so close that her breasts brushed against his arm. Then she stood in front of him, those same breasts thrust provocatively forward.

'She reminds me of someone,' he replied.

Her eyes flickered. 'Who?' When he smiled, without answering, she pouted. 'I can be whomever you wish, Guy. Come to me tonight, and I will make you forget her.'

'I have no desire to forget her, Lady Fenton.' But at that moment a stir in the ballroom dragged his attention away, and he was dismayed to see Maria Carberry in a glittering scarlet gown that made every other gown seem indifferent. She was at her most glorious, her flaxen hair piled up on top of her head, her neckline plunging so much further than Lady Fenton's that her full breasts seemed they were barely contained. Plumes streamed from her head, and she glided like an Irish galleon in full sail. It was an arrival *par excellence*, and she enjoyed every moment as she approached Guy.

A hush had fallen over the ballroom, and the orchestra's playing gradually died away as it became clear that very few would partake of the next dance. Guy faced her reluctantly, alert to the glitter in her eyes. In recent days she had been trying unsuccessfully to resume their liaison; now he guessed she was intent upon stirring things in public. She halted dramatically before him. 'Well, if it isn't my English rover.'

He inclined his head. 'Maria.'

Her eyes flickered toward Lady Fenton, whom she accurately assessed as a rival. 'Well now, with breasts like that you'd be a success on the stage.'

There were gasps, and Lady Fenton was outraged. 'How dare you, madam!'

'I dare because you're shoving them in everyone's face. Why, a short man would suffocate. If you don't want them commented on, put them away.'

'I wish you to leave, Miss Carberry.'

'Oh, so you know who I am?' Maria preened.

'I saw you as Lady Macbeth. Until then I had no idea it was a comedy.'

'I'm surprised you understood enough to think anything,' Maria retorted.

'I understand when an overblown has-been makes a fluff of her lines and totters because she's inebriated.' Lady Fenton's capacity for vitriol was a match for Maria's.

'Inebriated? *Inebriated*?' shrieked the actress.

Lady Fenton's lip curled unpleasantly. 'Irish bitch,' she declared.

'English sow,' was Maria's swift riposte. 'Do titties range all down your belly too? It wouldn't surprise me, given that you have such a snout.'

Guy stepped between them. 'Enough!'

'She started it!' Maria cried.

'No, she didn't, you did. You came here to be troublesome, and you've succeeded. Now I suggest you leave quietly.'

'Will you come with me?' she whispered.

'No. It's over, Maria.'

'I suppose you're dibbling *her* now?' She gazed at Lady Fenton with loathing.

'No, nor will I be,' he said, for her ladyship's benefit. 'I sleep alone now, and that's the way I intend it to remain. So fight on if you both wish, but it will do neither of you any good where I'm concerned.' He stepped aside again, and bowed to them both. 'Goodnight, ladies.' Then, as cool as the proverbial cucumber, he left the ballroom.

Chapter Twelve

On late July, on the eve of the wedding at Gloucester Cathedral, Jane had cause to wonder if marrying Thomas Welland might be a grave mistake, but love being blind, she ignored the warning. The incident happened at Whitend after breakfast, when she had changed into her riding habit for an agreed ride with her husband-to-be and his son, who, for some reason, was disposed to accompany them. She went down to the hall in full expectation of the plan proceeding.

The main staircase was wide, shallow and creaking, and there wasn't much light from the small windows paned in red and blue. At the bottom her riding boots echoed on the smooth stone flags of the oblong hall, which was brightened by a magnificent oriel window. Neither Thomas nor Rowan was waiting for her, so she went to the fireplace, where the tilt of the tarnished mirror above the Jacobean chimneypiece revealed her reflection. She adjusted her spruce black hat and rearranged the net veil that shaded the upper half of her face. She still had her looks, she decided approvingly, and would make a noteworthy bride tomorrow. Ivory silk and lace were perfect for a bride of her age and widowed status, even if her decision to reside at Whitend before the marriage had offended many prissy principles. Still, she was about to become Lady Welland, so what did she care?

At last she heard Thomas's gruff voice approaching the front entrance. He'd been with his bailiff and his tone was edgy. The doors were flung open unceremoniously and Thomas strode in, closely followed by the bailiff, whose red face and ears suggested he'd received an unpleasant tongue-lashing. Seeing her, Thomas halted. 'You surely don't imagine I have time to indulge in a pretty little jaunt around the park, do you?' he asked patronizingly.

'I was under the impression that we'd arranged just that with Rowan.'

'Today nothing could be further from my thoughts. I have half-a-dozen tenants clamouring for lower rents because they cannot pay their way; the bank in Gloucester has closed its doors; my shares in armaments have become virtually worthless overnight, and *you* wish to go riding!'

'Put like that, it does seem a little like Nero fiddling while Rome burns.'

He glowered, suspecting her of facetiousness, and then stomped into the library, followed by the hapless bailiff. The door slammed, and she heard him shouting again. Well, better the bailiff than her.

The butler opened the outer doors with a flourish, and she swept past him like a frigate before the wind, her sapphire riding habit bright as she emerged into the sunshine from beneath the two-storey porch that hunched its shoulders against the house. Whitend was surrounded by a moat adorned with lily pads and exotic waterfowl, and spanned by a flat wooden bridge upon which peacocks sunned themselves. Beyond the bridge the scenery was very different from that up at Tremoille House. Low, flat acres of parkland extended for 200 yards to the banks of the Severn, the serpentine course of which was marked by pollard willows and the wild pear trees that made the vale so famous for perry. On the far shore of the river were the rolling foothills of the Forest of Dean and, in the hazy distance, the Welsh mountains.

Crossing the bridge to the fresh-raked gravel circle where carriages turned at the end of the drive, she looked up at the façade of the house. Whitend was so much part of its surroundings that it might have grown out of the rich Severn clay. Grey and rather imposing, it was far from beautiful, rising slab-like through four storeys to a stone-tiled roof with five plain gables and ugly chimneys. Jane glanced around. The air was too clear, so rain was on the way. She could see the steeple of Frampney church a mile or so to the south, and a curl of smoke that presumably came from the forge where Jake Mannacott now worked, as Bolton had discovered. It was hard to imagine her delicate, well-bred stepdaughter between the sheets with a blacksmith. A groom appeared from the stable block behind the house, leading three horses, including Thomas's favourite mount, and at the same moment the front door opened again and Rowan came out. 'Your father is not joining us, I fear,' she said.

'So I gather. Am I supposed to murmur something regretful? The less I see of the loathsome old goat, the better,' he replied, donning his top hat and kid gloves.

She thought he looked very handsome in his green riding coat and tight cream breeches, his long curling hair clinging to his collar. Youth was on his side, endowing him with the strength and vitality to overcome the results of his numerous over-indulgences. Even now he was suffering the after-effects of too much alcohol last night, sherry, wine, liqueurs, cognac, the latter to great excess, but apart from being tired, he was master of himself. How long would it be before he became a drunkard? 'Do I pass muster?' he enquired, seeing how she studied him.

'You'll do, I suppose, although it escapes me why you're coming on this ride.'

'For your charming company, of course.'

A few minutes later they cantered slowly along the banks of the Severn, following the river around a loop toward the estuary. The tide was out, exposing vast bars where seabirds congregated at the water's edge. The hard, flat sand invited a stretched gallop, and Jane urged her horse forward, scattering lapwings skyward. Rowan kicked his heels and followed. He soon caught her, and for a while she tried to outrun him, but with no chance of success, so she reined in. 'I'll allow you victory!' she cried, above the racket of some squabbling herring gulls.

He turned his capering horse. 'You have no choice in the matter, madam!'

'How gallant.' She rode a little closer. 'Why *have* you come out today, Rowan?'

'To tell you I do not like you, or want you as my stepmother.'

'Well, that is honest enough, I suppose. I, on the other hand, can put up with you, spoilt and selfish as you are.'

'*Touché*, but perhaps I should also inform you that I am acquainted with Guy Valmer. Actually, he's a cousin.'

Oh, wouldn't he be! 'Ah, and you choose to believe what he says of me?'

'Naturally, but please don't overlook the fact that any woman who could send someone like Beth into penury must be entirely bad. There, I've said my piece, Jane, so I trust you no longer have any illusion about how I feel about you.'

She raised an eyebrow. 'So, you don't like me, nor do you like your father, so why on God's own earth you have consented to walk me to the altar tomorrow?'

'Because I wish to see the whole sorry business over. Just don't seek ever to encroach upon *my* preserve, Jane dear, for that I would not tolerate, and I can be even more unlovable if I choose. I am no Beth, to be forced out penniless.'

She stroked and patted the horse. 'I won't encroach, Rowan, I only want your father. I've *always* wanted him.'

'Well, after tomorrow you can lust legally. I won't be here to give a damn.'

'You're leaving?'

'La, how the lady's eyes suddenly shine. Yes, Jane, I'm running back to London, to fritter the rest of my mother's fortune as best I can.'

'And be in your grave before you reach thirty? How admirable an ambition.'

'It will be my own choice,' he answered.

'Have you no thought for your birthright? It is up to you to provide the next generation.' Jane watched his firm young body yielding effortlessly as the horse shifted. He was a little too pretty and boyish for her taste, but there was an attractive air of virility about him. Perhaps his passion for pugilism was not a bad thing after all, for it kept him very fit and agile. Of course, it might yet give him a broken nose and cauliflower ears, but for now he was still a young god.

'My birthright is mine, whatever I do, so dear Papa can go to hell, and hopefully take you with him. Come on, it's a fair distance back to Whitend.'

He kicked his heels and sent his sweating horse away from the river, toward the unfinished canal embankment about a quarter of a mile inland. They followed the canal all the way back to the house, and arrived just in time to share a light luncheon with Thomas, who complained and carped throughout. It would be different once they were married, Jane thought. She would make him happier and more content than Diana ever had. It didn't cross her mind that she was committing the most naïve female sin of all – believing her love would transform a man.

The open landau was as white as the horses that drew it, and so garlanded with bridal flowers that it resembled a bower. A rather surly crowd waited in the cathedral close, where the carriages of Gloucestershire society were drawn up. Necks were craned as Rowan, looking particularly poetic and romantic in a dove-grey coat and cream trousers, alighted to help Jane down. Elegant in the ivory silk and lace gown that pleased her so much, with a veiled pink bonnet and carrying pink roses, she was indifferent to the simmering hostility of the onlookers. This was her day, and she wasn't about to let anything spoil it. She glowed, as was most becoming for all brides, of no matter what age, and there was confidence in the way she accepted Rowan's arm to enter the cathedral, from whence the sound of organ music resonated gently.

Rosalind was with Phoebe among the crowd. 'Lord Welland's son is very dashing, isn't he?'

Phoebe nodded 'And from all accounts he's a proper gentleman too.'

Rosalind's glanced moved to Jane. 'She looks beautiful.'

'Past her prime, like me,' Phoebe replied shortly.

'Well, her nasty stepdaughter said she was ugly and horrible.'

'I see. Well, last night your Dad told me all about him and Beth. Lord above, your jib's trailing on the ground again, even at the mention of her name. What did she do to you that was so bad, eh? Beat you with a stick? Starve you?'

'She had no right to come between me and Dad!'

Phoebe frowned. Jake had spoiled the girl, who needed taking down a few pegs if she was to learn anything of life. 'Rosalind, will you listen to yourself? The love between a father and daughter is not the same as between a man and his sweetheart. You know that well enough when you're not being a mule. Your father loved Beth, and loves her still; you can see it in his eyes. And you can't say it happened too soon after your mother's death four years back of the same pox that took my daughter.'

'Nothing you say will *ever* make me like that woman.'

'Cluck that often enough and you'll start laying eggs,' Phoebe replied drily.

'She lied about her stepmother.'

'You think so? Rosalind, from all accounts Mrs Tremoille may be a picture on the outside, but inside she's a witch. You're childish to talk of hatred, and no young man of worth will admire you, certainly not Rowan Welland.'

Rosalind went a little pink. 'I'm not childish.'

'Oh, yes, you are, my girl, and what's more, you should be grateful – really grateful – to Beth Tremoille for teaching you to read, write, and speak properly. Now then, we'll have to put on a trot if we're to get to Johnno's wagon in time.' Phoebe began to push her way toward King Edward's Gate and, after stealing a last look at the cathedral entrance, Rosalind followed.

Johnno was on the point of leaving. He was impatient, and spat out a plug of tobacco as he saw them. 'I'll leave you here if you like! Darned women. Squawking I suppose, with a whole lot of other fowls.'

'That's enough of that, Johnno Walters,' Phoebe said primly, waiting deliberately for him to help her up into the back of the covered wagon. He obliged, giving her a hearty smack on the rump as he did so, but when he turned to Rosalind, she scrambled up quickly before he could touch her. He grumbled under his breath, and reached in his smock pocket for some more chewing tobacco before taking his place on the wagon box. Giving a piercing whistle, followed by a flick of the whip, he coaxed the oxen into life, and the wagon rumbled slowly up toward the Cross.

Gloucester was some way behind when Johnno discarded his tobacco and decided to select a blade of grass from the roadside. Phoebe was incensed. 'Get on, Johnno Walters, we want to be home this side of Christmas!'

'Hold your noise, Phoebe Brown, you're worse than my wife! Nag, nag! Haven't you got any Christian thoughts to occupy your mind?' He didn't see the two dogs bounding along the road toward the wagon, and when they began to snap around the legs of the oxen it was too late. The frightened beasts heaved forward and sideways, and in a trice the wagon had tipped over into the water-filled ditch that ran alongside the road. Rosalind screamed and clutched at a dangling rope, and Phoebe slid to the floor where the nearest sack of flour burst and spilled over her.

As soon as the wagon had come to rest, Johnno scrambled through the back. 'Are you all right?' he cried anxiously, dragging several barrels aside to get to the two frightened women. He helped Phoebe out first.

She was trembling. 'Lord above us, Johnno Walters, you're a danger to folk!'

'It was your fault, you foolish biddy, if you hadn't gone on and on at me I'd have paid attention to what I was doing!'

'That's right, blame someone else, anyone so long as it isn't you!'
Phoebe retorted, trying to shake the flour from her clothes. He made the
mistake of trying to help her and got a smart slap for his pains. 'Keep your
paws to yourself! I'm fine, except for my dignity. How about you,
Rosalind?'

'I think so.' Rosalind allowed Johnno to lift her down to safety.

Then the hapless wagoner gazed at his stricken livelihood. 'Now what
am I to do? Repairs will cost me a small fortune.'

Phoebe was dismayed as well. 'And it's a terribly long walk home.'

Rosalind glanced back toward Gloucester. 'Maybe something else will
come along soon,' she said hopefully, but the usually busy road was quiet.
Then her sharp young eyes picked out an approaching rider, and at the
same time her heart leapt a little, because she recognized the prancing
cream-coloured horse. 'I – I think Master Robert is coming. Yes, I'm sure
it's him.'

'That cocky young bugger!' Johnno spat roundly on the ground. 'We
can kiss goodbye to any hope of *him* stopping to help!'

But he was wrong, for Robert reined in as he reached the overturned
wagon. 'What happened, Johnno?'

'Damned loose dogs worrying around the oxen, sir.' The wagoner
snatched off his floppy straw hat.

'The George and Dragon has a wagon, has it not?' Robert spoke to
Johnno, but smiled at Rosalind, his eyes wandering quite obviously over
her. Phoebe glanced anxiously at the girl's flushed face and shining eyes.

'Yes, Master Robert,' Johnno replied, turning the hat in his hands.

'I'll inform them when I reach Frampney.'

Johnno was taken aback. 'Well, thank you, Master Robert, thank you
kindly.'

'It's the least I can do.' Robert was still looking at Rosalind. 'Will
someone worry if you don't return when expected?'

He knew she did, she thought, but answered politely. 'Yes, sir, my
father, and Matty Brown will be worried about Phoebe.'

'Well, we can't have that, can we?' He held his hand down to her
suddenly. 'Prince can more than carry the two of us, Miss Mannacott, and
then you can inform them in person that all is well and they are not to be
anxious.'

Phoebe grabbed Rosalind's arm warningly, but he swung the girl up
before him, looked down at Phoebe for a moment haughtily and then
kicked his heel.

Johnno exhaled slowly. 'She's a mite young, Phoebe.'

'You think I don't know that, you daft curmudgeon? Oh, damn you,
Johnno Walters, you and your blasted grass! He took her right under my
nose!'

Johnno went to the wagon, produced a bottle and pulled the cork out with his teeth. 'Get some of this inside you and shut up for a bit, eh? I was watching that girl's face, and can tell you here and now that she was more than willing to sit up there with her arse pressed back against his—'

'Don't you say anything more, Johnno! Not one word!' Phoebe took the bottle, drank some, and then spluttered. 'Dear Lord, what *is* this?'

'Black rum.'

'I hate to think what makes it black!'

'I don't give a sod provided it gives me a nice glow. Well, there's nothing we can do except wait for the other wagon. Do you play cards?'

Robert's arm was around Rosalind's little waist as the horse cantered easily along the lane toward Frampney. 'Have you been to the wedding, Master Robert?' she asked in her best voice.

'Yes. To ignore such a glittering occasion would be to tread upon influential toes. The champagne was tolerable, but that's about all I can say.' He began to slow the horse. 'Why are we rushing these sweet moments away?'

She blushed. 'You shouldn't say that.'

'Why not? Doesn't Webb pay you compliments?'

'Jamie Webb means nothing to me!' she said crossly.

Robert smiled. 'Poor fellow, to be so utterly excluded from your thoughts. So if you're not Webb's sweetheart, whose are you?'

'No one's, nor have I ever been.'

She was a virgin? His interest quickened, and blood pumped into his loins. He'd like to be the first blade to pierce the flesh of this comely little peach. Through the soft stuff of her gown he could feel that she wasn't wearing stays, and he pulled her closer, the better to rub his arousal against her without her realizing. She thought it was just the saddle. 'May I call you Rosalind?' he murmured, his excitement increasing.

'I don't think that would be right, Master Robert.'

'Why? Who would know, except you and me?' he asked.

'Someone else might hear and tell my d— my father.'

He noticed how she corrected herself. She was better spoken than her father and could drop her Gloucester accent if she tried. He reined in. 'Soon there will be cottages and folk to see what we do, which will stop me taking payment.'

'Payment?' Her eyes widened apprehensively.

'A kiss. Just one kiss,' he begged sensuously.

She knew that if she had any sense right now she would slip down to the ground and tell him to ride on without her, but she couldn't. 'You shouldn't talk to me like that, Master Robert, it's not right.'

'Many of the best things aren't right. Don't you wish to kiss me?'

'Oh, but I do!' The foolish words slipped out.

'Then I shall grant that wish,' he murmured, taking her chin in his gloved hand and tilting her mouth to meet his. Her lips parted. His kiss was very soft; his breath tasted of cognac and she could smell the scent of lemons on his clothes. When he was sure of her response, his hand moved from her chin, slid down the whiteness of her throat, and then to her breast, cupping it expertly so he could take her nipple between his thumb and forefinger. She gasped nervously and began to pull away, but his arm was too strong about her waist. His lips claimed hers, and he continued to roll her nipple with his thumb and forefinger. Amazing feelings began to tighten her breasts and quicken her pulse. The pleasure she'd previously had to give herself now came of its own accord, making muscles twitch in her crotch and causing her senses to revolve. She felt both faint and fully awake, and wanted him to kiss her forever, but he brought it to an end. This little peach was one to consume at leisure, and to the full. So he smiled at her flushed face, kissed her forehead and without another word moved the horse on again.

Chapter Thirteen

On the first day of August, Beth looked critically around her newly decorated bedroom at the Dower House. Blue silk wallpaper, blue brocade hangings on the bed and a blue and beige carpet. Too much blue, maybe? She considered a moment. No, with the cream figured-velvet curtains at the windows it was utterly perfect – if a little extravagant. But she could *afford* to be a little extravagant. Her life was comfortable and moved from day to day with an ease she had almost forgotten. Billy had driven her to Barnstaple, where she stayed two nights in order to discuss her financial affairs and deposit her funds at a reputable bank. Her money had now been wisely invested. While in Barnstaple she had purchased everything for her new bedroom, and engaged a decorator to brighten the entire house. Mrs Cobbett and the new maid, Molly Dodd, had made curtains and cushions, and all in all everything now looked much better. The Dower House was beginning to seem like her home, not just the house she had rented.

The bedroom occupied the south-east corner of the house, and had two casement windows, one of which stood open. Mrs Cobbett had placed a bowl of dark red roses on the sill, and their scent was as warm as the summer air that breathed in over the thatched roof of the veranda, directly below the sill. Outside, a rocky shore stretched down to where the deep blue-green of the Bristol Channel sparkled at the lowest tidal ebb. This window also gave her a view of Rendisbury Hill, but she hadn't seen Landry Haldane again. The other window faced inland to the south, past Lannermouth and up the deeply wooded gorge to the heights of Exmoor.

She turned to inspect herself in the looking-glass on the dressing-table, straightened her frilled cap and fluffed out the delicate white-spotted blue muslin of her gown. Her thick dark curls were caught back with a blue ribbon; she had put on a little weight and her unblemished skin was beginning to look truly supple again. The waif of Fiddler's Court was fading, and in another month would surely have disappeared entirely. She was happy here, and hit it off with Mrs Cobbett, with whom she had made her only other excursions, to church on Sundays. There she had been subjected to a great deal of scrutiny, not least from the rector, Mr Bellamy, of whose daughter Harriet, whose name was linked with the major's, there had as yet been no sign. Billy was happy here too, especially since the arrival of the new maid, Molly, a plump twenty-year-old with large delphinium-blue eyes. His grandiose tales of city life impressed her, and she clearly adored him.

Beth smiled to herself. Contentment was a strange feeling after all that had happened to her. She no longer wondered what her father's letter contained, and even felt a little less vengeful where Jane was concerned. The prospect of being traced by Guy Valmer remained a constant threat, yet here, in this beautiful place, he didn't often cross her mind. Except at night, when he often came to her in her dreams.

'Miss Mannacott?' Molly tapped at the door and peeped inside. 'Miss Mannacott, Miss Bellamy's come calling.'

The elusive daughter? 'Please tell her I will be down directly, Molly.' After adjusting her hair ribbon, Beth went downstairs. The little drawing-room was directly below her bedroom. It was pale primrose, with green chintz furniture and curtains, and swathes of delicate sprigged gauze at French doors that were slightly ajar to the veranda and flower garden. Miss Bellamy, attractive and boyishly slender, sat rather uneasily on the edge of the sofa, glancing around as if trying to assess something. The tastes and quality of the new tenant, perhaps? She wore a ruby riding habit and her golden hair was worn short beneath a frivolous black hat with spiky feathers. Her hands, clasping her gloves, twisted and untwisted in her lap, and she leapt to her feet as Beth entered. 'Miss Mannacott?'

Beth smiled. 'Miss Bellamy?'

The rector's daughter smiled too. She had light-grey eyes that were flecked with gold, and there was a little mole at the corner of her mouth that gave her a certain appeal. She resumed her place on the sofa. 'I would have called before, but have been away and didn't hear about you immediately on my return. But here I am, hoping above hope that we might become friends. I hope you didn't come here to escape from people?'

'It's true I chose Lannermouth for peace and quiet, but I am certainly not averse to making new friends.'

'Oh, good, I'm so glad. Society around here boasts mainly dull married ladies and grizzled octogenarians. I'm only twenty-seven but I feel more like seventy-seven in such staid company. So please, can we forget the lengthy fuss of formality? Please call me Harriet; Miss Bellamy sounds uncomfortably like meat pies at the House of Commons, or something to settle the stomach.'

'Then you must call me Beth. Oh, Harriet, you are a breath of even fresher air than already exists in this wonderful place. I've hardly met anyone since arriving. There's your father, of course.'

'You made a favourable impression.'

'Really? I can't imagine why. He gives me stern looks when I go to church.'

Harriet giggled. 'He's short-sighted and probably can't see you at all.'

As they laughed together, Molly came in with a tray of coffee provided by the thoughtful Mrs Cobbett and, when the maid had gone and Beth began to pour the coffee, Harriet spoke again. 'You've met Major Haldane as well, haven't you?'

'Oh, yes. On the morning after my arrival.' Beth noticed the flush on Harriet's face, and remembered that Mrs Cobbett had said the major was expected to marry Harriet Bellamy.

'He speaks well of you,' Harriet went on, the blush deepening.

'Indeed? We only met for a few moments.' The gallant major was a sensitive subject. Better to change the topic. 'Is there a good dressmaker here? I need some clothes for the coming winter, a mantle or two, and a pelisse, maybe.'

'Dressmaker? Oh, yes. Miss Archer. She's a marvel. I've heard it said that she's as clever as any London dressmaker. She made this riding habit. I must visit her myself soon, perhaps we could go together?'

'I'd like that, thank you.'

Harriet glanced around. 'Will you make any changes to the house?'

'Well, I'm only the tenant, but I think I'd like a little summerhouse just over there.' Beth pointed out of the French windows toward the corner of the garden between the sea and the park.

'You'll have no trouble finding labourers and craftsmen, as there are so many out of work at the moment. My father was saying only this morning that the army and navy are about to discharge thousands more now the war is ended. I dread to think what it will be like soon, with so many out of work and prices reaching toward the sky.' They were both silent for a moment, sipping the delicious coffee. After that the time passed pleasantly as they talked of fashion, the most picturesque places to go riding, and the various local people Beth would soon meet, but then Harriet realized she had to leave. 'My father is lunching early today and he gets very cross if I keep him waiting,' she explained. 'I'm so glad I've met you at last, Beth. I'm sure you'll love living here.'

'I already do.'

The two women walked to the front door and Billy brought Harriet's horse. Beth watched her ride away down the drive, her red habit bright amid the greens of summer. As she disappeared over the bridge and into Lannermouth, Beth glanced along the shore toward the base of Rendisbury Cliffs, where low table-topped rocks jutting into the water seemed to offer a pleasant place to sit. The thought appealed, so she collected a book of Shakespeare's sonnets left by the house owner, told Mrs Cobbett where she would be, and then set off along the path at the edge of the park. The coast of Wales was lost in the summer haze as the incoming tide lapped between the rocks. She had yet to see the Bristol Channel in anger, and on a day like this it was hard to imagine crashing gale-whipped surf. At the end of the park, where the path curved sharply around the bouldery shore toward the deep water at the foot of the cliffs, lay the outcrop of flat rocks. She picked her way down to a particularly smooth one, and then chose a spot from where she could dip her fingers in a large rock pool.

Placing the book on the warm stone, she removed the ribbon from her hair and sat with her knees drawn up, her hands clasped around them. A playful, rather timid breeze stirred her hair, so that several strands caught across her face, and she brushed them aside, hardly realizing she was doing it. If she began to walk east along this shore now, if she walked and walked, the sea would become the Severn, which passed through Gloucester. She stared in that direction, recalling how she had walked hand in hand with Jake along the river-bank, hoping to see the tidal bore come rushing upstream, and how it had almost swept them away when it proved far larger than expected. The Severn passed Frampney too.

Taking a deep breath she picked up the book and began to browse through the sonnets, but the frequent expressions of love brought Guy to mind. She knew how foolish it was, but he exerted such a powerful effect upon her that it seemed he was always there, on the very edge of her past, waiting to step into her present. Then two lines in particular caught her attention. '*For I have sworn thee fair and thought thee bright, Who art as black as hell, as dark as night.*' This was how she should regard Sir Guy Valmer, she told herself sternly. 'Don't let him rule you, Beth Tremoille,' she breathed. 'Forget him and let your life move on.'

Suddenly a male voice hailed her from the path. 'I was told I'd find you here, Miss Mannacott.' Startled, she turned to see Landry Haldane. He removed his top hat to sketch a bow. 'May I join you?'

'Oh, I—' She was embarrassed to be caught outside with her hair loose.

He hesitated. 'You would rather I didn't?'

'I cannot claim squatter's rights, sir.' She watched as he made his way toward her. No longer in uniform, he wore a dark-green coat and tight buff breeches that cleaved to his hips and thighs. His face looked different, and she realized he'd shaved off his moustache and side-whiskers. He wasn't strictly handsome, rather were his even, quite ordinary features animated by immense charm. He was vital and confident, exuding virility, and she knew by the warmth in his light-brown eyes that he was attracted to her. He sat down, one leg drawn up, the other outstretched. His hat was in his right hand, tapping lightly against his riding boot, and he didn't say anything. Was it serendipity that he had come here just when she was instructing herself to forget Guy? Was fate telling her to break the spell? She smiled. 'You wish to see me about something, Major?'

'Just plain Mr Haldane will do.' He smiled too.

'You certainly no longer look a major.'

'I'll take that as a compliment. Anyway, I'm here because I believe you are seeking a good riding horse. Your coachman mentioned it in my game-keeper's hearing. I wish to sell just such a desirable mount. So that is my official purpose.'

'And your unofficial purpose?'

'Why, to make sure Lannermouth is to your liking.'

'It is indeed, Mr Haldane, and yes, I am seeking a horse.'

'Would a six-year-old Hanoverian gelding be of interest? I bought him from a Prussian officer two years ago. You've seen the horse. He and I do not get on.'

'And would *I* get on with him?' She wasn't that good a rider.

He smiled. 'Oh, certainly. He just doesn't like me very much, and occasionally makes that very plain by depositing my elegant hide on the ground. Ride him, to see what you think. His official name is Sleipnir, after Odin's six-legged steed, but I just call him Snowy. If you're interested I'll make arrangements for you to see him tomorrow.' He paused to glance at her book. 'The sonnets?'

'Are they to your taste?'

He held her gaze with his deep turquoise eyes and recited softly, '"*Shall I compare thee to a summer's day? Thou art more lovely and more temperate: Rough winds do shake the darling buds of May, And summer's lease hath all too short a date: Sometime too hot the eye of heaven shines, And often is his gold complexion dimm'd; And every fair from fair some-time declines, By chance or nature's changing course untrimmed: But thy eternal summer shall not fade, Nor lose possession of that fair thou ow'st, Nor shall death brag thou wand'rest in his shade, When in eternal lines to time thou grow'st: So long as men can breathe or eyes can see, So long lives this, and this gives life to thee.*"'

She was entranced. 'You know your Bard, sir.'

'Don't fall for hussar deceits, Miss Mannacott. I learned several such sonnets to further my cause with the fair sex. I'll spellbind my bride with such romance.'

Her lips parted. 'You are to be married?'

'I was speaking hypothetically.' He smiled again. 'You may be interested to know that our wild cliffs and leafy gorges have so far attracted Coleridge, Wordsworth and Southey. Oh, and Shelley.'

She stared. 'Shelley? The author of *Queen Mab*?'

'The very subversive fellow. Don't tell me you approve of *Queen Mab*, it's a blatant incitement to rebellion.'

'I don't approve of what it preaches, but I *do* think Mr Shelley is a great poet.'

'Hmm. Radical agitators who practise free love aren't much to my taste. Begging you pardon,' he added quickly. 'I was certainly glad to see him gone, for he could turn a cake recipe into an anti-establishment harangue. The government started to investigate him, and he fled across to Wales. I thank Heaven Lord Byron hasn't honoured us, for I couldn't abide his strutting.'

'He has a club foot,' she murmured.

'Very well, I couldn't abide his limping.'

They laughed together, and she felt as if she'd known him a long time. Being with him was palliative. How good it would be to lie back on the rock with him, gazing up at the flawless sky. He was amusing and unconventional, and conversing with him was to indulge in a subtle flirtation. She was aware that the wilful breeze played with the petals of her gown, allowing him glimpses of more bosom than was seemly. She ought to return to the house, but the irresistible force of her own sensuality kept her there.

He set his hat down and put his hand in the pool. 'Have you seen our mermaid?'

'*Mermaid?*'

'Yes. They say that when the moon is full she sits on a rock that is only exposed at low tide, and combs her hair while she sings.'

'Have you seen her?' she asked.

He grinned. 'No, not even after a medicinal measure of cognac.'

She could imagine him after a little cognac, his dark hair tousled, his eyes dark and amorous, his lips ready to kiss. Her wanton thoughts hurried on to imagine him without coat, cravat or waistcoat, just close-fitting breeches and a shirt that was unbuttoned to his waist. He'd be lying back on a bed, inviting her to do with him as she would. But she yearned more for it to be Guy who lay thus. Something must have shown on her face because he became concerned. 'Please say if you'd rather I left.'

'Oh, no, of course not.' Embarrassment made her hot, and she couldn't meet his eyes. 'I've seen so few people since arriving that I'm sure even the dullest conversation would be a pleasant diversion.'

He raised an eyebrow. 'So you expect only dull conversation from me?'

'I will be gravely disappointed if that proves the case, sir.'

'Miss Mannacott, I would have called sooner, but felt compelled to delay a second meeting until it would no longer cause undue comment. Please, don't misunderstand, it's just that Exmoor gossips are exceptionally zealous, and if I had come to the Dower House immediately on my return, your name would by now be rattling in adjoining counties. Rumour has betrothed me to so many young ladies that I've ceased counting. Believe me, the eyes and ears of the county will be fixed on Haldane Hall until I stand before the altar with my chosen bride.'

One set of eyes and ears were certainly turned in his direction, Beth thought, remembering Harriet. 'And now Snowy has given you just cause to call?'

'Something of the sort.' He glanced away. 'Cards on the table, Miss Mannacott: I seized upon Snowy because I very much wanted to see you again.'

Flattered and secretly pleased as she was with his frankness, Beth still thought of Harriet. 'It seems to be my day for visitors. Miss Bellamy left not long ago.'

'Yes, I waited out of sight until she departed.'

Beth regarded him. 'That is more than I needed to know, sir.'

'Is it? I would hate you to think that Harriet – Miss Bellamy – has expectations where I am concerned.'

'My housekeeper implies that she has.'

'Ah, yes, Mrs Cobbett. She it was who told me I'd find "Miss Beth" here.'

'So she's wrong about you and Miss Bellamy? There is no under-standing?'

'None.' He met her eyes, and she did not look away. She knew she should, but so determined was she to snap her fingers at Guy that she became guilty of implied encouragement. The air seemed to hang, and for a moment the sea was as calm as a millpond. Desire was in his eyes, and she felt her senses stirring too. She couldn't have Guy, but this man was here, wanting her – and she needed to be wanted. Neither of them moved. It was enough just to know.

The silent emotion became so great that she got up. 'I think it best I go now, sir. No, please don't get up. Please.'

'About Snowy. I'll call tomorrow morning at about ten, Miss Mannacott.' He caught her hand and turned the palm quickly to his lips.

'Yes, of course.' She climbed back to the path, and hastened away.

The blood pumped urgently through his veins as he gazed after her. 'I can wait, Beth Mannacott, I can wait,' he breathed. Then he paused until he was sure a certain part of his anatomy was quiescent again, before returning to his horse.

Chapter Fourteen

The next morning the smart yellow curricle skimmed along the narrow road up the gorge, and Landry laughed as Beth clung fearfully to the seat beside him. 'It's the fashion to drive at risk of life and limb, Miss Mannacott.' He flicked the whip at the pair of mahogany-bay horses. 'We'll go up to the moor, and approach Haldane from the other direction. The views are worth the trouble.'

The roar of rapids was lost in the noise of hoofs and wheels as he tooled the bays around a bend, scattering small stones over the dense roadside greenery. Occasionally the trees and leaves thinned enough to give a glimpse of foaming white water far below, but then the foliage closed again. The curricle's exhilarating speed brought colour to Beth's cheeks, and she had to hold on her black riding hat in case it vanished forever into the precipitous gorge. The cords and tassels flew behind her and the curled ostrich feather fluttered against her hand. She felt unvoiced thoughts and emotions swirling around them both, and had lain awake for half the night, trying not to think of Guy, but of every word she and Landry Haldane had said the day before. As the curricle jolted over ruts and stones, she was conscious of his body flexing to the motion, the fit of his clothes and the way his dark hair fluttered against the under-brim of his hat. The tautness of his kid gloves across his knuckles was so sensuous that she longed to be caressed by them. Not through clothes, but against her naked skin. For a heartbeat she was in Guy's carriage again, watching him remove his gloves to hand her some capon from the hamper. *Guy, oh Guy, I want you so much.* But Landry was here. Now.

At last they drove up out of the valley on to the open moor, where the golden gorse was glorious against the hazy blue of the sky, and in sheltered or south-facing spots the heather was beginning to glow purple. Landry reined in to give the sweating team a rest at a crossroads, where the signpost pointed west for Barnstaple, north to Lannermouth and north-west to Haldane. The wild scenery of Exmoor stretched into the distance, sometimes plunging into other tree-choked valleys, sometimes soaring over prominent hills. Landry glanced at her. 'Exmoor is a timeless place that invades one's soul and occupies it until the day one dies. It already steals your heart, doesn't it?'

'I believe it does,' she murmured. A string of nine pack-ponies, brown, bay and dun, moved slowly along an ancient track, each with an enormous load upon its back, plodding reliably and steadily toward an unknown destination. 'Where are they going?'

'Dulverford, probably. For the most part we Devon rustics are still obliged to move our goods around by the age-old method. I've built the new roads hereabouts, but for isolated hamlets and farms the wheel hasn't been invented.'

The perfumed air was beguiling and the summer warmth seemed intent upon stealing Beth's inhibitions. The way to exclude Guy from her heart was to replace him with someone else. She could never have Guy's love, and was becoming more and more aware that Landry was strongly attracted to her. But she was afraid of the past, the present, and the future. With so much to conceal and be ashamed of, would giving in to sexual temptation be her ruin? Was Landry Haldane worth that risk? The very reason for coming to the Dower House was to be isolated, alone and safe, and yet here she was, on the brink of casting caution to the wind. There was time yet to draw back from that fatal final step. Feeling his gaze, she hoped her emotional conflict didn't show. She had to say something. But what?

She was spared having to say anything, because a stag in full antler suddenly broke from a thicket to the south, and Landry commented drily, 'Perfect for the hunting season in a couple of weeks' time.'

His tone surprised her. 'You don't approve?'

'It's very hard to find anything commendable in stag hunting.'

'But you're a landowner, and surely *all* landowners indulge in such sport?'

He drew a heavy breath. 'Most do, but I'm the exception that proves the rule. Almost everyone hereabouts supports either the North Devon or the Greylake staghounds, or both. I offer succour to neither, and indeed would rather support Beelzebub's private pack than anything Greylake.' He didn't expand, but watched as the stag disappeared over the brow of a hill. 'Actually, it's very unusual to see deer at this time of the day. They prefer to come out at twilight and the very early morning.' He turned to point behind them, over the thick trees of the Lanner gorge to the fracture between the Haldane Cliffs and Rendisbury Hill. 'Do you see the position of Lannermouth and the Dower House? Look a little to the west and you'll see Haldane.' He moved the whip to indicate a shallow sheltered valley set high behind the summit of Haldane Cliffs. There, nestling from the full force of winter storms, was the large village that was visible from the Dower House as only chimneys.

The air was so clear that she saw everything in detail. Thatched cottages and small houses were built around a village green, where cows and tethered goats grazed. An old woman walking slowly toward her home, carrying an armful of kindling, paused to talk to a neighbour in his small vegetable garden. The church spire reached toward the sky, its gleaming new copper weathercock swinging slowly in the playful breeze, and there was a leafy churchyard, with a lych-gate overhung by ancient yews. Nearby stood a small Jacobean house, presumably the rectory where Harriet lived with her father. But the property that captured Beth's gaze was the splendid white mansion set in a beautiful park behind the church. It was built in the fashion of the early eighteenth century, and presented a serene and gracious façade, with canted bays and a particularly handsome pediment. It was far larger and more impressive than Beth had imagined, and she turned to Landry in astonishment. '*That* is Haldane Hall?'

He was amused. 'Yes. Why do you look so shocked?'

'It's so, well, large.'

'It'll do, I suppose,' he said.

'How can you be so matter-of-fact? It's truly magnificent!'

'I'm delighted you approve, although how much longer it will stay this way remains to be seen. By building roads, I've invited the outside world to enter.'

'There must be progress, sir. It's the way of things.'

'Maybe. Enclosure is considered progress, is it not? Soon it will be illegal for poor folk to gather wood or graze their beasts on the village green. Walls, fences and hedges instead of this magnificent untrammelled moor, and—' He stopped ruefully. 'Forgive me, I didn't mean to deliver a sermon.'

'There's nothing to forgive,' she assured him. 'But surely, you must be one of the few landowners not to want enclosure.' Her father had commended it for the benefits to his already bulging purse.

'I'm an oddity, eh? I don't like hunting or enclosures.' He smiled a little sadly. 'Life goes on well enough in these parts, and doesn't need that sort of change. Every acre that can be successfully farmed is farmed. I don't keep close and hard watch on my game, and even allow those in need to take what they will, for there's more than enough for my needs. It works, and I'm content to keep it that way.' He gazed at the moor again. 'Maybe I state my old-fashioned views too freely, I don't know, but when I look around me, *I know* I'm right. In these times, with recession striking at everyone, men jobless and their families hungry, the old ways remain the best.'

'Tell me, sir, why is Lord Castlereagh Prime Minister and not you?'

He laughed and flicked the team into action again, taking the Haldane road, which led in a gentle curve up toward the village. The hall was in view all the time, and then its gates and lodge appeared just before the village was reached. As Landry negotiated the sharp turn between the open gates, a little fair-haired girl leaned out of an upper window of the lodge, waving at him enthusiastically, but he didn't notice her. Beth glanced at the mythical beasts topping the tall, oddly uneven stone gateposts. 'What are they?' she asked, pointing.

'Cockatrices or basilisks, whichever you wish to call them,' Landry explained. 'They're fabulous reptiles supposedly hatched by a serpent from a cock's egg, and their breath and glance is believed to be fatal.'

In the park, a herd of red deer grazed beneath copper beech trees, and there were rhododendrons that must be a wonderful display in May and June. A ha-ha separated the park from mown lawns, and on the sheltered southern side of the house she could see hothouses and potting sheds. Beyond the house lay the stables, their gateway crowned by a huge clock tower, and it was toward this that Landry drove. The curricle clattered on cobbles beneath the clock tower, and entered a large quadrangle three sides of which were lined by white-painted stalls from which handsome horses looked out. As grooms ran from the house to take charge of the team, Landry alighted and came around to assist Beth down. 'Welcome to Haldane Hall, Miss Mannacott.' His hand was strong and steady, and might have become more intimate had not the head groom hurried over. 'Ah, Johns, have Snowy saddled – I believe my mother's side-saddle is still here – and then prepare Rollo as well, and bring them around to the front of the house.'

The head groom touched his hat and hurried away to the tack room, and Landry offered Beth his arm. They walked through a postern gate into the walled rose garden, where the air was almost soporific with perfume. A fountain played into a square lily pond, insects hummed, and a brilliant blue damselfly hovered over the lily-decked water. From there they went up some steps to a terrace, and then in through open French windows to the house itself. They proceeded to the cool green-and-white vestibule, where marble statuettes posed in golden wall niches, and a sunburst clock, copied from one at Versailles, ticked slowly into the echoing silence. A handsome gilt-framed mirror above the white marble fireplace gave the impression of more light and space, and a garniture of costly green-and-white Chinese porcelain spoke of wealth. The overall impression was very gracious and pleasing. Beth noticed a footman waiting discreetly in the shadows by the grand staircase that curved up to a balconied landing on the first floor. Landry's servants were in constant attendance, albeit at a judicious distance. Nevertheless she was conscious of surveillance, and wondered what was being whispered in the kitchens about the new occupant of the Dower House.

The elegant double front doors stood open to the summer, and Beth could see down the drive and the park toward the village. A horseman was approaching the house, and Landry was about to instruct the footman to bring refreshments to the nearby library, when he recognized the rider. 'Damn! What does *he* want?'

'Who is it?' she asked.

'Bradfield, the agent from Greylake,' he replied. 'With your permission, I will speak to him. I promise it will not be for long.'

'Of course.'

He went out as the rider reined at the foot of the portico steps. The Greylake agent was a sallow-faced man in a plain brown coat, and the crown of his top hat was too low ever to have been fashionable. Beth could hear as Landry took the cob's bridle. 'What is it, Bradfield?'

'The poachers in Granleigh Wood, Mr Haldane, they're coming on to Greylake land from your land, and making an easy escape back into your land. There'll be ill-feeling if it goes on.'

Landry looked away for a moment, his mouth tight. 'And what in God's own name does the master of Greylake miss from that wood? He has more than enough land to harbour half the game in England.' Dislike thickened his voice.

'Nonetheless—'

'I know, I know!' Landry was irritable. 'What would he have me do? Patrol my side of the boundary with hounds?'

'My master is not in residence at the moment, sir, so I am here on my own authority. If you could just let it be known that you will not deal kindly with anyone who crosses on to Greylake land for the purpose of poaching.' Bradfield suddenly smiled effacingly. 'As agent I have to ask this, you understand.'

'I understand, and will do what I can, but can't promise the desired result.'

'Due to Sir Daniel Lavington having been presiding, there were two poachers hanged at Taunton Assizes not long back, Mr Haldane. Maybe a timely reminder of that would instil a little caution?'

'And maybe if Greylake's boundaries were more effectively guarded by gamekeepers, there wouldn't be any need for you to ride all this way.'

'Yes, sir, but I need my master's permission to authorize such a change.'

Landry was gripped with barely suppressed rage. 'Bradfield, I despise your master with a venom you can only imagine. And I despise Lavington, whose mill at Porworthy has always been profitable, yet who nevertheless installs power looms and every new contrivance, throwing men, women and children out of work. Then, when the poor are forced to poach for their food, he sets mantraps; the poachers are caught and tried, and *he* sits in final judgment upon them. Men like him cannot see beyond the ends of their noses.'

Bradfield shifted uneasily. 'No doubt, sir,' he murmured, on what Beth believed to be a cynical note, as if he were taking Landry's words with a large pinch of salt. Or, to use another saying, did the agent think it was a case of the Haldane pot calling the Lavington kettle black?

Landry cleared his throat, realizing he'd been haranguing the man.

'I've said my piece, and you've delivered your message, so I think you may go.'

Relieved, the man touched his hat and turned his horse away, and Landry returned to the house, where Beth waited anxiously. 'I know it's none of my business,' she said, 'but it distresses me to see you so clearly upset. There must be great ill will between you and the owner of Greylake.'

'There is.' He drew a long breath and ran his fingers through his hair. 'Forgive me for displaying such a lamentable lack of control. It would have been bad enough to have sounded off to another gentleman, but to have done it to a mere agent is shameful.'

'Hardly shameful.'

He gave a penitent smile. 'There aren't many things on this earth guaranteed to enrage me, but anything to do with Greylake achieves it every time. I loathe everything about that man, and the feeling is mutual. Our lands adjoin, but we have as little to do with each other as possible.'

'What happened between you?' she asked.

'It's an old feud that goes back generations, but with this generation it has become unpleasantly personal.'

She put a tentative hand on his sleeve. 'I cannot believe there is anyone with whom you do not get along.'

He relaxed and grinned. 'My wit and charm render such a thing impossible?'

'Yes,' she replied truthfully.

His eyes were warm. 'Do they work upon you, Miss Mannacott?'

'Yes.' But there was a hesitation he could not help but notice.

'Indecision?'

'I cannot tell you about them, but there are reasons I escaped to Exmoor.'

'A cruel husband?' he asked.

'No, nothing like that. There is no one else.' *Just an impossible fantasy.*

'I won't press you for more than you're prepared to give.' Embarrassed, he ran his hand through his hair again. 'I swear upon my honour that I have never behaved as forwardly as this before.'

'Nor have I, sir,' she replied truthfully.

'It's ridiculous to be formal after what has just been said. My name is Landry, and I beg you let me call you Beth.' He glanced toward the ever-present footman. 'One has no privacy in one's own house,' he added, smiling.

The head groom and a boy led the horses around, and Landry again offered her his arm. His hand rested briefly over hers as they went down the steps to the gravel, where two grooms waited. He cast an appreciative eye over the Hanoverian. 'You've turned him out so well, Johns, that I'm almost of a mind not to sell him. However, take him up and down a little, to show Miss Mannacott his paces.'

The groom led Snowy around, slowly at first, and then at a run that stretched the horse to a quick trot. Beth held her breath as she watched. Snowy had been brushed until his coat shone, and his mane and forelock rippled. Landry smiled at her. 'A handsome lad, eh?'

'Quite magnificent,' she said, as Johns brought the horse back.

'We can ride along behind Haldane Cliffs and into Stone Valley, of which seeing is believing. You will never have encountered its like before. Anyway, we'll be able to give Snowy a good stretch.'

They rode down the drive toward the gates, and were almost there when a young woman and a little girl emerged from the lodge. The woman was blonde, blue-eyed and exceptionally slender, with an exquisitely delicate face and complexion. Her skin was so clear it was perfect, and her cheeks were flushed an unnatural pink. The little girl, who'd waved from the upstairs window earlier, was about nine years old, a solemn creature with the same colouring as the woman, who had to be her mother. Landry reined in and doffed his top hat, smiling. 'Good day to you, Carrie.'

'Good day, sir,' said the woman, her large eyes flickering to Beth.

'I trust all is well at the lodge?'

'Yes, all is well.' There was a definite Devon burr in the soft voice, and Beth could not but be aware of the warmth in her eyes as she looked at Landry.

'Be sure to send word to me if you need anything,' he said.

'I will, sir.' Carrie turned away suddenly to cough. 'Forgive me, sir, it was one of those tickles.'

He looked down at the little girl. 'And how are you, Katie?'

'I'm very well, thank you.'

'Are you looking after Mama?'

She looked at Carrie and then nodded at him. 'She's been very good.'

'I'm pleased to hear it.' He leaned down to put his hand under the girl's chin, tickling her briefly. 'And how is the puppy?'

She giggled and put a conspiratorial finger to her lips, then gestured for him to lean down again. 'Pompey wees on the floor and Mama gets very cross,' she whispered in a way that would have carried from the stage up to the gods.

He laughed. 'Sweeting, Mama is quite right to be cross. You must tap his nose if he does it again, or you must clean up after him. If you don't want to do that, you must make sure he doesn't wee in the house.'

Beth looked anew at Carrie. The woman hadn't taken her eyes from Landry. She did not bother to hide her love for him, and obviously did not care who else knew either. What of her husband? If there *was* a husband, of course. Beth's heart sank as a new possibility struck her. She watched Landry and Katie. Was there a likeness? Something in the line of the jaw and tilt of the head?

Landry gathered Rollo's reins. 'Well, good day to you both,' he said to mother and daughter, and tapped his top hat on again.

'And to you, sir,' Carrie replied.

Beth and Landry rode on through the gates, and then turned toward the village. 'Who are they?' Beth asked at last, unable to contain her interest.

His turquoise eyes were reluctant. 'To answer that I need to be painfully honest with you,' he replied, and her heart sank further, for she guessed what he was going to say. 'Katie is my daughter, and Carrie Markham, who was a housemaid at the hall, is her mother. Which proves me to be a hypocrite after all that righteous pulpit-thundering earlier.'

Perturbed, Beth didn't know how to respond. Until now she had not been able to imagine Landry had feet of clay, but it seemed he did. She glanced to the left, and saw they were passing the churchyard and rectory. The sunlight was glancing off the rectory windows, and she could see Harriet gathering roses in the garden, her face shaded by a gypsy hat.

'You disapprove, don't you?' Landry reined in and forced her to do the same. 'Well, so do I, but I am doing my best by them both. I seduced Carrie, I cannot deny it, and she bore my child. I have acknowledged Katie and I keep them both. They lack for nothing.'

'Do – do you still visit her?' The question slipped out before Beth realized it was in her mind. Heaven help her, she was jealous of Carrie Markham!

'No.' He regarded her for a long moment. 'Beth? Do you think me shabby?'

'You, sir, are a gentleman, and no matter how many children you sire, you will remain a gentleman. Carrie and her like are not only left with proof of your profligacy, but they lose their reputations as well. And Katie will have the stigma of illegitimacy.'

'If you imagine Devon to be littered with my by-blows, you are gravely mistaken. Katie is my only child. She is well cared for, has tutors and is being taught how to be a lady. At the moment she wants to stay with her mother at the lodge, and I am not monster enough to force her to come to me instead. When she is of age I will see that she has goodly sum, so she will attract suitable offers of marriage. If I marry and have legitimate children, she will be treated on an equal footing with them. As for Carrie's reputation, you have my word that she had lost it before I entered her bed. Having a child by me has been her salvation, because I will always care for her. Beth, I do not wish this to change things between us. I could have lied.'

'I'd already observed the likeness between Katie and you.'

'Then I'm relieved I chose to be truthful. Beth, I swear that I have done all in my power to be fair and kind to Carrie, and I love Katie as a father should love his child. I don't visit Carrie now, nor have I since Katie was born. I have no other mistresses dotted around the countryside, nor do I keep one in London. I am interested in you, and only you. Please say you believe me.' He leaned across to put a hand over hers, and she knew that it would be unfair to judge him; there were few gentlemen who had not reaped at least one crop of wild oats. It was clear he was treating Carrie and Katie well, and he'd been open about it as soon as she'd asked. What more could she expect of any man? His hand was warm through their gloves, and his thumb moved gently against her palm. 'I have never desired a woman as I desire you, Beth,' he said softly. 'My heart, body and soul sparked into harmony when I saw you that first time.'

Her heart rushed with excitement as she allowed her sensuality full rein. She didn't want to stop, and was determined to look past Guy's image to see Landry, in the hope that Guy would become more indistinct before fading altogether. But a stirring of guilt made her glance toward Harriet, who still didn't appear to have noticed them. 'I'd prefer to speak in more privacy,' she said.

He followed her glance. 'Very well, we'll ride on, but only if you assure me you do not harbour secret fears that Harriet Bellamy has some claim to wear my ring.'

'I don't fear it.' *I just know she loves you.*

'Good. Come on then.' He urged Rollo away at a slow canter.

Chapter Fifteen

*B*eth guided Snowy after Landry, and soon caught him up. They rode side by side through Haldane, causing quite a stir among those villagers who saw them. Within the hour news of Mr Haldane's ride with Miss Mannacott would spread everywhere. Apart from the area around the green, the few village streets were winding and narrow, with old stone cottages, several small shops and two taverns. And there was a smithy that again brought Jake into Beth's thoughts. She should have taken him into her confidence and told him she was leaving; it was the least he deserved. Now there were things she ought to say to Landry, but didn't dare to. She was a thief living under a false name, and if caught might also be charged with Joshua's murder. Common sense dictated she should keep herself to herself, and abandon all thought of taking this man, no matter how gallant and charming, as her lover. Far wiser to continue dreaming the impossible, that Guy was her devoted lover, and everything in her world was perfect.

Landry spoke. 'A penny for your thoughts,' he said, as they began to ride out of the village, past some fine new houses and a handsome classical villa that commanded panoramic views of the Bristol Channel.

She struggled to collect herself. 'I – I was thinking that Haldane seems to be enjoying new popularity,' she said, knowing how unconvincing it sounded. She gestured toward the villa.

'It's a new country home for the Dowager Lady Bettersden, an elderly lady who was my mother's childhood friend. She has always resided in London, but is soon to come here instead. I think she grows tired of the glittering lives of the *ton*.'

'Whose are the other new houses?'

'Mine, to be let to those who appreciate natural and picturesque scenery.'

'But excluding radical poets?' she answered mischievously.

He answered with a laugh. 'Especially not such alarming fellows!' He kicked his heels to urge Rollo faster.

The valley undulated gently for two miles or so, descending gradually

to low oak-clad cliffs around a rocky bay. Nothing was walled or culti-
vated now, there was just wild common land grazed by sheep and cattle.
A hare bounded away from a tuft of heather, and a rare black adder
basked on a flat, sunny rock. Blue butterflies fluttered over vivid yellow
gorse, and grasshoppers sang all around. Thyme and heather flavoured
the air, with the background freshness of the sea to invigorate the soul.
Sandstone and shale boulders were scattered on the grass as if by a giant
hand, while others were balanced on top of one another in strange natural
formations. Stone rested upon stone, slab upon slab, rising in bare crags,
pinnacles, towers and castellated turrets that resembled the ruins of a lost
civilization. It was a dry and desolate place, yet so hauntingly beautiful
and romantic that Beth could well imagine how it inspired poets like
Shelley. Then she looked at the summit of Haldane Cliffs and saw wild
goats. Surely not! But yes, there they were, billies, nannies and kids, all
agile and surefooted in their precipitous surroundings. Astonished, she
reined in. '*Goats?*'

Landry rode back to join her. 'The scourge of Haldane. Seventy-five of
their ancestors were recorded in the Domesday Book, and there are about
that many here now, and they're not well liked because their favourite
sport is to butt unwary sheep off the cliffs. Not an endearing trait.'

They rode slowly on toward a higgledy-piggledy tower of massive rocks
that rose like a huge crumbling lighthouse in the centre of the valley. A
buzzard soared around the summit, its screeching cries echoing along the
slopes. The horses slowed to a walk as they passed by, and Beth could hear
the sea breeze playing among the rocks. Beyond, where the valley dipped
again toward the rocky bay, they were confronted by the remains of an
ancient stone circle, some of the sarsens still standing, others lying on the
ground. Landry glanced at Beth. 'This is claimed by some to be evidence
of druidic occupation. There are supposed to have been pagan ceremonies
here, with human sacrifices hurled from the cliffs.'

'Death from the cliffs appears to be rather a risk hereabouts, what with
goat-butted sheep, lovelorn maidens turning into mermaids and now
human sacrifices.'

'Dower House tenants are perfectly safe,' he assured her.

'I sincerely hope so.'

'Well, what the circle may once have looked like is no longer known,
because over the centuries it has been plundered of its stones. My family
isn't blameless. The two tallest sarsens were removed by my great-grand-
father and used as gateposts at the original hall. That house didn't meet
with my grandfather's aspirations, so he demolished it and built anew,
keeping the old gates.' He gathered the reins again. 'Come on, we'll ride
to the top of Oak Bay, and then come back to take lunch. Well, more a
picnic,' he explained, 'at a particular spot with matchless views over the
sea. Up there.' He pointed back toward the top of Haldane Cliffs.

Beth was a little alarmed. 'Among those murderous goats?'

'We'll come to no harm.'

They rode on toward the bay, where waves broke around the rocks below, and excited gulls swooped upon hovering kestrels. There were sails out on the water, and across the channel they could see the crowns of the Brecon Beacons shimmering amid the inland heat haze of Wales. After pausing for a while to rest the horses, Landry grinned at Beth. 'The time is right for a cool white Chablis from a crystal glass. Come, let me lead you to my lair.' Returning past the stone circle and tower of rocks, he turned Rollo toward the foot of the slope behind Haldane Cliffs, and reined in by a knot of golden gorse bushes around a rock-shaded dip. Beth expected this to be where they would eat, but when Landry dismounted and came around to help her down as well, she realized there was no hamper or any sign of the promised refreshment. He indicated a narrow path that led up toward the cliff top. 'Our feast waits up there, where there is a secret little nook to which I have been coming since I was a child. It is perfect for a picnic, and you will be the first person I have ever taken there.'

'I'm honoured.'

'Indeed so, Beth, because you are very special.' He held his arms up, and she slid down into them. She was in his embrace for a second, alive to the contours of his body, and the fact that his lips were close enough to kiss. So much had happened to her since her father died, and she'd only felt safe and loved in Jake's arms. She needed to be loved, both physically and mentally, and Landry Haldane was here, now, with desire in his eyes. Would there *really* be any harm done if he were her lover?

He took her hand to help her up the slope, and they were almost halfway when she saw an antler lying under a clump of bright mauve heather. Landry smiled as she bent to retrieve it. 'Now you'll have good luck, for they are considered very fortunate. Let me carry it for you.' They reached the top to find the Bristol Channel spread matchlessly before them. The cliff fell sheer to the water some 600 feet below, so Landry made sure Beth kept well back from the edge as he guided her between two lichen-covered rocks. Then she saw the secret place, a small grassy hollow that was open to the sea, but otherwise protected by the cliff. From it one could look right across to Wales, as well as south-west along the edge of the cliffs toward Oak Bay, which was hidden by a small bluff. Beth sat down and made herself comfortable against a rock, and as she gazed over the sea, it was as if she were flying.

Landry was so relaxed with her that he took off his coat, undid his neck cloth and unbuttoned his brocade waistcoat, which flouted etiquette. But then so did an intimate picnic *à deux*. 'I came up here at dawn to prepare everything,' he explained, indicating a hamper tucked carefully in the shade, and the bottle of Chablis submerged in a little mossy pool of rainwater and dew beneath an overhanging tuft of thick grass and heather. He grinned sheepishly. 'You see, I schemed to be alone with you like this.'

Their gaze met, and the air became charged again. She was aware of the paler skin where he'd shaved off his moustache and side-whiskers, of the sunlight casting shadows through his eyelashes, and vulnerability of his throat; he was aware of her dainty beauty, the sweetness of her mouth, the mystery in her eyes, and the allure that seemed to pervade the very air around her. He wanted her so much that his body threatened to make his desire embarrassingly clear.

'This is happening too quickly,' she breathed, unable to look away from him.

He smiled. 'I've been waiting for you all my life, Beth, but you have my word that I will not do anything you do not wish.' But she wished so much, and couldn't trust herself to be strong. Or sensible. He took two stemmed glasses from the hamper, retrieved the wine bottle and set about opening it. Within moments he'd handed her a full glass. 'I'll wager wine will never have tasted as good before,' he said, sitting next to her.

No wine could be as good as a glass of Moselle handed to her by Sir Guy Valmer. She raised her glass. 'Your health.'

'To us.'

Their eyes met again, and she smiled. It was a signal and she knew it, but she had already slipped beyond the point of no return. Let fate take its course. As she sipped the wine, he dragged the hamper close and opened it. Suddenly she found herself back in Guy's carriage again. The illusion was gone in a moment, but not before she'd heard his voice. *Eat, I beg you, for I cannot bear the thought of your hunger.*

The cook at the hall had prepared an excellent picnic of ham, salad and some slices of pork pie, to be followed by fresh apricot tart. There was also a selection of delicious fruit, including a pineapple from the hall's pinery. They applied themselves to the picnic, talking idly of this and that, and then Landry poured their second glass of wine. 'Well, you know my shocking past, Beth,' he observed, leaning back again, 'but I know nothing of yours, not even where you lived before coming to the Dower House.' He smiled. 'I want to know all about you, you see.'

'I came originally from Gloucestershire.'

'I know the county a little. Where in particular?'

'Nowhere in particular, various places,' she replied vaguely, and then headed him off. 'How much are you asking for Snowy?'

He smiled at the change of subject. 'Keep him for a while, and we'll discuss prices later if he pleases you.' He sipped the wine and studied the view for a moment before looking at her again. 'Beth, something must be fixed for you to meet local society. Believe me, they'll be as curious about you as you must be about them.'

Her vulnerability returned. 'I'd rather not. I don't care for the social whirl.'

'We don't whirl hereabouts,' he said with a grin, 'rather do we turn a little now and then, and that with rustic simplicity.'

She had to laugh. 'What a picture you paint.'

'Beth, if you don't appear in society, it will be talked of.'

'I know.' She sighed.

'You're not alone; you have me, and Harriet will be to hand as well.'

'There'll certainly be talk if *you* escort me,' she reminded him.

'Then I will see to it that you are chaperoned by Harriet and her father. Nothing could be more proper than that.' His gaze was lazy upon her. 'You fobbed me off earlier when I asked about Gloucestershire, but I refuse to be left in complete ignorance. Beth, you must at least tell me something about yourself.'

'There is nothing to tell.' *There's nothing I dare tell.*

He raised an eyebrow. 'That cannot be so. Forgive me, Beth, but I'm consumed with uncertainty. You assured me you have no husband, but is there is someone else?'

'No, there isn't.'

'But there has been?' he pressed.

'Why do you think that?'

'Beth, you are a beautiful woman, and, forgive me again, you are at ease in male company in a way that tells me you've been admitted to the great secret.'

'Secret?'

'You've made love. You still have an innocence, Beth, a delightful air of not yet having been brought to full life by shared passion, but you are no longer a virgin either.'

Colour suffused her cheeks. How well he described her, she thought, astonished that he'd perceived so much. 'Will you think less of me if I admit it to be so?' she asked, almost wishing he would recoil, and give her a reason to depart in high dudgeon and thus save herself from her desires.

'So there *has* been someone?' he pressed.

'Yes.' Jake smiled in her memory, but Guy could not be denied either.

'Does he still matter to you?'

She shook her head dishonestly. 'It's all in the past.'

'Is that the truth?'

'Were you truthful when you said you no longer visit Carrie Markham?'

He smiled. 'Yes. And I know you do the same.' He set his glass aside, and then leaned across the hamper to take hers as well. When both were safely propped on the grass, he pushed the hamper away and pulled her down on to the mossy ground. Still holding her hands, he leaned over her. 'Look at me, Beth.' She obeyed, tingles of pleasure dancing through her as his thumbs caressed her palms. 'I don't care what is in your past,' he said, 'provided there is no one who can return to your life and take you from me.'

'There isn't anyone,' she insisted.

'If you wish me to stop now, you have only to say,' he whispered, gathering her gently to him.

Stop? No, she wanted to plunge over the precipice into carnal bliss. A heady blend of excitement and apprehension consumed her, and her flesh and senses thrilled almost unbearably as she raised her parted lips. He cupped her face in his hands and kissed her long and slow. His mouth was strong and yet pliant, commanding and yet teasing, and moved richly to and fro over hers. Her skin quivered as his thumbs caressed, persuaded and tempted her with sexual promise and, as she felt control slipping away from her, she made no effort to call it back. She wanted desire to carry her away with utter and complete gratification, so she returned his kiss with a fire that seemed to burn white-hot within her. The taste of his mouth was ambrosia, the food of the gods, and his body was strong and vibrant. He smelled of the moors and the ocean, of heather and the onshore breeze, and tasted as sweet and fresh as sun-warmed strawberries. She exulted in his weight and hard contours pressing against her, and remembered rhythms returned as she undulated erotically against his arousal. He wanted her as much as she wanted him, and the knowledge intensified her craving. She felt wild and uninhibited, an untamed she-creature that must mate at the height of the sun or the full of the moon. The stone circles in the valley behind them seemed to whisper to her, urging her on, denying her the wit or will to call a halt to what was happening. Her pent-up sexual craving now found release in a savage coupling that was the swiftest route to ecstasy.

Landry's ardour was spurred on by the intensity of her response. She neither gave him the chance to be gentle nor invited such consideration. If he was shocked by the eager fury of her lovemaking, he gave no sign. He matched her kiss for kiss, intimate caress for intimate caress, fumbling with her jacket buttons in order to reach the soft mounds of breasts that waited to be freed so that he could draw her hardened nipples into his mouth. She shivered as delicious sensations quivered through her, and her body stretched up beneath him. Her hands roamed over his back. How strong and warm he was through the rich silk of his shirt, and how exciting. Then her hands moved down his back, and for a moment she held his buttocks, pulling his hips against her. Shivers of joy scattered over her as she felt the urgent outline of his masculinity, hard and potent, kept from her only by the few layers of their clothes. How soon it would be released now, and at last she would feel the most vital part of a man within her. She kissed his hair as he nuzzled her breasts. He raised his head and kissed her on the mouth. His face was flushed, his eyes dark with desire, and his hair dishevelled by her caresses. He was ready to take her, his excitement such that it strained the front of his breeches to a peak. He rolled aside to undo the falls, but her impatience was too great and she did it for him, in order to fondle him before he entered her. His erect member sprang out the moment the breeches were undone, and she groaned with delight at its hardness. He was so ready for her that he might explode at any moment. As she smoothed her palm over the tip, he gasped and rolled to straddle her again. Her thighs parted eagerly, and her riding habit skirt opened as if designed for just this. Slowly he lowered himself between her legs, and electric sensations engulfed her as she felt him at the entrance to her body. He slid forward, pushing in until he filled her completely. Rapture overwhelmed her, and she sucked in her breath to prolong the moment. This was what she wanted so much, what she needed so much. Ever since that last time with Jake, she had become prey to these yearnings. Now she wanted to cry and laugh at the same time, but most of all she wanted him to raise her to the heights of utter elation. But it was Guy who held her. Reality disappeared, and she was dreaming once more. With Guy. Guy.

She was a wild being again, writhing beneath him, clenching him within her, sucking and nibbling whatever part of him she could reach. His strokes were long and deliberate, but he thrust harder and harder as all control left them both. He drove himself in with a force that shook them. She clawed his back, squirming against him, kissing his throat, his neck and his shoulder. Torrents of ravishment began to flood through her, melting her flesh and burning her soul. She could feel him coming too, and as they became weightless she almost cried out Guy's name. They clung together as they rode the tide, and when the waves washed them ashore, they lay together as the pounding of their united hearts gradually subsided.

I'll find you again, Beth Tremoille, I'll find you! Guy's voice spoke within her, like a distant church bell through an autumn mist, and with it came not only guilt that she had used Landry to quench the power of her desire for Guy, but that she had done so with such animal abandonment. She hadn't merely surrendered to Landry's advances, she'd been so ferocious, intense and unstoppable that she'd displayed all the talents of a whore. Where now Miss Mannacott, lady tenant of the Dower House?

Landry drew out of her, and rolled on to his back. He smiled and reached for her hand. 'Beth, I didn't know a woman could be so—'

'Depraved?' she finished for him. Her face was now branded with mortification. How could she have been so licentious? So utterly unprincipled and immoral? What did he really think now? How could he possibly respect a woman who behaved as she had? One kiss and she had become a wanton slut.

'No, Beth, not depraved,' he answered, his fingers tightening over hers, but she pulled her hand away and scrambled to her feet. She was shaking so much she could barely button up her jacket, but somehow she managed. 'Beth, for pity's sake!' Realizing she was going to flee, he got up as well, pushing himself back into his breeches and trying to straighten his clothes.

She hesitated agitatedly, the tears now wet on her cheeks. 'I've just allowed myself to behave so appallingly that I cannot even look you in the eyes.'

'Please, Beth, there is no need for this.'

'There is every need if I am ever to hold my head up again.' She retrieved her hat and pinned it back into place on her untidy but still netted curls.

'Please don't run away,' he begged, but she started to make her way out of the little hollow. She was silhouetted briefly against the sky, and then had gone. Landry breathed in deeply, and then exhaled, trying to collect his thoughts. 'Oh, Beth,' he whispered. All he'd been trying to say was that he hadn't realized a woman could enjoy the sexual act to such a degree. He had just experienced the most magnificent lovemaking of his life. Her eagerness had released something in him, and the satisfaction was such that it had been like his first time. Perhaps it *was* his first time; everything that had gone before was a sorry imitation of what he had with Beth Mannacott. She had electrified his life, transformed it, set him so by the ears that he hardly knew himself. But it was already finished.

His glance fell on the antler, which was still propped against the rock. Luck? With a curse he hurled it over the cliff into the sea far below.

Chapter Sixteen

As Beth fled in shame, her stepmother was no happier. Jane's marriage to Thomas had already turned sour because he'd cast off his cloak and she finally saw him for the irredeemable maggot he really was. The scales had fallen from her eyes at last. Too late, of course, because she would lose everything if she left him now. All she could do was contemplate how sweet it would be to turn back the clock, never have donned her wedding clothes, never driven to Gloucester Cathedral and certainly never uttered those imprisoning vows before the altar. Now she was jailed in her own house, and her guard was an embittered, drunken pig who had legal possession of all that was hers, and felt free to treat her with cruelty and contempt. Beth would laugh at such poetic justice.

Jane sat in a window seat, trying to enjoy the afternoon sunshine. A volume of Lesage's *Gil Blas* lay open on her lap, but she wasn't reading. The August day was hot and hazy, and everything down in the vale shimmered like a mirage. How breathless it would be down there. Jake Mannacott crossed her mind. The Lord help him if he was in the forge on a day like this. Even up here on the hills it was stifling. With luck there would soon be a storm to freshen the air. What a strange summer this had been, sometimes so cold and wet it was like March, sometimes so humid as to be unbearable. And there were the astonishing sunsets and sunrises.

Her mind moved back to her unhappy situation. She had soon learned how real was Thomas's fear of water, because he had insisted on quitting Whitend to come up here. He ruined Tremoille House for her, ruined *everything* for her, and his behaviour was so irrational that the servants sniggered behind his back. His dread of water even extended to ponds, about which he displayed such abhorrence as to seem suitable for incarceration in an asylum. The marriage was descending into Hades, and she already felt the flames around her feet. He was in the room with her now, slumped despondently in a comfortable chair, staring at a miniature of Esmond on the over-mantel. A glass of cognac was to hand, as it always was from breakfast onward, and he hadn't spoken in over an hour. He just sat there, staring at Esmond. What was he thinking? Nothing good, that was for sure, and whatever it was boded ill for his hapless wife. She hated him. After adoring him ever since her early teens, now she wished she had never set eyes on him. She wanted a red-blooded man of constant passion; she had Thomas, Lord Welland, God rot him. At last she couldn't bear the silence any longer. 'You've hardly said a word all day, Thomas.'

'I'll give you a number of words. Copper's down from a hundred and eighty pounds a ton to only eighty, and iron from twenty a ton to only eight. All this and *still* the damned government leaves income tax on the statute books. That limp-wristed scoundrel Pitt promised it was only for the duration of the war. Ten per cent of everything! The government owns a wheel of every damned blasted vehicle on the roads! *And* it takes three-pence ha'penny on every fivepenny pot of beer.'

She groaned inside. 'I know your financial position has been affected, but surely not as much as it affects those with less.'

It was an error of judgement, for he erupted from his chair and stomped furiously to a drawer, which he unlocked with shaking hands. He snatched the sheaf of documents lying inside, and strode over to her, waving them aloft before dropping them on her lap. 'It could be, madam my wife, that I too will soon have much less than now, eh? In short, I may soon only be master of what was mine anyway. Is that not so?'

How she wished she'd kept her mouth shut. 'I don't understand, Thomas.'

'Don't you? Well, I've been thinking about how Tremoille gained this property, and about your insistence that you are his sole heir. Is Beth the real heir after all?'

'I've already told you—'

'But you're a lying bitch,' he interrupted bluntly. 'Don't test my temper, Jane, because I'm in no mood! Let me begin with this house. Does Sir Guy Valmer stand a chance of reclaiming it?'

She flushed and got up from the window seat to put the documents and Lesage on a nearby table. 'Be reasonable, Thomas. Esmond had this estate *before* I married him! It was because his lands abutted yours that I chose him in the first place!'

'You knew him long before that, my dear,' he said menacingly. 'I *know* you were involved, and unless you tell me now, so help me I'll beat it out of you.'

'Thomas, there was nothing illegal about it. Esmond told me he settled Sir Richard Valmer's gambling debts in return for this house and estate. Sir Richard accepted the offer, knowing his wife was heir to the vast fortune of an elderly relative close to his deathbed. Sir Richard didn't *need* this house, just the money.'

Thomas looked at her. 'The rumours all concern a fishy royal flush, but you expect me to believe this?'

'I've told you what I know. I believe it to be true.'

'Madam, you wouldn't know the truth if it jumped up and bit your tits off!' he snarled, clenching his fists until the knuckles turned white. 'There are two packs in this, a pack of lies and a pack of cards!'

'No, Thomas. Sir Richard didn't want the *monde*, particularly his wife, to know he had numerous duns on his track. He wanted the deal to be done without the truth getting out. It was preferable for him to pretend he'd had one lapse at the gaming tables, not that he'd been dim-witted enough to squander his wealth over several years.'

He gazed at her, his eyes small and porcine, and then he grunted and went to replenish his glass. Her heart sank. He hadn't finished yet. He swirled the cognac, sniffed the bouquet and then drained it in a noisy gulp, before slamming the glass on the table. 'Which leaves Beth. Does she have a claim upon her father's estate?'

'No.' She returned his gaze a little wearily. 'Thomas, how many times must I tell you that there isn't, and never was, a second will.'

'That had better be so, my dear, because if not I'll tear your tongue out.' With that he stomped from the room, bawling to Bolton to have his horse saddled.

Robert Lloyd shifted his position, his riding crop tapping against the back of his boot, his top hat crooked on his blond hair as he waited in the Frampney forge. A groom was with him, holding the reins of a fine red bay thoroughbred. Robert wasn't sure if Jake had seen him or not, but suspected he had. A faint smile lurked on the young man's lips. Mannacott needed a little reminding of his station in life.

Jake continued to hammer the glowing poker, his body gleaming with sweat in the fiery heat. He was deliberately taking his time because he'd disliked what he'd heard of the young man even before the incident two weeks before with that fool Johnno and his wagon. Rosalind had been taken severely to task for riding home with the squire's lecherous son. She hadn't come to harm, but she so easily might, and for that she'd been punished and forbidden to go outside at all. Until today. And now here was the strutting young hosebird to stir up the memory. Jake thrust the poker into the fire before turning. 'You want me, Master Robert?'

'The nag's lame, take a look at it.' Robert indicated the horse's off-foreleg. The sunlight lay brightly across his hair, and its unusual length framed his handsome face as he watched Jake wipe the dirt away from the animal's hoof and rub a dirty thumb slowly over a hairline crack that split the horny wall.

'Sand crack,' Jake said, releasing the hoof. 'I can burn it from going further, but this one's out of any racing for a while. Needs a new shoe too. Best take it off and let him rest until the crack's grown out.'

'No. He's racing next week. Put a new shoe on.'

'Master Robert, I'm a smith. I look after horses; I don't patch them up carelessly when they're lame. I won't put a new shoe on for you to race him and leave him fit for nothing but feeding to dogs.'

The groom's eyes widened and Robert's blue eyes were chill. His hand tightened on his riding crop, but he didn't raise it. 'Are you defying me, Mannacott?'

Jake wasn't intimidated because the horse was the squire's, not Robert's. 'Yes, sir, I am. Race another horse,' he said, prompting the groom's jaw to drop.

'So,' Robert breathed furiously, 'you're not only disobeying me, you're also taking it upon yourself to *order* me to ride another horse?'

Jake returned to the half-finished poker, picking it up with his tongs and preparing to hammer it again. 'I treat Squire Lloyd's horses with care, Master Robert. It *is* your father's horse, isn't it?'

Robert's face reddened and for a moment he hesitated, clearly of a mind to give Jake a thrashing, but then he thought again. The smith was big and very strong. Better to get him another way. 'You'll be sorry for this, Mannacott,' he said, his voice shaking with suppressed rage, and then turned on his heel to stride away.

Jake spat into the fire. 'Damned snotty hosebird!' he muttered contemptuously. Hell would freeze over before Jake Mannacott accorded Robert Lloyd any respect.

The groom hesitated before leading the horse out. 'You've done it now, Mannacott. He'll get you good and proper.'

'I'm a match for him.'

'Oh, he won't take you on face to face, he's too smart for that, but whatever he does, you'll be sorry.'

The sun was beginning to make long shadows over the meadow that evening as Rosalind lay on her stomach on the bank of the stream, between two clumps of elder, watching small fish dart among the waving fronds of green weed. She could see the evening sky in the water, not the bright flawless blue of a normal August, but oddly pink and salmon. Her purpose in coming out had been to gather elderberries for Phoebe's wine-making, and two fully laden wicker baskets were on the grass beside her. Now she was lingering, enjoying the open air, the gentle stream, and the tall grass and flowers that would disappear tomorrow when the meadow was mown for hay. It was good just to lie there, listening to the grasshoppers and skylarks, and the gurgle of the water among reeds. She sighed comfortably. The water mill clanked downstream, and upstream, just beyond the tall redbrick wall that bounded the manor grounds, the doves cooed and flapped around Squire Lloyd's dovecote. Here, midway between both, she was in her own small world. If she sat up and looked across the stream, she would be able to see the chimneys of mad Lord

Welland's house at Whitend. He and his new wife were up at Beth's beloved home. Rosalind hoped Beth knew, and was cut to the quick. She rolled over and looked up at the sky. Two weeks of being kept in the house had been stifling, but it would have been much worse if Dad knew she'd let Robert Lloyd kiss her. Well, no one else had seen what had happened, so Dad would never find out. She thought of Robert all the time, and of what it would be like if he were her lover.

A dog barked somewhere in the manor grounds, and she sat up hopefully, because she knew it was Robert's Irish setter. For a moment she couldn't see anything, but then someone came out of the postern gate in the wall. It was Robert! He'd dispensed with a coat and his shirt was very white against the pale blue of his waistcoat. He wasn't wearing a hat, and the slanting sun blushed on his unmistakable hair as he paused to make safe the rifle over his arm. His riding breeches sheathed his hips and legs in a manner that was quite indecent, or so Phoebe said. Rosalind disagreed, because she liked to see that one part of him that she could not put from her mind. Tight smallclothes made it stand out, a compelling shape that concentrated her thoughts like nothing else. It caused a strange feeling between her legs, a needful sort of feeling that took her over.

She watched him stroll along the wall, the setter at his heels. He was hated in the village. Jamie's sister had killed herself in the mill sluice when Robert denied going with her. That was why Jamie hated him so much. But why should Robert say he had if he hadn't? Other girls lied about Robert because they didn't want the world to know they'd parted their legs for labourers or farm workers. No, far better to say it was the squire's son who got them that way. Rosalind wouldn't hear ill of him. He'd been honourable with her that day coming back from Gloucester, and she believed in speaking as she found. Her heart skipped a beat as he reached the stream and then turned toward her. He was *bound* to see her! What would happen? Would he be bold enough to kiss her again? Oh, how glad she was that she was wearing her rose-coloured gown. She glanced around swiftly, fearful that someone else was near, but there was no one, so she lay down on her stomach again, pretending to be watching the stream. She heard him coming through the grass, and the setter's regularly panting breaths, but still she gazed into the water as if unaware of his approach.

'Good evening, Rosalind.'

She gasped and twisted around, being sure to do it gracefully, with the swell of her virginal breasts displayed to advantage by her gown's low neckline. 'Oh! Good evening, Master Robert.' She knew her face was flushed and that she sounded green and nervous, but at least she could use the proper voice Beth had taught her.

He smiled, his gaze moving slowly over her and then studied her breasts. 'My,' he murmured, 'what delights one finds when out of an evening.' He rested the rifle up against one of the elder bushes and ordered the setter to guard it, and then lay on his stomach on the grass beside her to gaze into the stream. 'What were you looking at?'

'I was just watching the fish,' she said, remembering their last meeting, and the things he'd done.

'Fish? They're only tiddlers.' He grinned at her.

'Well, it's only a little stream,' she replied.

'Ah, how she defends them.' He turned on to his side and propped himself on an elbow to look at her. 'Sometimes you speak remarkably well for a blacksmith's daughter. Your father is so Gloucester he could be rolled down Cooper's Hill like a cheese, but you have a much more correct grasp of English. Who taught you? I know it wasn't your father, so who? Your mother?'

'Yes,' she answered, rolling to face him. 'She was from a good family.'

'Really?' He raised an eyebrow. 'And that family is?'

'The Tremoilles,' she answered, hating herself for choosing that name.

'And which Tremoille was your mother?' he enquired disbelievingly.

'She was the daughter of the late Mr Tremoille's cousin.' No one could disprove *that* on the spur of the moment, she thought a little smugly.

'How disappointing to be a mere Mannacott.'

'It would have done me no good to be a Tremoille, for I'd have been thrown out penniless by the new Lady Welland, like my cousin Elizabeth.'

He searched her face. 'You certainly know your Tremoilles,' he murmured, 'and I find I'm actually prepared to believe your claims. What a shame you only have that one gown to set off your well-bred beauty.'

'How do you know I only have one gown? I might have a whole wardrobe.'

He laughed. 'Do you? I confess that if that's true, I'm not only amazed you live in rooms at the forge, I'm *astounded* not to have seen you in a different colour of the rainbow every day.'

She plucked at the grass. 'Well, maybe I don't have a wardrobe yet, but I could. I have money my mother left me.'

'Don't ladle it on too thickly, my dear, for it spoils the flavour.'

'You were wrong about the Tremoilles, so perhaps you're wrong now.'

'I was wrong to kiss you that time as well,' he pointed out softly.

'Yes, you were,' she replied, with rather ridiculous prudishness.

'I didn't notice you protesting too much.'

'Are you laughing at me?' she demanded.

'Why on earth would I do that?' He smiled again, and drew a finger against the hair at her temple. 'You're very pretty when you're angry.' He traced a gentle line to the corner of her mouth, then tarried, pushing just a little between her lips before moving back across her cheek to follow her jaw. A torrent of excitement began to pour through her, and she could feel her breasts tightening until their hard tips showed through her flimsy bodice.

He saw too. 'Oh, Rosalind, I do believe you like me more than you should.' He lowered his hand to undo the drawstring of her bodice. The rose material fell away and her upturned breasts were revealed. Oh, how delightful they were, he thought, so very young and untouched, their nipples sweetly aroused. These village girls were all so fresh and unwary, so tight and satisfying. Now his fingertip slid over her nipple, and he heard her breath snatch with pleasure. He smiled. This was going to be a very pleasant interlude – and such sweet revenge on her insolent giant of a father.

For Rosalind the flood of desire was almost too much to bear. Her legs shook and her mouth was dry. She couldn't stop herself from looking down at his loins. The interesting mound had changed, and was now so rigid and long that his breeches strained over it. He knew where she was looking, and caught her hand again. 'Have you ever touched a man there before?'

'No,' she whispered.

'Would you like to?'

She could hardly breathe. Her heart pounded like a mad thing, and she felt as if none of this could really be happening, but she nodded. He put her fingers over the hardness, and her breath escaped on a soft shudder. 'Would you like to see it?' he asked quietly.

Her eyes lifted to meet his. 'I'm afraid,' she whispered.

'No one need ever know.' He lay on his back again to undo his falls, but held them in place until he was on his side again. 'Now then,' he whispered, reaching for her hand.

She held her breath as he allowed his quivering erection to be seen. Closer and closer he guided her hand, until, finally, he could press her palm against it. She was speechless with excitement and wonder. It was too big for her. Surely it could not possibly fit inside, and yet babies were much, much bigger. He was so hard too, yet also felt warm and silky. And the tip was moist, with more moisture glistening its way out into the fading evening light. Muscles she did not know she had began to quake uncontrollably between her legs. Emboldened, she clasped him to explore with unsteady fingers.

'Do you really want to feel it?' he breathed. 'Properly, where it should be?'

'I shouldn't.'

No, but you're going to, he thought, easing himself closer to her, and pulling her skirts up. The gown was all she was wearing, she didn't even have stockings. All the better to do as he wanted. He pushed her gently on to her back again, and then leaned over her. 'Let me show you what it's all about, Rosalind. I promise it won't hurt, and that I will pleasure you.' He bent his mouth to her right breast, and sucked the nipple. She writhed beneath him, so excited that she cried out. His hand pressed over her mouth. 'No noise now, sweeting, for we don't want the village to find us, do we?' He moved further over her, so that his erection was pressed to the soft forest of hair at her loins. She moaned and squirmed, so swept along by desire that she hardly knew what she was doing. He kissed her mouth, pushing his tongue inside and sliding it voluptuously against hers. She responded eagerly, doing the same to him. He wanted to prolong the pleasure, but he wasn't good at that. Once cocker was ready, there was no holding back.

Shifting himself down her a little, he put his hand down between her legs. She started with surprise, but he caressed the entrance to the virginal shrine, where all was all warm, moist and prepared for desecration. He parted her legs and savoured the knowledge that he was the first to be here, the very first. No other man had been admitted to this secret place. He pushed slowly forward, at last reaching the threshold, and sweet resistance. She was almost wild with passion her hands roaming over his back, her legs as wide as she could so that he could come in. He couldn't control himself any more, and with a grunt forced himself into her. She gave a cry of pain, but then he was thrusting in and out and the pain ceased to matter. Amazing sensations shuddered over her, and she exulted in the joy of his urgent strokes. Faster and faster, harder and harder, until suddenly he came, pulsing in to her and collapsing on to her at the same time. His whole body twitched and she could feel the pulsing gradually slowing and, as it did so, he began to soften within her. She clung to him, holding him tightly as waves of pleasure engulfed her too. He began to pull away, but she wouldn't let him. Her body moved richly against him, her muscles clenching and unclenching around his used virility. He was soft now, but still long and thick, and she could feel him inside her, lying snug. She was one with him; for this wonderful moment she and Robert Lloyd were one living thing. She tightened and relaxed her newly discovered muscles several times, just to feel him more. The hunger had gone, and she was warm, sated and happy.

He pulled away again, and this time she couldn't stop him. Rolling over on to his back, he began do up his breeches again, and then got to his feet. As he reached for the rifle she realized he was just going to walk away. 'Robert?' She touched his thigh.

He was cold with her. 'It's Master Robert to you, my dear, so don't presume to touch what you'll never have again.' He moved beyond her reach.

'Don't touch? I don't understand.' Humiliation seeped acidly into her veins.

He gave a slight laugh. 'My dear, I've had what you had to offer, and it was an agreeable few minutes, but that is the end of it.'

'I thought you liked me.'

'I'd decided to have you, yes, but not only to scratch an itch. Your father was impertinent to me today, and now I've had my revenge.' Robert enjoyed being cruel.

The air seemed to echo sickeningly. 'You did this because of my *father*?'

'I fear so. In part, anyway, but I thank you for making it such a pleasure.'

She was too devastated to answer. Only now, when it was too late, she realized that everything she'd heard of him was true. How stupid she'd been to sneer at those other girls. Now he'd tricked her as he had them, and stolen that which could never be replaced. She felt defiled, and so small and foolish that she could only turn her head away in shame. He clicked his tongue to the setter, and then she heard the rustle of his retreating steps through the meadow grass. When he'd gone, she curled up into a ball and sobbed her heartbreak. What a gull she'd been, believing it to be so beautiful, so meant to be, when all the time he was just using her. And now she couldn't even confide in Phoebe, because that was bound to mean her dad finding out.

At last she could no longer postpone going home. Phoebe would be wondering where she was. Praying she could conceal what happened, she sat up to dip her hem into the stream to pat her reddened eyes. If anyone noticed she'd been crying, she'd say a branch had swung back across her face. Getting up, she reluctantly picked up the baskets to make her way home through the colour-drenched evening.

The forge was quiet because Jake and Matty had gone to the George and Dragon for a jar, but Rosalind still had to run the gauntlet of Phoebe in the kitchen. The latter looked up from her crocheting. 'Where on earth have you been for so long, Rozzie? Surely elderberries don't take that much gathering?'

'Oh, I just sat by the stream for a while.' Putting the baskets on the kitchen table, Rosalind hoped her reply was in a light and carefree tone.

But Phoebe looked sharply over her spectacles. 'What's up?'

'Up? Nothing.' Rosalind began to walk to the door to the steep staircase.

'Not so fast, miss. Let's have a look at you.'

Rosalind's heart plummeted. 'I'm all right, honestly.'

'Did I say you weren't? Turn around.'

With a sinking feeling that made her feel sick, Rosalind obeyed.

Phoebe studied her. 'I'll ask again. What's up?'

'Nothing.'

'Don't lie to me, Rozzie. Your eyes are—'

'Oh, that. I was holding back a branch and it slipped from my hand and smacked me right across the face.' Rosalind attempted a light laugh.

'I'll have the truth, if you please,' Phoebe said, folding her spectacles and putting them aside with her crochet work. 'Something upset you when you were out.'

'No, honestly.' But Rosalind's face suddenly crumpled.

Phoebe got up quickly and went to her. 'What on earth is it? Tell me now.'

'I c-can't.'

Phoebe took the girl's face in her hands. 'Yes, you can. I can see you're all of a rattle, and it's my place to find out what it is and put it right.'

'It can't be put right,' Rosalind whispered tearfully.

A suspicion of the truth began to dawn on Phoebe. 'You've been with someone?' Rosalind bit her lip and looked away. 'Oh, you silly girl!' Phoebe shook her. 'Who was it? Jamie Webb?'

'No!'

'Who then?' Phoebe's mind was racing, and then she gasped. 'Oh, no, not that mangy tomcat Robert Lloyd?' Rosalind couldn't speak, but guilt shone in her tear-filled blue eyes. Phoebe's hands fell away. 'You silly, silly child,' she whispered. 'After all the warnings and being kept in, you *still* went with him? Your father's going to half kill you!'

'Oh, don't tell Dad! Please, Phoebe!' Rosalind was distraught.

'You want me to sit back and say nothing? What if in nine months your little jaunt brings forth some unwelcome results, eh? What then? That hosebird hasn't admitted to any of his bastards yet, and I doubt he'll start with you!'

Rosalind leaned against the table, her whole body trembling. 'Please, Phoebe,' she whispered, her voice breaking, 'please don't tell Dad.'

'Rosalind, I can't *not* tell him.'

'I won't do it again! I won't ever do it again! And I'm near my time this month.'

'Oh, God above, what am I to do?' Phoebe drew out a chair and sat down heavily. 'How near are you?'

'Three days. Maybe four. Something like that.'

'Well, I suppose you *might* be all right.'

Rosalind saw a chink in her armour. 'Please, Phoebe. I'm begging you. Just wait a little. If my monthly comes, there'll be no need for Dad to ever know.'

'A week then, Rosalind, I'll give you a week.' Rosalind began to sob with relief. 'But mind now, you're not going out of this house on your own again, and you'll account to me for every minute of every day. Do you hear me?'

'Yes, Phoebe.'

'And if that young ram comes anywhere near you—'

'He won't.' Rosalind sniffed miserably, and so far forgot Beth's lessons as to wipe her nose with her sleeve.

'You seem mighty sure.'

'I am. He only did me to get back at Dad.'

Phoebe exhaled. 'Oh, my dear.'

Chapter Seventeen

By the second week of August the weather at Lannermouth had changed completely. The warmth and blue skies gave way to clouds and a chill north wind that turned the sea to a choppy grey. Fishing boats bobbed and swayed in the harbour, smoke was torn from cottage chimneys, and the wind moaned around the chimneys and eaves of the Dower House. It was so unseasonable and wretched that late one morning Mrs Cobbett set Molly to kindle a fire in the drawing-room, where Beth was sketching by the window. The racket of the incoming tide was audible, and torn petals whirled beneath the veranda thatch as she tried to capture the weather and the view with her pencil. She didn't draw very often, but every now and then found it a quite a tonic. Certainly she needed a tonic. She was still mortified about what had happened on Haldane Cliff, and hadn't left the house since. When Landry called she had refused to receive him, and then she'd ordered Billy to return Snowy to the hall. The horse had been promptly returned.

The concerned housekeeper observed everything, and at last went to the parlour to speak to her mistress. Beth looked up from her drawing. 'Yes, Mrs Cobbett?'

'Have you remembered that I'll be going over to help my sister this afternoon, Miss Beth?'

'I hadn't forgotten. I hope she's better soon.'

'Might I speak to you in private?'

Beth immediately set her sketching aside. 'Why, yes, of course you may, Mrs Cobbett. Is something wrong?'

'Well, I don't know for certain, Miss Beth, because this is about you. I'll come straight to it. I can help you after what happened with Mr Landry.'

Colour flew into Beth's cheeks, and she rose in a fluster of pink-and-white gingham. 'I don't know what you mean, Mrs Cobbett, and would thank you not to go around repeating such things!'

'Please, Miss Beth, I'm not a fool. You've not been at all yourself this past week, and you've sent Mr Landry away. It takes no great brain to guess what went on between you, and I imagine that now you're worried about what may come of it.'

Beth's shame deepened, and her eyes filled with tears. 'Oh, Mrs Cobbett.'

'Just tell me one thing. Were you willing?'

'Yes. Oh, please don't think badly of Mr Haldane. I was my own fool, not his.'

The housekeeper put comforting arms around her. 'Mr Landry is a real charmer, so I can understand your weakness. Now then, there's no need for any of this to get out, or for you to worry about having a child out of wedlock. I know herbs to bring you on.'

The wind blustered around the veranda, and rattled one of the windows. It was a hollow, lonely sound that suited Beth's unhappiness. 'There is no need for your herbs, Mrs Cobbett, because I can't have children.'

'You can't possibly know that, my dear.'

'I can. I lived with a man, a widower, who already had a daughter by his late wife. He was virile enough, but I was never even late.'

Mrs Cobbett's mouth opened and closed, and then she cleared her throat. 'Miss Beth, I don't understand you. You lost your maidenhead long before you came here, and you went willingly to Mr Landry, safe in the knowledge that you'll not bear a child. So why are you brought so very low and unhappy? It isn't that Mr Landry has lost interest.'

Beth bit her lips to stem fresh tears. 'Because I'm ashamed, Mrs Cobbett. I was more than just willing, I was eager, and now I can't face him again.'

'But he still wants to see you, Miss Beth, and there isn't any gossip, beyond the fact that you and Mr Landry went riding together, but that's all. Somehow you managed to ride back here, all of a fluster, without being seen. If I hear one word out of turn, I'll sort it out. I'm a fearsome old biddy when my dander's up and bristling.'

Beth had to smile. 'I cannot believe that of you, Mrs Cobbett.'

'Oh, you mark my words, I'm a force to be reckoned with.' The housekeeper smiled fondly. 'So don't you fret, Miss Beth, things will go on like before. Now then, I'll make you a nice cup of tea, and soon you'll feel a *lot* better.'

'Thank you, Mrs Cobbett.' Beth hugged her.

Mrs Cobbett smiled with pleasure. 'Think nothing of it, my dear.' She went to the door, and then remembered something. 'I almost forgot. Billy and Molly want to know if they might take this afternoon off. There's a fair over at Porworthy.'

'Five miles there and back in this weather? Well, it wouldn't do for me, but yes, of course. I won't need Billy today. Tell him he may take one of the horses if he wishes. I'd offer two, but I'm sure he'd rather have Molly riding double with him.'

'Oh, yes, I'm sure of it too,' the housekeeper replied. 'Well, I'll be back here come teatime, so you won't be left alone for long.'

'Don't worry about me, Mrs Cobbett, I'm quite capable of being on my own. You stay with your sister as long as you like. I insist.'

'Very well, Miss Beth.' Then the housekeeper spotted something outside. 'Well, I do believe that's Miss Harriet's chaise coming down the drive. Yes, it is. Do you want me to tell her you're indisposed?'

Beth considered it, but then shook her head. 'No, I'll receive her.'

'Very well, my dear.'

Harriet had not called merely to pay a sociable visit, but to persuade Beth to accompany her to the dressmaker, Miss Archer. The rector's daughter was very elegant in a light-blue lawn gown, navy-blue velvet spencer, and straw bonnet tied with white ribbons. 'Well, Beth, I promised to introduce you to Miss Archer, so here I am. Only the examination of fashionable fripperies will drive this weather away. I insist, Beth, because you haven't set foot over your own threshold in far too long. And when I saw Mrs Cobbett just now, she virtually ordered me not to take no for an answer.'

'She is about to make tea.'

'No, she isn't.' Harriet grinned. 'You may as well give in. Do accompany me, Beth, for I would cherish your opinion of the winter gown Miss Archer is making for me.'

'You're always stylish, Harriet, and don't need me.'

'I'm stylish because Miss Carter subscribes to *The Ladies' Temple of Fashion*,' Harriet confessed ruefully. 'Please, Beth?'

Beth submitted, but as she left the parlour to get ready, she found Mrs Cobbett waiting in the passage with her mantle and bonnet. 'You two really *are* set upon winkling me out, aren't you?' she said, as the housekeeper helped her with them.

'Yes,' they replied together.

A moment later she and Harriet emerged into the daylight. The wind snatched at their clothes, and almost whisked Harriet's bonnet from its pins as they climbed into the chaise. It began to rain as they drove off. 'This summer is very mean-spirited,' Harriet declared.

Beth nodded. 'Autumn has come early.'

'We've certainly been having wondrous sunrises and sunsets. Actually, they've been making me uneasy,' Harriet confessed. 'I mean, what do they signify?'

Beth adopted a very solemn face. 'The end of the world,' she said gravely.

'Oh, don't even jest about such a dread thing!' Harriet gave a rueful smile. 'Anyway, enough of that. It won't take us long to reach Miss Archer's, and she'll soon serve us some good hot Pekoe. Oh, there's just one thing, I have to call upon Carrie Markham first. I need to give her something, and will only be a moment.'

Beth's apprehension returned as the chaise climbed up the steep road to

Haldane. What if they encountered Landry? The closer they drew to the village, the more monosyllabic her responses became, but if Harriet noticed she didn't say anything. At last they halted by the lodge, but as the driver came to open the door for Harriet to alight, the horse started forward unexpectedly, and she dropped something. Beth retrieved it for her. It was a gold medallion on a faded blue ribbon, bearing on one side a picture of St Michael slaying a dragon, and on the other a three-masted ship sailing before the wind.

As Harriet hastened to the lodge and went inside, Beth sat back, trying to keep out of sight in the shadows. She knew the medallion's purpose. Her father had worn one as protection from consumption. Carrie Markham's cough and her delicate face with its exquisite colour and almost porcelain fragility, now told a truth that Beth felt she ought to have recognized before. She gazed sadly at the lodge, because the talisman hadn't helped her father. Harriet returned, her skirts blowing as the waiting driver opened the door to help her back in. Rain scattered over Beth, and the smell of the moor was strong before the door closed again and Harriet had resumed her seat. As the vehicle drove on into the village, Harriet looked at Beth. 'I know you recognized the medallion. Please don't speak of it to anyone. Carrie is trying to keep her illness secret.'

'Does Mr Haldane know?'

Harriet hesitated. 'Why do you ask?'

'I went riding with him and met Carrie and her daughter.' Beth glanced out of the rain-washed window.

'You know, don't you?'

'That Katie is his child? Yes.'

Harriet lowered her eyes. 'I hadn't realized you were close enough to Landry for him to have told you.' She bit her lip. 'I sometimes wish you'd never come here.'

The other's pain was so evident that Beth felt dreadful. 'Please don't say that.'

Harriet was immediately contrite. 'Oh, forgive me, I didn't really mean it. It's just that – that—'

'That you are in love with him?'

'Is it that obvious?' Harriet smiled ruefully. 'It's all quite hopeless, of course.'

Beth felt culpable. She and Harriet were still barely acquainted, but what had been done on the cliff could not be undone. Landry swore there was no understanding with Harriet, and it was clearly true, but even so it was hard to look her in the eye.

'I knew when he first met you that he was more than a little interested,' Harriet continued. 'He can be disconcertingly honest, you know.'

'Yes, I've discovered that.' Rain was driven against the windows as the wind gusted through the village streets.

Harriet went on, 'Father grows vexed with me for mooning after a man I will never have, and now my cousin John Herriot has made a good offer of marriage. At least if Landry gets you to the altar—'

Beth interrupted hastily. 'I hardly know him!' *No, but you've already spread your legs for him and behaved like a savage!*

'At least my hand is being forced,' Harriet continued. 'I'm bound either to marry my cousin or become an embittered old maid.'

Beth endeavoured to use levity to fend off the returning gloom. 'My friend, it may be that spinsterhood is infinitely preferable, because if you marry your cousin, you'll be Harriet Herriot.'

Harriet gave a little laugh, and then glanced out. 'Ah, we are at Miss Archer's.'

Beth saw that the dressmaker's was also the village haberdashery, but as she and Harriet hurried in, laughing because of the wind and rain, the first thing Beth noticed on a table was the latest edition of *Lithgow's Journal*. Was the notice still being published? She didn't want to look inside to see, but knew she would.

It was the late evening of the same day, and the weather had worsened. The setting sun, reflecting as if upon a watery mirror, frilled the low, racing clouds with vivid shades of autumn, and the surf was tremendous as the tide roared in. The lights of Lannermouth flickered wanly through the gale and rain, and the trees in the Dower House park heaved and swayed as if intent upon hauling themselves from the earth, but Beth's parlour was firelit and cosy. A draught sucked down the chimney so that the flames flared noisily in the hearth, and brilliant sparks fled up toward the stormy night sky. She was alone. Mrs Cobbett hadn't yet returned from seeing her sick sister, nor had Billy and Molly come home from the fair. On such a night she thought it would be morning before she saw anyone.

She was on the settle by the fire, her hair loose, wearing a primrose muslin chemise. There was a glass of Madeira in her hand, and her face was illuminated by the flames. Why, oh why, had she opened the journal? She had so wanted the Dower House to be a haven, but it had been spoiled, first by her unbridled misconduct with Landry, and now by revived fears of the past. The London lawyers still sought her. Guy would be after her too. Mrs Cobbett's cat padded into the room to join her, but instead of settling down comfortably as usual, it sat upright by the hearth, staring in a penetrating way that summoned more thoughts of Guy. The gale rattled the French windows, and she got up to make sure they were properly closed. Through the rain-distorted glass she saw a bedraggled horse, head low, trudging slowly into the drive from Rendisbury Hill. Billy and Molly! Appalled that they'd come five miles in such conditions, she went to the kitchen just as footsteps hurried to the back door and Billy ushered Molly inside. Beth had expected to see two bedraggled, tired, wet people, but was unprepared for the maid's ashen, mud-stained face and torn clothes. 'Oh, whatever has happened, Molly?' she cried.

Billy removed his dripping hat. 'There's been trouble over at Porworthy, Miss Beth. The fair didn't even start on account of it. Sir Daniel's mill was fired by an angry crowd, all of them in hoods. It was nasty.' He glanced back outside. 'Reckon I'd better settle the horse. Molly will tell you what happened, Miss Beth.'

Beth led Molly into the parlour and sat her on the settle by the fire, before pouring her a glass of Madeira. 'Tell me about it, Molly,' she said gently, forgetting her own problems as she sat next to the maid.

'Well, when we got there we supped at the Bell and Fox first, but saw that the fair wasn't going on as it should. There weren't any women and children around, just men. They stood in quiet groups, and had something about them. No laughing or light chatter. More and more men arrived and gathered in front of the Bell and Fox. Billy got worried, but as we were going to leave, someone blew a whistle and the men put on hoods. They grabbed staves and other weapons they'd hidden, then got torches and marched on the mill to put it to flame. The fire took a grip in spite of the storm, and there was smoke, a lot of shouting, windows breaking and doors being kicked in so machines could be wrecked. They destroyed everything they could find, and not one of them could be recognized because of their hoods. When the fire became too dangerous, they began to parade through Porworthy with Sir Daniel's likeness on a pole, then they burned that as well and began to dance around and screech like they were possessed.' Molly took a gulp of the Madeira and wiped the back of her hand across her trembling lips. 'We watched from the inn, and the landlord, Mr George, told us it was happening because Sir Daniel had brought in even more power looms and steam presses, putting another twenty men out of work, eight of them forced to go on parish relief. Sir Daniel sentenced Porworthy men to hang for poaching a while back, so he's really *hated*. Anyway, he must have realized early on what was happening, for the next thing there were screams; some women and children appeared through the smoke shouting that the army was coming. We ran to the stables for our horse just as mounted soldiers poured into the street. I was knocked down and my gown was ripped and my stockings torn. I was covered in mud and so frightened I couldn't move. I just lay there as the army cleared the streets. It was harsh, Miss Beth, with deaths and injuries. Sir Daniel will sit in judgment again, and hang even more.'

'Oh, Molly, it must have been dreadful.' Beth didn't know what else to say.

'On the way back, we had to keep leaving the road to hide in bushes so the army wouldn't find us and think we'd been involved. They're out everywhere, Miss Beth. I felt like a criminal.' Tears streamed down Molly's dirty face.

Billy returned, and came to crouch attentively in front of the maid 'It's all right now, Molly my love, you're back here at Lannermouth and it's all done with. Come on, we'll go to the kitchen and have a bite to eat. It will do us good.'

Beth sensed his anxiety to leave the parlour, and then realized why as a shadow moved in the doorway behind him and she saw Landry's cloaked figure. Molly gasped, discarded her glass and hurried out with Billy, and Landry closed the door behind them. He removed his wet hat and cloak, revealing a brown coat, scarlet waistcoat and fawn trousers. 'I've had the army at the hall, alerting me to events at Porworthy and warning me of possible repercussions in this area.'

'You think there will be?'

He shrugged. 'No one on my land has just cause to stir up trouble, but it only takes one discontented bell-wether to lead a flock.'

'Well, the army hasn't called here. I wouldn't have known anything about it had it not been for Billy and Molly having gone to Porworthy fair.'

'They were fortunate to get back without being arrested. The army isn't particular about who it takes, or how. Anyone out tonight is suspected.' Without asking, he replenished Molly's glass and drank it all. 'By God, this is a miserable day for everyone. It will be some time before the mill is rebuilt, so Lavington won't get the income and his people will be out of work, so the hedge priest who dreamed up tonight's trouble should be hanged from the nearest crossroads.' The gale rattled the windows and he went to look out. 'There are trees down in a number of places, and two of my hothouses have been blown to perdition. Both Lanners are danger-ously swollen as well, but at least the tide isn't expected to be high enough to cause problems. What a summer this is.' He turned to look at Beth. 'How calm you are. Clearly Gloucestershire storms put our small breezes to shame. And speaking of that county, yesterday I received a letter from someone you may know. Lady Welland.'

'Lady Welland has been dead for years.'

He removed his coat. 'I gather this is the second Lady Welland. She was Mrs Tremoille when I wrote to her.'

The names reached out like vengeful wraiths. Beth froze. So Jane had married Thomas Welland. Poor Rowan, to have acquired the worst of all stepmothers. 'I know of whom you speak. Why – why are you correspon-ding with her?'

'Oh, I heard she had a good stallion for sale, but I was too late. Someone got there before me, at least two months ago.' He drew a long breath. 'Well, that's by the by, and tonight, considering the storm, I decided you should not be on your own.'

'There is no need, for I have Billy and Molly.'

'Who are more concerned with each other than with you.'

'There is still no need for—' She gasped as the storm increased its endeavours, wailing so strongly down the chimney that it shifted the fire, sending a shower of sparks over the stone hearth.

'You were saying?' he prompted quietly.

'Please, Landry, what happened between us was wrong and best forgotten.'

'Even to the point of trying to return Snowy?'

'You intended to give him to me, didn't you?' she demanded.

'And if I did?'

'Can't you see that such a gift would be like payment in kind?'

'*In kind*?' He looked at her in astonishment.

She turned away. 'I wish you would understand how ashamed I am.'

'Beth, how can I understand if you don't explain? What did I do wrong? Did you perceive an insult that wasn't intended? Help me, Beth.'

'It wasn't you, it was me. All me.' She turned away as the gale shrieked its howling crescendo, and there was a splintering crash from the park as a tree was brought down. Its leaves were being hurled away on the air – just like her new life.

He stood behind her. 'Beth, to me what happened was precious and quite unforgettable.' He rested his hands on her shoulders and his cheek against her hair. 'I know you have secrets, and I suspect your heart has been given to another, but it doesn't matter. In a short time you've come to mean everything to me, and in order to be with you I'm prepared to agree to whatever conditions you set. Please, Beth, at least concede that what we shared on the cliff was exceptional. You were demonstrative and honest in a way I have never encountered before.'

'I was no better than a she-cat.'

'Stop it!' His fingers tightened. 'You behaved like a woman, and showed me that you have your own passions. It awakened me, and my open eyes see only you. Don't send me away.'

His voice and touch were enticing, and she closed her eyes. 'Please don't do this, Landry,' she whispered.

'Why? Because you're afraid of being hurt? I would rather die than hurt you, Beth,' He turned her to face him. 'I'll never have you as completely as you have me, and your secrets, whatever they are, may eventually take you from me, but until then I will accept whatever terms you set.' He bent his head to try to put his mouth lovingly to hers, but she put a finger to his lips.

'Whatever terms?'

'Yes.'

'I have already admitted to secrets that I cannot confide, but I have denied that there is anyone else. Landry, there *is* someone else, but he doesn't love me. He's not my husband, my fiancé or even someone with whom I have an understanding, nor is he someone else's husband, but he *is* a threat to me. I fear him, but I love him too. Given all this, do you still want me?'

'I won't pretend it doesn't hurt that you love someone else, but I have no pride or shame. I want you, Beth, and even knowing I could lose you at any moment in the future is better than being without you now.'

'You shame me, Landry. Your motive is love, whereas mine—'

'— is purely physical?' he interrupted.

She closed her eyes. In this at least she had to be painfully honest with him. Guy had given life to something vital deep within her, and only he would ever satisfy its needs, but she had to exist without him; things carnal were essential to that existence.

'Yes, Landry. I can desire you, but I cannot love you in the way I think you love me. If that is sufficient for you, then we can be as we were on the cliff.'

He caught her to him, but she placed her hands against his chest and leaned back, her hazel-green eyes serious. 'Are you really sure, Landry? Unrequited love is not to be taken lightly.' He was going to be another Jake. Another Jake.

'I'm sure,' he whispered, crushing her in a kiss as fierce and unstoppable as his love. He didn't care about anything, except that she was his for now.

For her a weight had been lifted because she had been forthright and because he didn't think ill of her for what had gone before. The relief warmed her blood and her lips softened and parted beneath his. His embrace lifted her from the floor, and she could feel that he was aroused too. He carried her to the door and pressed her back against it, his kiss more imperative and fervent, his hips thrust forward to bury his straining erection against her. His mouth moved from her lips to her eyes, her cheeks, her throat, and all the while he moved against her, to their shared pleasure. Her body began to sing with desire, and it felt so good to surrender honestly that tears stung her eyes. Loving gratification beckoned, and she floated sensuously into its velvet weightlessness. He raised his head to look into her darkened eyes, and she sought his lips again, tasting him, fusing with him. He drew back, his turquoise eyes rich and warm.

'Oh, Beth, all this from mere kisses,' he whispered, setting her on her feet again, for fear he would take her here, up against a door.

'Make love to me between lavender-scented sheets, Landry,' she breathed, and went to get a candlestick from a table and hold it to the fire. When it was alight, she returned to take his hand. The flame guttered, and threads of smoke ribboned in the air as she led him up to her room. Once they were inside, she pushed the bolt across and then placed the candle on a table. It was much cooler up here, and the storm howled around the house, carrying the thunder of the sea only yards away from the foundations. She turned to face him untying the ribbon drawstring that fastened her chemise gown under her breasts. The primrose muslin slithered softly from her shoulders and subsided in soft folds around her feet. She wore nothing else, except silk stockings fixed with little blue garters.

He gazed at her. 'You are so beautiful,' he breathed, holding out a hand to her. She went gladly to him and they kissed again. His hands moved adoringly over her body, caressing and exploring, until she drew away and began to unbutton his waistcoat, then removed it and tossed it to a corner. Next she dispensed with his neck cloth, and finally his shirt. He smelled of rosemary and leather, of clean perspiration and the fresh air, and as the shirt parted, her arms slid around his waist and her lips pressed to the soft dark hairs on his chest. She moved her nipples against him and breathed deeply of his scent. It was so vital and exciting that her heart seemed to adjust its beat to match his. He removed his boots, stockings and riding breeches, and at last they were naked together. He drew the bedclothes back, and gathered her up in his arms to place her gently on the sheet. She lay back on the pillow, her body ready to welcome him, and he heard her sigh of pleasure as he joined her, supporting himself on his arms as he lowered his hips toward hers, down and down until she felt the tip of his hot masculinity against the soft lips between her legs. 'I love you, Beth,' he whispered, moving until he was at the threshold of her innermost place. She gasped and closed her eyes, knowing it would be Guy she held, Guy to whom she made love. As Landry sank slowly into her, it was Guy's lips that found hers in a searing kiss that threatened to turn their blood to fire. Slowly Landry drew out again, then in, out and then in, long, rich satisfying strokes that made her flesh quiver with ecstasy. Each leisurely thrust was exquisite, imparting such ravishment that she thought she would lose consciousness. Her soul seemed to break free, soaring away into the wild, stormy night, and the waves of pleasure that undulated through her body were stronger and more rhythmic than those of the high tide beyond the window. Their passion and need was too great for either of them to want to prolong the pleasure, and they cried out together as the final moment came. Weightless and in ecstasy, she clung tightly to him. Their bodies shuddered and undulated together. It was so magnificent, liberating and euphoric that more tears glistened on her cheeks as she drew him down into a tender embrace. Warm satisfaction enveloped them both like a comfortable blanket, and she wrapped her legs around his, so that his virility was still against her most secret places. She put her lips to his throat and tasted the salt on his skin, remembering the dashing and gallant hussar officer she'd first seen only a few days ago. Now, here they were, naked and sated, and more intimate than either of them could have dreamed.

'Oh, Beth, my beloved Beth, I worship everything about you,' he murmured, his fingers stirring sensuously in the hair at the nape of her neck.

She curled against him and closed her eyes again, trying to shut out that other face she loved and feared so much.

Chapter Eighteen

'By all the whores of Babylon, that was some storm last night, eh?' Rowan settled back in Guy's town carriage and tossed his top hat on the seat opposite.

'How disgustingly bright you are, to be sure,' Guy muttered.

Rowan grinned. 'What's this, a surfeit of wine and women or a bad session at the green baize?'

'Neither, just a restless night and lurid dreams. Too much Wensleydale for supper,' Guy replied.

'A few rounds with Taffy Hughes would sort you out.'

Guy grimaced. 'I refuse to square up to some sweaty fellow in a prize ring.'

Rowan was curious about Guy's private life, or lack of it these days. 'I know you've escaped from La Carberry, but it's not like you to be celibate.'

'Cards provide danger enough.'

'Danger? My dear cousin, money adheres to you as a tick to a dog.'

'What a pleasant analogy,' Guy murmured.

Rowan scrutinized him. 'I will be direct: why don't you have a fair lady?'

Guy smiled. 'Perhaps I find you more to my liking.'

'Well, I know *that* isn't so, for I can smell a deviant at sixty paces. Believe me, with looks like mine, it was a vital lesson! So the truth, sir, why are you always alone?'

'You don't really know whether I am or not, Rowan.'

'If you are not, then who is she?'

Guy paused. Maybe the time had come to tell Rowan about his quest for Beth. 'There isn't anyone, Rowan, but I am definitely pursuing a particular lady. You know her, as it happens. It's Beth Tremoille.'

Rowan's jaw dropped. 'Beth? But why?'

'I've found her father's elusive last will.'

Now Rowan stared. 'How? When?'

'I found it in Gloucester.' Guy explained where it had been all along.

'And you didn't tell me?' Rowan was miffed.

'Don't take umbrage, my friend, because my silence was out of consideration to you. I didn't want to make things awkward for you at the wedding. And now I want you to promise that you won't say anything to anyone else.'

'Damn it all, Guy, you insult me!'

'Not intentionally. I simply need to really impress upon you that I don't want anyone else to know.' Guy omitted to add that he was well aware that when in drink, Rowan's tongue could get the better of him.

Rowan ran his fingers through his hair as he tried to digest what he'd been told. 'So, I take it the will makes Beth sole heir?'

'It does.'

Rowan eyed him. 'But you don't want her simply to present her with her father's will, do you? You want her to marry you, with Tremoille House as her dowry?'

'How well you know me,' Guy observed wryly.

'What if she refuses?'

'I'll cross that bridge when I come to it.' *And force her if I have to.*

Rowan pursed his lips. 'Beth isn't to be trifled with, Guy.'

'You fear you may have to call me out?' Guy smiled.

'I will if I have to.'

Guy was at his most amiable. 'Oh, do calm down. I'm quite sure this will all work out splendidly. Now then, you requested me to accompany you to Putney Heath. Are you still intent upon taking on "Bull" Baldwin?'

'Er, no, actually. It would seem that the prospect of confronting me was too much for him. He's cried off, pleading a sprained knee. His minion arrived before breakfast this morning.' Rowan grinned. 'But I still get the purse. I was most insistent on that before accepting the challenge. If low fellows wish to smash my aristocratic features, they must pay for the privilege.'

'You're too lightweight and he'd have pulverized you.'

'What kind words of encouragement from one's second,' Rowan murmured.

'Is that what I am? Well, being your second doesn't preclude me from disagreeing with your actions. A broken nose would seriously mar your pretty face, and a well-aimed fist might put your lights out forever.'

'I'll take that chance.' Rowan glanced out. 'Why are we going this way?'

'I never go anywhere these days without making Easterden Street part of the route.' Guy told him about having seen Beth there.

'More things from which I've been excluded?' Rowan was a little disgruntled. 'And you hope to see this short fat fellow again?'

'Finding him is not beyond the realms of possibility.' The carriage negotiated another crossroad, and then turned left into Easterden Street.

Dickon slowed the team to a walk, and Guy leaned forward to observe the crowded pavements.

Rowan sat forward too. 'London has many short, fat fellows,' he grumbled.

'Yes, but only one that looks like *that*! There! Do you see him? Over there, purchasing a newspaper from the boy on the corner!' Guy rapped his cane against the carriage roof and soon alighted to thread his way toward the corner. Rowan slid across to the nearside of the carriage to watch.

Henry Topweather, the newspaper tucked under his arm, was just about to cross the busy carriageway to his offices when he was almost jerked from his feet by a hand seizing his shoulder. 'I say—!' he squeaked in alarm, and then gaped as he turned to see the hand was attached to Guy's fashionable, immaculate figure.

Guy released him. 'Forgive me, sir, but I've been looking for you for some time. Allow me to introduce myself. Sir Guy Valmer.'

'Henry Topweather.' The agent was nervous. 'Looking for me, sir? Why?'

'I need to find the whereabouts of a certain young lady. Her name is Miss Elizabeth Tremoille, or perhaps you know her as Miss or Mrs Alder?'

The agent's tongue passed over his lips. 'I've never heard of her, Sir Guy.'

'You were talking to her one night, right here in this street. It was at the time of Waterloo. She's very beautiful, with dark hair, and was wearing an emerald-green gown. She was in a yellow-and-black chaise.'

'I'm sorry, Sir Guy, I can't help you. You are mistaking me for someone else.'

'Oh, no, it was definitely you.' The more Guy looked at the fellow, the more certain he became.

'Sir, I'm convinced that I would recall such a lady. In my profession—'

'Which is?'

'I'm an agent for the sale and lease of property around the country.' Topweather indicated the upper window opposite, with his name in faded gold.

'And this lady did not come to you in your professional capacity?'

'She did not come to me at all, Sir Guy. I know of no one named Tremoille or Alder, and certainly did not speak to a beautiful woman here at night.'

Guy was unconvinced, but knew that while the fellow continued to deny any knowledge, there was little he could do. Except, perhaps, secretly inspect Mr Henry Topweather's records for that part of June. He gave the agent a bland smile. 'Very well. Once again, I ask your forgiveness.'

Relief reddened the other's plump visage. 'Not at all, Sir Guy, not at all.'

Guy turned and walked back toward his waiting carriage, and Topweather watched until it had driven away. His little eyes were sly and thoughtful. This incident merely confirmed what he already knew. The mysterious Mrs Alder was not what she seemed. Sir Guy Valmer was seeking her, and she clearly did not wish to be found. *Eliza Mary Alder, née Wilkes, widow of Jacob James Alder, sea captain. Presently staying at the Swan with Two Necks in Lad Lane, but formerly of Queen's Crescent, Scarborough.* Skilful lies. She was more likely the Miss Tremoille Sir Guy mentioned. Now what might she pay for Henry Topweather's silence, eh? On that pleasant thought, he made his way across the street to his offices. A visit to North Devon would be very pleasant at this time of the year, he mused.

In the carriage, Rowan raised an eyebrow. 'Well? Was it the right fellow?'

'Yes.'

'So you now know more about Beth?'

Guy shook his head. 'No, because the greasy porker denied any knowledge of her. One thing of interest, however, he is an agent for leasing and selling properties. Now why, I wonder, might the delectable Miss Tremoille be associating with such a person? She has money and wishes to begin a new life. What better than to take a lease in some remote part of the land?'

'Money? Beth? There's yet more you haven't told me, isn't there?'

Guy sighed. 'Yes.' He related the story of the theft of the thousand guineas and how he'd first found Beth.

Rowan was uncomfortable. 'Guy, after everything else you've told me today, you now expect me to believe that Beth – *Beth?* – stole that money and might even be guilty of *murder?* You're mad!'

'View her in a bowl of roses if you wish, my friend, but I know better. I'm not so sure about her having had a hand in Joshua's demise, but she definitely took the money, and had it hidden in a basket beneath a damned pheasant when I conveyed her to Gloucester. I had her, damn it.' Guy's fist clenched on the carriage sill.

Rowan watched the emotions cross the other's face, and exhaled heavily. 'So, what now? You'll offer Topweather a bribe?'

'No. We'll pay his premises a visit tonight. If Beth took out a lease with him, the documents will be in his office.'

Rowan's jaw dropped yet again. 'Pray pass me the sal volatile! You're going to break into his offices and you expect *me* to help you?'

'It will keep you out of mischief.' Guy's humour returned a little.

But that night, when the moon was clear and the stars bright over London, Guy and Rowan found nothing at 15 Easterden Street. There was a notice pinned to the outer door, informing anyone interested that Mr Henry Topweather was out of town on business. Once inside, a thorough search proved fruitless. Except, perhaps, for a gap in the files between the names Albrighton and Alford. It was too much of a coincidence, and Guy knew a name was missing; Alder. Topweather had gone to Beth. To warn her? Blackmail her? And where? Where on God's own earth was Beth Tremoille?

Beth and Landry returned separately from another assignation at the secret hollow on the cliff. The army searched Stone Valley a few times, but never when the lovers were there, and three days after the Porworthy riot the soldiers returned to barracks. Beth and Landry went to the hollow as often as they could, to make love and lie naked together, safe in the knowledge that no one would see them. They could be sure because Landry now brought a trusted servant to guard the horses and make sure no one climbed to the cliff top.

The villagers of Haldane knew something was going on, and Beth was aware that the Dower House tenant was under constant scrutiny. They were unlikely to approve of a young woman who accompanied him up to the cliff top where they were alone and out of sight for hours. She felt as alive as she could be without Guy, but deep down knew she was living in a fool's paradise. This became abundantly clear when she arrived back at the Dower House to find Mrs Cobbett kneading dough on the table, thumping it busily from side to side and singing as she worked. As Beth entered, the housekeeper indicated a letter behind a candlestick on the mantelshelf. 'That was pushed under the door, Miss Beth. I found it about half an hour back. I didn't see who brought it, and there's nothing on it to say who sent it. The wrong name is on it, but I reckon it's probably you. A Mrs Alder?' The housekeeper's attention returned prudently to the dough.

Beth was seized with apprehension. Who would write to her? Trying to appear unconcerned, she took the letter to the privacy of the parlour to break the sealing wax and read. *It's time for partners to meet again, but not on this occasion in connection with Belvedere's. Be at home at eight o'clock tonight.* There was no signature, but the hand could only be Henry Topweather's. What could he want? The apprehension settled coldly into the pit of her stomach.

Time passed on leaden feet for the rest of that day. Beth's anxiety was so intense that she felt ill, but at last it drew close to eight o'clock. The sun was hidden behind thick clouds, so the evening had closed in earlier than usual. A new breeze ruffled the surface of the bay, and the choppy waves along the shore were tipped with white as Beth, unable to bear the house any longer, strolled along the path toward the rocks where Landry had found her only two weeks before. It was a little cool, but such was her unease that she didn't feel it. She kept glancing toward the top of the drive, and eventually a horseman rode into view, a rather fat horseman on a broad black cob. She recognized the agent, and reluctantly returned to the house.

Billy emerged from the stables to attend to the cob, and Topweather dismounted, slowly easing his bulk down from the saddle, obviously aching and uncomfortable. Beth felt no sympathy. He may have been instrumental in her acquisition of more money through Belvedere's, but he revolted her, and she was certain that his visit now did not bode well. Seeing her, the agent made his way along the path that led around the Dower House garden. He wore a tall hat, brown coat, black waistcoat and ridiculously tight breeches that emphasized his bulging belly. She went into the shadows of the garden, which was on a side of the house well away from Molly and Mrs Cobbett in the kitchens. This meeting had to be a private as possible, for fear of what he might have to say. She faced him by a pink climbing rose that twined around one of the veranda posts.

'Why do you wish to see me, sir?'

He smirked. 'Well now, that's hardly a friendly opening, Mrs Alder. Or is it *Miss* Alder? Perchance even Miss Tremoille?'

A shaft of ice pierced her. 'I'm afraid I don't know what you're talking about.'

'So you're not even going to offer me the hospitality of a cup of tea?' His eyes were small and hard. 'And don't insult my intelligence by playing the innocent, madam. I haven't come all this way to be fobbed off. I mean to get what I want.'

'Which is?'

His hot gaze moved over her, pausing on the curves of her breasts. 'You're a very beautiful woman, quite the most lovely thing I've ever set eyes on. Fanciful dreams about you keep my right hand very busy at night, but I want a lot more than dreams, my dear. I want to get into your bed with you.'

She tried to conceal her revulsion behind a mask of indifference, but the sickness in her stomach was turning to dread. 'And why do you imagine I would consent?'

'Because I know you're not who and what you say you are, and you came dishonestly into your original money. Sir Guy Valmer badly wants to know where you are, and said you might call yourself Alder or Tremoille. Now then, what do you say to that?'

Her mouth was dry, the palms of her hands were cold and damp, and her whole body trembled. In the sudden silence she could hear a horse by the stables, and knew Billy was walking the black cob to be sure its legs didn't stiffen after a long ride over the moor from Dulverford, where she would later learn the agent had lodged at the Cross Keys inn. 'I – I have nothing to say to you, Mr Topweather,' she answered at last, aware that in spite of her efforts the tremble extended to her voice.

'It's my guess that you're the same Miss Tremoille that solicitors in Caradine Street have been seeking for months now. Why are all these persons looking for you? It seems to me that you might wish to buy my silence. A night enjoying you would certainly ensure my discretion for a while.'

'But you'd come back again and again. I'm not a fool, so please go to hell.'

'First let us consider the alternatives. For instance, if I go away from here unsatisfied, I guarantee that Valmer will immediately learn of your whereabouts. I'm sure he'd pay well for such information.'

'Do that and I will broadcast your duplicity in the St Clair case.'

'You'd have to prove it, my dear, and my associate in that instance has rather more power and influence than you realize. And he likes to keep things in the family.' Mr Justice Baynsdon, she thought, as he continued, 'I'll say it just once more, either you're nice to me, sweetheart, or I spill the lot to Valmer, who doesn't seem the sort of cove to offend, eh? Cool, calculating and cruel, is how I'd describe him.' He moved closer to her, close enough to put his hand to her throat and stroke her skin with his damp thumb. She froze, almost gagging on the smell of cheap cologne and sour sweat. Interpreting her inaction as acquiescence, he began to paw her. 'Come on now, it's just a few steps to the house.' He groped at her right breast, applying his other hand to his genitals, rubbing busily as his excitement began to mount. Suddenly his mouth was over hers. His lips were wet and sloppy, and his breath so repellent that her stomach heaved. He was so abhorrent that at last she resisted, beating her fists against his head, clawing at his eyes and kicking his shins. The dread and nausea almost choked her, but no matter how she fought and tried to scream, his strength and weight proved too much. He clamped a hand over her mouth, and tore at her flimsy gown with the other. He grunted as he tried to thrust his groin against her, but his thick girth hampered him. He fumbled with the falls of his breeches to expose his swollen member, and began to force her down on to the lawn beside the veranda. Her gown caught on rose thorns, and petals and leaves fell on to her face as she continued to resist him. His fingers pried roughly between her legs, trying to push inside her, and he continued to rub his erection against her. His breaths were shorter and swifter, and she knew he was close to ejaculation.

Revulsion almost robbed her of consciousness, but then, quite suddenly, she heard a thud, and suddenly his strength gave out and he slumped heavily on to her, his breath rattling in his throat. What was wrong with him? A heart attack? The rattling ceased, and he became utterly still. With a frightened cry she managed to push him off and scramble away.

Someone helped her to her feet. 'Are you all right, Miss Beth? Miss Beth?' It was Billy, who'd been alerted by her muffled screams.

'Oh, Billy,' she whispered, gripping his arms to steady herself.

'You're safe now, Miss Beth, he's out cold. I whacked him with a log.' Billy put his coat around her to hide her torn bodice, which now exposed far more than was seemly. Then he knelt by Topweather, slapping him to bring him around. Beth looked at the log, and then at the blood oozing from the wound at the back of Topweather's head. There was something uncannily lifeless about him and, as the thought crept over her, Billy looked up, frightened. 'Oh, my Gawd, I've killed him! He's dead, Miss Beth, he's dead!' She began to shiver violently, and glanced around fearfully, wondering if there had been any witnesses. But they were in a very private part of the garden. The only place from which they might have been seen was the top of Rendisbury Hill, but the road was deserted. 'Miss Beth?' Billy was panic-stricken. 'What'll I do, Miss Beth? I don't want to swing!'

'I won't let that happen!' she cried, but her shocked mind was numb.

At that moment the French doors from the parlour opened and Mrs Cobbett emerged, brandishing a saucepan. Molly peered from behind her. 'What's going on out here?' the housekeeper demanded, and then her face changed as she saw Beth. 'Miss Beth? Oh, my dear life, is that a body?' She stared at Topweather's body.

The little coachman was distraught. 'I did it, Mrs C. He was attacking Miss Beth, and so I clouted him with that log. Now he's dead! Oh, my Gawd, he's dead!'

Molly gasped and hid her mouth with her hands, but Mrs Cobbett had her wits about her. 'Who is he?'

Beth answered, 'The London agent from whom I leased this house. He believed he knew something about me that would force me to – well, I think you can guess.' She parted Billy's coat to show her torn bodice.

Mrs Cobbett was appalled. 'The dirty, misbegotten dog,' she muttered, and then looked around urgently. 'There's no one about now. Do you think you were seen?'

Beth shook her head tearfully. 'I'm sure not, Mrs Cobbett, although any number of people might have witnessed him coming here.'

The housekeeper pushed the saucepan into Molly's hands and stepped down from the veranda to put her arms around Beth. 'It's all right now, my dear, we'll sort this out.' She glanced up at the darkening skies. 'It's lucky it's such a lowering evening. Not many will be out. Molly, you get on over to my sister's and tell her I need the pony and trap urgently. She won't ask questions, and you can drive it back here.'

'I can't drive!' Molly cried, bursting into tears.

'Billy, you go with her. But first, did the murdered man come by horse? He did? Then we'll use it to help with the climb up to the Porworthy road. I'll get the second harness out when you've gone, and I'll go with you, Billy. We can leave the body by the wayside, with the horse. A couple of highwaymen were busy along there early in the year, and folk will think they've started up again. Well, get on with it then, the sooner we get this done, the better for all of us. Bring the trap right here to the garden gate. We'll lift the body into the back and cover it with something.' As Billy and Molly hurried off, Mrs Cobbett looked fondly after them. 'That soft hosebird Billy thinks he's done a murder, when all he did was save you, Miss Beth.'

It seemed an age before Billy and Molly led the pony and trap around to the garden gate, together with Topweather's black cob, which they harnessed in front of the pony. Then, with some difficulty he and the three women managed to get the agent's body into the trap and cover it with an old blanket. When they'd finished, Billy rode Topweather's cob and Mrs Cobbett drove the trap for the laborious climb up Rendisbury Hill. As the silhouettes disappeared at the summit, Beth and Molly went back into the house. Molly touched Beth's arm timidly. 'Billy won't be in trouble for this, will he? I mean, Mrs Cobbett's plan will work, won't it?'

'Of course it will,' Beth replied reassuringly, but with more resolution than she felt, for only time would tell. They adjourned to the kitchen, and it seemed a lifetime before they at last heard the trap returning. Billy attended to the pony and trap, and Mrs Cobbett came inside. 'It's done,' she said, 'and without a soul around. We left him half in the heather, half on the road, by the Rendisbury church signpost.' She took a purse from her pocket. 'And we relieved him of this too, to make it more convincing. Open up the range, there's a good girl, Molly. Much as it grieves me, I'm going to burn it.' She faced the two seated at the table. 'Now then, I've been over and over it all with Billy, and he knows exactly what to say if we should be asked anything. I'll say it again, so we *all* know what we should.'

Beth smiled gratefully at her. 'You've been a tower of strength tonight, Mrs Cobbett.'

'I told you I was a fearsome old biddy when my dander's up and bristling. A clear head in times of crisis, that's me. Besides, I'll do whatever's needed to preserve our little household. Whatever's needed. From now on we'll all act as normal as can be when we go out, and when we're in church come Sunday, we'll sing like larks. No one is going to know from our faces that we've anything to hide.'

Beth nodded, but already the enormity of what had happened filled her with fresh guilt and terror. Had this night's events added involvement in a second murder to her tally of crimes? She closed her eyes, for all the stars in Heaven and beyond had crossed this summer, which was to have seen the happy transformation of her life.

Chapter Nineteen

og closed in from the Bristol Channel over the following days, a clammy grey cloak that created an air of eeriness. Topweather's death shocked the area. His identity was established through the cob, which belonged to the Cross Keys in Dulverford. Posters were put up offering a reward for information leading to the arrest of the culprit or culprits, and several local men were suspected until they proved they were elsewhere during the relevant hours. The hue and cry died down within days, but rumour and speculation ran a longer course. No one came to the Dower House to ask questions, and no one appeared to have seen Topweather riding through Lannermouth. The awful crime was blamed upon highwaymen.

When Sunday came, Beth's red chariot left the Dower House in good time for morning service. It was warm and sunny, with a light breeze that rustled the trees and set the wayside grass dancing. Mrs Cobbett and Molly, both in their best clothes, were inside with Beth, who wore a pale-green silk pelisse and gown. The rector's congregation came from miles around to worship, but although there were traps and gigs by the lych gate, most arrived on saddle horses, cobs and ponies. Beth saw Landry's mount, Rollo, tethered to the great oak that overhung the churchyard wall. People were standing around in groups, and few appeared to have gone into church already. Vehicles like the chariot were still a novel enough sight for talking to cease as Billy manoeuvred it to a halt. Attention wasn't only on the vehicle, but on Beth as well, and Mrs Cobbett looked at her kindly. 'What they know is nowhere near as much as they guess. Believe me, if there was chatter, I'd know about it.'

Billy came to open the door, and as Beth alighted she saw Harriet, wearing dark-brown muslin, a cream spencer, and a straw gypsy hat with cream plumes. She also wore what Beth considered to be a rather forced smile. 'Good morning, Beth.'

'Good morning.' Beth paused, noting that in spite of the bright greeting, beneath her hat's wide, shady brim, her friend's eyes were red from crying. 'Is something wrong?' she asked in concern.

Harriet gave a smile that was supposed to be carefree. 'Not unless you consider a proposal of marriage to be something wrong.'

'A proposal? From whom?'

'My cousin John Herriot, but I haven't accepted yet. John arrived the day before yesterday, at my father's secret invitation, and has been bombarding me with attention and love tokens since the moment he stepped over the threshold. Castle Harriet is under siege.'

'Do you dislike it?'

Again the slightly false smile. 'Of course not, for it flatters my vanity.'

'Will you accept? The truth now, Miss Bellamy.'

Harriet looked at her. 'The truth? Probably, especially after this morning.'

'What happened this morning?'

There was a long pause. 'I had a falling out with my father when I discovered that he intends to follow the North Devon Staghounds tomorrow. He isn't as young as he once was, and I'm afraid he'll break his foolish neck. So we had words. I've begged John to go too, to keep an eye on him.'

'I'm sure you and Mr Bellamy will soon be fast friends again,' Beth said reassuringly, not convinced she'd been told the whole truth. She hoped Harriet did accept her cousin, if only to alleviate Beth's conscience over Landry.

'You'll meet John in a while, for he's already gone into the church,' Harriet explained. 'He's tall and thin, with a pale square face topped by a shock of spiky blond hair that simply will not obey the comb. You'll like him, for he's very kind and charming.'

At last everyone began to file beneath the lych gate toward the church porch. Once inside, Harriet drew Beth down the aisle to the Bellamy pew at the front to introduce her to John Herriot, who proved to be exactly as described, but with thick freckles too. Beth liked him, and thought he and Harriet went well together. Or was that another instance of wishful thinking? Taking a discreet glance at the gallery, where Landry stood alone, as he always did, Beth smiled and he smiled back. She was still looking at him when his eyes moved slightly to her right and his smile became awkward. Harriet had also glanced up at him, her face unsmiling, and her eyes almost sorrowful. Beth concluded that something had happened between them, and it was only a small leap to conclude further that Landry, not John Herriot's proposal or Mr Bellamy's penchant for stag-hunting, was the real cause of Harriet's tears.

The hymns, which were suitably doleful in a week when a traveller had been found apparently robbed and murdered, were clearly not the ones the congregation had expected for this particular Sunday in August. As the organist commenced the opening bars, those with hymn books made much fuss about turning their pages, and the singing was a little off-key and ragged until everyone settled. Harriet's father had also composed his sermon around the Sixth Commandment, *Thou shalt not kill,* and delivered it as if he suspected the entire congregation of having had a hand in Topweather's demise. Mr Bellamy was a tall, heavily built man of about fifty. Everything about him was heavy, even his voice, which rang through the church like a tolling bell. He was balding, his hair little more than a monk's tonsure, and he had a rather gloomy face, which went well with the mood of the service.

When everyone eventually left, greeting the clergyman as they emerged from the porch, Harriet and her cousin paused to stay with him, but Beth slipped on by to linger in the shade of one of the two ancient yew trees that had stood in the churchyard for 700 years, or so it was believed. She hoped that when Landry emerged he would come over to speak to her. He lingered only a few moments with the group by the porch, and then came to join her. Fearing to appear too intimate in public, he and Beth strolled openly around the churchyard, being very proper and not doing anything to arouse comment from the many watching eyes. Beth could tell he had something on his mind, but he seemed set upon not coming to the point of it. She halted at last.

'What's wrong?' she asked for the second time since leaving the Dower House. 'Is it something to do with Harriet?'

'Why do you ask that?'

'Because I'm not a fool. She's been crying, and tried to convince me that it concerned proposing cousins and stag-hunting fathers, but there was something very false about it all. Then I saw how your face changed when she looked up at you in the gallery. What is going on?'

He sighed. 'Very well, I'll tell you. I called at the rectory after breakfast, to tell her how I feel about you. I couldn't leave it any longer. She has a right to know.'

'I thought she had no rights.'

He looked at her. 'Just the rights of an old and dear friend.'

Beth felt rebuked. 'Did you tell her *everything*?' She sincerely hoped he hadn't!

'Well, no, of course not, although I think she guesses. She's heard the whispers too, and can hardly imagine we play cards up on the cliff. I needed to tell her, Beth, because I know how she feels about me. I live in hope that she will get over me and find someone else. I pray she accepts her cousin.' Landry glanced at the porch, where Harriet and John were laughing together about something.

'Maybe she will. She hinted as much,' Beth said.

Landry removed his hat in order to run his fingers through his dark hair. 'Beth, I haven't confessed all about Harriet and me. Once, over ten years ago, we became lovers.'

Beth was thunderstruck. 'Lovers?' she whispered. More feet of clay?

'It's not something of which I boast, and I'm only telling you because I want everything to be open between us.' She glanced away. The thought of confiding her past had been difficult enough before this week, but Topweather's death made it utterly, absolutely and completely out of the question. Oh, what else did this star-crossed summer have in store for her? Landry took her silence for condemnation. 'Don't censure me without hearing it all, Beth. It happened the afternoon I heard of my elder brother Gerald's death. We were both in the army. I was about to rejoin my regiment when news arrived that he'd been killed in an accident while his regiment was embarking at Cork for Gibraltar. Harriet was with me when I received the tidings, and she could see how devastated I was. She tried to comfort me, and one thing led to another. It was a moment of extreme emotion, Beth, and I'm ashamed to say that the following morning I rather skulked away to my regiment.'

Beth lowered her eyes. 'Do you expect me to commend you?'

'No. No, of course not, but I don't want you to despise me either. Letting my emotional and physical needs rob me of gallantry is not something of which I am proud. On returning a year later I was uneasy, not wanting to hurt her, but at the same time needing her to understand there would not be a resumption of physical intimacy. She and I were meant to be good friends, not lovers or spouses. So I behaved as if nothing had happened, and to my relief she didn't say anything about it, and seemed as anxious to forget as me. I've always wanted to marry for love, Beth, not duty. Maybe by the strict rules of our society my duty was to marry her as soon as I'd robbed her of her virginity, but as my wife she could never enjoy the sort of fulfilment she needs, because I could never give everything of myself. Do you understand that?'

Did she understand? Oh, yes, she did. Only too well. She also knew that there were now two women with a prior claim to him, Carrie Markham *and* Harriet Bellamy.

At that moment Harriet hailed them. 'Landry? I have decided that you and Beth must be the first to congratulate us,' she declared happily, and they turned to see her approaching on John Herriot's arm.

Landry bent forward to kiss Harriet's cheek. 'I'm delighted for you.'

Her eyes closed as his lips brushed her skin, then opened again with almost dazzling brilliance. 'I couldn't be happier, Landry. How could I have dithered so long?'

Next Landry reached out to pump John's hand. 'Congratulations, sir! I vow that you have snapped up one of the two most splendid ladies in the whole of Devon!'

'That would appear to be so,' John replied, beaming.

Harriet turned to Beth. 'I've been such a fool, not seeing the happiness that was right under my silly nose. As I was talking to John just now I suddenly saw what a dear thing he is. He makes me laugh so, and can be so tender that I knew I would always regret not accepting him. So I decided there and then.'

Beth hugged her. 'I'm so glad, Harriet.' She smiled at John too. 'I wish you and Harriet every joy, Mr Herriot.'

'Thank you, Miss Mannacott.'

For a second Beth's mind went utterly blank. Mannacott? She was on the point of correcting him that her name was Tremoille when wit returned and she bit back the traitorous words. Harriet looked curiously at her. 'Beth?'

'Mm? Oh, nothing, I was just remembering something.'

The four exchanged the usual pleasantries and small talk, and then Harriet murmured about it being time for lunch at the rectory. She and John took their leave and walked off, heads together as if in tender conversation.

'Do you think Harriet is truly happy about this?' she asked Landry.

'Yes, of course. Why? Do you doubt it?'

'I don't know. It's just that it follows on the heels of your visit this morning.'

'Does it matter?' he asked softly. 'She has made her choice and is to marry her cousin. He is clearly considering jumping over the moon, and she seems, well, relieved to have come to a decision.'

Beth watched Harriet and John disappear beneath the lych gate, and then heard the tinkle of Harriet's laughter from the roadway beyond. Her doubts faded and she smiled a little sheepishly. 'You're right. Guilt is making me unsure of everything.'

'You have no just cause to feel guilty.' He drew the back of his fingers softly down her cheek. 'Before Harriet and her cousin joined us just now, I told you that I didn't love her and could never marry her. I say it again now. You're my other half, the lover I have always sought, Beth Mannacott, and I want you to be my wife.'

Her green eyes widened. 'Marry you?' she repeated.

'You told me you'll never have the man you really love, so why not accept the man who loves you? I don't care what secrets you have, but I can help you face them. I want to look after you, protect you and love you, and I think that you already know we will do well together. I can be content with being second in your heart, provided I am first in your life. So Beth, make that possible by becoming my wife.'

She couldn't speak. The things he'd said made it all so very tempting. She was afraid of her past, but with Landry at her side, she— Her thoughts halted. She had to be practical. Yes, she could marry him, and maybe they'd be happy for the rest of their lives, but she couldn't tell him everything about her past, not when two deaths were involved. And what if Guy were to trace her? What then? Better it was Beth Tremoille who faced the consequences of her actions, than Mrs Landry Haldane, with all the shame it would bring to her husband.

He'd been watching her face. 'Beth, when I say I don't care about your secrets, I mean it. I need to be at your side, and I really do mean it. Being with you is infinitely more important than anything else. *Anything* else. I want you as my wife, and I will keep on asking until you accept.'

She gazed at him. 'Landry, I can't have children.' She hadn't even realized she was going to say it.

'Children? Damn it, Beth, I don't want you to ensure the next generation of Haldanes, I want you for yourself!'

He didn't ask her how she knew she was barren, nor had he asked about the man she really loved, and her secrets were hers to keep if that was what she wished. So great was his love that he wanted to overlook everything. Under those terms she could give enough of herself to be fair to him, and in return she would be loved and cherished. Temptation spread enticingly before her.

'Beth? Let me provide you with security and a loving marriage. Believe me, my reward will be eternal happiness. Accept. Please.'

Suddenly the summer seemed less star-crossed as she was swept along by new emotions. For once, Guy was nowhere in her thoughts as she flung her arms around Landry's neck. 'Yes,' she breathed, 'yes, I accept!'

He gave a jubilant laugh and caught her around the waist to swing her up into the air. 'Oh, Beth, Beth, you've made me the most blessed man on God's own earth!'

Late that evening, during another dramatic sunset, Harriet slipped out of the rectory with a basket of fresh-baked cakes for Carrie Markham at the lodge. She walked quickly, her eyes downcast, her shawl clutched around her shoulders. Her heart should have been light and happy because of John, but instead she felt low and depressed. There was no going back, and in due course she would become Harriet Herriot. Oh, what a mockery of a name! Reaching the gates, she wondered if Landry was at the hall, or down at the Dower House with Beth. Salt tears pricked her eyes. She had loved him all her life, and would never stop loving him, but Beth Mannacott had won him with a single smile. Fate was so cruel. She knocked at the lodge door, and Carrie answered, holding a lighted candlestick and wearing a long-sleeved grey muslin dress, unadorned and simple. 'Miss Harriet? Come in, do.'

'I've brought some of Katie's favourite cakes.' Carrie's deteriorating health was plain to see, and she'd wasted away visibly in the week since being given the medallion. Even her voice, still so pleasantly Devonshire, was frailer. Harriet stepped straight into the little parlour, which was furnished with items from the big house. They looked unlikely in such a small dwelling. Katie had been playing with a wooden doll, but was allowed one of the cakes before being despatched to bed. Then, when they were alone, Harriet came to the point. 'Carrie, have you heard of the two betrothals that—?'

'Two? I've heard that you are to marry your cousin. Is it true?' Harriet nodded. 'Well, it's not the wisest decision you've ever made.'

'Wisdom is not my greatest asset,' Harriet observed wryly, 'and now it's time to get on with my life.'

'Not this way. You should be marrying Mr Landry.'

'Well, that brings me to the second betrothal: he is to marry Miss Mannacott.'

Carrie was appalled. 'That cannot be so!'

'It is so, Carrie. They came to the rectory after church service to tell us. It will be made official at a grand betrothal ball at Haldane Hall just before Christmas. The nineteenth of December, I believe, as it's Miss Mannacott's birthday. Anyway, he proposed to her just after I'd accepted my cousin. So you see, it's all too late now.'

'It won't be too late until the wedding band is on her finger.'

'Please don't, Carrie, for it's all settled.'

'Miss Mannacott will need many midwinter lights if she is to fend off—'

'Stop it!' Harriet became agitated. 'I'm the rector's daughter, Carrie, and have no truck with pagan superstition.'

'It is not pagan or superstition, but common sense. Everyone hereabouts knows it to be so. If you dance at midwinter, you need many lights to see your way. I do not think Miss Mannacott will ever have sufficient light.' Harriet fell into a stony silence, and after a moment Carrie glanced at Katie's doll, which lay where the little girl had left it. 'And what happens when I go? What then? It's no good, Miss Harriet, he *must* be told.'

'No, Carrie. Leave things as they are.'

Carrie suppressed a cough. 'And – and you think all will be well? That the new Mrs Landry Haldane will welcome Katie into her home? Jealousy is a monstrous thing, Miss Harriet, and I believe Miss Mannacott to be no more free of it than anyone else.'

'She would never be cruel to a child.'

'How can you say that?' Carrie coughed again, more agitatedly this time. When it had subsided, she looked at Harriet. 'What do you really know of her? What do any of us know of her? She's come out of nowhere to take over.'

Harriet lowered her eyes. It was true, what *did* they know of Beth? Even Landry hardly knew her, and yet intended to spend the rest of his life with her.

'Miss Harriet?' Carrie's hollow eyes were upon her.

'Miss Mannacott knows all about Katie, and would never be unkind.'

'He should still be *made* to do the right thing by you,' Carrie repeated.

'No, Carrie. Promise me you won't interfere. I beg you, let sleeping dogs lie.'

'Very well, Miss Harriet, if that's your wish.' But Carrie's face was shadowed.

Chapter Twenty

It was a fine mid-September morning in Frampney, and smoke rose from the forge as Jake and Matty went about their daily business. Phoebe was waiting in the kitchen as Rosalind returned from the vegetable garden with potatoes and runner beans for the evening meal. Rosalind thought – hoped – that Phoebe had gone to the village store for some provisions, and could not hide her dismay on finding the older woman seated at the table. 'Oh, Phoebe, I – I thought you'd gone out.'

'Put those vegetables down and take a seat,' Phoebe instructed.

'But, I've things to do, and—'

'Do as you're told, Rosalind.' Reluctantly the girl put the basket down and wiped her hands on her coarse brown apron before sitting down. 'Now then,' Phoebe said, 'it's been more than a month since that foolishness with Master Robert, and you haven't washed any cloths from your monthly bleeding, so I have to ask if you've come on at all.'

'Yes,' Rosalind lied, 'yes, I came on within a week. It wasn't really heavy, and I used the cloths as usual.' She spoke well, knowing it pleased Phoebe.

'And washed them too?'

'Yes, of course.'

'Then where did you dry them? I saw nothing on the line.'

Rosalind lowered her eyes quickly. 'I – I get embarrassed, Phoebe, so I dried them by the window in my room.'

'Did you now?' Phoebe studied her closely. It might be the truth; on the other hand, it might be the lies of a girl too frightened to admit to anything. 'I don't know that I can take your word for it, Rosalind.'

'Are you saying I'm lying?' Rosalind leapt up.

'No, I'm saying I've seen no proof that you've had your bleeding. Your word isn't enough. I owe it to your father to let him know about all this.'

Rosalind's eyes widened with horror. 'No! Oh, no, Phoebe, please!'

Jake suddenly spoke from the doorway behind them. 'Let me know about what?'

Rosalind's eyes waxed as round as saucers, and she whipped around with a dismayed gasp. 'Nothing, Dad! Honest, it's nothing!'

'It doesn't sound like nothing, Rozzie,' he answered slowly, glancing at Phoebe and then at his daughter again. 'Now, I'm not moving from here until I'm told.'

Rosalind could only stare at him, struck dumb with fear, and it was left to Phoebe to let him in on his daughter's guilty secret. 'Be calm now, Jake, because you're not going to like what I'm about to say, but—'

'Don't, Phoebe, please!' Rosalind cried desperately. 'It's nothing, Dad, I swear!'

'Enough, Rozzie. Go on, Phoebe.'

'Well, I'm not sure whether or not Rozzie's with child.'

A deathly silence fell upon the room, interrupted only by the sound of hammering from the forge, where Matty was making a new weathervane for the parish church.

Jake stared, his mind emptied of all thought, but then he seized Rosalind's arm. 'Have you been with someone?' he demanded, but she was shaking so much she couldn't answer. 'Answer me, damn it!' he cried, anger beginning to thicken his voice.

'Yes, yes, I have!' she whimpered, shielding her head from the expected blow.

'Who?'

She was filled with dread. She'd been warned and warned again about Robert Lloyd, and had still gone with him. Now, faced with her father's fury, her tongue froze.

Phoebe answered for her. 'The squire's son,' she said quietly.

Jake shook Rosalind as a dog would a rabbit. 'Is that right, Rozzie? After all that was said, you *still* went with him like a whore?'

'Yes! Oh, yes, yes! You're hurting me, Dad!'

'I'll do more than that, you damned little slut!'

'I'm no more a slut than Beth was!' she cried, trying to fight back.

'Don't speak of Beth like that!'

'Why not? She went with you time and time again. I saw you. She's a slut, but not me. I only went with Master Robert once!' Her head jerked back as he struck her, and he would have struck her again had not Phoebe intervened anxiously.

'Enough now, Jake, for she's only a slip of a thing and you don't know your strength. And what point is there in lamming her? What's done is done.'

Jake turned away, but his anger hadn't left him. He looked at Rosalind again. 'Don't *ever* speak of Beth like that again, do you hear, girl? Right now you're not fit to mention her name!' He strode from the room, slamming the door behind him and, as his angry steps diminished down the path to the forge, Rosalind burst into tears.

Phoebe went to comfort her. 'There now, child, don't take on so. It's out in the open now. The truth now, you haven't come on since that day, have you?'

Rosalind shook her head. 'But I'm going to, I *know* I am,' she sobbed. 'I can feel that tugging in my belly, and my breasts are sore.'

'Pray God you're right, Rosalind, because I don't rightly know what your father might do if he finds he's to be a grandfather.'

'Do? To me?' Rosalind's breath caught with alarm.

'No, dear, to Master Robert Lloyd.'

Matty watched Jake hammer the horseshoe as if to consign it to perdition. Glancing at Jamie, who held the squire's cob, the old blacksmith sat in his chair and lit his pipe. 'Unless you watch it, Jake Mannacott, you're about to smash everything to pieces, forge and all,' he observed. 'I like to see a craftsman, not a madman.'

Jake paused, his muscles wet and shining in the firelight. 'If I don't beat all hell out of this, Matty, I'll do something far worse.'

'Oh?' Matty puffed on the pipe. 'And what might that be?'

'Choke the bloody lights out of Robert Lloyd.' Jake threw the hammer down, and plunged the shoe into the bucket of water.

Jamie soothed the nervous cob as Matty sat forward in the creaky chair. 'What's that mangy hosebird done this time?'

Jake glanced at Jamie, but then decided to blurt the truth anyway. 'Messed with my Rozzie, that's what.'

Jamie's jaw dropped, but Matty's brows drew together. 'Is she—?'

'She says not, but Phoebe's obviously none too sure.' Jake rounded on Jamie. 'And if one word of this gets out, I'll break your neck!'

'It won't get out on account of me, Jake, I promise you that, but it's long past time something was done about Master Robert.'

Matty was uneasy. 'That's dangerous talk, Jamie, so hold your tongue. The likes of us have to put up with the likes of him.'

'This is a new score to settle, on top of all the old ones.'

Matty was sympathetic. 'Your Jenny?'

'Yes. I didn't do for him like I should back then, so this is my fault.'

Jake put out a hand. 'Steady on, you can't go thinking like that. This isn't your fault. You're right about one thing, though, it's high time Lloyd was brought to book.'

The sun was setting as Robert urged his father's bright bay thoroughbred, Jupiter, along the deserted exercise track, accompanied by his setter. He was intent upon the gallop because he'd rashly issued a challenge to Lord Welland's jockey, Sam McCullogh, to a match with Welland's top stallion, Galahad, over five miles at the Burford racecourse up in the Cotswolds. A great deal of money already rested on the outcome, so he needed Jupiter to be at the peak of fitness for the beginning of October, but when he spurred the horse for a blistering last hundred yards, the animal had nothing more to give. Reining in with a scowl, Robert tugged the horse's mouth viciously before alighting. 'What's the matter, damn you?' he breathed. Jupiter stamped, snorted and danced around nervously, his eyes rolling toward a gate, where last week he'd been stung by a wasp. 'Oh, so you remember, do you?' Robert muttered, pushing the inquisitive setter away as he tried to examine the horse. He found nothing wrong. Still muttering under his breath, he tethered Jupiter to some bushes before taking out a flask of brandy and flinging himself on the grass, where the setter joined him. He wished he hadn't issued the challenge, but it was too late now and he'd lose face if he withdrew.

Emptying the flask, he removed his hat to lie back. The late evening sun was warm, and the brandy felt fiery in his belly. He relaxed a little. If only he had a girl with him now, a ripe virginal receptacle like the Mannacott wench. Ah, yes, sweet Rosalind. He moved his hand to his groin, and rubbed gently as he remembered how eager and rewarding she'd been. His excitement mounted, and he opened his breeches to masturbate. The setter growled, but he took no notice. In his imagination he was bucking inside Rosalind again, storming her maidenhead and taking his selfish pleasure. But as he twisted sideways to soil the grass and not his clothes, he became aware of Jupiter's uneasiness and then the setter's renewed growling. Turning back, his dangling member still exposed, he found himself dazzled by brilliance of the fading sun, but then two shadows loomed over him and a forked stick stabbed one time down on either side of his throat, almost closing his windpipe. 'A voice he didn't recognize spoke with a contemptuous sneer. 'Well, if it isn't Onan giving his cock another tug.'

He struggled helplessly and, as the shadow moved again he found himself staring up at Jamie. 'Webb!' he choked. 'Are you mad? I'll see you dead!'

The setter's growls became more menacing, and suddenly it leapt at Jamie, but a second figure, much larger, plucked it from the air and put great muscular hands around its throat. Robert's light-blue eyes were wide with fear as the setter struggled and squirmed, but was no match for Jake's strength. Gradually its movements became weaker, until at last they ceased, except for an occasional lifeless twitch.

'Sweet God, sweet God,' Robert breathed, trying to free himself from the fork.

'You're not going anywhere, Lloyd,' Jake said softly, tossing the dog aside.

'You'll pay for this, Mannacott. And you, Webb.'

Jake gave a mirthless laugh. 'No, my fine fellow, we'll not pay even a farthing, because you're going the same way as your dog. You've shot your load for the last time.'

'Please—!'

'Oh, so you're begging me now, eh? Well, that's something pleasant to remember you by.' Jake's teeth flashed white in a smile that terrified a coward like Robert.

Jamie suddenly took fright, unnerved by the darkness he saw in the blacksmith's eyes. 'No, Jake, let's just rough him up a bit.'

'Don't be daft, Jamie, he's seen our faces now! Damn it, Rozzie's right, you *are* a fool. Do you imagine he'll walk away from this and kindly forget about us?'

Jamie swallowed. 'No.'

'Right. I came here to see this bastard die for the things he's done, and there's no one here to stop me, right? If you've no stomach for it, you'd best go now, but if you've any respect for your Jenny, you'll stay.'

'I'll stay.'

'Then keep that stick in place.'

Realizing that his life was about to be snuffed like a candle, Robert tried to scream, but Jake shoved a dirty kerchief into his mouth. 'That's enough of that. You've fancied yourself such a fine arrogant fellow, so it behoves you to act like a man now, not like one of the poor wenches you've ruined. If I could tie a knot in your prick, I would, but there's not much there to get a grip on, eh? I'd be ashamed to own such a skinny worm of a thing. And to think you used it to ruin my Rozzie. Well, you won't ruin any more wenches. Breathe your last, tomcat,' he said softly, reaching down to Robert's throat.

Robert was so terrified that he lost control of his bladder, but it was the last thing he did before Jake's fingers snapped his neck like a twig.

Jamie turned away, retching, but at the same time a wild exultation began to hunt through him. It was done at last. Jenny, and all the others had been avenged.

Matty, Phoebe and Rosalind waited in the kitchen, where only the ticking of the old clock on the mantelshelf broke the silence. They all turned nervously toward the door as Jake's steps approached. He came in and leaned back against the door. 'Robert Lloyd isn't going to bother anyone again. We got him on the exercise track. It's nice and quiet there.' Jake's smile was a travesty.

Rosalind hid her face in her hands and began to sob, and Phoebe got up to fill the kettle and hang it over the fire. 'Rozzie came on not half an hour since, Jake.' He breathed out with relief, but when he went to put his hand on Rosalind's shoulder, she shook free and ran up to her room.

'Why insist that I drive you?' Rowan asked, steadying Jane's arm as he tooled the cabriolet speedily over another rut in the Frampney road. After an overnight frost had come a fine crisp October morning, with blackberries and old man's beard in the hedgerows and gossamer in the air. There was a smell of woodsmoke from a perry apple orchard, where several trees had been uprooted in the August storm, and through the open entrance of a cottage lean-to they saw two old women working a pear press.

Jane gripped the side rail and the handle of her folded lace parasol, and trusted an overhanging bramble would not ruin her silk hat. 'I need a second opinion, and understand you are a good judge of horseflesh,' she answered.

Rowan raised a sly eyebrow. 'Was dear Papa otherwise engaged?'

'I have no idea because I have not approached him. He has become the very last person with whom I wish to spend time, which is why I have decamped to Whitend. And is also why you have joined me rather than stay at Tremoille House.'

'Repenting at leisure, are we?'

'Gloat away, it is your prerogative,' she responded, frowning as dust flew over her jade pelisse and white muslin gown.

'So you prefer your ne'er-do-well stepson to his sire?'

'Needs must,' she murmured, 'for the Devil is certainly driving.'

'I'm a dashing blade, Stepmama dearest, incapable of driving sedately.' He laughed. His top hat was tipped back on his dark curls, and he was dressed as splendidly as all country gentlemen should, but his handsome face was battered and bruised, and there were bandages around his knuckles. 'Why are you interested in this horse? What's its name? Jupiter?' Rowan asked, urging the high-stepping horse to greater effort.

She nodded. 'I'm interested because the squire's son was to have raced it against McCullogh on Galahad.'

Rowan slowed the cabriolet to a more acceptable trot. 'Galahad, eh?'

'Yes, and McCullogh admitted to being a little worried about the outcome. Galahad may be Lancelot's full brother, but he isn't Lancelot.'

'His offspring may prove in Lancelot's mould,' Rowan pointed out.

'One can but hope. Anyway, I'm of a mind to acquire Jupiter.'

Rowan remembered something. 'You said his son *was* to have raced it?' He knew Robert and disliked him.

'Lloyd the younger was killed last month. Murdered, it seems. He'd been out exercising Jupiter and was found with a broken neck, pinioned to the grass by a fork. Oh, and with his penis on show to the four winds,' she added.

'Good God.'

'Anyway, Squire Lloyd no longer wishes to keep the horse, hence the sale.'

'And I thought life in the country was peaceful and bucolic.'

Jane looked at his bruised face. 'What would *you* know of a peaceful life?'

'Not much. Folk pay well to see Lord Welland's heir getting a good drubbing. Each new shiner means a fat purse.'

'Rowan, you're destroying your looks. You're such a handsome boy that it grieves me to see your face resembling a shambles.'

'Do you have designs upon my virtue, Stepmama?'

'What virtue?'

He laughed. 'Jane, I want to despise you, but you make it damned difficult!'

'Don't tell me I'm forgiven for throwing dear sweet Beth out in the cold?'

'Hardly.' Her words were an immediate damper upon his humour, reminding him that her cold ambition took precedence over everything else. He was ashamed of having briefly enjoyed her company. 'Have you heard anything of Beth?' he asked.

'No, unless you count her shameful decision to become a blacksmith's mistress.' She eyed him. 'From your question, may I deduce that Sir Guy Valmer hasn't found her?'

Rowan hesitated. 'Yes,' he said then.

She hid her relief, but not well enough, for he smiled grimly. 'Ah, how you worry, Stepmama, as well you might, since you told Papa such fiblings about Esmond Tremoille's final will and testament.'

'You aren't privy to anything, Rowan, nor is Sir Guy. There wasn't another will. Esmond disinherited Beth in my favour, and that is that.'

Rowan suddenly wanted to unsettle her. It was an impulse he couldn't resist and immediately regretted, but was done in a trice and could not be undone. 'Ah, but you and I know there *is* another will. Why else would you go to London to see old Withers?'

Her lips parted. 'I had no idea my private appointments with a solicitor were being made public. I will have to remonstrate with the loose-tongued fellow.'

'So you admit it?'

'That I went to ask him about the will? Yes, of course. Rowan, I am as intrigued as everyone else to know what Esmond wrote in the mysterious letter to Beth, and of *course* I wondered if there might, after all, be another will. But now I am sensible again and accept that Esmond intended me to have everything.'

The Devil still perched on Rowan's shoulder, prodding him into an irresponsible disclosure. 'You're wrong, madam. Your late husband decided to cut you out and reinstate his daughter. The will is irrefutable, and is now in Guy's possession. All he lacks is Beth to complete his plan. Where will that leave you, Jane? If Papa merely sulks with you now, he'll be deranged when he learns once and for all that you lied in order to marry him.'

Jane managed not to react overtly, but it took such an effort that she felt sick. 'Sir Guy has forged it. Even if he finds Beth and makes her his wife ten times over, the inheritance remains mine, as I trust you will inform him.' At last the Devil flew away, and Rowan was appalled to have broken his word to Guy. His silence aroused Jane's curiosity, but she couldn't read him. 'By the way, how long will you be in London?' she asked.

'I, er, have no idea. Possibly until the new year.'

'Hmm. Well, it would please me if you were to come home for Christmas. And, if my intuition serves me well, it would also please your father. It is in your own interest to be snug with him again. Better to have title, country pile *and* fortune.'

'I rather thought *you* had your sights on the pile and the fortune,' he observed.

'Rowan, all I ever wanted was your father.'

'You took Beth's home and fortune,' he reminded her.

'A crime for which I am now endeavouring to make amends by being on guard for you. Rowan, did you know that your father has an illegitimate son? Slightly older than you from all accounts.'

Rowan was stunned. 'Who is he?'

'I don't know.'

'Damn it, Jane, you can't come out with this and then refuse to say more!'

'I'm not refusing to say it, Rowan, I really and honestly don't know any more.'

'How did you find out?'

Jane smiled a little ruefully. 'Well, one of my great failings is that I do not trouble myself with other people's privacy. I found the drawer of your father's desk open and his diary inside. He is considering sending for this son to replace you. No title, of course, for that is not transferable, but certainly the young man, whoever he is, would have the lands and fortune.'

'I must read that diary.'

'You'll be wasting your time. I read it from cover to cover and only found the bald reference to the young man. So take care, Rowan, common sense must prevail.'

The first cottages of Frampney came into view, but Rowan's consternation made him headstrong, and he cracked the whip to fling the horse forward again. The cabriolet flew, as did the dust, and Jane sat rigidly, wondering if Rowan was intent upon an overturn? As they emerged into the wide stretch of the village green, the horse's head came up suddenly and its pace became uneven. 'Damn and blast, I think it's a cast shoe,' Rowan muttered, reining in.

'How fortunate that this should happen almost within heat of the forge,' Jane declared, seizing the opportunity to climb down to *terra firma*. She needed to compose herself, and could do so more satisfactorily under pretence of straightening her clothes and shaking them free of dust. Her heart was pounding, her mouth was dry, and all she could think was that Guy Valmer had the will she'd prayed was lost forever. If he located Beth as well, Jane, Lady Welland was well and truly undone. Snapping open her parasol, she turned to Rowan, who was examining the horse's off-foreleg. 'You go on to the forge. I will walk a while.'

'But I thought you wished to inspect Jupiter.'

'I'll trust your judgement, Rowan. If you think he'll be an asset to the stud, I'll pay whatever price you agree. Oh, and by the way.'

He looked curiously at her. 'Yes?'

'Did you know that Beth's former lover, Mannacott, is now blacksmith here?'

'Yes, as it happens, I do. Guy told me.'

'I see.' Without a backward glance, she turned to stroll across the green in the opposite direction from the forge, and after a moment Rowan persuaded the horse to move on. He was shaken to discover he had a half-brother, and his stomach churned as much as Jane's. The darkness in the smithy was dense before the flames flared brightly and he saw an old man with a paunch working the bellows as a younger man, tall, muscular and good-looking, held a red-hot shoe in the glowing heart of the fire. A groom waited nearby with a docile hunter. Rowan watched in silence. So this was Beth's rough lover. It was difficult to imagine Beth Tremoille, so dainty, elegant and refined, rolling in the hay with such a brute, although there was probably a great deal to be said for the fellow's splendid body. He'd make a good prizefighter.

As Jake thrust the shoe into a pail of water, he felt the newcomer's scrutiny. 'Can I help you, sir?'

'My horse has cast a shoe.'

'I won't be long, sir.' Rowan nodded and leaned back against a wall. Jake glanced at him. 'What brings you to Frampney, sir? It's a mite off the beaten track.'

'My stepmother is interested in acquiring Jupiter.'

'Ah, yes.' Jake held his gaze. 'A fine horse, but I'm afraid you're too late. Jupiter was sold yesterday to the Duke of Beaufort. I fear you've made a wasted journey.' So that's that, Stepmama, Rowan thought as Jake finished shoeing the hunter, and then attended to the cabriolet horse. As he unharnessed it the smith recognized the small W branded on its flank. 'A Welland nag, eh?'

'I'm Lord Welland's son.'

'Indeed? So, your stepmother is the former Mrs Tremoille.' The flat tone revealed Jake's opinion of that lady.

Rowan seized his opportunity. 'Do you know where Beth is?'

Annoyance clouded Jake's face. 'Hasn't the fashionable world got anything better to do than ask questions about Miss Tremoille and her common farrier? No, I don't know where she is, and as I said to Sir Guy Valmer, if I did, I wouldn't tell. You wait outside now, sir, for this is no place for a gentleman. Your horse will soon be ready.' Rowan knew he'd been dismissed, and had to hide a smile as he went back into the sunlight where the cabriolet's fittings gleamed like silver. He could see Jane in the distance, her parasol twirling slowly, almost thoughtfully, as she strolled near the village ponds, but then a young girl of about seventeen in a rose-coloured dress caught his attention. Her long, straight, blonde hair hung loose beneath her simple mobcap, and she carried a basket over her arm. She walked gracefully, her hem lifting in the light breeze, and there was something about her that completely engaged his interest. She drew nearer, and he realized she was approaching the forge. He cleared his throat and automatically began to fiddle with various parts of the cabriolet, but then a bag of flour fell from her basket and burst on the ground. 'Oh, no! Oh, no!' she cried in dismay, and Rowan ran to assist.

'Let me help,' he said, as she tried to scoop as much of the flour as she could.

'Phoebe will kill me, flour being the price it is,' she said, allowing him to help as he could. She spoke well, having recognized him from outside Gloucester Cathedral.

'The ending of the war hasn't made for a cheap loaf of bread, has it?' he replied, noticing her diction.

At last she looked up at him, taking in his cuts and bruises. 'Oh, dear,' was all she said.

He was a little self-conscious. 'Pugilism isn't the daintiest of sports, but I promise I'm not as disreputable as my appearance might suggest.'

'Fisticuffs, you mean?'

'Yes.' He smiled. She was so pretty that he was quite captivated.

Satisfied she'd salvaged as much flour as possible, she straightened, and Rowan did the same. Her glance went past him toward the forge, and he saw the quick nuance of unease that passed through her eyes. 'I – I must go now, sir,' she said, managing to give him a shy smile in return.

'Please stay.'

'I daren't, sir. My father won't like it. I'm not to speak to gentlemen.'

As she hurried away he called after her. 'What's your name?'

'Rosalind, sir. Rosalind Mannacott.'

'I'm—'

'I know who you are, sir.'

Rowan gazed after her until she'd disappeared into the white wisteria-swathed house behind the forge. 'Rosalind Mannacott,' he breathed.

As soon as she was inside, Rosalind hurried to the parlour window to watch as Rowan walked away. How handsome he was, even with those terrible bruises, and to think that he'd wanted to know her name. 'And what are you looking at so intently?' Phoebe was in a fireside chair darning some stockings.

'Oh, nothing,' Rosalind replied hastily. Too hastily.

'Really? Well, I know a fib when I hear one, especially from you.'

Rosalind sighed. 'Well, as I was coming back I dropped the flour, and Lord Welland's son helped me pick it up.' She pointed outside.

'Lord Welland's son?' Phoebe's needlework tumbled to the floor as she hastened to the window in time to see Rowan. 'Yes, that's him, all right.'

'He's so handsome,' Rosalind sighed.

Phoebe noticed. 'Oh, no, my girl, don't you go getting more ideas. Master Robert should have taught you all you need to know. The gentry only want girls like you to lie back with their legs open, so put this one from your mind.'

'Yes, Phoebe.' But Rosalind glanced outside again.

Chapter Twenty-one

Thick fog shrouded Hyde Park, and the street lamps of Park Lane were barely visible through the frosted gloom of the December night. Guy was asleep in his town house, alone, as he had been every night since ending his liaison with Maria. He wasn't alone in the house, however, because Rowan had been lodging there since October, and occupied the guest wing facing over the gardens. Guy's bedchamber, situated in pride of place above the porte-cochère, had gilded dove-grey walls and rich crimson velvet curtains drawn tightly across balconied French windows that looked toward the park. A solitary carriage drove slowly past, and the sound became part of his dreams, taking him back to the stormy June afternoon when he'd become Beth Tremoille's Good Samaritan. This time she hadn't fainted by the roadside, but was standing in the pouring rain, the leaf-green muslin gown of the portrait clinging to her body, her dark curls wet and dripping about her shoulders. The carriage halted beside her, and he climbed down. 'Miss Tremoille? May I offer you the comfort of my carriage?'

She held out a slender hand, and he helped her up. Her fingers were wet and cool, and the soaked muslin gown cleaved so close that the soft green was blushed with pink where it lay against her skin. The atmosphere changed as he climbed in, becoming as charged as the lightning that shattered the gloom outside. Her beauty was spellbinding, her lips full and sweet, the lines of her jaw and throat as sensuous as the softest tendrils, and the swelling of her breasts as enticing as dew-soaked peaches. She was Oberon's daughter, an almost ethereal presence, otherworldly and translucent, defying him to touch her. If he reached out, if he dared to caress her, would she welcome him? Or would she melt away, like frost before the morning sun? Her hazel-green eyes, captivating and yet unfathomable, were upon him. 'Are you only pursuing me for my inheritance, Sir Guy?' she enquired, as the carriage moved on.

He couldn't bear the reproach in her voice. 'No, I want you for yourself as well.' Did he mean it? Or was he simply saying it to soothe her?

'Why should I accept you?' she whispered, her voice almost lost in the drumming of the rain on the carriage roof.

'Because you want me as much as I want you.' He reached across at last, and pulled her into his arms. She was light, almost weightless, and ... were those fairy wings he glimpsed folded so delicately down her back? She curled up against him, her lips only inches from his, and the perfume of a summer meadow filled his nostrils. Her mystery and magic twined around him like a delicate vine from the heart of an enchanted forest.

'You must prove you want me, Sir Guy,' she breathed, her lips now so close that sometimes they brushed his as delicately as a butterfly. Slowly, softly, he kissed that butterfly, and felt its gentle flutter, as if it was trapped by his desire. Her gown was so flimsy she might have been naked in his embrace. She was lithe and supple, slender and exquisitely formed, and he wanted to crush her so close that his body would absorb hers. She was the woodland deity in whose shrine he would offer his entire life force; where he prayed his oblation of love and honour would be cherished.

There was such a pulsating rod springing from his loins that he felt he would never find relief. Could such intoxicating desire ever be truly sated? Surely the moment of release would lead to fresh need, as urgent and compelling as ever? Was this what was meant by endless love? His hand moved to her breast, confined so loosely by her damp bodice. How perfectly it rested in his hand, and how sweetly her nipple reached toward him, at once hard and delicate, erect and so feminine that he could only take it between his lips and adore it. She gasped as ripples of delight washed through her, and her hands wandered over him tenderly, as if she could not believe that she was in his arms at last. He kissed the fullness of her breasts, and buried his face into the seductive valley between them. He could feel her heartbeats, gentle, rhythmic, quickening with excitement as he undid his breeches to liberate the quivering shaft that now erupted from the forest of hair at his groin. He guided her hand there, and her breath caught as her fingers began a gentle investigation, first sinking into the jungle at his groin, now working their way up the thick, rigid pole to the glistening head, which she massaged with rich enjoyment, her body arcing against him. He kissed the pulse at her throat, the sweet line of her jaw and her eagerly parted lips, and his hand moved between her legs, stroking, stimulating, adoring.

Ecstasy tingled all around and through him, teasing his desire until he thought he would explode of need. Then she was no longer Oberon's daughter, but flesh and blood, needing him as he needed her. Caresses were no longer enough, there had to be union. Her hunger matched his as she wriggled until she could kneel over him on the seat. He leaned back, his masculinity erect and throbbing as he pushed the green muslin up her pale thighs until the dark tangle of hair was revealed at her groin, then, slowly and luxuriously, she guided him into her body and sank down upon him. The pleasure was pure bewitchment, an invocation of every spirit of the greenwood, the realization of every hidden yearning. Her muscles enclosed him as she raised herself a little and then sank down again, her thighs taut and firm, her movement fluid and beguiling. He was in her thrall, spellbound by sexual joy, and when he knew he could not hold back any longer, his lips joined with hers in a kiss that laid souls bare and imprisoned hearts. Together they were swept to a peak of euphoria, seemingly soldered together by the heat and intoxication of their excitement. He came with a pulsing joy that made him cry out, and provided even more thrills as he felt her share his climax. Then, as the tide of passion slowly receded, she collapsed against him and they held each other, rejoicing in the echoes of their hearts.

His lips found hers again, this time in a gentle, lingering kiss that revealed the depth of his feeling for her, but to his dismay, she was becoming hazy and indistinct, as if some unseen force commanded her to leave. 'Beth?' But he spoke to the empty air. She'd gone, leaving only the redolence of flowers and crushed leaves, and the imprint of her lips upon his. 'Beth! Don't leave me!' he cried, and this time his own voice was so clear that he awoke. The banked fire glowed in the hearth, and everything was silent. He knew he'd called Beth's name in his sleep, and knew exactly what he'd dreamed. He breathed out slowly, and closed his eyes. If it was true that one's dreams revealed the truth, then he was deeply and irretrievably in love with Beth Tremoille. If only he could believe in the truth of dreams. After lying awake for a while, at last he fell asleep again, this time without dreams, and on awakening the next morning had forgotten the erotic fantasies from the hidden depths of the night.

Going down to breakfast, he paused on the staircase half-landing to look out at the chilly capital, still enveloped in fog and frost. He shoved his hands into his dressing-gown pockets and continued down to find Rowan already at the table. 'Good God, haven't you been to bed?' Guy enquired, selecting his breakfast from the sideboard.

Rowan looked up from his newspaper. His face was newly bruised and his swollen right eye almost closed, the result of defeat after fifteen rounds with Taffy Hughes on Clapham Common. 'Don't be facetious. I'll have you know I toddled off to bed at a respectable hour last night, and arose at an even more respectable hour this morning. And this in spite of being disturbed by your yelling some time after midnight.'

Guy paused and turned. 'My yelling?'

'Yes. Don't ask me what you said, for I couldn't make it out, but something certainly bothered you. If I had to guess I'd say you were calling someone.' Rowan looked at him curiously. 'Don't you remember?'

'No.' Guy brought his plate of bacon and scrambled eggs to the table and sat down. 'I thought I slept rather soundly, actually.'

'Well, I came to your door to listen, in case you were in distress, but you'd clearly gone back to sleep.'

'I might have been lying there with my throat cut and my virtue in tatters.'

'Then you'd have been beyond help and I could go back to sleep.'

'How unfeeling.' Guy selected the pepper from the cruet set. 'Well, this being St Nicholas's Day, I am saddened to find that you have not left me a little present for being such a good boy throughout the year.'

'I didn't like the present you didn't leave me,' Rowan responded.

'How childish, to be sure.'

'My father calls me a beastly spoilt brat, and as he is the fount of all wisdom, I suppose I must be.' Rowan folded the newspaper and then pushed it across the table and tapped a small notice. 'I think you ought to see this. It seems Topweather is no more. No, don't look at me like that, for it's true. His body was found on the North Devon coast road, west of Porworthy. It seems he was set upon and left for dead. Highwaymen have the blame. Anyway, if he knew where to find Beth, the secret died with him.'

Guy looked at the brief article. 'It's old news, Rowan. He was found in August.' Breakfast forgotten, Guy sat back thoughtfully in his chair. 'He must have left London at the very time I collared him about Beth. Would that be coincidence, one wonders?'

'What do you mean?'

'He knew I was seeking her, and when you and I searched his premises it was obvious a file was missing – the Alder file, I firmly believe. Then he travelled with some haste to the area of Porworthy. My somewhat suspicious nature leads me to conclude that he definitely did know Beth's whereabouts and was decided on blackmailing her.'

'Which, if true, means she is somewhere in that area.'

'Well, it seems probable, and so I will toddle along to Porworthy before Christmas and make enquiries. I have to leave anyway to attend to overdue estate and business matters. My search for Beth has made me neglectful of my duties.'

Rowan's guilty conscience stirred. 'Guy, if you do find her, I have to warn you that my dear stepmama will not give up without a fight.' He was about to say that Jane would say the rediscovered will was a forgery, but realized this would raise questions about how she even knew the will had been found. So he spoke vaguely instead. 'She's prepared to say and do whatever she thinks necessary to demolish your case.'

'My dear friend, your father's second wife has spent her entire life lying. The truth would have to sodomize her to be noticed. Once I have Beth, I will regain Tremoille House and the fortune, a goal that has driven me ever since I learned my father was tricked. It will be Valmer House again, and Tremoille will cease to exist.'

'Except through Beth,' Rowan reminded him.

Guy deliberately changed the subject. 'Will you leave Town as well?'

'Er, well, as it happens I think it best if I go home to sing carols with Papa. It wouldn't do to be replaced by his bastard.'

'Bastard?'

'It seems I have a half-brother, but no further information is available. I only know of him because my stepmother was imprudent enough to read my father's diary.'

'Do you believe her?'

Rowan nodded. 'Yes, I do. I want *all* my inheritance, Guy, not just the title.'

Guy smiled. 'Welcome to a rather exclusive club, my friend.'

Snow drifted from the frozen heights of Exmoor and the morning was very chill as Beth and Harriet drove to Miss Archer's for a final fitting of Beth's gown for the betrothal ball the next day. Beth wore cherry-red trimmed with white fur, with a matching hat, and her hands were sunk warmly in a white fur muff. Harriet, in royal blue, was at pains to let Beth know of her happiness with John Herriot. She chattered about the wedding gown she was about to order from Miss Archer, and the arrangements that were in hand for the wedding in February. Then she looked at Beth. 'Who is to be your bride-maid when you marry Landry?'

'I hadn't thought.'

'Then think now, for I wish you to be my bride-maid, and I would regard it as a great honour if you permitted me, a wife by then, to be your maid of honour.'

Beth was startled. 'Is that what you *really* want?'

'Yes, of course. Beth, you will have to start accepting that I am happy with the way things have turned out. I would still be marrying John even if you hadn't come here to snap Landry up. There, do you believe me at last?'

Beth laughed. 'Yes, I do, and of course we will wait upon each other.'

'Have you decided on a wedding date yet?'

'Well, we intend to let you and John enjoy all the attention first. We thought perhaps early April.'

'When the daffodils blow? It will be beautiful.'

'Well, you will have snowdrops.' Beth looked out at the snow. 'Mrs Cobbett vows the spring will be warm, settled and early. Something to do with her sister's big toe and the way the smoke goes up chimneys at midnight.'

'Then considerate it gospel,' Harriet answered with a laugh.

'She also read my tea leaves and told me that the betrothal ball will be the talk of Devon for years.'

'Indeed?' Harriet laughed again. 'Then it is going to be a splendid success!'

'You think so? Well, she also muttered something morose about needing many lights because it was midwinter. It was most out of character.'

Harriet groaned. 'Oh, no, not that old belief again. If you dance at midwinter you'll need many lights to show the way. It's superstition, Beth, something about the darkness of the season. It's all nonsense. The evening will go off brilliantly.'

'If I survive meeting so many people.'

'You'll deal with them all as befits the future mistress of Haldane.'

Beth pulled a face. 'Or they'll deal with me for the upstart I am.'

'Please don't worry,' Harriet replied soothingly. 'Oh, Beth, I *do* envy you the ball. Landry is going to such extraordinary lengths to make it an occasion to remember, what with a fancy French chef from the Pulteney Hotel in Piccadilly, an orchestra that has played at Almack's, and so many hothouse flowers that I believe he must have sent raiding parties to every estate in the south-west. Such roses, carnations, orchids and lilies, such exotic greenery and mosses, such— Oh, words fail me.'

'Thank goodness, because you make it sound as if I will need to fight through the undergrowth in order to tread a measure of Sir Roger de Coverley,' Beth replied with a forced grin. Haldane House was already filled with guests from all over the west, and more than anything she dreaded encountering an old acquaintance. The past stepped close again. It was never far away.

Harriet spoke again. 'You haven't invited anyone, have you?'

'No. I have no family now, and as I came here to start a new life, I haven't invited any former friends.'

Harriet shifted a little awkwardly. 'May I ask you something *really* personal?'

'Yes, of course.'

'Well, aren't you concerned that there will be talk because you and Landry often spend the night together?' Beth didn't know what to say, and her cheeks were suddenly on fire. Harriet smiled. 'Forgive me, it's just that I hardly imagine you sleep separately, and that being so, aren't you in the least concerned, well, that you may conceive?'

'I can't conceive,' Beth replied, still hugely embarrassed, but at the same time seeing little point in pretence. 'Don't ask me how I know, just take my word for it.'

Harriet leaned across to touch her hand. 'I don't disapprove, Beth. If I thought I could get away with enjoying physical love with John, then I would, but my father has developed a thousand ears and eyes.'

Beth laughed then. 'Oh, Harriet, you are incorrigible.'

'True. Now then, I will ask you something much more proper. Have you been practising with the Haldane diamond ring? How are you getting on?'

'It's a struggle. I have to wear it over a glove, or it keeps falling off. I know Landry is going to have it made smaller, but it can't be done in time for tomorrow.'

'Persevere, my dear, because the larger the diamond, the more to flaunt. It's been worn by every Haldane bride since before the dawn of time.'

Beth laughed. 'It's as delicately wrought as a Norseman's axe.'

'True. It's strange really. If Landry's elder brother Gerald hadn't been killed, then *his* bride would have worn it.' Harriet gazed out at the snowflakes idling through the brittle air, and Beth lowered her glance, knowing what had happened when Gerald died. The chariot halted outside a familiar door, now decorated with Christmas evergreens, and Harriet spoke briskly. 'Ah, I do believe we are at Miss Archer's. I hope your gown is ready, because I'm looking forward to seeing you in it.'

'I am no longer sure that silver-sprigged green silk was a good idea.'

'It's perfect. Do stop fussing. Besides, it's too late now, and even Miss Archer's nimble fingers couldn't produce another gown by tomorrow evening.'

Miss Archer welcomed them both inside. A bowl of holly stood on the counter, and a garland of ivy and mistletoe was draped along the mantel above the small welcoming fire. It was discreetly festive. 'Oh, ladies, ladies,' she cried, 'the gown is finished. I was up all night stitching the pearls, and the result is exquisite, truly exquisite.' She ushered them to the inner sanctum, her grey taffeta skirts rustling as she lifted a linen-shrouded gown down from the picture rail. Removing the cover, she draped the gown expertly over the back of a chair and awaited admiration.

Both Beth and Harriet stared in wonder. Rapt, Beth ran her finger-tips over the beautiful silk. The gown's low, square neckline was thickly embroidered with silver thread and edged with tiny pearls, as were the little puffed sleeves and hem, and the effect was delightful. Harriet spoke first. 'Oh, Beth, it's worthy of royalty. You will surely put my nasturtium tissue to shame. It's like frost on new spring leaves,' she declared romantically. 'Oh, you're going to steal everyone's thunder tomorrow night.'

After midday, when the snow had stopped and the sun came out for a while, Beth decided to go for a ride. The white countryside was dramatic as she made her way up to Haldane again, intending to ride in Stone Valley and be back at the Dower House before dark, but on the way she encountered Carrie Markham and Katie, who was carrying her King Charles puppy, Pompey.

Beth reined in. 'Hello, Miss Markham. Hello Katie.'

The little girl beamed at her and responded politely, but Carrie only gave a cool nod. The blue ribbon holding the amulet was still around her fragile neck, but she was a living corpse. 'How are you, Miss Markham?' Beth asked.

'We're looked after properly,' Carrie replied, as good as telling Beth to keep her nose out of what didn't concern her.

Katie put the puppy down, and he immediately gambolled away into the woods beside the steep road. 'Oh, naughty Pompey!' she cried, hurrying after him.

Carrie became anxious. 'Don't go out of sight, Katie!'

'I won't,' the little girl called back.

Shouting made Carrie cough, and the phlegm rattled in her wasted lungs. She reached out to support herself against a wayside tree, and Beth began to dismount in concern, but Carrie stopped her. 'No, I'm quite all right, thank you. It will pass in a moment.' She'd put a handkerchief to her mouth, and when she drew it away again it was thickly spattered with blood.

'You ought not to have come out on such a cold day,' Beth said gently.

'The child needed a walk.'

'If there's anything I can do to help?'

'There's nothing. All that can be done has been done. Except....' Carrie's eyes burned with a mixture of dislike and anxiety. 'Miss Mannacott, will you still allow Katie to be taken in at the big house?'

'Of course. Miss Markham, I will not do anything to harm Katie's future. She is Mr Haldane's daughter and will be accorded every privilege. I will try to be as good and loving a stepmother as possible, if she'll have me.' Beth smiled a little, hoping her words were a comfort to the dying woman.

Carrie suddenly came over to grasp Snowy's bridle and look up at her urgently. 'Miss Mannacott, there's something important you should know. I—' She broke off as Katie's scream rang from the woods.

'Mama, Pompey's got a thorn in his paw!' The little girl ran toward them with the puppy in her arms, and Beth dismounted to see what could be done. Carrie's alarm brought on another bout of coughing, so Beth attended to the thorn, which thankfully came out easily. When Carrie's coughing subsided, Beth expected her to finish what she'd been about to say, but she didn't. Instead she murmured something about it being too cold after all, and then she and Katie began to retrace their steps toward the lodge. The incident dampened Beth's interest in the ride, and she turned to go back to the Dower House. What had Carrie been on the point of telling her? Well, if it was that important, no doubt it would eventually be divulged.

It was as well she cut short the ride, because by the time she reached home the skies had clouded over again and heavy snow began to fall. When darkness approached, the clouds were livid as the winter sun sank beyond the horizon in another veiled blaze of unnatural and unsettling colour.

Chapter Twenty-two

*S*now had fallen in Gloucestershire too, and by the following morning was lying thickly over the Cotswold escarpment. Drifts blocked roads and silence presided over the hills. Some flakes still floated down as Jane sat at her embroidery frame in the drawing-room at Tremoille House. She didn't particularly like embroidery, but ladies were meant to do such things, and she, God help her, was now officially a lady.

There were Christmas decorations festooned around, holly, mistletoe, ivy and evergreens, but yuletide joy was most definitely absent. She had been endeavouring to make her peace with Thomas by joining him for the so-called festive season, and some progress had been made, until Rowan's return from London two days ago. Now there was friction, and it was clear that father and son would never mix. She glanced up at Rowan, who stood by the window. Even at this early hour there was a glass of Esmond's best cognac in his hand. His dark hair was ruffled and his clothes dirty because he'd just returned from helping with some distressed deer in the park. Why was it that a man was always attractive, regardless? If a woman appeared in a similar state, she would simply look bedraggled. Bruises notwithstanding, Rowan Welland remained handsome. He had a romantic air, and a warmth and winning charm that would one day wreak havoc. And his lazily sensuous way of glancing suggested he observed his cousin Guy.

'Is my coiffure a little awry, Stepmama?' he asked suddenly.

'I beg your pardon?'

'You're staring.'

'I'm pondering the trouble you'll cause when you enter the lists of love.'

He raised an eyebrow. '*Moi*? I'll be as virtuous as a monk.'

'That will be the day, sir.' Maybe the moment was right to reason a little with him. 'Rowan, you *know* how it annoys your father when you mix with the labourers.'

'An extra pair of hands made the difference between those deer living or dying. I hardly stained my birthright by such a commonsensical act.'

'Nonetheless—'

'Damn your nonetheless,' he replied with studied amiability.

Her lips twitched. 'Don't you think it's a little early to be drinking?'

'It's never too early, and I'll know when I've had enough because I'll fall flat on my well-bred arse. Besides, I have Papa's example to follow, although, of course, he has the brass neck to accuse *me* of being a drunkard.'

'You both drink too much.'

'Not according to him, Stepmama.' He downed the remainder of the cognac and then went to replenish the glass. 'Look, I paid attention to your advice and returned here for the joy of Christmas, but from the outset it's been clear that my father and I will never get on. We'll always loathe each other. Let him call upon his bastard son.'

'Hush! We're not supposed to know anything about that.'

'Tell me something, Stepmama, if you could turn back the clock, would you still have become Lady Welland? The truth if you please.'

'No, I wouldn't. Never has any woman more regretted allowing her youthful dreams to obscure the unpleasant truth. Your father is a toad, he's always been a toad, and he always will be a toad. I wish I'd realized that sooner rather than later.'

'Would you still have turned poor Beth out in the cold?'

Jane pretended to select another thread and compare it shade for shade with her stitches. 'Beth and I didn't hit it off,' she murmured.

'That doesn't answer my question.'

'I don't know what I'd do, Rowan.'

'Ah, the blessed chirrup of a stirring conscience.' Rowan raised the full glass to her. 'So it grates upon you when dear old Papa whines that the bottom has dropped out of half the world's finances, that thousand upon thousand of soldiers are discharged into unemployment, and that the banks are closing their doors because finance is so rickety.'

'Well, those things are only too true.'

'Indeed so, but I've heard your sharp little teeth grind when he starts. If he's so bothered about money, why does he keep the Tremoille *and* Welland studs, as well as maintaining Whitend and this great Cotswold barn? Ah, but I was forgetting, he's terrified to get rid of Whitend, in case this little palace is snatched away by Guy. And he's terrified of Whitend in case it becomes submerged.'

'You're always such entrancing company, Rowan,' Jane murmured.

Rowan grinned suddenly. 'Well, I'm off to Gloucester,' he declared. 'Coming?'

'In this snow? Certainly not.' She looked at him. 'Why on earth are you going?'

'Taffy Hughes.'

'Who?'

'The mad Welshman who blotted my pretty face a while back. He's taking on all-comers at the winter fair, and I'm of a mind to have some revenge.'

'Oh, Rowan—'

'No, my mind is made up. Besides, if I don't beat the daylights out of Hughes, I'm in danger of doing it to dear Papa.'

Thomas's voice growled from the doorway. 'Doing what to dear Papa?' He stood there, still in his gold brocade dressing-gown, his wide-set eyes bright and suspicious. There was an almost hunted alertness in his stance, and his fingers were constantly moving. He was obviously far too tense and agitated, but so far had refused to listen to anyone's entreaty to visit his Cheltenham doctor. 'Doing *what* to dear Papa?' he demanded again, blocking the doorway so that Rowan could not leave.

'Asking you to accompany me to see Hughes take on all-comers in Gloucester,' Rowan replied smoothly.

'Liar! The truth, damn you.'

'I've told you the truth,' Rowan insisted, and Jane nodded.

'He is, Thomas dear.'

'I'll not be lied to under my own roof! I have enough to contend with without my heir setting himself against me!' Thomas chewed his lip, and spittle flecked his chin.

Rowan exchanged a swift glance with Jane, and then gave his father an amiable grin. 'I'm not setting myself against you, Father, truly I'm not.'

'Then why did you stoop to helping with those damned deer? Eh? Eh? Why did you behave as just another labourer? You are supposed to be above that!'

Rowan strove to keep his temper. 'Would you rather I let the deer die?'

'Yes, boy, I would! You're going to be the next Lord Welland, and damn me you'll behave like it!' Thomas's voice was raised several notes.

'Behave like you? I'd as soon tread the boards as Desdemona!'

Thomas went pale, and then flushed almost purple. 'Don't presume to use your smart tongue on me, sir, for you aren't the only fish in the pool. Take care you don't alienate yourself completely, for I can replace you! The title goes to you, there is nothing I can do about that, but the estates and fortune I can bestow as I please.'

Here it comes, Rowan thought, awaiting the threat of his half-brother.

Thomas's eyes had become small and rather piggy. 'You aren't my only son, you know.' He waited for Rowan's shock, but there was none. 'Have you nothing to say, boy?'

'What is there to say? You've sired a bastard, and now dangle this illegitimate spawn in an attempt to bring me into line. Well, fuck you, sir, and fuck your by-blow!'

Thomas's face waxed crimson with passion. 'You, sir, are the bane of my life,' he bellowed, beside himself with outrage. 'Why the Almighty saw fit to inflict *you* upon me as well as all my other trials and hardships, I really cannot—!'

Rowan was incensed. 'Trials and hardships? You don't *begin* to know hardship!'

'And you do, I suppose?'

'Not personally, but I have recently heard of hardship caused by an act of God so tumultuous and terrible that many thousands of people are dead, and even more homeless and starving.'

Thomas looked blankly at him. 'What the Devil's arse are you talking about?'

Jane was also bemused. 'Yes, Rowan, what do you mean?'

'I attended a prizefight on my way here, and encountered a sea captain in the pay of the Dutch East India Company. He was newly come from the Indies, and vowed he would never return there, not even were the Company to pay him in gold sovereigns. At the beginning of April he collected a cargo from Sumbawa, and was on the way to Sumatra when thunderous detonations were heard in the distance. Ash began to fall from the heavens and more detonations sounded. There was a hellish stench on the breeze, and great waves devastated the island's shores. While at anchor off Sumatra the captain learned that the volcano of Mount Tambora on Sumbawa had exploded in a mass of molten flame, killing thousands of people. The sun was blotted out, and when the Dutch East Indiaman continued her voyage there was darkness night and day. At last daylight returned, but with strange sunrises and sunsets of the most violent hues, and the Dutchman's crew were terrified that God was sending the Angel of Death. Father, that captain hasn't been sober since reaching England, nor does he intend to be again.'

Thomas was unimpressed. What happened the other side of the world was of no interest to him, unless it affected his financial situation. 'The fellow should be in Bedlam,' he muttered callously.

Now Rowan was truly incensed. 'Damn you, Father! The horrors the *fellow* witnessed, the death and deprivation, the squalor and utter misery, make the shallow complaints in this country seem trivial. As trivial as your problems, most of which are of your own creation. Sink in self-pity if you wish, replace me with your bastard seed if that is what you want, but don't prate to me of your woes, because they are as nothing to what happened because of Mount Tambora. *That*, sir, is misery!' Slamming down his glass, Rowan strode toward the door.

For a moment his livid father considered squaring up to him, but there was something in Rowan's eyes that made discretion seem much the better part of valour. Thomas stepped aside, and Rowan walked straight past.

As Rowan prepared to ride to Gloucester, Phoebe and Rosalind were also on their way there, huddled in the back of Johnno's wagon. They intended to do a little Christmas shopping, and then visit Phoebe's cousin, but Rosalind was hoping to wriggle out of visiting in order to go to the winter fair that had been set up on the river-bank at the bottom of Westgate. Rosalind scowled at the lazy flakes that still floated in the icy air. 'Phoebe, do I *have* to come with you? Can't I go to the fair?'

'Go alone to a fair? Certainly not!'

'Please, Phoebe. I promise to be good, truly I do. Dad always let me go alone.' This wasn't true, because she'd lied that she was working late at Barker's Tavern.

Johnno, who was walking beside them, just the other side of the wagon's canvas cover, lifted the edge for a moment to look in. There was a rather hopeful sprig of mistletoe in his battered old hat. 'Aw, go on, Phoebe. Let the chit have some fun.'

'You mind your own business, and keep your eye on your work, before we end up in another ditch.' As he let go of the canvas and whistled at the oxen, Phoebe glanced at Rosalind. Mention of the ditch reminded her of Robert Lloyd, but the girl was leaning out of the wagon to touch a snowflake that floated within reach. 'Rosalind, have you thought any more about accepting Jamie Webb? He's steady and dependable, and in good employment now with the squire. It would be a good match for you.'

Rosalind scowled. 'Jamie's dull and long-faced. Be fair now, Phoebe, would *you* want to marry him?'

'It's not me he wants to wed, Rosalind, and if you think you're going to snap up someone like Lord Welland's son, then you're a cuckoo.'

'That's not fair! Just because I don't want Jamie Webb!'

Phoebe felt a little guilty. 'Oh, well, it's your decision, I suppose,' she muttered, making much of shifting her position and tweaking her warm winter cloak.

'Please can I see the fair?' Rosalind knew when to play on Phoebe's conscience.

'We'll see,' was the brief reply, but Rosalind knew it was capitulation. A rush of excitement flooded her. She'd been feeling unsettled and restless again, just as she had before going with Robert Lloyd. The same craving had returned, gnawing deeply through her and making her tremble some-times between the legs. She wanted to experience that pleasure again, to feel a man inside her. But that wasn't why she wanted to go to the fair. There was a prize ring there, where she might encounter Rowan Welland.

Back in Frampney, Jake, Matty and Jamie Webb were sharing a jar of perry. Jamie's face was miserable. 'Well, Rosalind doesn't like me that way, and that's that.'

Matty clapped a sympathetic hand on the boy's shoulder. 'She'll come around, Jamie. You're about the best catch in these parts. She's not daft.'

'No, but she prefers finer folk.' Jamie glanced sideways at Jake.

Jake sat forward. 'She's learned her lesson, Jamie. You mark my words, Matty's right, Rozzie'll come around and we'll be seeing a wedding come the spring.'

Matty relit his cumbersome pipe and Jake frowned. 'I wished you'd give up that smelly old chimney, Matty. I caught you dozing off again yesterday. You'll have this place down in flames one day.'

'Aw, stop moaning,' Matty grumbled. 'It's coming up to Christmas; there are no womenfolk to chew our ears, so let's enjoy it, eh? Pour us another jar of perry.'

Jake laughed and reached for the earthenware pitcher, but Jamie dwelt upon Rosalind. *Had* she learned her lesson? He'd seen what happened when she dropped the flour by Lord Welland's son. She still had an itch for the gentry, and Rowan Welland was a very different kettle of fish from that pig, Robert Lloyd. Jamie's spirits were low. He loved Rosalind Mannacott with all his fool heart, but she wanted far better. Far better. He reached for his replenished jar. 'I think I'll get drunk tonight,' he muttered, and began to drink long and deep.

Darkness had fallen before Rosalind eventually reached the fair, and to her chagrin Phoebe accompanied her, having insisted they do the shopping and cousin-visiting first. Now they had two hours before returning to Johnno's wagon at the White Hart at six for the return to Frampney. The fair was bright with torches, lanterns and lamps, and the air smelled of toffee, fried onions and gingerbread. A wheel of fortune was ablaze with colour, the wooden roundabout creaked and the swing boats went so high that those inside squealed and shrieked. Men were selling holly and mistletoe from carts, and a choir from a local church was singing 'I Saw Three Ships'. The sweet notes were almost indistinguishable amid the shouting, laughter and rival racket from a fiddle, drum and cymbals. Audible only at close quarters were the chink of coins, the splash of beer from kegs, and the whir of paper windmills. Horses were always to be found at fairs, and an assortment of dogs, but Rosalind had never seen such a strange animal as one that was led past now. 'What's that, Phoebe?' she asked.

'Darned if I know.'

A man next to them explained. 'It's a camel, I'm told, like the Three Wise Men rode. Darned ugly thing, eh?'

'Where's the prizefight tent?' Rosalind asked.

'Over there, close to the bridge. It's all red-and-yellow stripes, so you can't miss it.' The man, whose face was as brown and wrinkled as a walnut, with teeth like broken tombstones, looked her over. 'Now what does a pretty thing like you want with fisticuffs? Got a fancy for the famous Taffy Hughes, eh?'

Phoebe was indignant. 'You mind your tongue, you rascal,' she warned, raising the umbrella she'd brought along for protection.

'All right, all right, you daft old trout,' he protested, and shuffled away.

Phoebe then turned her wrath upon Rosalind. 'That's what you get for encouraging strangers!'

'I didn't!'

'Yes, you did, when you asked him about the tent. Which is another thing, why *do* you want to know about that?'

'I'd like to see a prizefight, that's all.'

'It isn't ladylike,' Phoebe replied shortly.

Rosalind smiled and nudged her a little playfully. 'Oh, come on, Phoebe, let's go and watch for a while, if only to see how daft men can be.'

Phoebe hesitated, part of her as keen as Rosalind. Temptation had its way. 'All right, but don't you leave my side.'

The snow crunched beneath their feet as they threaded through the crowds to the tent, where a master-of-ceremonies was extolling the virtues of Taffy Hughes, the Mad Welshman. Phoebe's nerve almost failed when she saw the unruly and disreputable types flocking into the tent, but Rosalind urged her inside, where the smell of tobacco smoke, damp clothes and unwashed bodies was almost choking. Now Rosalind's sole concern was whether or not Rowan Welland was here. Please let him be. Please.

More and more people tried to enter the tent, but it was so full that they had to stay outside, disgruntled because they wouldn't see the renowned Welsh fighter. Rosalind kept looking around, but saw no sign of Rowan. The master-of-ceremonies forced his way to the ring and tried to be heard above the racket, but the crowd's response was to start chanting for Hughes. At last the man seized a metal tray and a large spoon from somewhere and began to beat them together like a gong. 'Ladies and gentlemen, I give you the finest fighter in the length and breadth of the king's realm, *Taffy Hughes!*'

There was pushing and shoving as the huge Welshman came from the back of the tent, surrounded by his seconds. He was jostled and whistled all the way to the ring, where he stood dead centre, his brawny arms folded, gazing around with strangely dark eyes. 'Oh, my lord,' Phoebe breathed, 'who'd be dippy enough to take *him* on?'

'Do we have a challenger? Do we have a challenger?' the master-of-ceremonies bellowed, and there was a cheer as a local giant named Basher Hancock held up his hand. He was pushed and elbowed to the ring, and the closer he drew to the Welshman, the paler his face became. Moments later he was formally announced. 'Ladies and gentlemen, I give you a worthy challenger, Basher Hancock, a coal heaver from Kingsholm!' The two men squared up and the fight began.

Rosalind had always known that pugilism was a bloody sport, and Rowan's bruised and swollen face had proved it, but even so she wasn't prepared for the sheer butchery of the ring. The sound of the Welshman's fist striking Hancock's face, the sight of the torn flesh around the challenger's eyes and the blood streaming from his nose and split lips were too much. It was the last straw for her when Hancock received an upper cut that not only sent him sprawling but made him violently sick as well. Blood and vomit spattered over the ring, and Rosalind caught Phoebe's arm. 'Let's go, this is awful.'

'I'm enjoying it,' Phoebe replied unexpectedly. 'I never thought I'd like a good scrap like this, but I do! Just get some air by the entrance, but don't go out of sight.'

Rosalind pushed her way toward the entrance, but then saw Rowan watching the bout. Snowflakes clung to his hair, his hat was under his arm, and his cloak tossed back over his shoulders as he leaned against a tent pole. He hadn't seen her, so she had a moment or so to simply look at him. Oh, he was so handsome, even with his bruises. How she'd like to lie in the grass with him. Desire welled through her, making her breath catch and her eyes shine.

Suddenly he noticed her and straightened quickly. 'Miss Mannacott?'

She moved closer and curtsied. 'My lord.'

He smiled and reached out for her hand, which he drew to his cold lips. 'I'm not Lord Welland yet, but thank you for the compliment.' He searched her face. 'You're a little pale. Is prizefighting too much for you?'

'A *lot* too much for me,' she answered. 'Please say you're not here to challenge that Welshman.'

'Well, that was the main idea. I've fought him before and been beaten before.'

'But he's so—'

'Big? And I'm so skinny?' he supplied.

'Something like that.' She smiled, liking him more each second.

At that moment Phoebe bustled up, having spotted what was going on. 'You come back now, Rosalind,' she instructed. 'Begging your pardon, sir.'

Rowan bowed. 'Madam.'

Some of Beth's advice on etiquette rang vaguely through Rosalind's mind. She had to introduce them. Yes, that was it. 'My lord, this is my friend, Mrs Brown.'

'Mrs Brown.' Not being churlish enough to correct Rosalind again, Rowan kissed Phoebe's hand as well. Then he smiled winningly. 'I assure you, madam, that Miss Mannacott is not in any danger while I'm here, but I'll certainly be in danger if she isn't. She's in the process of trying to dissuade me from challenging Hughes. You wouldn't want her to fail, would you?'

Phoebe simpered at him, and then nudged Rosalind. 'Don't go away, my girl.'

'Of course not.'

As Phoebe withdrew into the tent, Rowan smiled at Rosalind. 'I hope

I'm right, and that your mission *is* to save me from myself?' As she nodded, he went on, 'Well, since we must not move from here, I suggest you stand with your back to the ring, the better to obscure the carnage.' He glanced past her as the Welshman floored Hancock again and was catcalled for foul play.

'Did you really fight Taffy Hughes?' she asked.

'Fight? Well, I endured fifteen rounds before he knocked me into the middle of the following week. I earned my purse that day, I can tell you.' He chuckled.

'And now you're here for more? Why?' she asked.

He paused. 'To be truthful, I don't really know. It's a habit.'

'A very foolish one.' She became suddenly self-conscious. 'I – I shouldn't have said that. I'm a blacksmith's daughter and you're a lord's son.'

He gave her an impish smile. 'So, I'm not good enough for you?'

'Don't tease. We're different classes, you and me, and we don't mix.'

'You, Miss Mannacott, are a snob to worry about class. It makes no difference to me, so you, I fear, must be a snob.'

'If I'm a snob, it's because I'm too good to talk to gentlemen who like to get knocked around a prize ring,' she countered.

'*Touché.*'

'I beg your pardon?'

'It means "ah, there you have me",' he explained.

She lowered her eyes. 'You must think me very ignorant.'

'No, for you intrigue me. You speak well; have you been taking lessons?'

'I'd rather not say. I hate her and don't want to speak her name ever again.'

'Hate is a very harsh word,' he observed, 'especially when I imagine you're referring to Beth Tremoille.'

Her eyes flew guiltily to his. 'How—?'

'I know Beth, and that your father was her lover. She and I almost married.' He saw how she recoiled, and added quickly, 'It would have been an arranged match, but I certainly do like her, as I fancy she likes me. I can't imagine anyone *hating* her.'

In the tent things had begun to turn ugly as the Welshman and his seconds found themselves ranged against an angry Gloucester crowd. The verdict had gone against Hancock, and the onlookers didn't think the victor had played fair. Sticks and bottles began to be brandished, and then someone threw something that struck the Welshman on the head. The mood snapped, becoming dangerous and menacing. Several men rushed outside to inform the rest of the crowd what was going on, and Rowan only just had time to pull Rosalind aside as people surged forward. He pressed back into the canvas, holding her close and protected as people stumbled and pushed past. Someone had a lighted torch that came too close to a low-hanging rope, and suddenly flames began to leap. There was panic as everyone tried to get away. Rowan dragged Rosalind out of the way again. 'Come on, we must leave!'

'But Phoebe!'

'Has already escaped. Someone had a knife and cut the canvas, and she was among those that got out. She'll be all right. My concern is for you.' Seizing her hand, he ran toward the river-bank. The Severn's muddy water shone in the lights from the fair, and only a few folk chose this route to escape the violence. The water rustled through overhanging willows, and several skiffs rocked by a small landing stage. Rowan halted to look back. 'Well, trouble isn't hot on our heels,' he muttered.

Rosalind was suddenly aware of their isolation. 'I – I ought to find Phoebe. We're supposed to be at Johnno's wagon by six to go home.' Her lips trembled suddenly and tears sprang to her eyes.

Rowan was concerned. 'I'll see you to the wagon in time.'

'Will you?'

'Of course I will.' He touched her cheek. 'Please don't be frightened.'

She didn't reply. She wasn't afraid of him, but of her own desires. The brush of his fingers quickened her heart, and renewed the terrible ache between her legs. Oh, how she wanted to relieve that ache. 'You're the most handsome, gallant and kindly gentleman I've ever met,' she whispered. 'A lord with more charm than anyone ought to have, and I can tell that you like me, and I *know* that I like you. So it's dangerous for me to be here with you like this.'

'That's very direct,' he murmured, aware of things stirring that should not. He was supposed to be gallantly protecting her, not wanting to lift her skirt to despoil her.

'It's the truth.' At least she could kiss him, couldn't she? That would not be so terrible. Would it? She moved closer and lifted her parted lips. He hesitated, but his loins were filling with excitement and her mouth was so sweet and provocative that he bent his head to kiss her. Their lips quivered together, and then settled, moving tenderly and sweetly. He put an arm around her little waist and pulled her to him. How supple and slender she was, how small and firm her breasts. He pressed her against his arousal, unable to prevent himself from seeking at least some gratification, for as God was his witness he was determined not to let his weapon loose. His desire mounted and his kiss became more intense and sensual, but as she began to rub against him he realized she might not be as virginal as he'd thought. There was knowingness in her motion, and he knew when she came, for her lips softened beneath his, her breathing turned to gasps and her body undulated voluptuously. For a moment he considered undoing his falls and letting nature take its course, but then she seemed so over-come and weak that he had to catch her around the waist to prevent her from collapsing. She sank against him, her body soft and helpless, seeming almost drugged with satisfaction, and several moments passed before she rallied herself to pull away in embarrassment. 'Forgive me.'

'There is nothing to forgive.'

'I'm not a whore, truly I'm not.'

'I know.'

'And you know I'm not a virgin.'

He looked away. 'I guessed.'

'I've only done it once.'

'It's none of my business, Rosalind.'

'But it is, because I've just taken my pleasure of you. I'm afraid to do it properly with you because I'm not close to my monthly, but if you want, I'll do this instead. Her hand moved to undo his falls.

'Sweet Jesu,' he breathed as she reached in to handle him. She pulled his foreskin back gently, and then closed it again, pulled it back, and then closed it again. She pressed against him anew, and their lips were joined in a kiss that lacked all innocence as she stroked him to a climax. His body jerked with the force of it, and he kissed her as if he would suck out her very heart. They swayed together by the little jetty, both stealing every last sexual pleasure they could. Then she smoothed her palm over his softening masculinity and slid a finger gently over the exposed tip, shivering as unbelievably enjoyable sensations danced over her flesh. He gasped and twitched. 'Dear God, what do you want, my complete prostration?' Everything was so sensitive that he grabbed himself to prevent her from doing the same again.

She smiled and reached up to take his face in her hands. 'Will I see you again?'

'If I can stand the strain,' he replied, smiling too.

Her lips were over his again. She was learning quickly, testing her wiles, taking the pleasure she wanted. But it was so easy to learn with him. She couldn't bear to think of him marrying Beth, of him even liking her. She, Rosalind Mannacott, wanted him. 'Maybe next time,' she breathed, 'we'll do it all. I'd so like that.'

'So would I.' His lips moved against her hair. 'Oh, Rosalind, Rosalind, what have you done to me?' he breathed.

'The same as you've done to me,' she answered, looking seriously at him. 'I liked you from that first moment by the forge, and I came to the fair today because I hoped you'd be there.'

'Did you, be damned?'

The cathedral bell rang out, and she gasped. 'Six o'clock? I have to go!'

He hurriedly straightened his clothes and caught her hand to run back toward the fair, which was quiet again now because the militia had moved in to quell the trouble. It wasn't far to the White Hart in Westgate Street, where Phoebe and Johnno were waiting anxiously by the wagon.

Phoebe hastened to meet them. 'There you are at last, Rosalind! Where have you been? I've been going mad with worry!'

Rowan was apologetic. 'Forgive me, Mrs Brown, but in order to escape the violence we had to run along by the river, and then we waited until things settled again before running all the way here. I assure you Miss Mannacott was not in any danger, and that I have been with her throughout. She came to no harm.' Which is more than can be said for my own peace of mind, he thought.

'You've been most kind, my lord,' Phoebe declared, 'but now we have to go, Johnno won't wait any longer.'

He bowed gallantly. 'Good night, Mrs Brown, Miss Mannacott. I trust you have a very happy Christmas, to say nothing of a provident new year.' He watched them climb into the wagon, which began the slow trudge up toward the Cross.

It wasn't going to be easy to shake free of Rosalind Mannacott, he thought, but that wasn't what he wanted anyway. The last thing he needed was further trouble from his damned father, and an entanglement with a blacksmith's daughter was certain to send the old boy into apoplexy. But when Rosalind Mannacott smiled at him and raised her sweet lips for a kiss, he couldn't help himself. The thought of possessing her completely was almost sublime. Paternal fury or not, he'd have to see her again. He sensed an uncertain future opening before him, and knew he could close the door upon it right now, or grasp it with both hands to see where it led.

Chapter Twenty-three

Dickon was weary as he drove Guy's travelling carriage into Porworthy. The lamps swung through the softly falling snow as he negotiated the narrow streets and corners, making for the Bell and Fox inn. The road had been cleared of snow, but the gardens and surrounding scenery were white. Sir Daniel Lavington's burned mill rose starkly where a small river rushed down from Exmoor to lose itself in a thousand channels in the two miles of salt marsh that now separated the former port from the sea.

Christmas was much in evidence, from evergreens fixed to doors and windows to lighted candles and a proliferation of red ribbons, and as the carriage drew up in the yard of the inn, loud male singing could be heard in the crowded taproom. A large gathering of farmers and labourers was giving broad West Country voice to 'God rest ye merry, gentlemen', and the raucousness suggested a surfeit of beer and cider.

Hearing the carriage arrive, the landlord hurried out, wiping his hands on his brown leather apron. There was a sprig of holly in his coat lapel, and his round face was very red and shiny. He recognized the carriage and almost ran to open the door. 'Why, Sir Guy, this is a very agreeable surprise! Welcome to the Bell and Fox!' His breath was silvery in the bitter cold.

Guy alighted, wearing a black astrakhan-lined greatcoat. His top hat was tipped back on his rich hair, and he held an ebony cane topped with his family's lion badge. 'Good evening, George. I trust the rabble haven't devoured all the food?'

'Indeed not, sir. I can offer you a handsome haunch of venison, or—'

Guy smiled. 'Not the whole haunch, just a hearty plateful with all the trimmings.'

'And so you shall, Sir Guy. Will you be wanting to spend the night here?'

'Possibly. Tell me, the fellow Topweather, what do you know of the circumstances?'

'Topweather? Oh, you mean the body up by the signpost to Rendisbury church. Well, it's believed to be the work of highwaymen. It seems he was lodging at Dulverford, but no one there knew anything about him. He hired an inn cob and set off for Lannermouth, but no one in Lannermouth seems to know anything. Nor did anyone here, yet he was found on the road between both places. I reckon some local lips are sealed, not in Dulverford, but here in either Lannermouth or Porworthy, because it's highly unlikely he wasn't seen in either place. It's a mystery, and no mistake. Was that all you wished to ask me, Sir Guy?' The man wanted to get back inside, not stay out in the bitter cold.

'Not quite. I'm seeking a young lady who calls herself Tremoille or Alder.'

'The names mean nothing to me, sir. Is she a lady lady, or a doubtful lady?'

Guy smiled again. 'A lady lady.' *Unless one counted a rather demeaning lapse with a brawny blacksmith.* 'She's dark-haired, small and delicate, and very beautiful. Her first name is Elizabeth, but she prefers to be called Beth.'

The landlord's eyes changed. 'Well now, not that I've seen her personally, but I'm told that a lady of that description and first name is about to be formally betrothed to Major Haldane of Haldane Hall.'

Guy was startled. 'Holy Haldane is to take a wife? It would appear that miracles do happen. Can you tell me more?'

'Well, yes, everyone's talking about her, because she came from nowhere and has started whispers due to her antics with the major. Riding off alone with him to spend secret hours in Stone Valley, then letting him stay with her at the Dower House at Lannermouth. Folk have seen him leaving of a morning, and the shocked old biddies hereabouts have been clucking until they're well nigh egg-bound.'

Guy remained surprised. 'I'm amazed that Haldane has relinquished his principles to such a dismaying extent. One expects more of him, does one not?' The landlord wasn't sure whether to agree or not, then Guy went on, 'You mentioned the Dower House?'

'Yes, Sir Guy. At Lannermouth. She's the new tenant.'

New tenant? Guy's senses sharpened as he thought of Henry Topweather's line of business. 'How new?' he asked.

'She arrived there during the summer. June, July, somewhere thereabouts. Her surname's Mannacott.'

Guy could have laughed out loud. *Oh, Beth, Beth, if you're going to the trouble of changing your name, at least choose one that doesn't point such a very direct finger!*

The landlord searched his face. 'Is she the lady you seek?'

'I believe so, George.' Guy paused. It was still early in the evening, and now that he'd run his quarry to ground at last, he wanted to confront her at the earliest moment. 'Is Rendisbury Hill open to carriages?'

'Yes, sir, since this morning.'

'Well, you've heartened my appetite considerably, and the prospect of venison begins to make my mouth water. I'll take a room, but after eating I intend to drive on to Lannermouth. I must speak to Miss Mannacott without delay.'

'You won't find her at the Dower House tonight, Sir Guy. She and Mr Haldane are having a grand betrothal ball at the hall. Most of local society has been invited.'

'I know one notable name that will have been omitted,' Guy murmured. 'Well, it's only five miles from here to Lannermouth, and a mile further to the hall. The sooner you place the feast before me, the sooner I can get there. Have my room made ready now, for I will need to change into more suitable attire if I'm to go to the hall tonight. Oh, and I need a good rider to take an urgent message to Greylake Castle.'

At that moment the gathering in the taproom commenced the same carol again.

> God rest ye merry, gentlemen, let nothing ye dismay,
> Remember Christ our Saviour was born on Christmas Day;
> To save us all from Satan's power when we have gone astray.
> Oh, tidings of comfort and joy, comfort and joy;
> O – oh, ti – idings of co – omfort and joy.

As Guy went in to dine at the Bell and Fox, Beth was preparing to leave the Dower House in her ball gown and warm, fur-lined mantle. She wore long white gloves, and the ring with the Haldane diamond, and was now so nervous and trembling she hadn't been able to eat a thing since midday. 'Is my hair as it should be?' she asked again.

Mrs Cobbett looked at her fondly. 'You're as pretty as a picture. Listen to me now, Molly and I may not be fancy lady's-maids, but we've made you look *exactly* like that engraving in the journal. In fact your hair looks even better because of those rosebuds Mr Landry sent from the hall, so have done with the worrying.'

Molly, standing just behind the housekeeper, nodded eagerly. 'Miss Beth, I'd give *anything* to step out looking as you do right now.'

Beth smiled at her. 'Thank you, Molly, but I'm so anxious about tonight.'

'Don't be,' Mrs Cobbett said, 'for it will all come right in the end.'

Beth looked at her. 'What does *that* mean? That it will be awful first?'

The housekeeper smoothed her apron against the plain folds of her woollen gown. 'I won't pretend I'm happy about this engagement, but—'

'Why?' Beth interposed. 'What is wrong with me marrying Mr Landry?'

'Apart from you not knowing him long enough for a grasshopper to grow legs? I don't know, and that's the truth,' Mrs Cobbett confessed.

'Oh, don't look at me like that, for I'm not saying it for effect. I just have this feeling. First that crow tapped on the window; then the milk froze over; then—'

'What on earth is the relevance of a crow and a pail of milk?' Beth cried.

'Such things must be heeded, Miss Beth. They're portents, and I know they're connected to your betrothal. You'll know great happiness in the end, but it will be a long and difficult path before you get there.'

Beth was unsettled. 'There's something you're not telling me, isn't there?' A thought struck her. 'Is it anything to do with Carrie Markham?'

'Carrie? Why do you ask that?'

'I don't know really, except that she tried to tell me something, but didn't have time. Well, no, that's not strictly true, she wouldn't say it in front of Katie.'

'Oh, take no notice of that.'

Beth studied her. Mrs Cobbett, whom she had always trusted, had an inkling at least of what Carrie might have wanted to say. 'Mrs C, is there a good reason why I should not marry Mr Landry?'

'Do you love him?'

'Yes, of course.'

'There isn't anyone else in your heart?' The housekeeper watched as Beth lowered her eyes. 'Miss Beth?'

'No, there isn't anyone.' *Liar*!

'If that's so, Miss Beth, I know of no good reason why you shouldn't become Mrs Haldane. Love – true love – must always come first. Now then,' – Mrs Cobbett bustled to the front door – 'if you tarry here much longer, poor Billy and the horses will freeze to death. You go to the ball, like that Cinderella, and you get your prince.' She smiled at Beth. 'Go on, my dear, and look them all in the eye. It's your birthday *and* your betrothal day, and you've hooked the greatest catch in all of Devon, so make sure of him.'

Beth hugged her suddenly. 'Thank you, Mrs C. And thank you too, Molly.' With that she went out into the swirling snow, where Billy waited to help her into the carriage. He waited until she was seated before raising the rung and closing the door. Moments later the vehicle jerked forward to make its way down the drive toward the bridge over the roaring spate of the Lanner.

Beth sat back, her gloved hands plunged into her white fur muff, her toes against an earthenware jar filled with hot water. Her breath was misty as she looked out at the trees and lighted cottage windows of Lannermouth before Billy urged the team for the steep climb to Haldane. Was she doing the right thing? Was it honourable to marry Landry when she loved Guy so very much? The questions rang through her head as they had done since she'd accepted Landry's proposal. She had to remind herself that she'd been truthful with him, and he was under no illusions. But was she? Was she wearing blinkers, and thus failing to see what a mess she might be making for herself? Then she felt the proximity of the high moor, invisible and mysterious in the darkness, and suddenly found new resolve.

As the carriage turned between the lantern-hung gates of Haldane Hall, she glanced up at the stone cockatrices, but the light didn't reach them. There seemed to be hundreds of variegated lamps across the park, and every window of the house was brightly illuminated. She saw that a throng of fine carriages had already arrived.

Carrie watched Beth's carriage drive past, and then lowered the curtain to turn back into the little parlour of the lodge. She moved with difficulty, feeling so weak she had to support herself on the table in order to reach her chair. Katie had fallen asleep in another chair, with Pompey curled up in her arms, and a low fire burned in the hearth. Carrie eased herself down and then leaned back exhaustedly. Her breathing was harsh, and her cheeks the colour of wax. She knew she had not long left. Another carriage drove past, and she closed her eyes. This was a bad night's work. She should have told Miss Mannacott the truth when she had the chance. Tears welled from beneath her blue-veined lids. But it wasn't too late. Only the altar and a wedding band would do that.

Beneath his astrakhan-lined greatcoat Guy was finely attired in a black, corded-silk coat and cream silk breeches that might have been sewn upon his person. There was a top hat on his head and kid gloves on his hands as he emerged from the inn to find it was still snowing, although not so heavily that it would make the road impassable. His shirt was adorned with a great deal of costly lace, his cream satin waistcoat was a master-piece of elegant quilting, and his simple neck cloth sported a discreet solitaire emerald. He found Dickon waiting with a fresh team hitched to the carriage. 'Right, Dickon, I want you to make all haste for Haldane Hall.'

The coachman gaped, both at his master's formal attire and the instruc-tion. 'The hall, Sir Guy?' He'd heard about the betrothal ball when in the inn kitchens.

'Is there a problem, Dickon?'

'No, sir.'

'Good, because I have some ill-advised betrothal celebrations to ruin.' Guy climbed in and the coachman flicked the reins. The fresh horses managed a smart pace for the long, winding climb toward Lannermouth, past the signpost where Henry Topweather's body had been found, and then on across the cliff-top moor toward the dangerous descent of Rendisbury Hill.

Beth's carriage halted at the entrance to the hall, and those guests arriving at the same time realized who she was as a footman came to open the door and assist her down. Snowflakes brushed her face as she stepped on to the carpet of ivy leaves and rose petals that had been strewn on the portico steps. She could hear a *ländler* playing in the ballroom, and there were so many lanterns, lamps and candles that the house was dazzling. As she went slowly up the steps toward the vestibule, a gentleman's silhouette was caught momentarily in the doorway, and then he stepped forward. It was Landry. He wore a tight, black velvet coat embroidered with jet, and white silk breeches, stockings and black patent shoes. The top buttons of his white satin waistcoat were undone, allowing the rich frills of his shirt to spill out as plentifully as they did from his cuffs. His neck cloth, crisp, white and perfect, was tied in a suitably elaborate knot, upon which nestled a lavish ruby star. Smiling, he came down the steps to greet her, and she removed her warm hands from the muff to slip them into his. 'Welcome, Beth. This hall and its master are your willing slaves.'

They entered the magnificently decorated vestibule, where Christmas greenery vied with elaborate arrangements of hothouse flowers, and when a footman had relieved Beth of her mantle and muff, Landry conducted her slowly toward the steps that descended to the ballroom. On the way they ran the gauntlet of numerous guests. Fearful of a known face, Beth was nervously aware of introductions, greetings and whispers. There was so much to take in, so many questions to answer, doubters to reform and disapprovers to charm. Notoriety attached to her name, and reflected in the eyes of those who regarded her. They all wanted to find fault with Landry Haldane's bride-to-be, and she had to show them they were wrong. But *were* they wrong? Her secrets were shocking, and made her very unsuitable indeed. She felt as if her past were a heavy sack over her shoulder, weighing her down and reminding her that she was wrong to have accepted Landry. But no one else could see the burden; no one else knew her or could even begin to imagine how much she had to hide.

At last they reached the top of the white marble steps and could look down at the glittering and noisy white-and-gold ballroom. The music of the fashionable London orchestra was barely audible above the chattering, laughter and thunder of dancing feet on the marble floor. Golden scrolls and exquisite plasterwork panels adorned the walls, and the ceiling was brilliantly painted with Greek gods and goddesses. Dazzling crystal chandeliers shimmered in the haze of smoke from cigars and fireplaces, and the delicious smell of the cold buffet drifted from the supper room. Footmen in crimson and gold bore trays of champagne and lime cup, and the floral arrangements were so abundant and outstanding that the ball might have been taking place in Paradise itself.

The steward's staff rang out and she was announced. People strained for their first glimpse of scandalous Miss Mannacott, and Beth felt like a specimen under a microscope. She smiled nervously at Landry. 'Please let's go down and mingle.' He didn't hesitate, and they soon joined the main floor, where she was able to deal with only a few people at a time. She was introduced to more new faces. There was squat, ugly Sir Daniel Lavington, tall, forbidding Lady Bettersden, a gentlemen she only recalled as a Justice of the Peace from Barnstaple, Dr Carter of Porworthy, two elderly sisters whose looks and voices reminded her irresistibly of turkeys, and many, many more. Name after name went in her right ear and immediately out of the left again. She would *never* be able to remember everyone. But of one thing she was thankful, there were no old acquaintances.

She and Landry led the ball in a waltz, earning a ripple of congratulatory applause, and then they parted to dance with others. An hour or more passed before they partnered each other again, this time in another *ländler*, but then something at the side of the ballroom caught Landry's attention. 'What's afoot over there, I wonder?' He nodded toward Dr Carter, who had been urgently approached by a footman. The doctor's smile faded and he hastened out of the ballroom. 'No doubt some baby has had the poor taste to arrive early,' Landry murmured, as he and Beth continued to dance.

But then, as the *ländler* ended, the ball was brought to a startled halt by the steward's staff striking the floor to announce a very late arrival. His voice rang out. 'Sir Guy Valmer!' Beth's blood chilled, and she whirled about to see Guy standing at the top of the steps, playing idly with the rich lace at his cuff. He looked superb, and commanded everyone's attention as he surveyed the scene with an air of ennui. For Beth there was suddenly no sound at all, except the anxious rhythm of her heart. Nothing and no one else mattered, just him, and in those breathless seconds she knew she was wrong to marry Landry. The only difference between her feelings for Landry and those she'd known for Jake was the sexual attraction exerted by Landry, but the agony in her heart due to just *looking* at Guy was something extraordinary. Apprehension swept icily over her, yet at the same time desire scorched her flesh. His eyes suddenly came to rest upon her, and expectation quivered unnervingly between her legs. Her breasts became so sensitive that she could feel the flimsy material of her bodice against her nipples, and her mouth ran dry; it was a moment of such utter self-knowledge that she could have laughed or wept, because she knew he was her nemesis.

He descended the steps to approach Landry and her, and the ballroom parted before him like the Red Sea. His grey eyes were vaguely amused as he ignored Beth and addressed Landry. 'Ah, Haldane, I believe my invitation must have been mislaid, but here I am at last.' His voice stroked Beth like a lover, but still he didn't look at her, and she couldn't look away from his fingers as they continued to toy with the lace. Here was sensuality and sexual fascination on a scale that she could barely credit. He did not have to look at her to enslave her, and yet, did he care? Did he even *see* her in that way? She could not tell from his impassive face.

Landry was cold toward him. 'You imagine you were invited?'

Such rudeness made Beth look at him in astonishment.

Guy, on the other hand, could not have been more amiable and charming 'Come now, Haldane, put aside neighbourly feuds and introduce me to your intended.'

Landry's face was a dull red, but feeling the eyes of the ballroom, he choked back his fury. 'Beth, may I present Sir Guy Valmer of Greylake? Greylake, my fiancée, Miss Mannacott.'

Guy was the hated master of Greylake? Beth was startled, but Guy was smooth and unruffled. 'I'm honoured to make your acquaintance, Miss, er, Mannacott,' he said, extending a white-gloved hand. She hesitated and then allowed him to draw her fingers to his lips, although he was careful not to actually kiss them. Their eyes met for a moment, hers wide and apprehensive, his cool and calculating, and then he turned to Landry again. 'A prize indeed, Haldane, I envy you.'

'Envy? From you?' Landry could not have been more scathing, but he caught the eye of the leader of the orchestra and gestured to him to play again. A waltz struck up, and gradually the ball resumed, although everyone continued to observe the man who'd brought the occasion to a halt in the first place.

Guy raised an eyebrow at Landry. 'Do I perceive from your manner and tone that you're in a miff with me about something?'

Beth watched him as he played with Landry. He was like a cat with a mouse, and she knew that Landry would never best him. Guy Valmer's armour had no chinks, nor did the man himself. He might have been fashioned from marble and given the gift of life, so perfect, sensuous and unassailable was he.

Landry rose to the bait. 'Miff hardly begins to describe my opinion of you, Greylake. You have far too much game, yet Bradfield trots here like a docile pony to complain that poachers cross my land to get to yours.'

'*Game?*' Guy's lips twitched a little. 'My dear fellow, I provide amply for my people, allowing them what they need, but I see no reason to provide for yours as well. That, Haldane, is your responsibility.'

'I am not beholden to poachers!' Landry snapped.

'So your keepers have orders to shoot on sight, which means that *your* poachers invade *my* woods instead. All they need is food in their bellies, so please change your draconian rules.'

Beth was shocked. Landry had instructed his keepers to *shoot* poachers? She remembered the visit to Haldane of Guy's agent, Bradfield, who had quite clearly not believed Landry's protestations of innocent outrage. She found it hard to believe Landry would be so harsh, and yet there had been other matters which revealed him not to be quite what he ought to be....

Landry flushed, and Guy's smile broadened. 'This disagreement should not be permitted to blight Miss Mannacott's evening, so I will make immediate amends by requesting her to honour me with this dance. Miss Mannacott?' He held out a hand.

She looked to Landry for guidance, but he was too angry and turned his head away, leaving the decision to her. Provoked, she accepted Guy's hand and allowed him to sweep her into the throng of dancers. For Beth, Guy was the only thing in sharp focus, because the chandeliers became a brilliant blur, and the other couples a whirling rainbow of colour and jewels. She felt alone with him. *If you dance at midwinter you'll need many lights to show the way.* She needed no lights with Guy Valmer, for his very presence illuminated her darkness.

'So, we meet again, Miss Tremoille. Or is it Miss Alder? Ah, no, it's Miss Mannacott now, isn't it?'

From somewhere she found the spirit to fence with him. 'Please call me Beth; after all, I feel we know each other well enough now.'

'Do we?' Two small words, uttered so softly they could hardly be heard in the ballroom; uttered so softly they were like his breath upon her cheek. She was at his mercy, as was her heart.

She managed to answer. 'Don't you think so?'

'One question begets another?' He smiled. 'Very well, let me ask another still. Did you enjoy the visit of the late Henry Topweather?' When she didn't reply, he continued, 'Did you perchance despatch him as you did your stepmother's courier?'

'I confess to stealing the money, but had no hand in Joshua's death!'

'So, there have been two suspicious deaths which are connected with you, but you had nothing to do with either? Oh, dear, you're suddenly the colour of chalk. Are you about to swoon away? I do hope not, for I would have to pick you up and carry you, which Holy Haldane would not like.'

'Don't call him that.'

'No? Look at him, Beth, did you ever see such a petulant fellow? He practically *gave* your hand to me for this waltz.'

She flushed, because that was exactly how she'd felt.

'Ha, I see you agree. Haldane isn't quite the angel he likes to pretend.'

Feet of clay, she thought, and immediately felt disloyal. 'Stop playing with me like this, for I can't bear it. If you mean to have me arrested, please tell me!'

'Arrested? My dear Beth, that isn't my purpose at all, far from it. What I want from you is your hand in marriage.'

She halted, staring at him in astonishment. 'Marriage?' she repeated faintly.

'Unless you would prefer imprisonment for theft?'

'You wish to commit social suicide by marrying a woman you believe is guilty of two murders and theft? That's hardly sensible, Sir Guy.'

Admiration glimmered in his grey eyes. 'You have great spirit, Beth, but you aren't a social disaster, unless one counts your indiscretions with Mannacott. I may know of your links to Joshua's death and that of Topweather, but no one else does. Nor do they know how light-fingered you were with your stepmother's hoard, and believe me, your notoriety because of Haldane will soon be a thing of the past. So you see, you'll be perfectly acceptable as Lady Valmer. Therefore my proposal, and implied threat, remain the same.' The waltz came to an end, and he bowed to her. 'I don't intend to leave just yet, so please take time to think about it. But I do demand your decision tonight. One thing you have to realize is that you are not going to marry Haldane.' He indicated the diamond glittering on her white-gloved finger. 'Return that showy piece of paste, Beth, for it's even more vulgar than the gaudy ruby star Haldane has been tasteless enough to wear tonight. So, Beth, it's me, or gaol, and I imagine I am marginally preferable.' With that he turned and walked into the throng.

Beth was fixed to the spot with shock, until she realized how many curious eyes were upon her, at which she caught up her skirts to return to Landry. She walked in what she hoped was a carefree manner, and made sure there was a smile on her lips, if not in her eyes. Marry *Guy*? It was the last thing she'd expected. Why did he want her? What possible reason could he have for going to such lengths? Her mind darted in all directions at once. *It's me, or gaol, and I imagine I am marginally preferable.* What could she do? What *should* she do? Defy him? But was marriage to Guy such a vile prospect? She would be denying her own soul if she said it was. On seeing him tonight, she'd reached an epiphany, finally realizing how disastrous a second-best marriage to Landry would be. Now Guy offered marriage. It was something she could never have dreamed of, and now that it was before her, it was something she wanted. There was no doubt in her mind – or body – that becoming Sir Guy Valmer's wife was what she wanted. And yet … it would be marriage solely on *his* terms, and she had no idea how he really felt or what he thought. Clearly he had a very compelling reason for choosing her, but that reason did not touch upon love or desire. She was an instrument, for a purpose as yet unknown.

As she approached Landry, she saw that he was deep in conversation with Dr Carter, whose rosy cheeks suggested he'd had to go out in the cold for whatever emergency had called him away. Now both he and Landry looked grave, and she could tell that Guy's unwanted intrusion had been temporarily forgotten. Landry turned as if to hurry away, but the doctor shook his head and restrained him. She read the doctor's lips. *It will do no good.* What would do no good? What had happened? Her steps quickened and the two men broke off, the doctor in embarrassment, Landry in confusion. She looked from one to the other. 'Is something wrong?' she asked.

The doctor cleared his throat awkwardly, but Landry answered. 'It's Carrie, she has taken a sudden turn for the worse. Doctor Carter does not think she will see the dawn.'

Beth was dismayed. 'Oh, no. What of Katie? Is there anything I can do?'

Doctor Carter glanced enquiringly at Landry, who nodded. 'Speak as you wish, Doctor, for Miss Mannacott is aware of the truth.'

'I see. Well, Miss Mannacott, I have just attended to Miss Markham, not that there is anything I can do, except make her as comfortable as possible with laudanum, which she refuses to take until she has spoken to you.'

'Me?'

'Yes. She is greatly distressed about Katie, and I believe needs to hear from you that the child will be cherished here at the hall.'

'But, I've already assured her—' Beth broke off and nodded. 'Yes, of course I'll go to her. If I can offer consolation, I'll do so gladly. I'll go now.'

'I'll accompany you,' Landry said immediately.

The doctor shook his head again. 'No, sir. Miss Markham is most insistent that it should be Miss Mannacott alone, and I think that under the circumstances her wishes should be paramount.'

Landry gave in, but reluctantly, and contented himself with insisting that Beth take one of the footmen with her, to ensure her safety in the snow and darkness. She hurried away rather guiltily, aware of seizing upon Carrie's deathbed request as an excuse to postpone temporarily having to confront anything else. She despised herself for having reached such a point, knowing she ought to be distraught about the hurt she was about to deal Landry, just as she ought to have felt remorse for deserting Jake. She had a conscience about both men, yes, but her heart and soul told her she was right. A sense of destiny was upon her now, and that destiny was Sir Guy Valmer.

Guy had adjourned to Landry's library, which was as brightly illuminated as the rest of the house but blessedly deserted. He helped himself to a glass of cognac, and then went to the desk, flicked back his coattails and took a seat. Selecting a sheet of fine writing paper, he commenced a brief note to Jane Welland. *I have the missing will and the missing heiress, so Valmer House and its lands are as good as mine.* He smiled at the use of the house's original name. Jane, having been devastated by the beginning of the sentence, would be goaded by the sly sting in the tail. He continued to write. *Tell your husband what you will, but be warned that he is bound to learn that your fine dowry is no more. Be assured that our next meeting will be in a court of law. Valmer.* He recalled his meeting with Jane, at the time of buying Lancelot. It would be most agreeable to see her face when she received this little billet-doux. And Welland's, for that matter. Rowan's reaction he already knew, although to be sure the advent of a mysterious new lady love would appear to be occupying that young man's thoughts to the exclusion of all else. Or so it seemed from the hasty note that had arrived at Park Lane at the very moment he, Guy, was setting off for the West Country. Rowan was in love, but was curiously coy about the young lady's identity. Pray God she wasn't a dairymaid ... or someone else's wife.

After sanding the note, Guy was about to hold a stick of red sealing wax to the candle on the desk, when he thought again. Would it be more prudent to have Beth's acceptance first? One should never tempt Providence. Not that he was in any doubt about her response, because she had no real alternative. His confidence was such that he'd already despatched a Bell and Fox messenger to Greylake, with instructions that his late mother's rooms were to be made ready for Miss Tremoille. Further, he'd halted at the Dower House on the way here and instructed a thunderstruck Mrs Cobbett to pack her mistress's belongings, as Miss Beth would be leaving for Greylake before the night was out. Now he could even ape virtue by telling himself he was saving Beth from the unspeakable fate of marriage to Holy Haldane, a man whose exterior charm and self-crowned halo disguised a mealy-mouthed toad.

Guy smiled wryly. Given his confidence hitherto, why falter about sealing this note to Jane Welland? Providence could not be tempted now. He held wax and candle together above the folded letter, and enjoyed the way the molten wax formed a little pool that only awaited his signet ring. 'Well, Jane, we will soon face each other before the law's majesty, and with Beth *and* Esmond Tremoille's last will in my grasp, victory is bound to be mine.' He relished taking on the new Lady Welland, because Jane was a formidable woman and tricky adversary. Even now, with the odds stacked against her, he was sure she would fight him with everything in her power.

The footman's lantern jolted as he and Beth hurried toward the lodge, where a single small light shone at an upper window. Behind them was the dazzling brilliance of the hall, and all the lamps in the park. The night air was bitterly cold, and Beth shivered in spite of her mantle and muff.

At last they reached the lodge and, after removing her mantle and muff, Beth went upstairs, to find Carrie lying in bed, having just taken an infusion of honey and dried hyssop that had been prepared by a woman from the village. The woman, plump and swarthy, dressed in black, hurried out as Beth entered. Katie was asleep in her room across the tiny landing, and knew nothing of what was happening. Carrie's fair hair had been brushed neatly and spread upon the pillow, and her face was ghostly, the unnatural flush having faded from her cheeks and the brightness from her hollow eyes. 'Forgive me, Miss Mannacott, but I *must* speak with you.' Her voice was feeble, and there was a rattle in her lungs.

'There is nothing to forgive, Miss Markham.' Beth sat on the edge of the bed in her exquisite green silk gown with its silver threads and tiny pearls.

Carrie gazed at her. 'You're so beautiful, I can see why he loves you, but you've danced at midwinter, and can never light the darkness that will haunt you now.'

Beth gave a sad smile. 'I know that, Miss Markham. I discovered it earlier tonight.' *When the man I really love danced my darkness away.*

'I have to tell you something, Miss Mannacott, something so important that I'm breaking my word to a dear friend by telling you. Mr Landry is Katie's father, but I'm not her mother. Miss Harriet is Katie's mother, Miss Mannacott, and apart from you and me, there's no one else in the world that knows it.'

Beth stared at her.

'She went with him once, that's all, and then he went away to his regiment. Miss Harriet and I were always friends, we played together as children, and so she told me when she knew she was with child. I arranged for us both to stay with my aunt in Taunton, where Katie was born. We stayed there for months on end, and when we returned to Haldane we said the child was mine. It could have been, you see, because Mr Landry and I had shared a bed. My reputation didn't matter, for it was well known that I'd been his mistress, but Miss Harriet's reputation was spared. It's the way we both wanted it at the time. I loved him then as I love him now, and by being Katie's mother I was assured of his attention and kindness, if not his presence in my bed. Miss Harriet loves him too, but knows he doesn't love her.' Carrie closed her eyes for a moment, exhausted by the effort of speaking, but then struggled again. 'Do not think badly of him, Miss Mannacott, for he knows nothing of this.'

Beth lowered her eyes. Whether he knew it or not, the story did not reflect well upon his conduct. He'd put Harriet's reputation at risk when he lay with her, and on his own admission had been relieved when she didn't mention it afterward. Any man of true honour would have married her. Someone like Harriet warranted a gentleman's protection, not his casual indifference. Landry did not always behave nobly, a fact she, Beth, had contrived to ignore until now, but could no more. After everything else that had happened tonight, this was almost too much. Again she tried to assemble her thoughts in the face of circumstances beyond her control. It was easy to imagine what Harriet had gone through at the time, being with child out of wedlock, and Landry far away with his regiment. Fear of ruin was a terrible force, and ruined she most definitely would have been. And all because Landry Haldane had been less than a gentleman.

Carrie continued, 'All was well while I had my health, but now that I'm dying I can't let this go on. You may have stolen his heart, but it is Miss Harriet he should wed. She has always refused to tell him the truth because she felt it would force him to do the honourable thing.'

'You are right to tell me, Miss Markham, and I am sure that when he learns the truth, Mr Haldane will wish to rectify matters.' He won't *wish* to, he'll simply have no choice. But as she thought this, Beth knew this revelation was her own salvation too. Even if Guy had not come to the hall tonight, learning what she now had, she would not have been able to proceed with the betrothal. She would have had to remove Landry's ring. *Return that showy piece of paste, Beth.*

'Miss Mannacott? I know I ruin your life, but—'

Beth halted the words. 'No, Miss Markham, you don't ruin anything, rather have you confirmed something that I had already decided. Mr Haldane and I are not suited, and if I had not been so blinkered and foolish of late, I would have known it sooner.'

There were tears of relief on Carrie's cheeks. 'I have not been kind to you, Miss Mannacott, yet you are kind to me. I'm ashamed.'

'Don't be. Please.' Beth squeezed Carrie's hand. 'Would you like me to let Miss Bellamy know you've told me? Perhaps when she realizes I will not marry Mr Haldane anyway, she will see where her duty lies. I will tell Mr Landry for the same reason.'

'Would you do that? They *must* marry, Miss Mannacott. For Katie's sake. When I'm gone, that child will need her true parents. I know that their marrying now will not make her legitimate, but it's the next best thing.'

'I agree.' Beth thought of Landry, so unaware of the great upheaval that was about to change his life. But, like her, he must face the consequences of past actions. They both had feet of clay.

Chapter Twenty-four

Landry had found Guy in the library. 'Ah, here you are, Greylake. So tell me, why have you really come here tonight?'

'To take Beth Tremoille away from you,' was the blunt response.

'Tremoille?'

'That's her real name. Mannacott is the name of the blacksmith with whom she lived for a year in Gloucester.' Guy knew there was little point in concealing this scandalous fact, because Beth's liaison with Jake Mannacott was bound to come out sooner or later, especially as Jane Welland almost certainly knew of it and would use it to heap public scorn on the new Lady Valmer. The newspapers would be delighted, and soon the juicy titbit would be circulating throughout society.

Landry stared at him. 'A *blacksmith*? That's a lie, Greylake!'

'It's the truth.'

Landry flushed. 'I want you to leave.'

'No, you don't, because you want to know more. Sit down, dear fellow, for we may as well be comfortable.' Resuming his seat at the desk, Guy waved Landry to a chair, subtly reversing the role of host and guest.

'I'll stand,' Landry replied. 'Well, proceed with your poison.'

'We don't like each other, Haldane, and nothing will change that, but if you really do love Beth, then believe me, I am sorry for what I do tonight.'

'I'm all gratitude.'

'I'm sure.' Leaning back, Guy related an edited version of his pursuit of Beth, for he wasn't about to confide his reason for needing her, or the crimes of which she might conceivably be accused. 'Beth won't marry you now,' he finished, 'she doesn't dare to, being mistress of Greylake is a more palatable prospect than—' He stopped prudently.

Landry's face had grown more and more pale, and now he leapt to his feet. 'Than what? Are you threatening her? I'll defend her against you, Greylake!'

'How noble, but it won't come to that. She *will* marry me. Mark my words, before the hour is out, she will return your ring.'

'Why do you want her? Do you love her?'

'Love?' Guy chuckled. 'And what, pray, has that to do with it? You may be propelled by such a debilitating condition, but common sense has charge of me.'

Landry was almost beside himself with anguish. 'I'll wipe that smug smile from your face, Greylake!' he cried, beginning to step around the desk with his fist raised.

Guy rose. 'I'd think twice if I were you, Haldane, because I'm well able to take care of myself. And if you really *do* want there to be talk, you'll succeed if we emerge with cuts and bruises and Beth still returns your ring. Listen to me, now, here, where we are private, for I swear I'm quite prepared to carry on this conversation in the middle of the ballroom, with all of Devon and Somerset bearing witness.'

Landry halted, deterred by the quiet menace with which the words were uttered.

Guy smiled. 'Ever the dashing cavalier, eh, Haldane? How did you ever believe yourself worthy of Beth?'

'Have you ever lain with her?' Landry demanded, and then became triumphantly scornful when Guy didn't answer. 'I see not. Well, when you dip your proud wick in her sweet body, just remember that I was there before you!'

'Haldane, when that choice moment arrives, you'll be the last thing on my mind.'

'I've had her time and time again.'

'What a braggart you are, and so ungallant to boast at the expense of a lady. Well, it makes no difference to me. I want Beth for reasons other than love and desire.'

'I pity her,' Landry breathed.

'Then don't.'

'One day I will destroy you, Greylake.'

Guy smiled. 'Even insects can dream.'

Landry turned on his heel and marched from the library, slamming the door. Once outside he paused, his mind in turmoil. Beth. Oh, Beth. His heart felt as if it were splitting in two, its life force draining away. She was everything to him, everything, but he knew he'd lost her. The betrothal ball had become a farewell ball, and he had to swallow the bitter pill of knowing his most loathed enemy had taken her.

In the library Guy poured another glass of cognac, and then went to stand by the misted window, looking out at the lamps glittering in the park. There was a lacquered screen behind him, so that anyone entering the library would not know he was there. His thoughts were of Beth, and the regaining his childhood home.

On leaving the library, Landry, still smarting from his interview with Guy, looked for Beth, in order to demand an explanation face-to-face. But she had yet to return from the lodge, and then he was confronted by an inebriated and truculent Sir Daniel, who was determined to persuade him not to ban stag hunting from Haldane land.

Landry was still being thus lambasted when Beth slipped back into the ballroom, meaning to find Harriet first. She found her dancing a cotillion with John, and waited until the dance was at an end before drawing her discreetly aside. 'Harriet, I must speak with you,' she said quietly.

'Is something wrong?' Harriet looked anxiously at her.

'That depends upon one's point of view.'

'How mysterious.' An uncertain smile played on Harriet's lips.

'We'll go to the library, it's private there.'

'Beth, what on earth can you tell me there that can't be said here?'

'You have a very closely guarded secret that is secret no more.'

Harriet blanched, and without another word walked toward the library which was empty. Or so they both thought. Harriet turned as Beth closed the door. Her eyes were tormented, and her nasturtium tissue gown shimmered in the mixed light of fire and candles. 'Carrie has told you?'

Beth nodded. 'Yes, and she was right to do so.'

'It wasn't her secret to tell.'

'You know that's not true, Harriet. She's dying, and according to Doctor Carter may not even see the dawn.'

Harriet leaned weak hands on the desk. 'Oh, no, poor Carrie.'

'Landry is Katie's father, Harriet, but I now know that you, not Carrie, are her mother. It is up to you and Landry to do what is right.'

'But this ball celebrates *your* betrothal to him.' Harriet turned away agitatedly. 'Oh, it will all come out now, and I will be seen for the fallen creature I have always secretly been. What will Father say? And John! Oh, no, what of John?'

'If you and Landry marry, what will it matter if there's talk? As for John, well, sadly, he'll be a casualty.'

'He doesn't deserve this, for he at least is innocent of blame.' Tears shone in Harriet's eyes. 'You may find scandal easy to live with, Beth, but it frightens me. And you love Landry, so how can you urge this upon him?'

'No, Harriet, I don't love him.'

Harriet was shocked. 'Then why...?' She pointed at Beth's ring.

'I would have returned it to Landry tonight even had I not learned the truth about you. No, Harriet, don't disbelieve me, or think I'm trying to make things easier for you. My betrothal to Landry is no more, because I am going to marry Sir Guy Valmer.'

Harriet looked at her, as if at a fiend incarnate. 'You're what?' she repeated faintly. 'But *why*? What's Sir Guy to you? How do you know him? What's this about?'

'I know nothing of his reasons, except that passion and devotion don't figure on his side. *My* motives are ... such that I cannot refuse him.'

'You don't mean to tell me everything? Aren't we friends enough for that.'

'There are things that must remain between Sir Guy and me.'

Harriet searched her face. 'You've loved him all along, haven't you? Since before you even came here.'

For Beth, the question sailed uncomfortably close to home. 'Of course not,' she replied, a denial that might convince others, but never herself.

'Does – does Landry know all this?'

'Not yet. I mean to tell him next. Harriet, what I feel for Landry doesn't compare in any way with your deep love for him. You and he should be together, for your sake, and Katie's.'

'You have already accepted Sir Guy?'

'Not yet.'

Harriet still searched her face. 'You seem so calm.'

'I'm not really.' Beth was nervous about her new situation, and at the same time the erotic wanton in her was unbearably excited. She wanted Guy, even on these terms, and yet anger and resentment burned within her that he could and would manipulate her. At this moment she was his puppet, but a puppet that was flesh and blood, and aroused by the prospect of being his wife. She was a paradox, loving and deploring him at the same time. She met Harriet's eyes. 'This isn't about me, but about you and Landry. I was going to tell him of these developments, but maybe, because of Katie, it would be better coming from you.'

'Either way it will be cruel for him.'

'He should not have done what he did with you. The past catches up with us all, including me.' Beth went to hug her. 'Go to him now, Harriet.'

'Can't we go together?'

Beth shook her head. 'I'd rather tell Sir Guy of my decision.'

'Very well. But Landry doesn't *have* to marry me, you know, nor will he want to.'

'Nevertheless, he will.'

Harriet went reluctantly to the door and, as it closed softly, Beth leaned her hands on the desk, her head bowed. But she turned with a dismayed gasp as she heard Guy's soft tread from behind the screen. 'You!'

'I fear so. I did not hide deliberately, but was caught unawares when you and Miss Bellamy came in. And once you started talking—'

'— you kept quiet in order to eavesdrop!'

He pursed his lips slightly. 'The more you said, the more awkward it became to make my presence known. Haldane's lamentable lack of honour is hardly my concern.'

'Who are you to speak of honour? You're blackmailing me into marriage.'

'And who are you to complain?'

She coloured and turned the conversation elsewhere. 'Well, you already know that I will marry you, although why on earth you want me I can't imagine.'

'You'll learn in due course, and when you're Lady Valmer, provided you conduct yourself as I wish, we'll get on famously. Please, no blacksmiths, cordwainers or such.'

Now her face was fiery. 'I'm sure that even you would bed with a washerwoman if your belly was empty and there was no roof over your head.'

'What an interesting thought.'

'Ponder upon it when next you feel compelled to ridicule me.'

'Ridicule you? Maybe I am guilty of that, but my purpose is to make you realize that from now on you will never need to descend into such degradation. You were far too good for Mannacott.'

'And too good for Landry? Presumably I'm far too good for anyone except you?'

'Of course.' He smiled.

That smile almost undid her, and she looked away, afraid that her innermost thoughts might be revealed to him. She didn't want him to know how much she hungered for him, because that would put her even more in his power. 'What is to happen next?'

'We quit this place without further ado.'

Her gaze flew to meet his again. 'Now? But there is Landry, and—'

'Haldane already knows; we had a verbal set-to in here a little while ago. I think he really does love you, Beth, but he's spineless. Oh, and in case you did not know, in the past he's had a considerable weakness for drinking and gambling. He was quite dissolute in fact, which is certainly at odds with the angelic front he puts on now. He has overcome his vices in recent years, but it won't last. Now then, I've waited some considerable time to capture you, so this is not haste, merely a determination to conclude matters satisfactorily. You and I will travel to Porworthy tonight, and Greylake in the morning. Once there, we will be married as soon as it can be arranged. I intend you to be Lady Valmer before Christmas.'

And do you also intend me to be in your bed? The thought was there and she could do nothing about it. Looking at him now, hearing him now, it didn't matter how cold and aloof he was, or that their marriage would be simply one of convenience – *his* convenience. What mattered was that she would be his wife. *For better, for worse....*

She held his gaze. 'And will you be my husband, sir? Or merely my lord and master?'

'No man could be your lord and master, Beth. Catching you has been like pursuing a dream.' She bowed her head, thinking of what Jake had said. 'Beth?'

'It's nothing. You just reminded me of someone.'

'I hardly dare ask who.'

'More mockery? Well, how many whores have you bedded?' she demanded defensively.

'Oh, the usual full complement,' he replied with a glimmer of amusement, 'because such things are expected of gentlemen. Hugely unfair, I know, but there it is.' He paused. 'Are you ready to leave? Together, through the ballroom?'

Her nerve wavered. 'Can't we simply slip away and spare Landry's feelings?'

'Did he spare *your* feelings tonight? No, when I asked you to dance, he displayed his inherent pettiness. That is the measure of him, Beth. He's the sort of man who seduces a vicar's innocent daughter, gets her with child, and then turns his back.'

'He didn't know she had his child.'

'No? Didn't he have a tiny suspicion? Surely he knows how babies are made? And what was he thinking, idly bedding a young woman of Harriet's quality?'

Hadn't she thought virtually the same? But still she issued a sharp retort. 'Such acid must surely eat through you, Sir Guy.'

'Enough of this charming banter. I wish to leave Holy Haldane's domain and breathe fresh air again. I've taken a room at the Bell and Fox, and—' He broke off hastily. 'Oh, don't fear my unwelcome attentions tonight, for I will secure another room, or sleep on a settle. Your bed is your own. For the time being.' He came around the table and offered her his arm.

Slowly and with great trepidation, she accepted it. For a moment his hand enclosed hers. 'One day you will see this as providence,' he murmured, 'because you know deep down that Haldane isn't for you.'

'Perhaps I know that you aren't, either.' Such bravado, when her silly heart fluttered and her legs had become jelly.

'It's all immaterial anyway, because this is to be a *mariage de convenance*. Neither of us gives a fig about the other, but in public we will pretend we do.'

You might not give a fig, but I do. Oh, how I do. I love you, Guy, and want you to want me. He began to walk toward the door, but she held back. 'You may have the nerve to walk brazenly through the ballroom, but I don't.'

His fingers twined firmly with hers. 'Oh, yes, you do, Beth, you have the nerve for anything, as you've shown in all our previous encounters. We're both capable of facing down the Devil himself, so West Country society will be simple. Besides, they'll imagine that I have a prior claim to you.'

'And provided I'm a meek, obedient lapdog, all will be well?'

'Meek and obedient? *You?*' He laughed.

'Sir Guy, are you familiar with the local saying that those who dance at midwinter will need many lights to see their way? Well, you and I danced tonight.'

'I can afford all the candles in England, so our darkness with be well lit.'

She fell into silence as he opened the library door and they stepped through into the antechamber that led to the ballroom. Another waltz was in progress, but the moment they appeared – the future Mrs Haldane arm-in-arm with Sir Guy Valmer, his fingers linked lovingly with hers – the assembly's elegance and dignity dissolved into an utter shambles. Beth recalled Mrs Cobbett's doubts about tonight. Had the housekeeper fore-seen tonight's tumultuous events? She felt as if she and Guy trod a brightly illuminated stage, before a darkened auditorium where every seat was taken, every aisle crowded. She would better have worn scarlet tonight....

'Smile, Beth,' Guy prompted, 'for I will not have it thought that you are being *made* to marry me.'

'Heaven forfend,' was the brave riposte she knew must set the scene for the ensuing acts. She must be cool and remote, she thought, smiling obedi-ently for the benefit of those who'd gathered at Haldane Hall to celebrate her betrothal to Landry, only to see her depart on the arm of the man he loathed most. She must also be cool and remote with Guy, a goal not easily accomplished when his hand moved over hers in as loving a manner as could be imagined. Even this false caress affected her, exposing as it did how much joy he could impart to her ... had he been so disposed. She shivered secretly as shameless sensations invaded places they shouldn't. Her body and senses quickened; her imagination taunted her with thoughts of exqui-site carnal joy ... but such desires were fanciful, because Sir Guy Valmer didn't want her in that way. His affection and physical adoration could make her the happiest of creatures, but neither would be forthcoming. To him she was as much a matter of business as the purchase of Lancelot, and she wished she knew his motives; unless ... could it be connected with her father's missing will? Yes, of course! Why hadn't she thought of it before?

Tears sprang to her eyes. How cruel life as Lady Valmer was going to be. She would be the wife of the only man she would ever love so intensely, but in the face of his coldness would have to salvage her pride and self-respect by pretending indifference. Tormented, she hardly knew that her fingers wove between his, or that he glanced at her in surprise, as did the rest of the ballroom, around which a torrent of whispering now began to pour. Society was affronted by what conclusion it drew, and she knew she was branded. The rumours of the summer and autumn pierced the thin veneer that had hitherto cloaked this evening, and local society decided once and for all that Miss Mannacott of the Dower House had never been anything but a scheming, ambitious whore, who, having snapped up the considerable prize of Landry Haldane, was now setting him aside in favour of one far greater.

Guests moved silently aside, as they had on Guy's arrival, and as he and Beth mounted the ballroom steps, a babble of conversation broke out behind them. Somehow Beth managed to hold her head up as they entered the vestibule, where bemused footmen rushed to obey when Guy requested their outdoor clothes and that his carriage be brought to the main entrance. The mantle's fur lining felt cold against Beth's too-hot skin, as did the muff into the pristine white depths of which she plunged her hands. She hardly knew as she and Guy approached the outer doors, nor did she feel the chill of the snow-filled night as he assisted her down toward the waiting carriage. Snowflakes brushed her face, and clung to Guy's dark coat. The atmosphere of Christmas was all around, and she was sure that a trick of the wind carried the sound of carols from Haldane church.

But then she saw Landry and Harriet ascending toward them. Both couples halted awkwardly. Harriet had been crying, and Landry, who avoided Beth's gaze, looked as if he'd been struck by lightning, but Harriet's hand was on his sleeve, and his hand was over it, just as Guy's was over Beth's. 'Every hand tells a story,' Guy murmured to Beth as he made her continue the descent.

She looked back, and Harriet gave her a wan smile as she tried to suppress another sob; Landry proceeded stiffly toward the house. Beth wanted to call out and *make* him acknowledge her, but Guy sensed as much and forbade it. 'Leave the churlish fellow to his sulks, my dear,' he murmured. At the bottom she glanced back a final time, but Landry and Harriet had gone inside and the doors were closed again. Another chapter of her life had also closed, she thought. Guy paused by the open carriage door. 'Forget him, Beth, for he really isn't worth your regrets.'

'At least there would have been warmth with him.'

'You think me incapable of warmth?' he asked.

'I have no idea of what you are capable or incapable, Sir Guy. You present a mask to the world as you mock it. You are ice itself, sir.'

His grey eyes were unfathomable in the light of the carriage lamp, and she was so aware of him that desire seemed to have replaced the blood in her veins. Then he tossed his hat into the carriage and pulled her toward him. 'I'm not ice, Beth, but you won't believe that unless I demonstrate my skills,' he breathed, lowering his lips to hers.

Time stood still as he kissed her. How often had she dreamed of this? How often had she craved this man? Her own resolution mocked her. *Cool and remote, cool and remote....* But as his lips played with hers, and he gathered her body close, as if she were the most beloved thing in his world, it was impossible to abide by her promise. Her disloyal lips parted and softened as she returned the kiss with all the stifled passion she'd endured since meeting him. But this wasn't the same as her savage surrender on the cliffs, this was timelessly exquisite, a kiss shared with the man she loved to distraction. She felt the moisture between her legs, and the rich flow of desire over her entire body. She dissolved against him, exulting in the way his embrace tightened so that he lifted her from her toes. Their lips moved together, their hearts beat together, and she felt the desire that swelled at his loins. She was in ecstasy, drawing his tongue into her mouth and pressing to him in a way so wanton and abandoned that he surely could be in no doubt of her feelings for him.

If her fervour startled him he gave no sign, but with her still in his arms he turned to press her back against the carriage. She kissed him again and again, running her fingers into his hair, that wonderful hair that so set him apart. If only she dared tell him of her love ... but that would be to court his derision. He was simply proving a point now, and proved it only too well.

To save what was left of her self-respect, she had to pretend to be paying him in kind, so from somewhere she found the strength to draw back coolly. 'You see? Two can play at that game, Sir Guy,' she whispered.

His face was unfathomable. 'It would seem they can, Beth. I bow to your superior acting talents, for to be sure you are very convincing.'

She was glad of the poor light, because she knew there were spots of guilty colour on her cheeks.

He turned to Dickon, waiting discreetly nearby. 'The Dower House first, I think,' he said, and then helped her into the carriage. Moments later they drove out of the Haldane Hall gates and then down the steep incline toward Lannermouth. Her senses were in chaos as she waited in the carriage at the Dower House, where Dickon loaded her waiting luggage into the boot. Mrs Cobbett and Molly waited nearby, clearly in some confusion, but then the housekeeper hurried to the carriage. 'What's to become of us, Miss Beth?'

Guy answered. 'You will stay here as you are now.'

Mrs Cobbett looked at him nervously, but then became suddenly bold. 'I knew there would be dark goings-on tonight, Sir Guy, but I did not imagine it would be this. Take care of her.' The last words were an instruction, not a request.

Guy was amused. 'And if I do not?'

The housekeeper raised her chin. 'Dark goings-on require dark remedies.'

'Am I being threatened with a wisewoman's magic, perchance?'

Mrs Cobbett's lips parted to respond, but Beth spoke quickly. 'I'm quite all right, Mrs C. Please don't worry, for Sir Guy's motives are honourable. I'm to be Lady Valmer.'

The woman's face changed. 'Lady Valmer?' she repeated in awe. 'But—'

Guy cut her short. 'The only other thing you need to know is that you and the other two servants will be as secure in my employ as you were before.'

The luggage had been loaded, and the carriage shook as Dickon resumed his place. Guy closed the door on Mrs Cobbett, and the team moved forward again. Soon they were toiling up Rendisbury Hill, but at the top Dickon urged the horses along the coast road. Snowflakes swirled, and the sea and great inland expanse of Exmoor were lost in the darkness.

Another new beginning stretched ahead for Beth Tremoille, this time as the titled mistress of the great estate of Greylake. Tears stung her eyes. Oh, why did it have to be this way? Everything would be so based on deception and pretence that surely there would never be a moment to tell him how much she loved him. She had so much to give this man. If only he wanted it.